Hold Me One Last Time

Lois Jean Thomas

Seventh Child Publishing, LLC
Saint Joseph, Michigan

This book is a work of fiction. Names, characters, and incidents are the product of the author's imagination or are used fictitiously. Any resemblance between events or persons, living or dead, is coincidental.

Cover design by A. R. Thomas

Copyright © 2019 by Lois Jean Thomas

All rights reserved.

ISBN: 978-0-9976445-6-2

Library of Congress Control Number: 2019907505
Lois Jean Thomas, Saint Joseph, Michigan

In memory of Marjorie Lawson Derringer,
who struggled valiantly and loved abundantly.

CONTENTS

ACKNOWLEDGMENTS

My deepest gratitude goes out to my dear friend Mary Ruth Fox, a lifelong resident of Brown County, Indiana, the setting for this story. Throughout the writing of this book, I have turned to her for insight, information, and moral support. She has done a great deal of research and legwork on my behalf.

My thanks also go out to Rhonda Dunn from the Brown County History Center. I have incessantly pestered her with emails, and she has faithfully and expertly responded by forwarding me the information I have asked for. I also acknowledge my indebtedness to the Brown County Historical Society website.

And as always, I owe a debt of gratitude to my husband, who plays a vital role in any book I write. He lightens my load by doing research, by helping with formatting, and by providing valuable feedback on what I've written.

Hold Me
One Last Time

1907

I've only been married to Frank Kelly for three months, and I'm already carrying his child. Truth be told, I can't rightly say whether this baby was made before or after our wedding day. My belly is rounding out, more than you'd expect. People around here might be saying things, like maybe I'm not a nice girl. But I don't know any girl, no matter how upstanding she is, who could've said no to Frank Kelly.

My ma had warned me about the Kellys. They were the neighbors who lived a mile down from us on Helmsburg Road, in the house I'm living in now. I know I should've listened to her and guarded myself against temptation, although I'm not sure if I'm truly sorry about what happened. Only time will tell whether I have anything to regret.

The Kellys are Catholic, which made my folks leery of them from the get go. There's not more than a handful of Catholics here in Brown County, Indiana, not even enough to build a Catholic Church. Frank's sisters attend Mass at a church in Bloomington, over there in Monroe County. But Frank doesn't have any interest in that sort of thing anymore.

I can't say my folks are regular churchgoers, even though they're God-fearing people. Every now and then, weather permitting, my ma and pa and my sister Hazel and I pile into the spring wagon and drive down to the Christian Church in Nashville. With the roads as bad as they are, that takes a lot of doing, so we don't make it more than once every month or two. But in between times, Pa sits us down for a bit of scripture reading on a Sunday afternoon. And we pray every night at the supper table.

The Kellys always let it be known that they're Irish, as if they're proud of it. Most people around here don't talk much about where they come from. They've got their minds set on the business of keeping body and soul together. I can't say I fully know how we Sniders came to be in these parts. I've heard it said that my great-grandparents on my ma's side came from Kentucky way back in the 1830s, and that the folks on my pa's side came from Tennessee around the same time. I can hardly think what it would be like to make such a trip.

But I don't know where my people came from before that. Most likely, we're from German stock. We're down-to-earth, hardworking people.

From the time I was a little girl, Ma warned me that the Kellys were peculiar, and that it was best to steer clear of folks like them. "They pray to statues of saints," she told me once. "Mrs. Kelly used to have statues in the house that were nothing more than idols, and that's an abomination to the Lord."

The idea of our neighbors praying to idols sent a shiver up my spine. Like most people I know, I was taught to pray only to God and his son Jesus Christ.

Ma used to say that Frank's mother, Rose Kelly, was fey. Every time she'd mention that, she'd close her eyes and shake her head a little, like it was something she could hardly stand to think about.

"What does being fey mean?" I asked her one day about five or six years ago.

She looked up from the kettle of apple-butter she was cooking down on the stove, narrowing her eyes and chewing on her lip like she didn't know quite what to tell me. "Bertha," she finally said, "Rose Kelly saw things that no one else ever saw. Visions and nonsense like that. She saw things that are best left unseen. It's been said that she could predict the future. She took up with spirits and such, things not of this world. Things we ought not be messing with. And that's something I don't want any part of."

Then she pointed her wooden spoon at me, so serious that she didn't even worry about the apple-butter dripping onto the floor. "And I don't want you having any part of it, either."

I knew right then that I should never get too friendly with the Kelly girls, in case they tried to put strange ideas into my head. But that wasn't much of a problem, seeing as they were all so much older than me.

After that day when she was cooking the apple-butter, Ma started telling me all kinds of stories about Mrs. Kelly, as if she thought I was finally old enough to hear the full truth about our neighbors. As if she wanted to warn me away from any trouble that might be coming down the road.

I never knew Rose Kelly myself. She died almost twenty years ago, when I was hardly more than a baby. But people have kept on telling stories about her odd ways. Whenever Ma would talk about her, I'd just have to stop and listen, my mouth hanging open in wonderment.

Ma said that being around Rose Kelly made her feel peculiar, and that the Kelly house made her uneasy. "Something was lurking there," she'd say. "Something that made the hair on the back of my neck stand up."

She told me that Rose married her husband, Frank Kelly Sr., when she was just a little slip of a sixteen-year-old. Right away, she started having babies, all of them girls, one coming right after the other. Six of them in all, each one as pretty as a picture.

Ma said Rose Kelly had a knack for growing flowers, and that she was so devoted to her flower gardens that she practically worshiped them. Which, of course, wasn't right. Following in the pattern of having a flower name herself, she gave each of her girls the name of some kind of plant growing on their farmstead. She called the oldest girl Violet, and the next four were Iris, Ivy, Lily, and Fern.

When people would see those pretty little Kelly girls with their flowery names, they'd smile and say, "Isn't that the sweetest thing?" But when Rose gave her sixth daughter the ridiculous name of Clover, everyone thought she'd gone a bit too far.

Then she stopped having babies, and everybody figured the Kellys had all the children they were ever going to have. But then, a full ten years after Clover was born, Rose's belly started swelling with another child. Most decent women keep quiet about such things, but Rose talked about it with anybody who'd listen. She kept saying she was going to have a boy this time, but that she wasn't going to live to see him grow up.

People would say, "Now Rose, how on earth could you know such a thing?"

"It came to me in a dream," she'd tell them.

Everyone laughed at her prediction, saying that Rose Kelly had finally gone plumb out of her head. But when she passed away giving birth to a baby boy, it left everybody a little bit scared.

Rose had been saying ahead of time that she wanted to name her son Sweet William. But seeing as how she died when he was born, she ended up not having a say in the matter. Mr. Kelly insisted that his son be named Frank Jr. That was probably a good thing, as any boy growing up with a name like Sweet William would've turned out to be a sissy. I can tell you that Frank Kelly is no sissy.

After their ma's death, the Kelly sisters kept house for their pa. Some of them were pretty much grown by that time. They raised their baby brother, doting on him something terrible, fighting over which one got to take care of him. I think all that attention gave Frank a puffed-up feeling about himself. He's always carried himself like he was something special, standing tall and proud with his head held high. Like he can do anything in the world he wants to do.

But aside from Rose being touched in the head, the Kelly family had another problem that made my ma and pa leery of them. Frank Kelly Sr. was given to drink. His battle with liquor took him down a wrong road, and at this point, you could say he's gone completely around the bend. The liquor has a hold on him, and he has no power to leave it alone anymore.

My pa brings his jug of whiskey out of the root cellar whenever company comes to call, but he's never been overtaken by drink the way Mr. Kelly has. Pa has no regard for a man so weak in his resolve. Nowadays, everyone around here calls Frank Sr., "Old Man Kelly." The name shows what people think of him now. He no longer deserves the respect of being called Mr. Kelly.

Growing up, my sister Hazel and I never went to the Kelly farm. Not one time. That doesn't seem very neighborly, but my ma was bent on keeping her girls away from bad influences. She went on her own from time to time, to take them some fresh baked bread or some green beans from her garden. She never was sure the Kellys were eating right without having a wife and mother in the home. Ma's always been good about looking out for others, even if they aren't the kind of people she approves of.

Every now and then, I'd ask her if I could ride along when she went to see the Kellys. "I'll stay in the wagon," I'd plead with her. I'd think to myself that while Ma was in the house, I could have a look around, just to satisfy my curiosity about my strange neighbors. But Ma never would allow it.

When Frank was just a little boy, his older sisters started marrying off, one by one. Their husbands are well-to-do men from Bloomington, lawyers and businessmen and such. People say those girls ended up with better lives than they ever would've had if they'd married Brown County farmers. I guess that's the way things turn out for beautiful women.

The youngest of the girls, Clover, stayed home until she was twenty-six. She thought somebody needed to be there to take care of her little brother. People were saying it was a shame she was turning out to be an old maid, as she was the prettiest of all the Kelly sisters.

But I guess Clover finally decided she needed to look to her own future, as a couple of years ago, she married a rich widower. Hiram Henderson is twenty years older than her, practically an old man, and he has children that are almost grown. He owns the Henderson Mercantile in Nashville.

Hiram and Clover live in one of those fancy homes on Jefferson Street in Nashville. Whenever Pa would us to Nashville when I was growing up, we'd always go past those big houses, just to have a look. Pa would say that was where the rich people lived. To me, those homes seemed like the palaces of kings. They had so many rooms that I figured I'd get lost if I ever went inside.

After his first wife died, Mr. Henderson hired a maid to cook and clean and tend to his half-grown children. She kept on working for him even after Clover moved into the home. Now, Clover never has to lift a finger to do any chores around her house. People say they see her flouncing around Nashville on Mr. Henderson's arm, all decked out in her fancy dresses, smiling so pretty, looking like she's having the time of her life. Hiram's a heavyset man with a pocked face and a bulbous nose, so he's not much to look at. But he's as pleased as can be to have a beauty like Clover on his arm.

Clover getting married left Frank and his drunkard pa

to fend for themselves. By that time, Frank was pretty much running the farm on his own. My pa took an interest in him, trying to help him in any way he could. I once heard him say that even if the boy was a Kelly, he deserved respect, because he had the gumption to take care of a farm his good-for-nothing father had let go to ruin.

Frank was young to take on such a load of responsibility, a couple of years younger than me. Three or four times a week, I'd look out the front room window and see him come riding up Helmsburg Road on his chestnut Quarter Horse, his pair of fox hounds running alongside them. The whole thing made a handsome sight that set my heart to pounding.

Frank would be wanting to borrow some tool, or to get a piece of advice from my pa. Ma and Hazel and I would look out the window and watch the two men talking under the shade of the wild cherry tree in our front yard. My short, heavyset pa would be craning his neck to look up at Frank. He'd always give Frank a plug of tobacco, and every now and then, the two of them would spit out streams of ugly brown juice. Ma would shake her head in disgust, as she always held to the idea that chewing tobacco was a filthy habit.

Ma would never let Hazel and me go outdoors when Frank was there. She'd never say why. But I always knew it was because he was such a fine-looking young man, and she was afraid all our good sense would fly out of our heads if we went anywhere near him. Frank was a tall, lean fellow with a square jaw and a mop of curly black hair, and his face and forearms were dark from working in the sun. I always thought he had the bluest eyes I'd ever seen, eyes usually found in people with fair complexions. They seemed kind of startling in that dark face of his.

I knew Ma thought a man like Frank posed a danger to a young woman, and she wasn't happy about having him around. Still, she'd take pity on him, and would always send him home with something for his supper. She got to where she started grumbling that Frank was coming to talk to Pa just as an excuse for getting something to eat.

All my years of living on the farm with Ma and Pa and Hazel, nothing much ever changed about my life. But one morning this past April, a few days after I turned twenty-one, something happened that sent my life spinning in circles. I felt so dizzy that I couldn't find a way to stop what was going on. Truth be told, I didn't want it to stop.

On that fateful morning, I was out in the henhouse gathering eggs when I heard the sound of horse's hooves galloping up our road. They slowed to a clip-clop as they turned into our lane. I was curious as to who was coming to call so early, and I went to look out the henhouse door.

Wouldn't you know it, it was Frank Kelly. I was surprised to see him, as he usually came to talk to Pa late in the afternoon.

I knew I should duck back inside the henhouse, but I couldn't move. The sight of our fine-looking neighbor man had turned me to stone. I stood there holding my egg basket, staring at him.

Frank swung his tall body off his horse, tied the reins to the hitching rail, and then walked toward me. His startling blue eyes looked at me in a way that made me feel hot and cold at the same time. It was like they were saying things that words couldn't say. All I wanted to do was to answer those eyes, but I didn't know how.

"Morning, Bertha," he said.

I couldn't say anything back to him. It was all I could do just to nod.

He went on talking. "I never see you out here. What're you doing?"

I finally found my tongue. "Gathering eggs."

He kept walking toward me. It seemed like he wanted to look inside the henhouse, and I moved aside so he could step in. Then I did something I shouldn't have done. I followed him inside. Standing right next to him made me feel lightheaded.

"How many laying hens do you have?" he asked me.

"Six," I told him.

He looked around, nodding like he was pleased with what he saw. "My pa and I only have two hens left," he said. "One up and died just last week. I suppose I'm not tending to them properly."

"It's my job to tend to the hens," I said, feeling a little proud. "I like taking good care of them."

We kept on talking like that, not saying much of anything important. All the while, a tingly feeling was running through my body from my head to my toes. I was glad Frank had come in the morning, when I wasn't hot and sweaty from the day's work and my hair wasn't a mess.

All of a sudden, Frank said, "You're a good woman, Bertha." He stepped closer and brushed a wisp of hair off my cheek. Right then, I thought I was about to die and go to Heaven. If that would've happened, it would've been fine with me, as I'd just had the best feeling a person could ever have in this world.

Then he stepped back and headed toward the henhouse door. "It was nice talking to you, Bertha," he said. "Do you know where your pa is? I need to borrow a shovel."

"He's in the barn," I told him.

I stayed there in the henhouse for a good long while, trying to steady myself. It felt like somebody had grabbed me by the shoulders and shaken me so hard that I couldn't tell left from right or up from down. My heart was all aflutter, and I could hardly breathe. I prayed to God that Ma and Pa would never find out I'd been in the henhouse talking to Frank Kelly.

I'm ashamed to tell you everything that happened after that. Frank started coming to see me two or three times a week, mostly walking the mile between our two farms after dark so that Pa would never know he was there. We'd make plans to meet in one of Pa's sheds or in the barn, and I'd find ways to get around Ma's all-seeing eyes.

Before I knew it, I was letting Frank do things to me that he never should've done. It got to the point where all I could think about was when I was going to see him again. On the days he didn't come, I'd be down in the mouth, and Ma would scold me about needing to keep a cheerful attitude.

Looking back on it now, I can see that I wasn't myself. It was like Frank Kelly had cast a spell on me, and I went clean out of my head.

Frank told me he liked my big bosom. He shouldn't have, as that's not a decent thing to say to a girl. Even though his words made me blush, I liked hearing them. For the first time in my life, I felt pretty. At least for a little while, I could pretend I was the type of girl who could turn a man's head. But in the back of my mind, I knew my big bosom came with a thick waist, wide hips, and heavy legs, and that's not something most men are looking for.

All the while I was carrying on with Frank, I never thought about how things were going to end up. We were so caught up in our secret meetings that we got careless. When Frank would come down to borrow something from Pa in the middle of the day, I'd know to duck into the shed or the henhouse. Then, the minute Pa would go back to his work, Frank would come find me.

I should've known my secret sins couldn't be hidden for long, and that a day of reckoning would come. One afternoon in June, Frank and I were lying in each other's arms in the corner of the haymow, and I wasn't thinking of anything other than how nice it felt to be close to him. All of a sudden, I heard my sister's voice screech, "Bertha!"

I jumped to my feet and straightened my dress. Hazel stood there staring at me, her big brown eyes wide open in shock, one hand clamped over her mouth.

She was holding a kitten in her other hand, and I knew why she'd come up to the haymow. Hazel has a lazy streak in her, and when she's finished with the chores Ma has given her to do, she'd just as soon take a nap as to do anything else.

But Ma gets aggravated if she sees Hazel lying around the house, and she'll think up something else for her to do. So, Hazel goes to the haymow to escape Ma's watchful eye. She likes to take a kitten with her, one who's just finished nursing off its mother and is ready to settle down and sleep. Hazel lies down in the hay with the kitten on her chest, and the two of them nap together.

"Oh, Bertha," she whispered, "how could you?" She dropped the kitten, then turned and climbed back down the haymow ladder as fast as she could.

I knew for sure what my sister was going to do. She was going to run straight to the house and tell Ma everything she'd seen.

I looked at Frank, but he lowered his eyes, like he didn't want to face the trouble we were in. In a split second, he was down that ladder, too. Watching out the haymow window, I saw him cut across our yard and head for the road like a streak of lightning.

I felt so sick with shame that I fell down in the hay and buried my face in my arms. *Oh, Bertha,* I scolded myself over and over again. *How could you have been such a fool? Your ma taught you to have good sense. How in the world did you get yourself into such deep trouble?*

I must've lain there for an hour. I was scared to death to go into the house, because I knew the wrath of God would be waiting for me when I walked through the back door. But sooner or later, I was going to have to face Ma and Pa.

I felt the kitten nudging up against me, mewing pitifully. I figured it was getting hungry again. I picked it up, trying to comfort it, but it only cried all the louder. I started feeling worse than ever. On top of everything else I'd done, there I was, keeping one of God's little creatures away from its mother.

So, I climbed down the haymow ladder and found the mother cat in the barn with the rest of her litter. I put the kitten at her side so it could nurse. It latched on and started feeding like there was no tomorrow. I felt jealous of the kitten cozying up to its mama, knowing it wouldn't be nearly so easy to face my own mother. But I knew I might as well get it over with.

As I headed toward the house, I saw Ma standing at the back door, her hands on her hips, fire blazing in her eyes. "Bertha," she hissed, "I thought I raised you to be a good girl. Never in all my born days did I think I'd see a daughter of mine behaving so disgracefully."

Pa came into the house just a minute after I did. Ma pointed her finger at me and told me to go upstairs so she could talk to him. As I passed by her, she gave me a swat on my backside.

Ma was so mad that she couldn't keep her voice down. So, I heard every word she said when she told Pa that I'd been letting Frank Kelly take liberties with me.

My pa's a quiet man. He keeps his mind on his work and doesn't get stirred up much. But when he does get riled, he can put the fear of God into somebody. When he heard what Ma said about Frank and me, he stomped out of the house and slammed the front door behind him. I ran to my bedroom window to see what he was going to do.

He didn't even take the time to saddle up one of the horses. Instead, he tore off down the road on foot, practically running, going as fast as his short legs and big belly would allow him to. He looked so comical that I would've laughed if I hadn't been scared out of my mind. I knew exactly where he was going. Thinking about what would happen when he got his hands on Frank Kelly made me sick to my stomach.

Pa came back about an hour later, and I could hear the family sitting down to supper without me. Ma didn't even call me to come downstairs. I listened to the sound of their voices in the kitchen, and I knew they were talking about the terrible things I'd done. When Hazel came upstairs to our room, she climbed into bed and turned her back to me, refusing to say a single word.

I was so stirred up with worry that I couldn't fall asleep until the wee hours of the morning. When I awoke, Hazel was already up and gone, and when I went downstairs, the house was empty. I knew Pa would be out in the field. I went to look out the back door and saw Ma and Hazel hanging a tub of wash on the clothesline. Their faces looked hard and angry, and I knew they weren't done talking about me.

The feeling of terrible shame came over me again, making me so weak that my knees started to buckle. For a few minutes, all I could do was to sit at the kitchen table with my head in my hands, trying to think about how I was going to get back into everyone's good graces.

Just get to work, Bertha, I told myself. *Do all your chores, and a little bit extra. Help out wherever you can. Be a good daughter and a good sister, and maybe in a few days, Ma and Pa and Hazel will forget all about this.*

So, I set about washing the breakfast dishes and tidying up the kitchen. Then I went out to the garden with my basket to pick peas.

While I was crouched down beside the row of pea plants, I heard the sound of horse's hooves. I stood up, thinking I'd run and hide in the house, as I was in no mood to pass the time of day with a caller. But the visitor was none other than Frank Kelly. I was surprised that he had the nerve to set foot on our property. I looked around, thinking that any minute, Pa would come tearing out of the barn with his shotgun.

Frank got off his horse and walked over to me, looking like he didn't have a care in the world. As if nothing at all had happened the day before.

"Morning, Bertha," he said cheerfully.

For a minute or two, he stood there beside me looking out over the farm, as if he'd never seen the place before. Then he said, "I was thinking that if you want to get married, I'm willing to do that. I've already talked with your pa about it, and he's given his consent."

It wasn't much of a proposal. It was like he was commenting on the weather instead of talking about something that was going to last for the rest of his life. I wasn't sure his heart was in it.

But I said yes. After what we'd already done, I knew the two of us had no choice but to get married.

My ma and pa weren't happy about me marrying Frank Kelly, not a bit. But both of them were of the mind that once a woman has been with a man, she needs to stay with him for the rest of her life.

Ma refused to speak to me for the longest time. When she finally broke her silence, she gave me a tongue-lashing that lasted for the better part of a week. Once or twice, I thought she was going to cuff me.

"I've got half a mind to go out and cut a hickory switch and give you a good whipping," she said. "But you're a grown woman and you're too old for that. Even though you didn't seem to know any better than to go out and disgrace yourself with the first man that looked at you.

Besides, you might already be with child."

When her anger finally burned itself out, Ma broke down and had a good cry. All the while, I felt like a terrible daughter, making her suffer like that.

After she dried the last of her tears, she settled down and started thinking sensibly about everything. She asked me if I was late. I told her yes, but that it didn't mean anything, as I'd been late before.

She said I needed to get married right away, just in case a child was on the way. "Anyhow," she said, "Walter Thompson has been courting your sister Hazel, and they're aiming to get married next spring. It's only fitting that the oldest daughter gets married off first."

I knew she was thinking that since I was already twenty-one, I was fixing to become an old maid, and that since I had no other prospects for a husband, getting married to Frank Kelly was better than nothing. Ma said she and Pa took comfort in the fact that I'd be living just a mile down the road from them. That way, they could keep an eye on me.

Frank and I worked it out to get married two weeks later, on the first Sunday afternoon in July. The Reverend Rutherford Wade presided over our wedding ceremony at the Nashville Christian Church. When Frank's sisters heard about our plans, they kicked up a fuss, saying that their brother ought to be married in the Catholic Church. But Frank himself didn't seem to care one way or the other, and he went along with what I wanted to do. That seemed to make Ma and Pa feel a little better, like maybe their daughter hadn't gone completely wayward.

There wasn't enough time for Ma to make me a wedding dress. At first, she counted on me wearing the dress she wore when she married Pa, and she hauled it out of the cedar chest for the first time in years. But when I put it on, it was too tight, as I'm plumper than she was on her wedding day.

Ma said there was enough fabric in the seams to let them out, and she was getting ready to do that. But then, she spotted a tear in the skirt that would've looked unsightly if she tried to mend it.

"Bertha, there's nothing I can do to fix this," she said. "You're going to have to make do with something else."

So, I ended up wearing my going-to-church outfit, my gray skirt and my white shirtwaist with the pin tucks. Ma let me wear her cameo broach at the neck. Hazel helped with my hair. She took extra care in pinning it up, fixing some wispy little curls alongside my face to soften my features.

Not many people from the community came to our wedding, as we hadn't had time to spread the word about our plans. Frank's sisters and their husbands were there, along with a whole slew of their children. They took up half the benches in the church, so at least the place didn't look so empty.

All the sisters were sniffling into their hankies at the sight of their baby brother getting married. Some of them were outright bawling. I just hoped they weren't crying because they were disappointed in the woman their brother was marrying.

When I walked down the aisle with my pa and saw Frank standing up front next to Reverend Wade, I got tears in my own eyes. I couldn't believe that I was lucky enough to marry such a fine-looking man.

My husband-to-be was wearing a dark suit with a waistcoat and a colorful cravat, looking as dapper as any fellow I'd ever seen in a magazine. Later, I found out how Frank came by those fancy clothes. His sister Clover had taken one of her husband's suits to the tailor shop in Nashville and had it cut down to fit her brother.

The Kelly sisters, with their curly black hair and blue eyes, were all decked out in their lacy linen summer dresses. When I saw how beautiful they were, my heart sank. I've never been much to look at, with my stout figure and dishwater blonde hair. But at least on my wedding day, I was hoping that people would look at me and think I was a lovely bride. I knew that with the Kelly sisters there, all eyes would be on them.

Standing in the front of the church next to Frank, I felt like a brown sparrow standing next to a proud peacock. As a matter of fact, I felt like a sparrow in a whole flock of peacocks.

The preacher's sermon droned on and on as he talked about the sanctity of marriage, and how no one should enter into that state lightly. My nerves were so on edge that I could hardly take in what he was saying.

All of a sudden, I realized Reverend Wade was about to lead us through our vows. When he asked Frank if he took me for his lawful wedded wife, Frank hesitated for a second. I saw his eyes flick toward Pa, who was sitting there on the front bench scowling at him. Then he said, all in a rush, "I do, I do."

To get to the Kelly farm, you have to go down a long wooded lane. You can't see the house or barn or any of the outbuildings from the road, except for in the winter when the trees are bare. Riding past in my pa's wagon, I'd only ever caught glimpses of the house. So, as Frank drove us home after the wedding, I had no idea what I was heading into. My heart pounded as we turned into the lane toward my new home.

As we came near the house, I spotted a handsome black Morgan hitched to a carriage with bright red seats and a fringed top. At first, my heart leaped in my chest, as I thought maybe the carriage belonged to Frank, and that it was meant to be a surprise for me. I'd never ridden in anything so nice.

But as we drew closer, I saw Frank's oldest sister Violet's husband, Cyrus Richardson, sitting on the front seat of the carriage, looking aggravated and impatient. I figured he hated coming all the way over there from Bloomington, driving his fancy new carriage on our rutted county roads.

"Violet's come to get Pa," Frank explained to me. "She's probably having a hard time getting him out of the house."

All kinds of thoughts came to me at the same time, making me feel a little shaky. My silly flight of fancy about the carriage crashed to the ground, and I realized we'd still have to get along with Frank's spring wagon. Thinking about Frank's drunkard pa made my stomach churn. In the rush to get married, I'd almost forgotten about the old man. I was mighty relieved that I wouldn't have to put up with him in my new home.

"Let me show you around the place before we go inside," Frank said. He helped me out of the wagon like a gentleman, making me smile.

Looking around, I could tell right away that the Kelly family wasn't well off. But nobody around here has much to show for all their hard work. We don't do much more than get by.

The past few years, families have been leaving Brown County in droves, because there's not much good farmland around here anymore. That's because of the erosion of topsoil on the hillsides. Pa says that was bound to happen. He says that people moving up here from the mountains in Kentucky and Tennessee and West Virginia decided to settle on the hills, because that's what they were used to. Then they got foolish and cut down too many of the trees, clearing off the land for farming and selling the logs for a little extra money. And then the erosion started, and a lot of farmers can't grow crops around here anymore. Pa counts himself lucky to have a piece of flat land in the middle of all Brown County's hills.

I followed Frank around the house to the east side of the property, where he pointed out a grove of fruit trees. "You'll probably want to make applesauce," he said. "And maybe can some cherries."

He showed me the pasture where a pair of draft horses and four milk cows were grazing. Then we walked past several run-down sheds to get to the barn. We poked our heads inside before going around back to the hog pen.

I was surprised to see at least two dozen hogs rooting around in the mud, more than my pa ever owned. Frank pulled a few ears of corn from the corncrib next to the barn and threw them into the pen. The hogs rushed toward the food, grunting and squealing and nudging each other aside.

Frank gazed at the animals, a satisfied smile on his face. "Raising and selling hogs earns me more money than anything else on this farm," he said. "It'll get us through the year, even if the corn crop isn't good."

As we walked around the back of the house to get to the chicken coop on the west side, Frank pointed out the cornfield in the distance. Then he pointed to the woods on the far back of the property.

"That's where my pa makes his whiskey." He lowered his voice, as if he didn't want anyone else to hear. "We bring in a little extra money from that."

My pa had never made his own whiskey, so I'd never set eyes on a still. "Can we go back there so I can see?" I asked Frank.

A dark look came over his face. "That's not a place a woman should go," he said. And I knew right then and there that a part of my husband's life would forever be cut off from me.

Frank seemed anxious to change the subject. He pointed to the outhouse, saying, "You'll want to know where that is."

Then we came to the henhouse. "This is something for you to do," he said cheerfully, as if he was trying to make up for not showing me the still. "You can tend the chickens like you did back home."

After that, he showed me the well and the root cellar. Finally, he took me to a garden patch that was overgrown with weeds. It looked like it hadn't been tilled in years. "This was my sisters' vegetable garden," he said. "After Clover left, there was nobody here to take care of it. With all my other chores, I didn't have the time."

He looked at me and smiled. "But next spring, I'll till it for you, and you can plant anything you want." The tenderness in his voice made my heart flutter.

Then we walked around to the front of the house. Cyrus Richardson was still sitting there in his carriage, his head slumped against his chest. It looked like he'd grown tired of waiting and had fallen asleep.

Frank stopped for a minute, and I stood beside him, taking in the whole of the house. "My pa built this house for my ma and the girls," he said. "Way back in the early 1880s, before I was born." He looked wistful. I knew he was thinking back on the days when his pa was still keeping up the farm, before the liquor got the best of him.

Then he shrugged his shoulders and went on talking. "My great-grandparents were some of the first settlers in this county. They cleared this land so they could farm it, and they lived here in a log cabin. This home that my pa built was one of the first frame houses in Brown County."

I couldn't rightly see what he was so proud of. The porch was sagging, and one of the steps was broken. A windowpane in the front room was cracked. The place looked like it hadn't had a coat of paint in twenty years or more. My pa never would've let his place get run down like that. But I knew I wasn't seeing things through my husband's eyes.

Before going inside, we went back to the wagon to get my belongings. Ma had sent along a quilt she'd made for me years ago, meant to be a gift on the day I got married. At the last minute, she'd hustled around to gather together a few other things she thought I'd need for starting out in my new home: a set of sheets, two towels for the kitchen, some washing powder, and an extra scrubbing brush she had on hand.

Being mindful of the broken step, I followed Frank onto the porch and through the door. We passed through the front room and went on into the kitchen. An old man was sitting slumped over at the table. I could tell he was overcome by drink. Right away, I recognized that it was Old Man Kelly, even though I hadn't laid eyes on him since I was a young child.

His daughter Violet was fussing at him, clearly at the end of her rope. "Pa," she scolded, "you need to get up and come with me." She had some of his things stuffed into a pillowcase, and she was holding it away from her fancy dress like it was a sack of garbage.

Old Man Kelly was blubbering like a baby, saying he didn't want to go, that this was his home and he had a right to stay in it. It was the most pitiful sight I'd ever seen.

Frank walked over and laid his hand on the old man's shoulder. "Pa, Pa," he crooned, "you need to listen to Violet."

Violet glanced over at me, then said to her pa, "Frank's new wife is just starting out here, and she doesn't need to be putting up with the likes of you."

She took him by one arm and Frank took him by the other. Together, they raised the sniveling old man to his feet and led him out of the house to Cyrus's carriage.

As they passed by me, I could see that Old Man Kelly had once been a fine-looking man like his son, even though he'd lost all his teeth and his face looked like a wrinkled piece of old leather. I had to think how sad it was to see a human life go to such ruin.

After the others left the house, I stood alone in the kitchen, taking in a sight that made my stomach heave. For a moment, I thought I might have to rush out to the outhouse and vomit. I breathed deeply to settle myself, then forced myself to look at my new surroundings.

Before the wedding, I'd told myself that my new home might be a bit of a mess, and that it might take a woman's touch to get it back in order. But nothing could've prepared me for the shocking conditions I now faced. Flies crawled over the unwashed pots sitting in the sink. The stovetop was splattered with grease, and I could see mouse droppings on the shelf above the stove. I was pretty sure the table hadn't been scrubbed for the better part of a year.

Sickened, I turned and stepped back into the front room, my shoes catching on the sticky grime that caked the floor. Cobwebs hung from the ceiling in the corners of the room, and the furniture was covered with a thick layer of dust. Even though the windows were open, the air felt heavy and stale, and it reeked of whiskey. The whole place reminded me of death and decay.

I remembered my ma talking about the uneasy feeling she'd had when she visited the Kelly home. I could feel it, too. It hung there in the air, making my skin crawl.

"Oh God," I whispered. "I can't live in such a place. What am I to do?"

In my mind, I scolded the Kelly sisters for not having done something to keep the house in decent order. Surely, one of them could've come over from Bloomington from time to time, to scrub the floor and dust the furniture. At the very least, Clover and Hiram could've paid their maid to give the place a good going over.

All of a sudden, it came to me why Frank had asked me to marry him. My heart felt like it dropped to the floor with a terrible thud. I knew my new husband had no loving feelings toward me, and that the only reason he started paying attention to me in the first place was because he needed a good, strong woman to keep house for him.

I wanted to tear out of that filthy, spooky house and run up the road all the way back to Ma and Pa's place. I wanted to bust out crying, burying my face against Ma's shoulder, telling her that I'd made an awful mistake and that I wanted to come home.

But I could hear her voice in my head saying, "Bertha, you made your bed, and now you're going to have to lie in it." I knew I had no choice but to buck up and make the best of things.

Ma brought supper over that evening, a couple of slices of ham along with boiled potatoes, some fresh green beans from her garden, and a pound cake. "I knew it'd be hard for you to get around to cooking when you're just settling into a new place," she said.

When she looked around and saw the condition of the house, she clucked her tongue. "Rose Kelly ought to be rolling over in her grave right now," she said. "She might've been touched in the head, but she never let her home get into such a state."

Before Frank and I went to bed that night, I took out the broom and gave our downstairs bedroom a good sweeping. Watching me, Frank laughed a little, like he was covering up the fact that he was ashamed of the mess. "It was hard to keep the place clean with a fellow like Pa living here," he said. "Now that he's gone, it should be easier."

I was so aggravated that I didn't say anything back to

him. I just kept on working, stripping the filthy blankets off the bed and telling him to take them out to the burn barrel in the backyard. Then I had him help me turn the mattress over, and I made up the bed with the clean sheets and the quilt Ma had sent with me.

For the next week, I swept, dusted, and scrubbed. I tied a rag over the broom and swept the cobwebs off the walls and ceiling. One afternoon, Ma came over, bringing Hazel with her. We washed the cupboard shelves and scrubbed the grease off the stove and tabletop. Then we all three got down on our hands and knees and scrubbed the ground-in filth off the kitchen floor.

I showed Ma the mess in the mudroom: grimy old overcoats, several pairs of work boots with the soles coming off, a few broken baskets, and some old tools that should've been kept in the barn. She waved her hand in front of her nose to ward off the stench of a bucket of rotting potatoes. "Take these out and bury them in the garden," she told me.

When I came back inside, I found Ma rifling through the piles of junk. She had pulled out a scrub board and two wash tubs. "If you scour these out really good," she said, "they'll be just fine for doing the washing."

I pictured all the Kelly sisters using those new-fangled drum washing machines in their fancy homes. And here I was, stuck in their old, rundown house with the old-fashioned way of doing things. I couldn't help but feel bitter.

Ma picked up a tangled rope, then pointed out the back door to one of the clothesline poles that was leaning to one side. "Have Frank straighten that up and put up this line," she said.

She waved her hand around to include the whole of the mudroom. "Bertha, have your husband sort out what he needs, and then burn the rest. You don't want to start off married life by having someone else's mess putting a damper on your spirits."

She told me to take my time in cleaning the upstairs bedrooms, so that I didn't tire myself out too much. And that is what I did. It seemed as if I had the burn barrel going day and night, with all the old clothes and shoes and moth-eaten blankets I hauled out of those rooms.

After the house was clean from top to bottom, I felt satisfied with what I'd done. The place now has a fresh feel to it, as if all those uneasy feelings got swept out along with the dirt and the cobwebs.

This winter while I wait for the baby to come, I'll sit by the stove in the front room and embroider some samplers to hang on the walls. That'll brighten up this place. It won't be anything fancy, but it'll do just fine for Frank and me and our little one.

Sometimes, I worry that a woman like me can't keep a man like Frank happy. But he seems happy enough. He keeps to himself most of the time, and doesn't have a whole lot to say to me. I guess a wife doesn't need to know everything her man is doing. I know Pa would be aggravated if Ma tried to cling to him all the time. He'd get testy with her.

Anyway, Ma doesn't have time for that. She's got her own business to take care of. And so do I.

1908

This April morning is so beautiful that it's almost too much for a person to take in. It's like a little bit of heaven has come down here to Brown County. For the past month, spring has been showing its face, then hiding it again. But I know for sure it's finally here. I've been hearing the peepers, and yesterday morning when I went out to feed the chickens, I saw robins in the yard. A couple of days ago, Frank said he saw a flock of sandhill cranes flying over the pasture.

I opened the window in the front room to let in the fresh air, but only a crack. I don't want to chill this two-month-old babe I'm holding in my arms.

Just a bit ago, Frank came in from the milking. I was finishing up frying his eggs for breakfast when my little one woke up, crying to be nursed. She's gone back to sleep now. I should be putting her back in her cradle so I can clear the breakfast things off the table and get on with my day's work. But I can't seem to get enough of holding this precious little thing and gazing at her sweet baby face.

A minute ago, she opened her eyes and looked up at me, as if she was looking right into my soul. As if she knows her mama through and through. She has a way of doing that. Every time she does, it touches me so deep that it brings tears to my eyes.

My baby girl had such a hard time getting here. It's a miracle that she even made it. Every day, I thank God for sparing her life and mine.

When I knew for sure that I was carrying a child, Ma was the first person I told. Right away, she let go of all her bitterness about what I'd done and started talking to me woman to woman. She set it up for me to be under the care of a midwife, Hattie Patterson. Hattie lives over in Helmsburg with her elderly parents. She's never been married or had children of her own. But she's brought at least a hundred babies into this world. Probably more than that. I've heard it said that she considers all those babies to be like her own children.

Ma insisted on being with me every time Hattie came to call. Having the two of them looking after me calmed my nerves a little bit. Hattie would always ask me how I was feeling, and whether I was eating enough and getting enough rest. She'd warn me not to strain myself with lifting things. Then she'd check me over and tell me I was doing just fine, and that the baby in my belly was growing like it should. She told me my child was due to be born in late February.

But even with all the good things Hattie had to say, I couldn't help but worry. One day when I was sitting with her and Ma, I broke down and confessed what had been weighing on my mind. "I'm scared," I told them. "I'm afraid I might not be able to get through this. What if birthing a child is something I won't be able to bear? What if things take a turn for the worst?"

Hattie was quick to reassure me. "From what I've seen, big strong girls like you, with wide childbearing hips, have the easiest time of it. There's no cause for getting worked up. Try to keep your mind on happy thoughts."

But on a day in early February, two or three weeks before my baby was due to come, Hattie looked worried after she checked me over.

"What's the matter?" I asked her.

"The baby's turned the wrong way around," she told me. "At this point, it should be getting ready to make its way out, with its head down toward the birth canal. But your baby's head is up and the bottom is down. This could make for a breech birth."

I tell you, those words knocked the breath right out of me. I'd heard of breech births before. I knew that mothers and babies sometimes died during births like that.

Hattie could see how scared I was. "There's no cause for alarm yet," she said. "You've got two weeks to go, maybe more. This baby might still get the notion to turn itself the right way around."

I tried to take comfort in Hattie's words, but my mind couldn't help but run wild with fear. Ma took me in her arms and held me while I cried. "Bertha," she said, "at a time like this, a girl's mother should be close at hand. You have Frank come get me the minute you need me."

At the supper table that night, I was so out of sorts that I could hardly find a word to say to my husband. Frank generally pays no mind to whether or not I'm in good spirits. But that evening, he looked at me like he was a little worried. "Bertha," he said, "you look pale. Is something the matter?"

I opened my mouth to tell him about the baby being the wrong way around. Then I thought better of the idea, as I didn't want to get my husband worked up for no good reason. As Hattie had said, the baby could still get itself turned the right way, and everything would be fine.

"Nothing's wrong," I told him. And Frank went on eating, like he'd forgotten what he'd even asked me about. When he was done with his supper, he went out to the barn to tend to the horses.

I was doing up the dishes when my first birth pang hit me, so sharp that it made me double over. I knew right then that I was in for the hardest time of my life.

As soon as the pain passed, I threw on my overcoat and hurried out to the barn to find Frank. "You've got to go get Ma and Hattie Patterson," I told him, all out of breath. Then another pang came, and I clutched my belly and cried out.

Frank held up his lantern to look at my face. When he saw the state I was in, he said, "I'm going right away."

He led the horse out of the stall, getting ready to hitch it to the wagon. "Get yourself back into the house," he ordered me. As I headed inside, I heard the horse and wagon clattering down our lane.

I crawled into bed and curled up under Ma's quilt, more scared than I'd ever been in my entire life. Every few minutes, the pains came again, each one so hard that I thought it would be the death of me. I kept praying that Frank would come back soon, bringing Ma and Hattie with him. It seemed like two or three hours passed with me being alone in the house.

I began to wonder whether my husband had decided he couldn't face what was happening, and that he'd run off to escape the ordeal. I started thinking that I should go get Ma on my own. But when I stood up, another pain doubled me over, and I knew I'd never make it a mile up the road.

As I crawled back under the quilt, the kerosene lamp beside the bed sputtered and went out, leaving me in darkness. I hadn't gotten around to filling it before my birth pangs set in. I noticed it was getting colder in the house, and I knew the stove in the front room needed to be stoked with more firewood. I tried to get up to tend to it, but I couldn't.

My mind began taking a terrible turn. I started thinking for sure that I was one of those young women who were doomed to die in childbirth. Or that maybe I would live, but my child wouldn't. I knew things like that happened. My ma had lost two babies at birth, both of them boys. She ended up with only Hazel and me.

All of a sudden, Frank's ma came to my mind. I

realized she'd died giving birth in this very house, probably in the very room I was lying in. Probably in the very same bed. I thought about how terribly she must've suffered. Rose Kelly had never been more to me than the peculiar neighbor woman in Ma's stories. But at that moment, I felt a kinship with her, as if she and I were two souls going through the same tribulation. As if she was right there enduring the pain with me.

Just as another pang hit, I felt something sweet and soft brush against my cheek. Like a mother stroking the face of her beloved child. And a peaceful feeling came over me. Right then, it didn't much matter to me whether I lived or died. Either way, I knew I was going to be all right.

I never did tell Frank that his ma came to comfort me during my travail. It would've been too unsettling for him to hear that.

The birth pangs must've stopped for a while, and I must've fallen asleep, because the next thing I knew, I woke up to the sound of footsteps in the house. Ma came rushing into the bedroom, calling, "Oh Bertha, oh Bertha!" Hattie Patterson followed her.

Ma clucked her tongue in dismay as she set about refilling the kerosene lamp. I could hear Frank in the living room putting firewood into the stove.

Just as quickly as it had stopped, my pain started up again. After the first pang passed, Hattie checked me over. "The baby's still in the breech position," she said. "We're going to need Doc Murphy's help with this."

My peace of mind left me, and I was back to feeling scared. I knew Doc Murphy lived in Helmsburg, and that there was no telling how long it would take for him to get there.

Hattie left the room, and I heard her giving orders to Frank. "Go straight to Doc Murphy's house. There's no time to spare. Pound on the door if the doctor is asleep. Tell him he needs to get here right away." I heard Frank leave the house, the door slamming behind him.

Ma brought a kitchen chair to my bedside and sat there holding my hand. Again and again, great waves of agony came over me. The sound of my screams must've rattled the windows of our house.

"Stay strong, Bertha," Ma kept urging. "Squeeze my hand if you need to." I squeezed so hard that I almost crushed her bones, but she didn't complain.

It seemed like half the night passed before Doc Murphy finally arrived. He checked me over, then said, "I'm going to need to use forceps to turn this baby around."

He brought the instrument out of his bag. When I saw what he was about to put inside me, I screamed louder than ever. Ma had to shush me. "It'll be all right," she said. "Let the doctor do what he needs to do."

"I think it's best if I give her a little chloroform," Doc Murphy said. "She's beside herself from the pain, and I doubt that she can take any more."

"Will that be safe for her?" Ma asked.

"I'll use a small amount," he told her. "Just enough to calm her and dull the pain."

From that point, my recollections are hazy. It seemed as if I left the here and now and went off into the realms of glory. At times, I could hear Ma crying and praying, pleading with God to spare my life. Her voice seemed far away, even though she was sitting right there beside me.

But in the place I'd gone to, I knew everything was going to be fine, even if I was about to die. As a matter of fact, I thought I was dying, and that my baby and I were going to heaven together. I could see my child's face, and I knew it was a girl. I can't say how I knew that, but I knew it for sure. We were going to spend eternity together, my baby girl and me, and that seemed like a beautiful thing.

Then I heard a baby's cry, and it brought me back down to earth. I knew my child had finally been born. Later, Ma and Hattie told me that the baby wasn't breathing at first, and that they were afraid she wasn't going to live. So, they were mighty glad to hear her cry.

I tried to lift my head to see what was happening, but I was as weak as a newborn kitten. I'd never felt like that in my entire life. Not even when I'd had a bad cold or the stomach flu. I closed my eyes and drifted off to sleep.

I don't know how long it was before I woke up again. Hattie Patterson was there by my side. "Do you want to see your baby girl?" she asked.

"Yes," I whispered.

She propped me up in bed, then laid my baby in my arms. I looked my child over, taking in everything about her. She was long and thin, not properly filled out. Her tiny arms and legs seemed hardly any bigger around than my finger. Her little face looked pinched, and there were ugly marks on her cheeks. But she had the most beautiful blue eyes I'd ever seen, startling blue eyes like her father's.

Hattie told me the marks on her face came from when Doc Murphy used his forceps during the delivery. "Don't worry," she said. "The marks will disappear in a week or two. And when this baby fills out a bit, she'll be as pretty as a picture."

I looked down at the little stranger in my arms. I couldn't believe that she'd grown inside me. But she looked up at me with her bright blue eyes as if she already knew me. It seemed like she was trying to say, "Mama, I finally made it."

Then I realized it wasn't just me who'd struggled with this birth. My baby girl and I had gone through the ordeal together. I felt proud of the brave little thing, honored to be her mother. In that moment, I knew I'd give anything, even my own life, to keep her safe and happy.

Ever so gently, I caressed my baby's silky blonde hair and kissed her soft little cheek, my heart swelling with more love than I'd ever known before. I wanted to say to her, "Yes, my precious child, you're finally here. And I am so glad." But I couldn't find the words to speak.

I looked out the bedroom window and saw that the sun was high in the sky. So many hours had passed since my birth pangs had set in. I tried to think what day it was, as it would forever be my daughter's birthday. Then it settled in my mind: February 7, 1908.

All of a sudden, Frank walked into the room. I'd been so taken up with the baby that I hadn't known he was anywhere around. Without saying a word, he took my child from my arms, leaving me feeling so bereft that I wanted to cry.

While Ma and Hattie and I watched, he held her as he paced around the bedroom, crooning to her in a voice so soft that we could hardly hear him. I could tell he thought our baby belonged to him more than to me. I wanted to cry out to him that it wasn't fair, because I'd been the one to carry her and go through all the trouble of bringing her into this life.

Then he looked up at the rest of us and smiled, holding the baby out like he was showing her off to the world. "Katherine Rose Kelly," he said.

The mention of her first name didn't surprise me. I'd already decided on naming our baby Katherine if it was a girl, and Frank had agreed to it. But I hadn't yet settled on a middle name. I'd been thinking about Lena, after my ma, even though I hadn't brought it up with anyone.

But I could tell Frank was set on naming our baby after his own ma, and that he'd never let go of that idea. I knew it was his way of clinging to a mother he'd never known. And seeing as how Rose's spirit had paid me a visit during my time of suffering, I couldn't find it in my heart to go against him. I did wonder, though, what Ma was thinking about his naming a baby after someone who'd been touched in the head. It might've seemed to her like it wasn't a good way for a child to start out in life.

Soon after Frank left, Pa came by to see the baby, bringing along the cradle Ma had used for Hazel and me. Pa's not one to make a fuss, but I could tell he was taken with his new grandchild. He held the little bundle in his big arms and hardly wanted to put her down.

Then Ma and Hattie tried to teach me how to suckle my baby. Katherine didn't want to latch on at first, and I worried that she wasn't taking to me as her mama. Hattie told me not to fret. She said to let the baby sleep for a while, and that she'd do fine the next time I tried to nurse her.

I asked Hattie why my body still hurt so bad. She told me my insides were torn up from the ordeal of birthing Katherine. She said I might not be able to have a second child. I cried a little bit when she said that. But the way things went with this one, I'd be glad not to go through childbirth again.

Ma and Hazel took turns staying with me the first week after Katherine was born. Ma told me I needed lots of rest, and she made sure I stayed in bed. She didn't allow me to lift anything or strain myself in any way. She and Hazel did all the cooking and cleaning and washing.

Every time my baby would cry, I'd want to go pick her up from her cradle. "Don't get up," Ma or Hazel would say. Then they'd bring her to me for suckling.

I'd never had a time like that in my entire life. Truthfully, I started feeling lazy, lying in bed all day. I was glad when Ma finally let me get up one morning to fix Frank's breakfast.

Every day that first week, one or two of the Kelly sisters came over to see their brother's child. Ma got fed up with their fussing and their foolishness. She complained to me that they were in the way when she was trying to get things done.

Then, they started bringing up the subject of the baby being christened. I had no idea what they were talking about. "What's a christening?" I finally asked Violet.

She looked at me like I was stupid. "A christening means a baptism," she said. "Christening a newborn baby is what we do in the Catholic Church."

That whole conversation aggravated Ma to no end. I could see that she was ready to give Violet a piece of her mind, to tell her that our family wasn't Catholic and that her granddaughter wasn't going to be raised Catholic. I whispered to Ma to keep her thoughts to herself. I reminded her that I married into a Catholic family, and that there was no way of getting around some of the things they wanted to do.

To be honest, I wasn't keen on the idea of Katherine being baptized in the Catholic Church, either. I was hoping Frank's sisters would get tired of talking about it and let the subject drop. But then, Clover brought over something she called a christening gown, a lacy little white dress and a matching bonnet. She was so tickled with the idea of Katherine wearing it for her christening. She said Frank had asked her to be Katherine's godmother.

I couldn't imagine Frank doing such a thing, as he doesn't care about Catholic ways. I was pretty sure Clover had taken him aside, and that he'd given in to her when she pestered him about wanting to be the godmother. I realized things were getting out of hand, and that I didn't want anything else to happen to my child without my having a say in it. So, I started joining in with the Kelly sisters while they carried on with their plans.

The christening took place when Katherine was a month old. Frank's sisters wanted to have it done earlier, saying we shouldn't waste any time in making sure the baby was saved for all eternity. But Ma wasn't swayed by their foolish beliefs, and she put her foot down. She told them that if they expected me to make the long trip over to their church in Bloomington, they needed to give me time to build up my strength.

Ma and Pa didn't go to the christening, of course. I didn't expect them to go against their beliefs. But at the last minute, Hazel told me she'd go along. She said I needed someone to look after me, as she didn't know how good Frank would be at that sort of thing.

Violet said she didn't want the baby to travel in an open wagon, so she and Cyrus drove their carriage over from Bloomington to pick us up. I was mighty glad to have my sister by my side for the long trip. Frank wasn't paying a bit of attention to me. His mind was somewhere else.

When I walked through the doors of Saint Charles Borromeo Catholic Church, I was trembling from head to toe, both from my nerves and from being worn out. I'd never been in such a place before. Frank took Katherine from me, and Hazel held onto my arm to steady me.

All six of the Kelly sisters were there with their families, all decked out for the big occasion, clucking and carrying on like a flock of hens. They didn't bring their father to his granddaughter's christening. I figured they would be ashamed to have him around.

Frank's sisters knew I was a stranger to Catholic ways, and they kept giving me orders. "Do this, stand over there, say that." Like they thought I was dimwitted. Time and again, I had to bite my tongue to keep from lashing out.

When I looked around that church and saw so many strange things, the crucifix and the statues and the stained-glass windows, it didn't seem like a house of God to me.

As a matter of fact, I felt a little sinful just being there. Katherine squirmed and cried when the priest poured the holy water over her head. I thought it was a foolish thing to do, aggravating a baby like that.

After the christening was over, I was all done in, and I wanted to go home. But then we had to go over to Ivy's house, because Frank's family wanted to keep on celebrating Katherine's big day. Ivy and her husband Caleb had hired a couple of women to come in and prepare a big feast. I'd never seen a table loaded down with so much food. But all the commotion in the house made me so nervous that I couldn't eat more than a few bites.

All afternoon, Clover insisted on carrying my child around, bragging to everybody that she was her godmother. It was like me being the mother didn't count for anything at all. She'd hardly let go of Katherine long enough to allow me to nurse her.

By the end of the day, I was more than a little fed up with the whole affair. But I know that, being a married woman, I sometimes have to put up with my husband's family's way of doing things. It's hard to know when to give in and when to stand my ground.

Just a week after Katherine's christening, Frank and I got word that Old Man Kelly had died. Lily and her husband Hubert came over from Bloomington to break the news. I figured the old man had lost the will to live after he'd had to leave the home he'd known for so many years. That made me feel bad, because me marrying Frank had pushed him out.

The sisters had been passing their pa around between their homes, sending him to the next place when they couldn't abide him any longer. Lily said their pa had died at her house, in his sleep. She carried on and on about how she'd gone to wake him up and found his body as cold as ice. Like the whole thing had been a terrible trial for her. I knew she was making that big scene to cover up the fact that she was glad to have him off her hands. I imagine all the sisters are glad to have him gone.

Frank has taken it hard, though. He didn't say much to his sister when she told him what happened. But after Lily and Hubert drove off, he left the house. He didn't say where he was going. He stayed away for the rest of the day, and didn't even come in for supper. I was worried sick about him, but there wasn't anything I could do.

That night, for the first time since I'd gotten married, I went to bed without my husband. I laid awake, thinking he was gone for good. Little Katherine had been doing so well with sleeping through the night. But that night, she woke up and cried, as if she knew something was wrong.

I brought her to bed with me and let her nurse. When she fell back asleep, I kept her with me, just for the comfort of it. All the while, I was wondering what kind of turn life was going to take for my baby and me.

It was almost sunrise when Frank finally came in. When he crawled into bed with me, he had the smell of liquor on him. And he kept on drinking for the next three days. I had to be the one to go out and milk the cows. All he managed to do was to throw a little corn to the hogs. I hoped this wasn't a prediction of things to come.

But since then, he's pulled himself together. He's tending to his chores again. I'm glad about that.

I don't know what it's like to have a parent die. I'd hardly know how to go on living if something happened to Ma or Pa. My husband isn't but a young man of twenty. He's got no pa to look up to anymore. Come to think of it, he never did, with his pa being the way he was. Frank's always been like a fatherless son. Sometimes, I pity him.

I try to comfort Frank, but he won't have any part of it. He hardly talks to me at all. So, I just let him be. He'll come around in his own time.

Looking on the brighter side of life, my sister Hazel is getting married to Walter Thompson next month. Walter works at his family's general store in Helmsburg. He stands to inherit the business from his pa, so he's all set for his future. Ma and Pa are agreeable to the idea of Hazel marrying him.

Ma just finished up making Hazel's wedding gown. The last time Hazel came over, she brought along the dress to show me. It's a thing of beauty, with its tiered skirt and the lace trim on the bodice and sleeves. My sister will be a lovely bride.

I thought I might be bitter because I didn't get to wear such a dress on my wedding day. But I'm not. How could I be jealous of anything my sister has when I have this precious little bundle in my arms? After something as important as giving birth to a child, worrying about a wedding dress seems silly.

Having her second daughter getting married and leaving the house will be hard on Ma. So, I expect she'll make up for it by doting on her grandbaby more than she already does. Little Katherine tickles her so. Ma uses every excuse to come down the road and take her from my arms and hold her for a while.

I tease Ma, telling her she's not paying attention to Pa the way she should. But I'm thrilled to see her so pleased with my child. I know she's forgiven me a hundred times over for what I did with Frank. Any way you look at it, bringing this sweet baby girl into the world couldn't possibly be wrong.

Ma says every mother thinks her child is beautiful, even if it's the homeliest thing on God's green earth. But she says little Katherine is especially comely. She has the same pale blonde hair I had when I was a baby, except that it's curly like Frank's. And she has her father's startling blue eyes. When anyone sees her for the first time, those eyes make them stop for a second look.

I often think about the world my child will be growing up in. It'll be a lot different than what I've lived through. I've known nothing besides getting around in a horse-drawn wagon, and I've never hankered after anything else. But now, people are buying motor cars. I saw two or three of them when we were over in Bloomington for the christening. No doubt, Frank's sisters will be riding around in them soon. Maybe motor cars will be everywhere by the time my child is old enough to think about such things.

Everybody's talking these days about the Wright Brothers' flying machines. I can't even imagine what it would be like to see one. Maybe the time will come when my child will look up at the sky and see one every day.

Maybe someday, Katherine will marry a rich man, and she'll have a telephone in the house, and a nice washing machine, and all sorts of other things I can't even picture in my mind.

Before his pa died, Frank kept saying he was going to till the vegetable garden for me. But he hasn't mentioned anything about it since then. I think I've gained enough strength to where I'm ready to do some planting.

It's such a nice day. Maybe he'll get around to doing the tilling today or tomorrow. If not, I'll bring it up, kind of easy-like, so I don't rile him.

Maybe we can bundle up the baby and take a little trip into Helmsburg to buy some seeds. It would do my heart good to do something like that as a family. I'm thinking it would do Frank some good, too, if he'll only agree to it.

1910

Yesterday afternoon, a census worker came to the house, a man by the name of Mr. Gibson. Frank was gone at the time, off to Helmsburg running errands. He'd told me he was going to Thompson's General Store to buy chewing tobacco, and I asked him to pick up some flour and coffee while he was there.

When Frank mentioned going to the store, I knew he was trying to cover up the fact that he was planning on delivering whiskey to a couple of fellows, Sam Walker and Zebadiah Hawkins. I didn't say anything about it, though. It's a sore point between us, his dealings with the liquor. When my husband's gone delivering whiskey, I never know when he's coming home.

But I was glad he wasn't here when Mr. Gibson came. Frank doesn't like strangers coming around, and he's gruff with them. It made me proud to sit down with the census worker and answer his questions on my own.

The last time I'd seen a census worker was in the year 1900, when I was just a girl of thirteen. At the time, I hadn't paid any mind to what the man was doing, as Pa was answering all his questions.

I can hardly believe a whole ten years have passed since then. It shocks me to think that I'm a grownup now, instead of just being Ma and Pa's young daughter, and that Frank and I are in charge of our own household.

Mr. Gibson looked like he was chilled to the bone from being out in the January weather. I invited him to sit in Frank's chair by the stove in the front room. Then I offered him a cup of coffee and some of the sugar cookies I'd baked that morning.

While Mr. Gibson and I talked, little Katherine played with her rubber ball. She'd toss it down on the floor and go toddling after it. Then she'd pick it up and toss it down again. Mr. Gibson watched her with a pleased smile before he got down to the business of his census questions.

"What year was your husband born?" he asked me.

"He was born in May of 1888," I told him. "He'll be turning twenty-two."

Mr. Gibson wrote that down on his paper, then looked up at me. "And your year of birth?"

"1886," I said. "I'll be twenty-four in April."

He nodded and wrote that down. "And your birth place?"

"Both of us were born in Indiana, here in Brown County," I said. "As a matter of fact, my husband was born right here in this house. And I was born at my ma and pa's place just up the road from here."

I felt foolish about blabbing on the way I did. But I hardly have anybody to talk to, and when someone does listen to what I have to say, I can't keep myself quiet.

"How far did each of you go in school?" Mr. Gibson asked.

"I went to fourth grade and my husband went to fifth grade." Telling him that made me feel a little stupid, being so uneducated. I looked down at Katherine, thinking that I'd make sure my daughter at least got to high school.

"And what's your husband's occupation?" he asked.

"He's a farmer," I said, feeling proud.

Frank's come into his own with this farm these past two years. He's raised and sold more hogs than I can keep track of. He's added a few more cows to his dairy herd, and he's selling twice the amount of milk he was when we first got married. His field corn crops have been more than enough for feeding the hogs and chickens and making his whiskey. I suspect he's making a good amount of money from the liquor, although he never mentions anything about it to me.

And I've been bringing in a little money myself. I've got thirteen hens now, and they lay more eggs than the three of us can eat. I had Frank put up a sign at the end of our lane that says, *Eggs for Sale.* It seems like every day, someone comes knocking on our door, wanting to buy a dozen eggs.

I told some of that to the census worker, even though he didn't ask about it. Of course, I didn't say anything about the whiskey, as I'm not sure my husband is abiding by the law in what he's doing.

Then Mr. Gibson asked, "How many children are in the household?"

Katherine had stopped playing with her ball and had come over to me on the sofa. I picked her up and sat her on my lap. "Just this one," I said.

"And how old is she?" he asked.

"She'll be two next month," I told him. "Just a couple of weeks from now."

He looked at her a good long while, with that pleased smile on his face. Then he said, "Going door to door with my work, I see a lot of youngsters. Most of them are runny-nosed little ragamuffins with dirty faces. I can truthfully say I've never seen a child as lovely as this one."

His words made my heart swell with pride. Katherine wiggled off my lap and toddled over to Mr. Gibson, as if she wanted to get a better look at the stranger who'd come to our house. He reached out and tickled her under the chin. "Where'd you get those pretty blue eyes?" he asked.

"From her pa," I said, wishing I could claim they'd come from me.

After Mr. Gibson left, I had to sit there for a few minutes, wondering how an ordinary woman like me could've given birth to such a special child. It made me feel like I'd done something good. Like I'd made my mark on the world.

A lot of two-year-old children I've seen don't have much more than a little bit of wispy hair on their heads. But Katherine's hair has grown long. Her pale blonde curls already hang to her shoulders. I take care to brush her beautiful hair every day to keep it from tangling. She likes the feel of the brush in her hair. When she sees me take out the hairbrush, she runs to climb on my lap without me even telling her to.

I have to admit that my child's a little spoiled. She has so many people doting on her. About every week, one or two of Frank's sisters come over to see their little niece.

Just as I'd predicted, all of their husbands have motor cars now. Violet and Cyrus were the first to get one. When they had no more use for their fancy carriage, Cyrus sold it to Frank for a reasonable amount of money. Frank was so tickled to own a carriage. I know he's proud that he's come this far in the world.

When Katherine hears the sound of an engine coming down our lane, her blue eyes pop wide open, because she knows one of her aunts is coming to visit her. She climbs on the sofa and looks out the window to see who it is.

Frank's sisters keep bringing over dresses their own little girls have outgrown, things that had cost a pretty penny when they were new. Sometimes, they even bring over brand new things.

I keep thinking I should put the nice dresses back for special times, just keeping one or two out for the Sundays when Ma and Pa take Katherine and me down to church in Nashville. But then, I think about how fast my child is growing. Katherine is tall for her age, and slender like Frank. By the time I'd get those nice things pulled out again, they'd be too short for her.

So, I dress my child in something pretty every day. I

make sure to keep her face and hands clean. My baby girl is so pleasing to look at that I can hardly take my eyes off her.

More often than not, the aunt who comes to visit is Clover. Hiram sits in the car and sleeps while she's inside.

Clover's getting up in age, thirty-two years old now, and she's never had a child. It's starting to look like she never will. Some people snicker and say old Hiram isn't up for the job of giving her one.

It seems like Clover is pouring all her motherly love into my child. I understand that she needs a little one to dote on, but it aggravates me sometimes. She goes overboard in the way she caters to Katherine, and I'm afraid she's giving my daughter the wrong idea. I'm afraid Katherine will start thinking that everything in life will always go her way. Frank and I will never be able to provide that kind of life for her. It wouldn't be a good thing even if we could, as a person needs to learn to bear up under life's trials.

Every time Clover comes to visit, she brings along the newest toy they have at Henderson's Mercantile. Katherine now has a stuffed bear and a stuffed rabbit, a couple of baby dolls, a Jack-in-the-box, a top, several rubber balls, and building blocks with the ABCs on them. Clover likes to take out those blocks and sit down with Katherine to see if she can get her to name a few of the letters. She likes to hold Katherine on her lap and show her the picture books she brings over.

Some of the things Clover brings Katherine aren't meant for a two-year-old. I've had to put back a few things until Katherine gets older, a china tea set and a doll with a fancy dress and china head. A toddler would break such things after a minute of playing with them.

Even though she has all those store-bought toys,

Katherine's favorite toy is the ragdoll Ma made for her. She drags it by one arm as she toddles around the house, and she insists on taking it into her crib when she goes to bed at night.

A couple of months ago, Pa built his granddaughter a toybox to keep all her toys in. And right now, he's working on building her a tiny table and chairs for when she's old enough to play with her tea set.

But so far, all that doting hasn't spoiled Katherine's spirit. She's a sweet-natured child, and she hardly ever cries. Sometimes, her not crying seems unnatural to me. I remember when my sister Hazel was little. She'd hang onto Ma's dress, fussing and crying all day long. Ma would try to shush her so she could do her work in peace. She'd end up having to hold Hazel on her hip while she washed the dishes or stirred something on the stove.

Katherine doesn't fuss for my attention. She's content with her own self. It's like she's a person who was born with a heart full of happiness, and she hardly needs to be soothed by anyone else.

There's one thing that aggravates me, though. Katherine favors her pa over me. There's no doubt about that. She can be happy as a lark with me all day long, but the minute Frank comes into the house, she runs to him, holding up her little arms to be picked up. "Papa, Papa!" she says.

Frank always gets a big smile on his face when she does that. He picks her up and swings her around, making her squeal. Then he holds her close, and she lays her head against his shoulder, as if her papa's arms are the best place in the world for her to be.

I admit that I'm jealous when I see that. Sometimes, I have to look away so I don't get myself too upset. But underneath my bitterness, I'm glad for my husband. Having Katherine is the best thing that's ever happened to

Frank. She's warmed up his heart in a way that no one else ever could. The way she loves him teaches him how to love in return. She's done more for him than I've been able to do.

My sister has two children already, one-year-old Annabelle and a newborn boy named after his papa. With one child coming so soon after the other, it makes me wonder how many Hazel will have before she's done with childbearing.

I'm not expecting to have any more children myself. There's the matter of what Hattie Patterson told me, that my insides were torn up during Katherine's birth. But the other thing is that Frank pretty much leaves me alone. That puzzles me. A young man has needs, and I wonder at the fact that he doesn't come to me to meet those needs. When he was sneaking over to Ma and Pa's place before we got married, he couldn't get enough of me.

Maybe he's put off by the fact that I'm heavier now than I was back then. Hazel's lucky enough to take after our slender ma, while I take after Pa with his portly frame.

It seems the only time Frank wants anything to do with me is when he's had too much to drink. It's like he can't muster up the will to touch his wife without being fortified by liquor. It doesn't do my heart any good for him to be fumbling for me at times like that, and I'd just as soon he stays on his own side of the bed.

Sometimes, the thought crosses my mind that he might be taking up with some other woman. I can't allow myself to dwell on such matters. I have to keep my mind on cheerful things.

I know my husband doesn't love me the way a husband should love a wife. But I do know that he loves our child, and for that reason, he's content with our family life. I suppose that's the best I can ask for.

And I'm happy with having just one child, my darling Katherine. I hate to say this, but in my opinion, she'll be worth more than all of Hazel's children put together.

When the weather warms up a bit, I'll take the carriage out and go visit my sister in Helmsburg. Katherine is old enough now to sit on the seat beside me. It'll be a nice outing, just her and me.

Frank didn't much like the idea of me driving the carriage at first. But it's something I insisted on. He doesn't need it for his work day, as he uses the spring wagon for carrying farm supplies. There's no reason the carriage should just sit there.

Anyway, a wife has a right to some say in a marriage. My ma has always respected Pa as the head of the household, but I've seen times when she's put her foot down about something.

Hazel will appreciate having the company. With those two little ones, it's hard for her to get out. She's at home all day while Walter's working at the store, and I'm sure she gets lonesome. Yup, I'm looking forward to Katherine and me getting out a couple of months from now. The thought of that helps me get through my days.

1912

This August has been scorching hot, and so muggy a person can hardly breathe. The kitchen has been miserable with me canning applesauce and tomatoes. Yesterday evening when he came in for supper, Frank complained when he saw the jars of tomato juice cooling on one end of the table.

"This kitchen is hot as hell," he growled at me. "Do you have to be doing this right now?"

I didn't much appreciate his use of a curse word, especially in front of Katherine. "I can't help when things get ripe," I snapped at him. "If I don't get these tomatoes canned now, they'll all go to waste."

The air felt heavy and unsettled, and I knew a storm was coming. After supper, I hurried up and took the last of my canned goods out to the root cellar, just before the rain started.

The storm was a mighty one, with the thunder and lightning keeping me awake half the night. When I got up this morning, I was relieved to find that the temperature had dropped by twenty degrees. The air felt fresh and crisp, reminding me that fall was just around the corner.

For weeks, Katherine had been listless and cranky from the heat. But this morning, she woke up full of energy. She bounced around the house singing the little nursery rhymes that her Aunt Clover had taught her: *Twinkle, Twinkle, Little Star* and *Mary Had a Little Lamb.*

I smiled to myself, thinking that I'd make it a good day for the two of us. It was time to put my work aside and take Katherine on an outing to see her Aunt Hazel and her little cousins. When I told Katherine what I had in mind, she jumped up and down and clapped her hands.

She was so excited about our plans that she could hardly eat the bread and butter sandwich I fixed for her lunch. But I made her stay at the table until she was done. Afterwards, she could barely stand still to let me wash her hands and face. Then she was out the back door, lickety-split. I ran out after her, laughing when I saw her scrambling up into the carriage like a little monkey.

"Hurry up, slowpoke," she called to me. "Hitch up the horse so we can go."

We headed out for Hazel's house in Helmsburg, both of us feeling lighthearted. I took along one of the apple pies I had baked this morning, as my sister has no time for baking these days. Just a month ago, she delivered her third child, little Ernest.

I have to say I was taken aback when I walked into Hazel's house and saw the state of things. Hazel has always been one to keep herself up. As a matter of fact, I used to think of her as being vain. But today, she didn't seem like her usual self. It looked like she hadn't taken the time to properly pin up her hair, and it was flying out in all directions. The front of her dress was stained from where the baby had spit up on her. She had dark half-moons under her big brown eyes, and she seemed nervous and upset.

I could tell she was worn out from taking care of her little ones, and that there just wasn't enough of her to go around. Three-year-old Annabelle was still wearing her nightgown, and her hair was a tangled mess. Two-year-old Walter's face looked like it hadn't been washed in days. The floor in the front room needed sweeping, and the children's toys were scattered all over the place.

"I'm sorry about the mess," Hazel said. Her voice was hardly more than a whisper, as if she didn't have the strength to speak any louder. "The baby isn't sleeping at night, so I'm not getting any sleep myself."

I thought about how easy I had it with just one child, and I felt sorry for her. "You're all tuckered out," I told her. "Why don't you go lie down for a spell while I tend to the children?"

Hazel shook her head. "No, Bertha, I need to tell you something. I can't rest until I get this off my mind."

The worry in her voice told me that something was troubling her deeply. I sat down next to her on the sofa. "What is it, Hazel? Tell me everything."

Then Hazel burst into tears. My sister has always been one to cry at the drop of a hat. And it seems as if her children are taking after her. When Annabelle saw her mama's tears, her lower lip trembled and her little face puckered up, and soon she was crying as hard as Hazel. Little Walter looked at his sister, and then he started crying. All the commotion woke up baby Ernest in his cradle, and he commenced to wailing at the top of his lungs.

My Katherine had never been around people carrying on like that. She stood there staring at all of them. Then she went over to Annabelle and Walter and put her arms around one and then the other.

"Hush, hush," she said, patting their little backs. When her cousins settled down a bit, she said, "Let's go play outside." Then she took their hands and led them out of the house.

"You make sure to stay in the yard, Katherine," I called after her. I knew she'd be okay, as she pays attention to what I say.

I picked up baby Ernest from his cradle, rocking him in my arms to quiet him. But he couldn't be soothed, and kept on crying. Hazel wiped her eyes on her dirty hankie and then blew her nose. "He needs to nurse," she said. I handed Ernest to her, and she put him to her breast.

She was quiet for a few minutes, closing her eyes as if

she didn't have the strength to keep them open any longer. I thought maybe she'd forgotten about what was troubling her. I had in mind to take the baby after he was done suckling and send her off to lie down.

But then she looked over at me and said, "Bertha, Walter told me something that has been heavy on my heart, and I think it's only right that I tell you."

Her words shot through me like a bolt of lightning from last night's storm. I knew she was about to say something that wouldn't sit well with me. My heart pounded while I waited for her to go on.

She stared down at her nursing baby, as if she was afraid to look me in the eye. Then she whispered, "Bertha, Walter's heard people talking at the store. They're saying things about Frank."

Looking back on that moment, I wish I had stopped her right then and there. I wish I would've said, "I don't want to hear any gossip about my husband."

But I didn't. Instead, I asked, "What are they saying about Frank?"

"Things that aren't very nice," Hazel said. "They say he's carrying on with the Hawkins girls."

Nothing in my life has ever hit me so hard as those words. I felt my heart drop to the pit of my stomach.

Ever since the day we got married, I've had the feeling that something isn't right with the way my husband behaves. The way he's gone for hours on end without giving me any reason for it. As if what he does and where he goes should be no concern of mine. The way he pays no attention to me, not saying a word to me the whole day long. As if I have no purpose in his life other than cooking his meals and washing his clothes and taking care of his child.

Still, Hazel's news seemed impossible. I couldn't take it in.

No one around here thinks highly of the Hawkins family. Zebadiah Hawkins is a worthless drunk. His wife Sally has become so downhearted that she's given up on caring about anything. She turns a blind eye to what her daughters are doing, and everybody knows they're full of mischief. Sometimes, I've thought about paying Sally Hawkins a visit, just to cheer her up. But I've been too ashamed of the fact that my husband brings over the liquor that keeps her husband drunk.

And now, could it be true that my husband was tied up with the Hawkins family in another way? How could he think of messing with those girls, who were only fifteen and sixteen, when he was a grown man of twenty-four?

Shame crept over me, scorching my skin and scalding my insides. Hazel put out a hand to lay it on my arm. "I'm so sorry, Bertha," she whispered.

I jerked my arm away from her. "It's just gossip," I snapped. "You know how people talk."

"Walter's heard about this more than once," she said. "At least four or five times."

"That doesn't make it true," I shot back at her.

"Bertha," she said, her voice rising a bit. "You know Frank for who he is. You knew the way he was before you married him. You knew he was bent on sneaking around."

Right then, I wanted to reach over and slap my sister in the face. To get a grip on myself, I got up and went to look out the front window, pretending that I was checking up on the children.

Anger boiled inside me. I hated my sister for bringing up the fact that I'd carried on with Frank before we got married. I hated myself even more for having been so foolish. For having fallen under the spell of a man who had no good intentions toward me.

"Bertha…." Hazel's voice sounded shaky, as if she was afraid to say anything more to me. "What will you do if Frank gets one of those girls in a family way?"

"How could you even think such a thing?" I growled at her. Without turning around, I could tell she was crying again, as I could hear her choking back her sobs.

I couldn't bring myself to sit down next to her again. Instead, I sat in the rocking chair across the room. "Have you said anything about this to Ma and Pa?" I asked her.

She shook her head.

"Don't tell them." I tried to keep my voice low so as not to upset her more. "Promise me you won't tell them. If Pa ever hears such a thing, he'll be coming after Frank with a loaded shotgun."

"Okay," she said. Her face was red and wet with tears, and I remembered that I'd been planning on taking the baby so she could rest. But I didn't have it in me to do that anymore.

We sat there for a good long while, not finding much of anything to say to each other. I told Hazel that I'd put the apple pie on her kitchen table, and I asked her if she wanted a slice. She said she wasn't hungry.

Then the children came in. Their cheerfulness eased the strain between Hazel and me. Katherine had a fistful of wild daisies that she'd found at the edge of the woods. She handed them to her aunt, and Hazel smiled through her tears.

"It's time to go," I said to Katherine.

"Why?" she asked. "I'm not done playing with Walter and Annabelle. And I never even got to hold baby Ernest."

I cast about in my mind to find a reason for leaving in such a hurry. "We need to get home to dig some potatoes for supper," I told her.

She pouted a little, but not for long, as she likes going out to the garden with me to harvest vegetables.

On the drive home, it felt as if a heavy cloud was hanging over my life, darkening the sunshiny day. My sister's words played over and over in my mind. I tried to tell myself that Hazel had said those terrible things because her nerves were on edge and she was beside herself with exhaustion. I've heard it said that some women have trouble with their minds after giving birth, and that it takes a while for them to get back to their old selves.

I shouldn't give this another minute of thought, I told myself. *I should put this completely out of my mind.* Still, I couldn't shake off the dark feeling that had settled over me.

Katherine kept up a steady stream of chatter, pointing out cows in a pasture and black-eyed Susans growing alongside the road. "Look out, Mama," she called when a farmer in his mule-drawn wagon approached us from the other direction. "You have to pull over so he can pass."

I had to smile, as my four-year-old already knows how people need to drive on these narrow country roads. She waved to the man, and giggled when he waved back at her.

She prattled on about playing with her cousins, saying, "Annabelle did this. Walter did that." All of a sudden, she scooted close to me and linked her little arm through mine. "Mama," she said, "when am I going to have a baby brother like Ernest?"

Oh, child, I wanted to say to her. *Such a thing is never going to happen.*

But I didn't want to dampen her sunny spirits. I thought carefully about what I wanted to say so as to make her feel good about not having any brothers or sisters. "Sometimes," I said, "God gives a mother only one child. And that child is so special that she doesn't need any more children. That's the way it is with our family."

My answer seemed to satisfy her. She laid her head on my lap and fell asleep. I stroked her blonde curls, wishing our family life was the way I'd made it out to be. I dreaded to think of the day that would surely come, the day her little heart would be broken by the truth.

The minute I pulled the carriage up to the barn, Katherine was wide awake. "Let's go dig the potatoes!" she sang out.

I laughed at her eagerness. "Give me a minute to get my bearings, child," I said to her. "Let me put the horse away first."

I wasn't in the mood for digging potatoes, but I went ahead with it because I'd given Katherine my word. In the garden, she crawled around on her hands and knees in the dirt, waiting to grab the potatoes as I turned them over with my shovel. As if each one was a buried treasure.

"Oh, look! This is a big one!" she'd squeal. Then she'd put it in the bucket for me.

Once, my shovel sliced a potato in half. Katherine grabbed the two pieces and tried to fit them together. "Oh no!" she cried.

"It's okay," I told her. "I have to cut the potatoes to cook them anyway."

She looked up at me, and the late afternoon sun hit her little face in such a way that it took my breath away. Her arms were dirty all the way up to her elbows. Her cheeks were smudged, and her tangled curls were hanging in her face. But her startling blue eyes were shining in the middle of all that, and I thought I'd never seen anything so lovely. It was like I was looking at an angel. I could see that no amount of mess could ever hide my child's glowing spirit.

Right then and there, I felt a love I'd never known before, a love so strong that I didn't know what to do with it. It lay there in my heart alongside all the bad feelings I was harboring toward my husband.

And then, I was overcome by a terrible fear. Something so beautiful as this angelic child couldn't possibly last long in this harsh world. I felt like my own life didn't matter at all, and that my one and only purpose on this earth was to keep this little one safe and protected.

I watched Katherine lift a nightcrawler from the dirt and hold it in the palm of her hand, looking at it in wonder. "What's this doing here?" she asked me.

"Worms live in the ground," I told her. "They make the garden soil better."

She scratched at the dirt with her tiny fingers, digging a little hole. Then she laid the wriggling worm in it, covering it with dirt and patting it down. "There," she said. She looked up at me and giggled. "I put the worm to bed."

Oh child, I thought, *this farm isn't the fairyland you make it out to be. This world is hard and cruel and unfair. This world is going to break your heart someday.*

Of course, I knew better than to say such a thing to an innocent child. If Katherine can stay happy and shielded from the world's ugliness for as long as possible, it'll give her a better start in life.

Frank hurried through his supper this evening and was getting ready to head out the back door again. But Katherine grabbed hold of his hand, looking up at him with sorrow in her big blue eyes.

"Where are you going, Papa?" she asked. "Can't you stay here with Mama and me?" She's gotten used to asking questions like that.

I saw a flash of hurt in Frank's eyes. "I've got business to take care of," he mumbled. He bent down and kissed the top of his daughter's head, and then he was gone.

He didn't tell me where he was off to, or when he'd be back. I don't expect that from him anymore. As a matter of fact, I was glad he was gone, as I couldn't abide his presence in the house. I needed time alone to think things over.

Katherine was all tuckered out from her big day, so I put her to bed early. I've taught her to kneel by the side of her bed to say her prayers. It seems as if those prayers keep getting longer. She always asks God to bless Grandma and Grandpa. Then she names off all her aunts on Frank's side. Sometimes, she mentions Clover two or three times, as if she wants to make sure she doesn't forget her. Then she prays for her Aunt Hazel and her Uncle Walter, along with Annabelle, little Walter, and Ernest.

This past spring when one of Frank's heifers gave birth for the first time, Katherine was so taken by the little calf that she kept going off to the barn all day long. She insisted on seeing it time and again. I had to keep dropping what I was doing to run after her, as it's not safe for a little one to be alone in the barn.

That night in her prayers, she asked God to bless the little calf. It seems as if that got her started on something. Now, every time a new animal is born on this farm, she asks God to bless it. After the calf, it was a litter of kittens. Then, it was the fox hound's puppies. Then, some newborn piglets. Her prayers are getting out of hand, and sometimes I'm afraid I'm going to fall asleep kneeling there beside her.

Wouldn't you know it, tonight she asked God to bless the worm she found in the garden. If I hadn't been so worried and downhearted, I would've laughed out loud.

She finished up her prayer by saying, "And bless Papa wherever he is tonight. Amen."

That brought tears to my eyes. I knew that in her innocent little mind, my child understood that something was wrong. In my own mind, I added to her prayer: *God, please bring my wayward husband to his senses.*

After I was sure Katherine was sound asleep, I slipped out the front door and sat on the porch steps. Looking up at the starry sky, I started pondering on what I needed to do.

Should I break down and tell Ma and Pa about what Frank's been up to? I know they'd never stand for me living like this. They'd take Katherine and me home with them in a heartbeat. I know Pa's been keeping his eye on things, and that he's getting fed up with Frank's running around the county the way he does. It wouldn't take much more to make Pa put his foot down once and for all.

But what if the rumors Walter heard at his store aren't even true? It would be a foolhardy thing to uproot my life and the life of my child for the sake of nothing but gossip.

Before I do anything else, maybe I should bring this up with Frank. Maybe I should ask for his side of the story.

But what if that makes him so angry that he tells me to leave right then and there? And what if he won't let me take Katherine with me? What if Pa comes to get us and Frank grabs his shotgun and points it in Pa's face?

My mind flashed back to something that happened last March, just a month after Katherine turned four. We were having a late winter snowstorm, with the wind howling something terrible.

The first snowfall of the season is always so beautiful. You get up in the morning to find everything blanketed in white, unspoiled by footprints or wagon wheel tracks. The world seems peaceful and pure.

But late winter snowstorms feel like nothing more than a hardship to endure. I always have my mind set on spring, and I can't bear it when winter hangs on and on.

So, I was feeling out of sorts that evening. Frank had come in from the barn and was warming himself in his chair by the stove. Katherine had set up the dollhouse Clover had given her for her birthday, and she had the little dolls and furniture spread all over the front room floor. She was caught up in her play, chatting to her dolls, not mindful of anything else. And she kept inching her little bottom closer and closer to the hot stove. She's so thin, I figured she was craving the heat to warm her bones.

"Katherine," I scolded, "you need to move away from

the stove before you burn yourself."

She glanced up at me and scooted herself away, then went back to her play. Before I knew it, she was right up next to the stove again.

Three times, I had to tell her to move away from the stove. I knew she wasn't disobeying me on purpose. She just wasn't paying attention to what she was doing.

Not only was I out of sorts from the weather, I was uneasy about having Frank so close at hand. I'd gotten to the point where having him in the house made me so nervous that I didn't know what to do with myself.

So, the fourth time Katherine almost burned herself on the stove, I wasn't thinking about what I was doing. I jumped up off the sofa, grabbed her by the arm, and yanked her up, intent on giving her a whack on the backside. Like Ma would've done with a misbehaving child.

But I stopped when I saw the fear in her eyes. Her little lip trembled, and I could see she was fighting back her tears. Frank bellowed from his chair, "Bertha, leave her be."

Frank often says, "Leave her be," when I scold Katherine for a little bit of mischief. As if I have no right to do the things a mother is supposed to do. But that night, he said it in such a harsh way that it scared me, and I let go of her arm.

"Come here, little one," Frank said to Katherine. She went to him and climbed onto his lap, whimpering. In a few minutes, she was asleep. Then Frank closed his eyes and fell asleep, too.

I looked at the two of them so peaceful with each other, and I felt so alone that I wanted to cry. It was like Frank and Katherine had their own little world, and I was shut out of it. I went to stare out the window at the falling snow, feeling low-down and ashamed of myself, vowing to never lay hands on my child again.

While I was remembering all that, the sound of Katherine's voice broke into my thoughts. "Mama, Mama," I heard her cry through the open window of her upstairs bedroom.

Jumping up off the porch step, I ran into the house and up the stairs. I found my little girl standing in the middle of her dark room, looking like a tiny ghost in her white nightgown. I held out my arms, and she ran to me.

"What is it, sweetheart?" I asked as I scooped her up.

She wrapped her arms around me and laid her head on my shoulder. "Papa's gone," she said. "And I thought you were gone, too."

In that moment, I knew for sure that there's nothing more precious in this world than a child's heart. It's like a delicate flower, something that should never be crushed or trampled on.

I tucked Katherine back into bed and lay down with her until she fell asleep again. Then I tiptoed down the stairs to my own bedroom.

Lying here alone in bed, I can't keep myself from falling back into troubled thoughts.

I can't take Katherine away from her papa. I can't be the cause of ruining the life on this farm that she loves so dearly. What if she would take her papa's side and turn against me? What if she would insist on staying with him?

Clover would love that. She'd jump right in and take over raising my child, and Katherine would grow to love her aunt more than she loved her own mama.

I know that I never could bear to lose the affection of my precious child. Never, never could I live through such a thing.

What is a woman to do, then? Just pray for strength, I suppose. Just pray every day for the strength to keep carrying on.

1914

I guess you could say that my husband and I have found a way to live with each other these past few years, even though there's no love between us. We've gotten into the habit of giving each other a wide berth. That way, we avoid any fussing and fighting in the household. Frank minds his business, and I mind mine.

I ask him no questions other than what's necessary for running this farm. I've come to the point where it doesn't matter to me whether I go to sleep alone or whether my husband is lying on the other side of the bed. He never reaches for me anymore. I wouldn't allow it anyway, as I never know where he's been.

But even though her mama and papa have no love for each other, Katherine is growing up just fine. I'm glad about that, and I'm pretty sure Frank is, too. Our child's gotten old enough to where she can help her papa with his chores. Sometimes, I stand on the back porch and watch her tagging along after him in the barnyard, chattering like a little magpie, asking him all kinds of questions.

She has no idea what a scoundrel her papa is, and she loves him with all her heart. I don't want to stand in the way of that. And I know he loves her, too. I suspect she's the only person in this world who means anything to him.

Katherine has already learned a lot from her papa about raising horses, cows, and hogs. She loves all the barnyard animals and insists on helping Frank take care of them, especially the puppies and kittens and baby pigs.

From me, she's learned about tending chickens and growing a vegetable garden. She's a well-rounded child who loves her life on this farm. She doesn't even mind the ugly chores, like carrying the table scraps out to the hogs or emptying the chamber pot in the outhouse.

Sometimes, I want to tell her that life on this farm isn't as wonderful as she makes it out to be. And that there isn't much reward from all our hard work other than keeping ourselves alive. But I don't.

When Hazel and I were growing up, we called our parents Ma and Pa. Those are the terms most folks around here use. But Katherine seems to be settled on calling Frank and me Papa and Mama. It sounds sweet coming from her, like there's some special love in it. So, I let it be. As far as I'm concerned, she can call me Mama until I'm an old woman.

Katherine's blonde curls now hang down to her waist. I thought her hair would darken as she grew older, like mine did. But so far, it hasn't. It's still so pale it's almost white, and so beautiful a person can hardly look at it.

About a year ago, I started braiding her hair. I figured it would be easier to keep it out of her face when she runs around the farm. At first, she didn't like the braids and complained that they felt too tight. But she's gotten used to them.

Now, when she runs out to the barn after her papa, or when she plays on the rope swing Frank hung for her on a branch of the oak tree in our backyard, her braids go flying.

Even though Clover keeps bringing her toys, Katherine likes to make her own little dolls with twigs, corn husks, and a bit of twine. In the summer evenings when the fireflies come out, she dances around the yard with them, pretending she's somewhere magical. I smile when I see her carefree ways. I know they can't last for long.

Katherine plays so hard that she's filthy by the end of the day. Her dirty little hands and feet keep me knowing that she's a child of the earth, not the angel from heaven I sometimes make her out to be. Every day, I fill a bucket with water from our outdoor pump, then let it sit in the sun to warm up. In the evening, I bring it to the back porch, and I have Katherine wash her hands and feet before she goes to bed.

On Saturday nights, I fill a washtub with water I heat on the kitchen stove so that Katherine can take a bath. I usually have her bathe in the mudroom. But when it's cold outside, I set the tub by the stove in the front room so that she doesn't get chilled. She loves her bath, and she's learned to wash herself properly.

Every couple of weeks, I wash her beautiful long hair in the kitchen sink. That takes some doing. It's going to be a while before she can manage that on her own.

Whenever Katherine gets mosquito bites or chigger bites or a little bit of poison ivy, I scrub her with the lye soap my ma makes. If she gets a bad rash on her arms or legs, I put a mixture of lard and sulfur on the area and wrap it in clean rags.

Sometimes, she gets stickers in the soles of her feet from running around the yard barefooted. I have to pick them out with a needle from my sewing basket. Katherine hollers when I do that. I tell her that if she would wear her shoes when she plays outside, she'd never get stickers. But she won't have any part of shoes during the summertime.

One day this past July, Katherine gave Frank and me quite a scare. She was playing in the front yard when I went out to call her in for supper. I went back inside to put the food on the table, expecting her to come running right in. Frank was already sitting there, waiting to eat.

All of a sudden, I heard a thump and a cry, and I ran out on the porch to see what was the matter. Katherine had caught her bare foot on the broken porch step, and had fallen backward onto the ground. Her foot was twisted to one side, and was bleeding badly. Her head was lying on one of the stepping stones that lead to the house. She wasn't moving.

I hollered for Frank, and he came rushing out of the house. When he saw Katherine lying there, he cried out in a way I'd never heard before.

He squatted down beside her, and very carefully, he worked to free her foot from the broken step. "Go get something to wrap it in," he said to me.

I ran inside and grabbed a clean dishtowel. Frank wrapped it around Katherine's foot. Then he picked her up and carried her out to the carriage. I followed him, as I knew he was aiming to set out for Doc Murphy's office. I wasn't going to let him take my child without me.

All the way there, I held Katherine in my arms. She stared up at me with glassy eyes, as if she didn't know where she was or what was happening to her. "Mama's here, sweetheart," I kept saying. "You'll be all right."

That probably aggravated Frank, me not mentioning that he was there, too. He could've spoken up to comfort her himself. But he didn't.

When we got to Doc Murphy's place, he let us right in and had us lay Katherine on the table in his office. "What happened?" he asked as he looked at her foot.

I glanced over at Frank, wondering if he'd say something. When he didn't, I spoke up and said, "She caught it on a broken porch step."

Doc Murphy cleaned up the wound, put antiseptic on it, and then wrapped it in a bandage. He told us her ankle had been sprained, but that she hadn't broken any bones.

Then he checked her all over to see if she'd hurt any other part of herself. When he touched her head, she winced. I told him she'd hit her head on a stepping stone.

"She has a lump on the back of her head the size of a goose egg," he told us. "She's got a concussion. That's why she's so dazed. She's probably so dizzy that she can't see straight."

"What should we do for her?" I asked him.

"Keep her in bed for a few days," he advised. "If she's up and playing too soon, she's likely to get dizzy, and she could fall and hurt herself again. Keep her off that ankle until the swelling goes down. And if you see any signs of infection in the wound, bring her back right away."

Then he gave Frank a stern look. "You need to get around to fixing that broken step. With a growing child in the household, you need to keep your place in good repair."

Frank nodded, hanging his head. I'd never before seen him look so ashamed of himself. On the way home, I didn't say anything else to him, as I could tell he'd taken the doctor's words to heart.

My husband's always done anything he's wanted to do, I thought. *And he's never felt bad about any of his wicked deeds. But now, he's full of remorse about not having fixed that broken step. He knows he's to blame for his child getting hurt, and he's got a heart full of sorrow over it.*

The very next day, Frank was out on the front porch taking measurements of the steps. Then, he went off to the lumberyard in Helmsburg to get supplies. Not only did he build brand new porch steps, he replaced the rotting boards on the porch as well.

It seemed like he was in a frame of mind to keep on fixing things. Because the day after he finished with the porch, he brought his friend Sam Walker over to the house, and the two of them replaced the cracked pane in the front window. And before the summer was over, he'd given the entire house a new coat of white paint. Instead of running out in the evening like he usually did, he stayed at the job until the sun went down.

I was thankful for everything my husband had done, even if it took my child getting hurt to get him started on it.

I figured he had a right to know how much I appreciated his hard work. So, one evening at the supper table, I told him that. He gave me a strange look, as if what he'd done had nothing to do with me.

The evening after he finished with the painting, I walked all the way around the house, just taking it all in. Then I stood in the front yard, looking at the new windowpane and the new porch steps. I told myself that no matter what else was wrong with my life, at least I had a nice place to live. I knew I needed to take comfort in that.

Katherine bounced back from her mishap in short order. In a week's time, she was as good as new. But I haven't been able to get over what happened. If I lose track of my child for more than a minute or two, my heart starts pounding, and I have to stop what I'm doing to go and look for her. I know now that a mother can lose her child in the blink of an eye.

Whenever Frank takes the wagon into Helmsburg to pick up supplies, Katherine begs to ride along with him. He doesn't always take her, but when he does, he tries to time the trip so they can watch a train pull into the station.

Helmsburg's train station is a busy place, with four trains coming and going every day: two from Indianapolis and two from Illinois. The trains carry freight and mail and even passengers. When I was growing up, I never could've imagined such a thing happening in our neck of the woods.

I'm glad Katherine gets the chance to see all that. But I can't help but worry that something might happen to her. I remind Frank over and over to keep hold of her hand so that she doesn't wander off when she wants to look at something.

My child thinks the train station is the most exciting place in the world. She comes home and tells me about seeing the train cars full of coal and lumber and gravel. Sometimes, she gets to watch the men load cars with logs cut from Brown County's forests.

Next to the station are stockyards that hold cattle, hogs, and sheep. Frank has mentioned that he can hardly pull Katherine away from looking at the animals.

Mostly, though, Katherine likes to watch the passengers getting off the train. The last time she went to the station with her papa, she came home and told me about everyone she saw.

"There was a tall man with a big mustache," she said. "He had a little boy with him. And there was a woman in a red dress. She was wearing a beautiful hat with flowers and feathers on it. She was holding onto a man's arm. He had a big belly like Grandpa's. There was a carriage waiting for them. They got into the carriage and rode away. I asked Papa where they were going. 'To Nashville,' he said, 'where your Aunt Clover lives.'"

Knowing she's so interested in all of that makes me think my child will someday get out and see the big world. Her life will be so much different than mine.

I wish I could go and see the train myself. Once, I asked Frank if I could ride along with him and Katherine. He looked at me funny and said, "Don't you think you have enough to do around here to keep you busy?"

That hurt my feelings so bad that I've never mustered the nerve to ask again.

A few months ago, Hazel had her fourth child, little Ruby. I hope she and Walter slow down some so that she doesn't wear herself completely out. As often as I can, I devote a day to helping her. Katherine is old enough to help mind the little ones, which lets Hazel and me get something done in her house or garden.

Hazel and I have restored our sisterly love. Since that

day two years ago, we've never spoken about what wicked things Frank might be doing behind my back. Hazel knows I'm handling the matter in my own way, the best I can.

When the weather is nice, Katherine and I like to go walking up the road to visit Ma. More often than not, I help Ma with a quilt she's got set up, while Katherine tags along after her grandpa. Sometimes, Pa grabs a piece of pine or oak or cedar, whatever kind of wood he has on hand, and sits down to whittle an animal for her. She gets excited and tries to guess what he's making.

My folks and I have started going to the new Oak Ridge Christian Church, that little white church about a mile or so north of Helmsburg. What with Helmsburg growing the way it is, people were thinking this community needed another graveyard. So, they started one on a plot of land on Oak Ridge Road.

Then, they figured they needed to build a church next to the graveyard. I'm glad they did. There are some real nice folks that go to the Oak Ridge Church. Keeping company with other people warms my heart, making up for the fact that I get no love from my husband.

I've also taken to going to prayer meetings and hymn sings at the church. At the prayer meetings on Wednesday evenings, the Reverend Isaac Barnes gives a little talk about living a Christian life. Then, we pray for the sick, the needy, and the wayward. People bring up the names of those in special need of prayer.

Truth be told, I think the prayer meetings give people a chance to gossip. Someone's always bringing up something about Zebadiah Hawkins and his problem with liquor. They say he gets out of hand and beats his wife when he's drunk. Or they say something about Maynard Mitchell's oldest boy, Willis. He has an unruly nature, and from time to time, he runs away from home. His mother

Nellie worries herself sick over him.

I never bring up praying for Frank, even though I rightly should, as I don't want to call attention to what's going on in our family. I don't want tongues to start wagging even more than they do now. Whenever people ask me about Frank, I tell them something about what he's doing on the farm. I try to sound like I'm pleased with him.

The prayer meetings get long. We have to turn around and kneel over the benches to pray, and that's kind of hard on those of us who are a little heavyset. After a while, my knees start hurting. Sometimes, I hope certain people don't get started praying, because they go on and on and don't know when to stop.

Katherine gets weary of it all, and she fidgets. If the evening is warm enough, I send her out to play with the other youngsters in the churchyard. During quiet moments in the meeting, we can hear the little ones in their outdoor games, playing tag or hide-and-seek among the gravestones. Sometimes, we hear their little voices singing *London Bridge* or *The Farmer in the Dell.*

If it's cold and she can't go outside, Katherine ends up crawling under the bench and falling asleep. I'm glad she does that, as I don't want her tender little heart troubled by what comes up during the prayers.

But she loves the Sunday evening hymn sings, and she stays awake for every minute of them. She likes to share the hymnal with me. Even though she can't read the words, she holds one side while I hold the other.

Ma goes to the hymn sings with us. Pa doesn't come along. He says he needs some peace and quiet after a week of hard work, and he can't abide all the caterwauling.

He does have a point. There are certain people who get carried away with their singing, and they're hard to listen to. Old Gertrude McDonald is the worst of all. She has a crackly old voice that wanders off tune, and she's always three beats behind the rest of us.

One Sunday evening, Katherine and I were sitting on the bench next to Gertrude. When it came time to sing *The Old Rugged Cross,* the old woman closed her eyes and threw back her head and sang with all her heart.

Katherine couldn't bear it, and she covered her ears. I tried to pull her hands away from her head, whispering to her that she was being naughty. But she wouldn't let go. So, I had to pick her up and carry her out of the church to have a talk with her.

"Why does Mrs. McDonald have to sing that way?" she complained when I scolded her. "She's too loud."

"She's old," I said, "and her voice isn't good anymore. But she still likes to sing because she loves the Lord."

Katherine seemed to understand. She didn't fuss about it anymore, and she behaved herself for the rest of the service. But later that week, while she was playing with her dolls, I caught her singing to them the way Gertrude McDonald sings. I had to walk away so she wouldn't hear me laughing.

One day last summer when Clover came over for a visit, she took me aside for a talk. "I want to start taking Katherine to Saint Charles Barromeo Catholic Church in Bloomington," she said. "Where she was baptized. It's time she starts getting some proper Catholic instruction."

I was fit to be tied. "Absolutely not!" I said. "She goes with me to the Oak Ridge Christian Church."

A dark look came over Clover's face, and I knew she wasn't going to let the matter drop. Wouldn't you know it, she went straight out to the barn to have a talk with her brother. When Frank came in for supper that evening, he said, "I gave Clover permission to take Katherine to Mass with her next Sunday."

"Why would you do that?" I said, raising my voice at him. That's something I hardly ever do.

He raised his voice back at me. "I have a say in what my child does."

Of course, Clover had talked with Katherine about it, too, and had gotten her all worked up. Truthfully, Katherine had no idea about what goes on in the Catholic Church. All she was thinking about was getting to ride in Clover's motor car.

Clover doesn't count on Hiram to drive her around anymore. Whenever she gets the notion to go somewhere, she drives herself. She's a bold woman, and I'm not sure everything she does is proper.

I gave up fighting about the matter of Katherine going to the Catholic Church. I knew I'd never win with Frank and Clover joining forces against me. That Sunday morning at the Oak Ridge Church, I hated having to explain to Ma and Pa why my child wasn't with me. They both looked sorrowful, and I felt awful about letting them down.

All morning long, I kept worrying about what Katherine was doing in her strange new church. In the afternoon, I was on pins and needles waiting for Clover to bring her back home. It wasn't until suppertime that Clover's car finally came rumbling down our lane.

I was so glad to have my little girl home that I picked her up and held her on my lap. She was all smiles about the adventure she'd had.

"Clover says I'm Catholic because I was baptized in the Catholic Church," she blurted out. I could tell she didn't know what she was talking about. She was just repeating the words her aunt had said. And she had no idea that she was hurting me something terrible.

"As far as I'm concerned," I said, "you're Christian. That's the kind of church you and I have been going to."

"Maybe I'll be both," she said. "But I think I like the Catholic Church better."

"You're just saying that because it's something new," I told her.

She got a serious look on her face. "No, it's because I know God in the Catholic Church."

I could hardly believe my ears when she said that. "You mean you don't know God at the Oak Ridge Church?" I asked her. "With all the singing and praying we do?"

"Yes," she said, "but I know God better in the Catholic Church."

Right then and there, I felt like nothing in my life was good enough for my child. I've never felt good enough for Katherine.

What am I to do about this? I asked myself. But no answer has ever come to me.

Since then, Katherine has kept on going to the Oak Ridge Church with me. Most of the time, anyway. I'm glad about that. But every now and then, Clover comes to get her and takes her to the Catholic Church. She never brings her home until it's late, and I don't know what kind of ideas she's putting in my child's head.

The last time Clover came to get Katherine was a couple of weeks ago, before the winter weather got too bad for her to take her fancy car out on these awful roads. When Katherine came home, she was carrying a string of beads with a cross dangling on one end.

"What on earth do you have there?" I asked her.

"It's a rose…." She looked down at the beads like she was trying to remember the word.

Frank had just come into the house after talking with Clover in the yard. "It's a rosary," he said.

"It's a rosary," Katherine repeated. "Aunt Clover said

I should use it when I say my prayers."

My first thought was to take such a ridiculous thing away from her. But Frank shot me a look that let me know he'd never allow that. So, I let her be.

And now, whenever we kneel by her bed to say her nighttime prayers, my child has that little rosary in her hand. She doesn't know how to use it the way it's meant to be used, but she hangs onto it as if it's something important. I have a feeling it's a habit that's going to stick with her for the rest of her life.

1915

Late last summer, I had to focus my attention on getting Katherine ready to start school. She was looking forward to it, and pestered me with questions about what was going to happen.

"What will I do at school?" she asked one day.

"You'll learn to read," I said. "The way your papa and I know how to read."

"Oh, goody!" She clapped her hands. "What else?"

"You'll learn arithmetic," I told her. "You'll learn to add and subtract numbers."

She nodded, as if she was taking it all in. Then she got a worried look on her face. "What if I get hungry? Who will fix me food for lunch?"

"Don't worry," I said. "I'll pack you a lunch, and you'll take it to school with you."

"What if I need to go to the outhouse?"

"There's an outhouse right there behind the school. Matter of fact, there are two outhouses. One for the girls and one for the boys."

"But what if I miss you and Papa? What if I get sad?"

Her question tugged at my heart. "You'll just have to be a big girl," I told her.

Even though I tried to build her up so she'd be sure of herself, it worried me terribly to think of my child being away from me all day long. Here on the farm, I'd been able to watch her almost every minute of the day, making sure she was safe. I knew full well I couldn't keep on doing that year after year. I needed to get her ready for the world, to teach her something more about life. But all I could think to tell her was to wash her face every day and to keep her hands clean.

I did take comfort in the fact that my child would be going to Owl Creek School, which is a couple of miles down from us on Helmsburg Road. It's the same school I went to when I was growing up in these parts, so at least I knew something about it.

I kept on worrying until an idea came to me. One morning in August, I took Katherine by the hand, and we walked a mile down the road to the Sawyer farm. My ma and pa, the Sniders, live on the farm the farthest north on Helmsburg road. Then it's Frank and me, the Kellys. Just south of us are the Sawyers, and south of them is the Mitchell farm.

"Where are we going?" Katherine asked me. She was used to walking north to see Ma and Pa, but we'd never gone the other direction.

"We're going to have a talk with Amanda Sawyer," I told her.

"About what?" Katherine asked.

"About her looking after you when you start school," I said.

The Sawyers have four children. Amanda, the oldest, is ten. Her little brother Benjamin is seven, and both of them go to school. Then there are two others still at home. I've always known Amanda to be a good girl. She's her mother Hannah's right hand helper, and she knows how to take care of little ones.

When we got to the Sawyer farm, Hannah Sawyer invited us in. I couldn't help but admire what a nice house she kept. Amanda was sweet enough to bring us glasses of water to drink after our walk.

After we passed the time for a few minutes, I explained to Hannah and Amanda the reason for our visit, that I needed someone to look after Katherine when she started school. Amanda nodded, as if she was serious about the matter. She walked over to sit next to Katherine on the sofa and put her arm around her.

"Don't worry," she told Katherine. "I'll watch over you. I'll hold your hand at recess, and I'll take you to the outhouse whenever you need to go. And I'll make sure the Mitchell boys don't bother you."

Maynard and Nellie Mitchell have nine big strapping boys, each of them ornerier than the last. It looks like they aren't stopping anytime soon, as the last time I saw Nellie, she looked to be in a family way again. She had a weary look on her face, as if she knew full well what she was in for, birthing another ruffian.

Even though Maynard Mitchell hollers at his boys and beats them with hickory switches, he can never count on them to do their chores right. Once, the boys let their hogs get out, and the animals ran all the way up the road to the Sawyer farm. They rooted around in Mrs. Sawyer's vegetable garden, eating all the watermelon and squash and cucumbers. Since then, there's been hard feelings between the Sawyers and the Mitchells.

While I was thinking those thoughts about the Mitchells, Amanda said to Katherine, "If the Mitchell boys ever get out of hand, I'll be sure to tell Mr. Fox."

Mr. Clarence Fox is the teacher at Owl Creek School. He might not be the best at teaching the three R's, reading, writing, and arithmetic, but he knows how to handle the big boys in the classroom. That's an important thing around here. There are always boys looking to get the upper hand with the teacher, and at Owl Creek, it's the Mitchell boys.

I've heard it said that almost every day, there's a go-round between Mr. Fox and the Mitchell boys. Willis, the oldest, and Rueben and Herschel, the twins who come right after him, try to whip Mr. Fox every chance they get. But Mr. Fox is a rough and tough fellow, and he keeps control in his classroom.

There's a whole lot of schools here in Brown County, maybe seventy of them or more scattered around in the hills and hollows. When my ma and pa were growing up, they went to log schools. We've come a long way since then, as now all the schools are frame buildings. But some of them are closing down because of so many families moving out of the county.

I've worried some about Owl Creek closing down, wondering where Katherine would go if that happened. You need to have at least a dozen children in a school district in order to keep a school open. One good thing about having the Mitchell family living here is that with Nellie Mitchell constantly birthing baby boys, there's no chance of Owl Creek closing down any time soon.

A lot of the teachers in our Brown County schools board with the families of their pupils. Clarence Fox boards with the Sawyer family during the school year. I'm sure he's comfortable there, with how nice Mrs. Sawyer keeps her house. I gave a moment of thought to how it would be to board a teacher in my home. We have an extra bedroom upstairs next to Katherine's. Frank and I could move up there and let the teacher have our downstairs room. It would be nice to have a learned person in the home to talk to.

But then, I thought about how with Frank gone almost every evening, it wouldn't look proper to have another man in the household. I'd only want to board a woman teacher. And with the Mitchell boys at Owl Creek, no lady would ever want to take on that job.

Besides, when I thought about Mr. Fox with his dark, ugly face, his fierce-looking eyes, and his big-knuckled hands that always look like they're ready to crack some boy across the mouth, I decided I wouldn't want the likes of him sitting at my supper table. So, I'd just as soon the Sawyers keep him.

I'd been planning on sitting down with Katherine to teach her the ABCs before she started school. But before I had the chance, Clover took it upon herself to do it. Even though that aggravated me, I had to admit that Clover's better at that sort of thing than I am. By the time Katherine went off to school, she was so good at her ABCs that she could say them forward and backward. She could also print out her full name, Katherine Rose Kelly, and the day she was born, February 7, 1908.

She'd already learned to count a few years back, with hardly any help on my part. She went through a spell where she wanted to count everything. First, it was the heads of cabbage in the garden. Then, it was the eggs she helped me gather. After that, it was the cows in the pasture and the hogs in the pen. She'd get so aggravated with the hogs because they'd never stand still, and she'd have to start her counting over and over again.

So, last September when I sent her off for her first day of school, I knew she was ready. In fact, I was pretty sure she was way ahead of some of the other youngsters her age. I was downright proud of her.

Clover wanted to make sure her niece had plenty of nice clothes for starting school. So, she brought me yards of calico from the mercantile in three different prints: blue, red, and yellow. I took the material up to Ma, and she sewed Katherine some school dresses. Clover and I were both pleased by how nice they turned out.

Then, to top everything off, Clover brought over some ribbons for Katherine's braids. So, when she set off for school on her first day, Katherine was the prettiest little girl I'd ever laid eyes on.

When my child is a little older, I might allow her to walk to school. But for now, I can't bear the thought of sending her out on her own. So, every morning Frank hitches the horse to the wagon and drives Katherine to Owl

Creek. Along the way, he picks up Amanda Sawyer and her little brother Benjamin, and then the Mitchell boys. In the afternoon, Mr. Sawyer brings all the children home in his wagon.

The Mitchell boys don't live that far from the school, and those big strapping fellows ought to be walking. But if they weren't delivered to school in a wagon, they'd be likely to forget themselves and run off into the woods on the way there. Then, they'd spend the day jumping out from behind trees and hurling clods of dirt at the horses and wagons passing by on Helmsburg Road.

So, it gives Frank some satisfaction to deliver the hooligans into the care of Mr. Fox, where he knows they'll get what's coming to them.

My husband hardly ever confides in me. But those first few weeks of driving the children to school, he was fit to be tied, and I suppose he needed someone to talk to. He told me that prissy little Amanda Sawyer, with her banana curls and her hair bows, hated the Mitchell boys. She complained that they didn't wash themselves properly. Any time one of them sat too close to her in the wagon, she'd turn up her nose and hitch herself away from him. The Mitchell boys soon learned how much fun it was to aggravate her, and before long, Amanda's squealing and the boy's laughter was driving Frank clean out of his mind.

To get her away from the rowdy fellows, Frank started having Amanda sit next to him on the wagon seat. Every morning, she'd tell him all about the terrible things the Mitchell boys had done at school the day before. One morning, she told him that Harold Mitchell had pulled Katherine's braids at least six times while Mr. Fox wasn't looking. Finally, Katherine couldn't bear it any longer, and she'd laid her head down on her desk and cried.

When Frank told me this, I said, "Maybe Amanda is just telling tales to get the Mitchell boys in trouble."

He shook his head. "Knowing those boys, I'd believe anything she'd tell me, and a whole lot more."

"Let's ask Katherine," I said.

So, we sat our child down and asked her about the hair-pulling. Her eyes welled up with tears, and she told us it was true.

"Your papa will take care of this," Frank said to her.

And the next morning when the Mitchell boys came tearing out of their house, Frank stood beside the wagon with his arms crossed, glaring at them. He told them he hadn't made up his mind whether he was going inside to talk to their pa about how they'd been acting, or whether he was going to tan their hides himself.

When he told me about that, I laughed out loud. I was downright proud of my husband. For a few minutes, I forgave him for all his shortcomings.

After that, things settled down, and Katherine got along just fine at school.

Mr. Fox likes to visit the home of each one of his pupils. He came by to see me a few weeks before last Christmas. He looked so stern that I was afraid he was going to tell me Katherine was misbehaving at school. But the first thing that came out of his mouth took me by surprise. "You have a very bright child," he told me. "Right now, Katherine's keeping up with the third graders."

After Mr. Fox was gone, I pondered on his words for a good long while. I thought back on how learning my letters and numbers had come easy to me. But no one had ever said of me that I was bright. Seeing as how I only went through fourth grade, I never had the chance to know how bright I really was.

But I know that with Katherine, it's a whole different matter. She lives in a different world than the one I grew up in. They built a high school in Helmsburg in 1907, the year before she was born. It seems like it was meant just for her. I'll do anything I can to make sure she goes there. Someday, my bright, beautiful daughter will end up doing something important in the world.

Katherine loves school so much that I'm afraid she may not want to stop for the summer. Every day, she comes home telling me about something new she's learned. She's picked up games from the other little girls, like jump rope and jacks.

Even though I've taught my child that begging for things isn't polite, she asked Clover for some jacks. And just as quick as I could snap my fingers, Clover brought her some from the mercantile. Frank found some rope in the barn, and he cut her off a length for jumping.

Since the weather's warmed up, Katherine's been taking a stick and drawing hop scotch squares in the dirt on our lane. She tries to get me to play with her, but I feel foolish hopping around like that, heavy as I am.

My child likes to play school up in her bedroom. She lines up her dolls and her stuffed animals and pretends like they're her pupils. She brings home her first-grade reader and reads the stories to them. She acts like she's teaching them to count and say their ABCs. Sometimes, I hear her scolding one of them for not counting right.

Almost every day, I hear her singing the ABC song she learned at school. She makes it fancier than what it is, putting some little trills and flourishes in it.

She keeps her bedroom door closed while she does all this, as if it's a private matter. Whenever I open the door to check on her, she puts her finger to her lips and says, "Shhh. We're having school."

Even though I'm so proud of Katherine, every now and then I see something in her that has me a little worried. She seems to have the same spirit her dead grandmother had. I don't want her to go down the wrong road with it, to go around the bend like Rose Kelly did. But at the same time, her spirit is too beautiful to crush.

Last month, she found a couple of daffodils blooming alongside the pasture fence, something left over from the days when Frank's ma did her flower gardening. There are still signs of Rose Kelly's gardens on this farm. I'd keep up with the old flowerbeds if I could, but I have no time for that. Anyway, Rose's own daughters didn't keep up with them, and by the time I moved into this place, they were all grown up in weeds.

Katherine was so tickled to find those flowers. She came running into the house to get me, then led me out to the pasture to show me. "It's a miracle!" she said. I think she's heard that term at the Catholic Church, even though she doesn't fully know what it means.

"No," I told her. "Those flowers were planted a long time ago."

"Who planted them?" she asked.

"Your grandmother."

She looked at me, puzzled. "You mean Grandma Snider came down here to plant them?"

"No," I said. "Your other grandmother planted them. The one who used to live here. Your papa's mother. She used to plant all kinds of flowers."

Right away, I wished I'd never opened up that subject, as Katherine started asking me one question after another. "Where's my other grandma now? Why don't I know her? Why doesn't she ever come to see us?"

"She's dead," I said. "She's been dead a long time."

"How long?" she asked.

"Ever since your papa was born," I told her.

Katherine looked so sad that I thought she was going to cry. She bent down and kissed the daffodils. Then she took my hand, and we walked back to the house.

From that day on, I've overheard her talking about her grandmother while she plays, saying, "My Grandma Rose did this. My Grandma Rose did that."

Seeing as how I never mentioned her grandmother's first name, I know she's had a talk with Frank about his ma. It's hard telling what he's said to her. He probably let her know she was named after her grandmother. So now, she's making up stories in her head about somebody she's never met.

Of course, Clover's probably talking to my child about such matters, too. I never know what she's putting into Katherine's mind, and that gets me worked up every time she comes to get her.

The newest thing people around here are talking about is the artist colony that's forming down there in Nashville. Folks with common sense aren't keen on what's happening, as artists aren't always the type of people to live upright lives. But Clover's gotten caught up in all that artist nonsense. She likes to carry on and on about how she invited this or that artist to her latest dinner party. I think it makes her feel important. I've been worried that she's taking Katherine around those people, and I know they can't be a good influence.

A few weeks ago, around the end of April when the weather was getting nice, Clover came over to take Katherine to Mass. When she brought her home in the evening, she took me aside in the front room to talk. She looked a little sheepish, which surprised me. Clover is always so sure of herself.

"Bertha," she said, "what would you think of the idea of me having Katherine's portrait painted?"

I was so shocked that she could've knocked me over with a feather. "Where on earth did you come up with that idea?" I asked her.

"We had Mr. Elkins over to the house this afternoon," she said. "He's the most talented artist in the colony. People say his work is brilliant."

Then she seemed to forget herself, and she got a dreamy little smile on her face. "When Mr. Elkins first laid eyes on Katherine, he said, 'Mrs. Henderson, you have an extraordinary child.'"

I tell you, my blood started boiling. That was just like Clover, claiming my child as her own.

She kept on talking. "I said to him, 'Oh, no, Mr. Elkins, this beautiful child is my niece.' All afternoon, he couldn't take his eyes off her. At the end of the day, he said, 'Mrs. Henderson, I'd like to paint your niece's portrait.' I said to him, 'That's a lovely idea, but I need to get permission from her mother and father first.'"

She looked at me, batting her eyes. "What do you think, sister? Do I have your permission?"

I've come to know that whenever Clover calls me her sister, she's trying to get something over on me. "Absolutely not!" I shouted at her.

As soon as the words left my mouth, I wondered why I'd said them. I guess it was because I'd gotten used to going against Clover. I started thinking about how nice it would be to have a picture of Katherine hanging in the front room. Everyone who came to call would comment on how lovely it was. It would be something to treasure for the rest of our lives.

I was just about to tell Clover that I'd had a change of heart when I heard Frank's voice coming from the kitchen. "I don't think that's a good idea, Clover."

Clover's face turned red, and she left the house in such a hurry that she didn't even take the time to say goodbye to Katherine. I watched her motor car rumbling down our lane, thinking how strange it felt to have my husband taking my side against his sister.

Of course, Frank saying no had to do with money more than anything else. We need everything we have to live on, and there's nothing left over for something so frivolous as having a portrait painted. Clover would be the one who'd pay for it, and she'd keep it for herself. She'd hang it in her own house so her dinner guests would make a fuss over it. I couldn't bear the thought of my child being on display for all the people parading in and out of Clover's fancy home.

Just a day or two after the ordeal with Clover, Frank came home from Helmsburg with a load of rocks in his wagon. That stirred my curiosity, but I didn't say anything to him about it. He gets aggravated when he thinks I'm sticking my nose into his business.

The next afternoon, I looked out the front window and saw him digging a hole in a low spot in our yard, a place that always gets a little marshy when it rains. My curiosity got the best of me, and I went outside to ask him what he was doing.

"I'm building a fishpond for Katherine," he said, "so she'll have something to enjoy this summer."

Right off, I figured Clover had put him up to it. "Whose idea was this?" I asked him.

He shot me an ugly look. "Mine. It was my idea."

I was so surprised by what he was doing. In a hundred years, I never would've thought of such a thing as building a fishpond. It touched me that Frank was doing something so special to please his child.

I have to admit, though, that I was a little jealous. He never does anything to please me.

Over the next few days, whenever he had an hour or two of spare time, Frank kept on digging, until that hole was four or five feet deep. When Katherine would come home from school, she'd run out there to watch him. I could see him talking to her, explaining what he was doing.

She'd get excited, wanting to peer down into that hole, and she'd move too close to the edge. He'd grab her by the arm to keep her from falling in, moving her back a little bit. Since she hurt herself on the broken porch step, he's more careful with her that way.

The next thing he did with the fishpond was to shovel gravel into the bottom of the hole. Then, he lined the sides with larger stones.

When he was finished with it, I went out to check on what he'd built. I was amazed at what a good job he'd done. Even though the fishpond wasn't meant for me, I was excited about it, and I couldn't wait to see what Frank was going to do next.

But he didn't do anything on it for a few days. I didn't know why he was just letting it sit, until I realized that ground water was seeping into the hole. Then, we had a good hard rain. Early the next morning, I found Katherine out there in her nightie, lying in the wet grass by the pond, splashing her hands in the rainwater that had collected in the hole. I went out and made her get up, scolding her for getting herself so dirty.

Later that day, Frank filled the pond the rest of the way up with buckets of water from our outdoor pump. Then he went down to Beanblossom Creek and dug up some reeds to plant alongside the pond.

Over time, he's brought in carp of different colors and put them in the pond. Two of them are gold, so big they're almost a foot long. They're Katherine's favorites. Some frogs and salamanders have come to the pond on their own, as if they've found themselves a new home.

I have to admit that Frank has built Katherine a thing of wonder. First thing in the morning, she has to run out to check on her fish before she can do anything else.

Today is Katherine's last day of school for the year. This morning, she got so caught up with different things that I didn't think I was ever going to get her ready to go.

First, she got excited when she found an iris blooming alongside the root cellar. She ran into the house calling, "I found another flower that my Grandma Rose planted." Then, she insisted on taking my hand and leading me out to see it. It was a puny little thing, almost choked out by the grass and weeds. Although I've seen hundreds of blooming irises in my life, I had to make a fuss over it to please her, acting like it was something special.

We went back inside, and I told her to hurry up and put on her school dress and her stockings and shoes so that I could braid her hair. I'd washed it last night, and it had been hanging loose when she went to bed.

She went upstairs to her room, but before I knew it, she was down again and out the front door. Aggravated, I stepped out onto the porch to call her back in.

And there she was, dancing around the fish pond, the morning sunlight shining on her golden curls. The sight was so beautiful that it took my breath away.

"Little fish, little fish, make a wish, make a wish," she was singing. Then her song gave way to words I couldn't understand.

I could tell my little girl's spirit was wide open to beauty and wonderment, and it seemed indecent somehow. And dangerous. It's a dangerous thing to be so wide open in this hard world.

Even though it was a chilly morning, Katherine must've gotten overheated from her dancing. She stopped for a few seconds to pull off her shoes and stockings and fling them aside. Then she went on dancing in her bare feet. Her skinny little legs were moving so fast they were almost a blur, and her feet looked as if they weren't even touching the ground. She looked like a fairy dancing in the forest of Ireland. I could almost see gossamer wings on her back.

I knew I had to put a stop to that. I stepped off the porch and called out to her, "Katherine, it's too cold out here to be barefooted. Get your shoes and stockings and come inside. You're going to make your papa late for picking up the other children for school."

She stopped dancing and hung her little head, looking like I'd slapped her in the face. I felt bad. It was like I'd dragged her down from heaven.

But scolding never really seems to touch Katherine's spirit. I see a hurt look in her eyes for a few seconds. And then she's back to the happy little world she lives in, a world I'm shut out of.

1917

When we were growing up, Ma would warn Hazel and me that we should never get too comfortable when life is going well. "A person never knows what's coming down the pike," she'd say. "You need to keep your mind ready for anything."

I guess I forgot that advice these past few years. Life wasn't really good, but it wasn't bad, either. I'd gotten used to the way things were with our little family on the farm. I'd grown a thick skin when it came to any unkind words Frank had for me. If he got ugly, I'd tell myself to pay him no mind. Long ago, I stopped looking to him to give me any loving. And whenever a worry would come into my head about what he was up to when he left the house of an evening, I'd push that thought away.

Some time ago, we started hearing talk about a war going on in Europe, with England and France fighting the Germans. Pa would go to Helmsburg to pick up a copy of the *Indianapolis Star* so he could keep up with what was happening. Then he'd sit out on the bench in front of Thompson's General Store, talking about the war with the other old men. Ma would tell me about it, shaking her head, saying the old fools would argue so much that they'd get hot under the collar.

Some of the men argued that we should go to war to help out our allies in Europe. They'd say England and France could never make any headway against Germany without the help of American soldiers. But Pa always came down on the side of our country staying out of the war.

"Woodrow Wilson's a man of good sense," I heard him say time and again. "He's not going to lead our country into war. What's going on over there in Europe is none of our business, and President Wilson's not looking to put our young men in harm's way."

But sometimes, I thought he might be a little more worried about the matter than what he was letting on. It seemed as if he always had his nose in the newspaper.

Personally, I had no interest in the war, and I got tired of people going on and on about it. "Why are you so caught up in all this war talk?" I asked Pa one day when I'd gone to visit him and Ma. "It's all the way across the ocean. Don't you think we should keep our attention on the problems we have right here in our own country?"

I felt proud of myself, being able to give my opinion like that. Ma jumped in and agreed with me. But Pa put us in our places pretty quick. "You never know when something like this is going to hit close to home," he said. "Only a fool would bury his head in the sand when a war as important as this one is going on in the world." Then he put his nose right back into the paper he was reading.

Some mornings, he'd bring the paper over to our place, and would sit down at the breakfast table with Frank. He'd shove the paper in front of Frank, pointing his finger at the headlines. Then the two of them would start talking.

I told myself not to get in the way of what they were doing. My pa had been leery of my husband ever since we got married, hardly even wanting to give him the time of day. Talking man to man about the war seemed to bring the two of them together, and I started thinking of that as a good thing.

It seemed to me that Frank was coming down on the side of America going to war, although he wouldn't say it outright. He knew that would rile Pa up. But once, I heard him say that it wasn't a matter of *if* our country was going to war. It was a matter of *when.* And him saying that made Pa's face turn red.

I tried to shield Katherine from all the talk about the war. But Mr. Fox took to bringing a copy of the *Indianapolis Star* to the school almost every morning, and he'd read news about the war to the children.

Some of the parents didn't like it, complaining that he was frightening the little ones. But Clarence Fox is so stern, it's hard to stand up to him.

Every now and then, Katherine would come home and mention something about what Mr. Fox had read from the newspaper. Seeing as she was only nine, she didn't grasp what war was all about. And I wanted to keep it that way for her.

Of course, at the prayer meetings at the Oak Ridge Church, someone was always bringing up something about the war. Most of the people would say we ought to pray that our country didn't get drawn into the mess. But that always got a few strong-minded folks worked up, and they'd stand up and say America ought to be doing its part. People's feelings got hurt, and I got to where I didn't even want to go to the prayer meetings.

One day toward the end of March or the early part of April, Katherine came home from school saying she had some important news. I was busy rolling out a pie crust, but I stopped and wiped my hands on my apron and sat down at the table to listen to her. Then she commenced to telling me all about how the Germans were sinking America's merchant ships that were headed toward England. She recited it very carefully, as if she'd memorized just the right way to say it.

"It's a terrible thing," she told me, shaking her little head.

I nodded, letting her know that I agreed with her. I hated that her innocent young mind had to think of such things.

Secretly, I wondered whether Katherine had it all

wrong. I hoped that was the case. But, wouldn't you know it, Pa came over with his newspaper the next morning, and he and Frank started talking about the very same thing. Katherine tried to join in with them, but I shooed her upstairs to get ready for school.

About a week later, Pa came tearing into the house while we were having breakfast, waving a copy of the *Indianapolis Star*. "The United States is at war!" he shouted.

I was dumbstruck by his news. Those were words I never expected to hear in my lifetime.

"How can that be?" I asked him.

"President Wilson asked Congress to declare war on Germany," he said.

My husband and my pa sat at the table talking about the matter for a full hour. I was so shook up that I couldn't sit still, so I got up and cleared the breakfast things away and did up the dishes. Even though I didn't want to hear it, I couldn't help but listen to everything they had to say.

Pa kept on coming over with his newspapers. I wanted to tell him to stop, that I didn't want any more talk of the war upsetting my household. But I didn't have it in me to disrespect him.

A couple of weeks after Pa first told us about our country being at war, Ma came to the house to tell Katherine and me she had a surprise for us. "Tomorrow, I'm going to take the two of you to Helmsburg to have lunch at the restaurant," she said. "We need to have ourselves a good time. With all this talk of war, everybody's getting down in the mouth."

When Katherine heard the news, she jumped for joy. "I've never eaten in a restaurant before," she said.

"Neither have I," I told her. "It'll be the first time for both of us."

Katherine decided to wear her favorite calico school dress for the occasion, and she made sure I tied the ribbons on her braids just so. "Wear your good Sunday dress, Mama," she said. "We have to look our best."

Then Ma came, and the three of us took the carriage to Helmsburg. We had ourselves a merry time all the way there. But when we drove into town, we were shocked. There were posters about the war all over the place: at the train station, the barbershop, Thompson's General Store, and even in the window of Doc Murphy's office.

The posters were things of beauty, all done up in bright colors. I would've enjoyed looking at them if they hadn't frightened me so. There were pictures of Uncle Sam, looking real stern, pointing his finger right at you and telling you to join the army, the navy, or the marines.

"Who is that man?" Katherine whispered to me.

"That's Uncle Sam," I told her.

She looked puzzled. "He's my uncle?"

"No," I said. I looked to Ma for help. She tried to explain to Katherine how Uncle Sam was a symbol of the United States government, but I don't think Katherine fully understood. She couldn't get it out of her head that Uncle Sam was a real person, and that somebody might be in trouble if they didn't listen to him.

Every time we'd pass one of those posters, she would look at it real seriously, as if she was trying to take it all in. She'd read off the words: I WANT YOU FOR THE U.S. ARMY. Or, I WANT YOU IN THE NAVY, AND I WANT YOU NOW. I could tell that the posters shook her up, and I wished Ma and I hadn't brought her with us.

There were also posters telling people to buy war bonds. Katherine didn't understand what that meant, and Ma had to explain that having people buy bonds was the government's way of raising money for the war. Katherine shook her head, more puzzled than ever.

Of course, there were posters in the window of the restaurant. But the minute we went inside, my child seemed to forget all about them, as she was caught up with taking in her new surroundings. The room was filled with tables covered in sparkling white tablecloths. Each table had a vase in the center with a flower in it, and the silverware and napkins were laid out just so.

"This is all so beautiful," Katherine said.

I'd been afraid she wouldn't know how to act in a restaurant, but she behaved nicely, sitting down on her chair so lady-like, smoothing out her dress. I could see other people in the restaurant smiling as they watched my pretty young daughter. I was downright proud of her.

We had ham sandwiches, along with vegetable soup and soda crackers, and apple pie for dessert. Katherine isn't a big eater, but she managed to finish every bite of her lunch. "This is the best food I've ever tasted," she declared.

"You mean you don't care for the roast beef and potatoes your grandma makes for Sunday dinner?" Ma asked.

"Now you've done gone and hurt your grandma's feelings," I told her.

For a minute, Katherine looked sorry. But then she saw Ma wink at me, and we all three had a good laugh.

"I could get used to this," Ma said. "Having someone else doing all the cooking and cleaning up."

"I could, too," I told her. Both of us felt like we were queens for the day.

From where we were sitting in the restaurant, we could look out the window and see the motor cars passing by. Katherine enjoyed that. "Mama, when are we going to get a car?" she asked me. Then a sad look came over her face, and she said, "Maybe after this terrible war is over." It was like she knew we were heading into hard times.

To pick up Katherine's spirits, Ma said she had something to tell us. "I've been aiming to keep it a secret," she said. "But I might as well come out with it." She smiled at Katherine and patted her hand. "Your grandpa is fixing to buy a car. A Model T."

I could hardly believe what she said. "How on earth is he going to do that?" I asked her.

"Your pa's been leasing a few acres of his farmland," she said. "He's getting a good price for it. That's how we came by the money for the Model T. Having a motor car will help us get around a little easier in our old age."

Katherine jumped out of her chair and ran around the table to throw her arms around her grandma. "I can't wait to ride in it," she said. "We'll take it to church, won't we?"

Ma hugged her and kissed her cheek. "Of course, we will, sweetheart."

Once the news about the car sunk in, I had to admit that I was excited, too. All in all, I counted that day as one of the best I'd had in a good long while.

When we dropped Ma off at her house, we told Pa about the posters we'd seen. He said he'd seen them, too. He didn't seem too happy about them.

"They're nothing but propaganda," he told us. "It's President Wilson's way of getting the country on board with a war we never should've gotten into."

Ma shushed him right away. "Be careful of what you're saying, Rupert," she scolded. "You never know who might be listening."

One day in May, Pa came over to the house more worked up than usual. I could tell he had more bad news, and I tried to brace myself for what he was about to say. "What is it now?" I asked him.

He tossed his newspaper down on the kitchen table. "President Wilson signed a new law," he muttered. "The

Selective Service Act. It says that every man between the ages of twenty-one and thirty-five has to register for the draft. I can't believe the government can do such a thing, forcing men to fight against their will."

He pulled out a chair and sat down facing Frank, looking him square in the eye. "This means you, too, son."

I'd never heard Pa call Frank *son* before. I figured it was because the matter was so serious.

Frank's face went white as a sheet. Pa went on to read the newspaper story to us. Then Frank reached out and pulled the newspaper over to where he could see it for himself. I watched him closely while he read, and I saw something change in his eyes.

Even though my husband hardly says anything to me, I've caught on to the way his mind works, just from being around him all these years. As he sat there reading that newspaper story, I knew full well what was in his head. He was thinking that if he got called to fight, it would give him the chance to go somewhere else in the world. My husband knew that he wasn't a young man anymore, and that his youth was passing him by. He was thinking about getting the chance for an adventure before it got too late.

In the early part of June, Frank had to go down to the courthouse in Nashville to sign up for the draft, along with a lot of other Brown County men. When he came home, I asked him what had happened. He told me they made him fill out a registration card, putting down things like his date of birth and what kind of work he did.

Then, he showed me the draft card they'd given him, something he was supposed to carry around with him all the time. He said that sometime soon, the government would be holding the first draft.

Hearing all that shook me up. Of course, we kept it from Katherine, so as not to worry her.

But then, something happened in our little community that turned my mind away from the war, toward a problem closer to home. Two days after Frank signed up for the draft, I went to the Wednesday evening prayer meeting. Of course, we spent a long time praying for the young men who were about to be called to go to war, some who would be giving their lives for the sake of our country. People got worked up over the matter, and many tears were shed. After all that, I was done in and ready to go home.

Then Reverend Barnes asked for the names of anyone else in need of prayer. And Doc Murphy's wife Eunice brought up Irene Hawkins. She wouldn't go on to say why Irene needed prayer. She just sat there with her mouth clamped shut, as if she was trying to keep some terrible words from tumbling out.

When I heard Irene's name mentioned, chills ran up and down my spine. Irene is the youngest of Zebadiah and Sally Hawkins' two girls. She's around twenty, I'd say, and the way people talk about her, she's never up to any good.

I'm not one for sticking my nose in other people's business, but something told me I needed to know more about Irene's problem.

So, after the service I moseyed over to where Eunice Murphy was standing and asked her why Irene Hawkins needed prayer. I tried to sound offhanded, like it wasn't that important to me.

Eunice looked uncomfortable. "I'm not sure I should say," she told me. "This isn't something to be spread around."

She looked one way and then the other, to make sure no one else was listening. Then she whispered in my ear, "Irene Hawkins is in a family way."

Right then and there, my heart felt like it fell out of my chest and onto the floor. I was so shocked by Eunice

Murphy's words that I couldn't say anything back to her. As a matter of fact, I couldn't even move.

"It's an awful thing, isn't it?" Eunice whispered. She patted my shoulder like she felt sorry for me, and then walked away.

I stood there like a stone. I knew I ought to be feeling bad about the news, but my insides were as cold as ice. Katherine came bounding into the church from playing outside with the other children. She took my hand and said, "Come on, Mama, it's time to go."

As I drove Katherine home in the carriage, the ice inside me gave way to fire. My blood boiled as my mind raced back to the day when my sister first warned me about Frank and the Hawkins girls. "I should've known this would happen," I whispered to myself.

"What did you say, Mama?" Katherine asked.

"Nothing," I said. I knew I needed to get ahold of myself for the sake of my child.

Just as I was pulling the carriage up to the barn, Frank came down the lane in his wagon. He walked into the house right behind Katherine and me, whistling under his breath. As if he'd just had himself a good time.

The sound of his whistling made my blood boil so hot that I thought I was going to blow up. I kept my eyes turned away from him, as I knew if I looked at him, I'd grab my cast iron skillet off the stove and give him a good going-over. If Katherine hadn't been standing right there, I might've done it.

Frank must've picked up on how upset I was. He stood there for a minute or two. I had my back to him, but I could feel him staring at me. Then, he turned and headed out the back door again. I was glad to have him gone.

After sending Katherine upstairs to bed, I went to bed myself. I lay there tossing and turning, rolling onto one side and then the other, kicking the blanket off when I felt hot and then pulling it back over me when I felt chilled. Every now and then, I'd give my pillow a few good thumps, and the feathers would go flying. I'd wish it was Frank's face that I was punching.

What in the world am I going to do about this? I asked myself over and over. *What is a wife supposed to do when her husband is having a bastard child with an unmarried woman?*

Just when I'd worked myself up into a terrible state, a thought came to me: *If a girl is the type to carry on with one man behind his wife's back, she might do the same thing with another man, and another and another. It could be that the baby isn't Frank's after all.*

That settled me down, and I told myself I shouldn't get worked up again until I knew the truth about the matter.

As it turned out, the problem of Irene Hawkins' bastard child was over before it hardly got started. Two weeks later at the prayer meeting, Eunice Murphy brought up Irene's name again. And after the service, she whispered to me that Irene had lost her baby.

"How far along was she?" I asked after I'd gotten over my first shock.

"My husband said about six or seven months," she told me. "He said the poor girl had a terrible time of it, and that she bled so badly she almost died. He got there just in the nick of time to save her."

She went on to say the Hawkins family wanted to keep the whole thing a secret. She said Irene's drunkard pa had put down his jug of whiskey long enough to build a little pine box, and that they buried the dead baby in their backyard.

"Doc says the little thing wasn't any bigger than the palm of his hand," she told me.

For a minute or so, I had to blink back the tears,

thinking about that poor dead baby in the pine box, a child who'd never gotten so much in life as a decent funeral. But I'm ashamed to say that I went home from that prayer meeting feeling like a weight had been lifted off my shoulders.

Toward the middle of July, just when I was starting to settle down about the matter of Irene's baby, Pa came over with his newspaper saying the government was about to hold its first round of drawings for the draft. Once again, my nerves were wound up so tight that my stomach was nothing but a knot of pain.

The day after the drawing, the *Indianapolis Star* listed the numbers of the men called up to serve. I cried out in relief when I learned my husband wasn't among the thousands of men being sent off to training camps. After falling on my knees and thanking the Lord, I felt like I could breathe again.

But I guess God didn't see fit to allow me more than a day or two of peace. Wouldn't you know it, Irene Hawkins' name was brought up a third time at the prayer meeting. And this time, everyone talked about the problem out loud. They said the poor girl wasn't herself anymore, that she'd gone clean out of her head, and that she was walking around Helmsburg acting like a crazy person.

After that, it seemed like all anyone could talk about was how Irene Hawkins had lost her mind. Something like that gets people's tongues going. Some low-minded people were even getting a good laugh about how she was acting.

Irene had taken to wandering around Helmsburg all day long, going in and out of the businesses: the sawmill, the gristmill, the cannery, the hardware store. Sally tried to keep her at home, but she couldn't. Word had it that she once shut Irene up in her bedroom and barricaded the door, but the girl crawled out through her window.

Hazel's husband Walter said Irene was wandering in and out of the general store three or four times a day. He said she always had a crazed look in her eyes, and that she'd start laughing or crying for no reason at all. She'd tell anyone she met that the devil had stolen her baby, and she'd ask if they'd help her find it.

Every time someone would look her in the eye, she'd commence to talking her nonsense. People started turning away when they saw her coming, so as not to get all of that started.

I saw her a time or two myself when I was in town. She looked so pitiful, thin as a rail, her face dirty, her hair flying every which way.

Folks started asking Irene who the father of her baby was. Most of the time, she'd say it was President Woodrow Wilson or General John Pershing. Sometimes, it was Charlie Chaplin. Once or twice, it was Winston Churchill. I got to thinking she must've been repeating the names of the famous men she heard people talking about while she was wandering around town.

People started catching on to this, and they'd ask who her baby's father was, just to see who she'd come up with. Just to get a good laugh out of it.

Sally Hawkins was about to lose her own mind, with her daughter being so out of hand. She asked Reverend Chester Wilkerson, the pastor of the Methodist Church in Helmsburg, if he'd have a talk with Irene and pray with her.

Reverend Wilkerson agreed to it. He's a kindly fellow, and Irene must've made something out of that. Because after he talked with her, whenever people would ask about the father of her baby, she'd say it was Reverend Wilkerson. The reverend was so shook up that he said he didn't want any part of her problems anymore.

As far as I know, Irene never once said the father of her baby was Frank Kelly.

The poor deranged girl took to going into the restaurant, trying to sit down with people while they were eating. The owner of the place was fit to be tied. He told her that if she ever set foot in his business again, he was going to have the sheriff arrest her, haul her off to Nashville, and lock her up in jail.

So then, she started wandering over to the train station, bothering the passengers getting off the train, grabbing people by their sleeves, trying to talk to them. She got to be such a nuisance that the station master told her she wasn't allowed there anymore. He told her that over and over again.

But she kept on going back to the station, as if she hadn't heard a word he said. I knew her mind was so far gone by then that she wasn't capable of understanding anything anymore.

The poor thing wandered around town all the rest of the summer and into the fall. And even in the winter, you could see her in her threadbare overcoat, trudging through the streets in the slush and the snow, her pinched little face red from the cold.

1918

Last Saturday morning, I woke up feeling better than I had in a long time. After months of winter weather, we were heading toward April, and I could tell the day was going to be a sunny one. When I looked out my bedroom window, there were only a few patches of snow left in the yard. I tell you, that bare ground sure was a welcome sight. I figured all of the snow would be gone by evening.

Before I went to gather the eggs, I walked around to the front of the house to see if the crocuses were coming up. A couple of years ago, Ma had brought over some bulbs she'd thinned out from her own flowerbed, and she'd helped Katherine plant them there along the porch. What with all Katherine's talk about her Grandma Rose's flowers, Ma figured she'd better do something more to make an impression on her granddaughter.

Sure enough, I found little green shoots peeking through the layer of rotting leaves blown up against the porch. *I'm going to show these to Katherine when she gets up,* I thought. *She'll be so excited.* Then I looked up, and the sky was so wide and so blue that all I wanted to do was raise my arms to heaven and sing out praises to the Lord.

I walked back around the house and out to the henhouse, thinking on how it would be a good day to wash the bedsheets and hang them on the clothesline.

It had been such a long while since I'd felt cheer in my heart. All winter, news of the war had crowded almost everything else out of my mind. The government was busy drafting soldiers and sending them to training camps, and then off to France to fight the Huns. According to the newspaper, people in Europe were saying that if America didn't get more soldiers up and trained and ready to fight, the Germans were going to beat back the French and the British once and for all.

Pa had gotten his Model T, and I'd been expecting him to drive Katherine and me to church and other places we wanted to go. But he protected that car like it was his own little child, and he wasn't about to take it out in the mud and the slush and the snow. Ma had to get on him, reminding him there was no reason to keep the car if he wasn't going to drive it.

So, I hadn't gotten out much during the winter months. I'd become so downhearted that it had taken a great deal of prayer just to keep putting one foot in front of the other.

But now, spring was in the air, and I told myself that life was finally going to take a turn for the better.

It wasn't more than a minute before I found out how wrong I was. Just as I was coming through the back door with the eggs, I heard the front door opening and footsteps coming through the house. When I walked into the kitchen, Pa was standing there. The look on his face told me he had news I didn't want to hear.

"What is it, Pa?" I asked.

He opened his mouth then closed it again, as if he couldn't get the words out. "It's Irene Hawkins," he finally said.

My heart pounded. "What about her?"

He looked down, shaking his head. "She's dead."

"What?" I screamed. "What happened to her?"

Pa took a deep breath, then blew it out through his lips. "Last night, they found her in the barn, hanging from the rafters with a rope around her neck."

I was so shocked that I started to swoon. The basket of eggs fell from my hands and crashed to the floor. I would've dropped to the floor myself if Pa hadn't grabbed me by the shoulders and sat me down in a chair. I watched in a daze as he paced around the kitchen.

"What else do you know?" I whispered.

Pa shrugged. "Not much, really. Doc Murphy's been out there at the Hawkins' place, and the sheriff, too. I suspect we'll know more in time."

He stopped pacing and turned toward me, a hard look in his eyes. "Where's Frank?"

"Out in the barn," I told him.

He glanced toward the back door, as if he was about to head out and tell Frank his terrible news. But he didn't. He headed for the front door instead. "I just got back from town," he said. "I haven't even been home to tell your ma about what happened."

After Pa left, I sat there wondering how much he knew about the ugly business of Frank and the Hawkins girls and Irene's dead baby. And whether he was blaming his son-in-law for the terrible turn Irene's life had taken.

A few minutes later, Katherine came down the stairs. She stopped short when she saw me sitting there in the chair with the mess of broken eggs around my feet.

"What happened, Mama?" she cried out.

"I had a weak spell," I told her. "I dropped the eggs."

I got up and began picking the eggshells off the floor and putting them in the garbage, my hands shaking, my stomach feeling as if someone had given it a good punch.

"Poor Mama," Katherine said. She got down on her hands and knees to help me.

I found two eggs that weren't broken, and after I wiped up the mess on the floor, I fried them for Katherine's breakfast. While she ate, I went out to find Frank. He was getting ready to hitch the horse to the wagon. I didn't ask him where he was going. I didn't care.

He shot me an aggravated look, as if I was interrupting something important. "What do you want, Bertha?" he snapped.

"I just came to tell you something," I said. "Irene Hawkins is dead."

He stood there holding the horse by the bridle, not moving a muscle, just staring at me. I didn't say another word. I turned my back on him and walked to the house. I knew he'd hear soon enough how Irene had died.

All day long, I couldn't get the picture of the poor girl out of my mind, her dead body swinging from the barn rafters. As I scrubbed the bedsheets on the washboard and hung them on the clothesline, the tears kept pouring from my eyes. Every time Katherine came around, I turned my face away so she couldn't see that I was crying.

I knew I wasn't going to get over this terrible thing until I let out all my sorrow. So, when Katherine was upstairs playing in her room, I went out to the henhouse and let myself wail out everything I'd been holding inside of me. Of course, this stirred up the hens, and they commenced to squawking and carrying on. I was glad, hoping all their commotion would drown out the sound of my crying. I didn't want Frank to hear me if he was anywhere around.

But I didn't see Frank all day long. When he finally came in late that evening, he was even quieter than he usually is. I didn't bring up the subject of Irene Hawkins taking her own life. I didn't want to hear anything he had to say on the matter.

For the next couple of days, people around here couldn't seem to talk about anything other than Irene's death. On Monday morning, after the children were off to school, Hannah Sawyer came up the road for a visit, and the two of us talked the matter over.

Hannah said Zebadiah was the one who found his daughter hanging in the barn. He cut the rope and laid her body on the barn floor, then ran into the house to get Sally and their other daughter, Ethel. Sally and Ethel stayed with Irene while Zebadiah rode off to fetch Doc Murphy.

Of course, Irene had long been dead by the time Doc Murphy got there. Then the sheriff came. He said he didn't see any signs of foul play. The county coroner ruled the cause of her death as suicide.

So, that's the way everybody around here has been telling the story. They all believe Irene's mind was so troubled that she didn't have the will to keep on living.

At the Wednesday prayer meeting, many tears were shed and many prayers were lifted to the Lord. Any time someone started bawling, they'd get others around them bawling, too.

Old Gertrude McDonald was the loudest of all, clutching her Bible to her bosom and calling out, "Lord have mercy, Lord have mercy." Seeing as her hearing is so bad, I wasn't sure Gertrude even knew what everybody was carrying on about. But she was bound and determined to take part in it.

I'm not one to make a scene when I pray, but that evening, I couldn't help but cry out, "Oh Lord, how much more would you have us bear?"

At the end of the service, when Katherine came in from playing with the other children, she looked around at all the red-faced, sniffling people and said, "What's going on, Mama?"

"We're all sad," I told her. "A young woman died."

Katherine got tears in her own eyes. "I know," she said. "Irene Hawkins. I heard about it at school. It made me sad, too."

On the way home, I wondered whether I should talk things over with Katherine, to speak to questions she might have about the terrible business of people taking their own lives. But I couldn't bring myself to go any deeper into the matter.

It's been a hard year for folks around here. Over the summer, Hannah Sawyer lost her mother. The old woman had been a widow, and she'd lived with the Sawyer family for the last ten years. Hannah says the house feels empty without her.

Hattie Patterson's pa died, and now she and her ma are on their own. Hattie's not doing much midwifery any more, as she needs to stick close to her ailing ma.

Six months ago, one of the Mitchell boys, Aaron, died when he was gored and trampled by their bull. That was hard on Katherine. Even though she never cared for the Mitchell boys, she told me she missed having Aaron in the wagon on the way to school.

All three of these departed ones have been laid to rest in the graveyard at the Oak Ridge Church. Irene Hawkins was buried there just a few days ago. I don't have the heart to visit her fresh grave. I won't do that until the grass grows over it and it looks like all the others.

For the first few days after Irene died, Frank seemed nervous and at odds with himself. I could tell he was mulling something over in his mind. I just let him be, figuring he was wrestling with his guilt and shame. I wasn't in any state of mind to comfort him.

On Wednesday, about the time Katherine and I were getting ready to go to prayer meeting, Frank jumped on one of his horses and rode away. He wasn't there when we came home, and he didn't crawl into bed until the next morning when I was ready to get up.

When I asked him where he'd been, he told me he'd been taking care of business. That's what he always says when he's been gone a while. But this time, I had a feeling he'd been caught up in business of an unusual nature.

All day Thursday, he seemed to be lost in his own thoughts. That evening, just as we were finishing supper, he said to Katherine, "Go on up to your room. I need to have a talk with your mama."

Neither Katherine nor I had ever heard him say such a thing. Katherine obeyed him right away. But as she headed out of the kitchen, she glanced over her shoulder at me, as if she wanted to make sure I was okay.

After we heard her footsteps going up the stairs, Frank turned to me. "Bertha," he said, "there's a contingent of Brown County men leaving for Camp Taylor in Louisville, Kentucky, on Saturday morning. I'm going with them."

I'd been bracing myself for what he had to say, but I had no idea such news was coming. All the strength drained from my body. It must've been two or three minutes before I could even speak. "But Frank," I said, "your draft number hasn't been called yet."

"I know," he said. "I'm enlisting on a voluntary basis."

"Why?" I choked out.

He stared down at the table, and I knew he didn't have the nerve to look me in the eye. "Because every man needs to serve his country. Now is my time."

My stomach started churning, and I knew I was about to lose my supper. I jumped up and ran out the back door, where I threw up every bite of the food I'd just eaten. When I came back inside, Frank was still sitting at the table. I rinsed off my face in the kitchen sink, then sat down across from him.

"What about Katherine and me?" I asked him. "You're up and leaving us with hardly a moment's notice."

"You're a capable woman, Bertha." He sounded like he was scolding me for being silly. "You don't need me here. You know everything there is to know about running this farm. And if you need any help, your pa's just up the road. He'll look out for you."

Once again, I realized how little my husband cared for

me. I jumped up, my hands clenched into fists. "Frank Kelly!" I shouted at him. "This isn't fair! You've done some low-down things in your time, but this is the worst!"

I thought for sure he was going to raise his voice and shout back at me, like he usually does when I get out of hand. But he stayed calm. "A man has to do his duty," he said, pushing his chair away from the table. "My country needs me." And with that, he got up and walked out the back door.

I knew full well that what my husband told me was a lie. He wasn't thinking about his country when he decided to enlist in the army. He wasn't thinking about anyone besides himself. He was looking to save his own hide. He knew that when all the crying and carrying on about Irene's death finally settled down, people would start looking around for somebody to blame. And he didn't want any fingers pointing at him.

It's interesting the way things sometimes line up in life. Like a young woman hanging herself in her pa's barn and some scoundrel having a chance to run away from it all by going off to war.

That night, I lay in bed awake, waiting for Frank to come home. "You'll have to be the one to tell Katherine," I said when he finally came in. "I'm not going to be the one to break her heart."

"I'll tell her," he said. His voice sounded gruff. As he climbed into bed, I turned my back to him, thinking that I'd never again care about what happened to him.

Around nine o'clock this morning, Frank and Katherine and I climbed into the carriage and headed off to the train station in Helmsburg. None of us said anything to each other on the trip there. Katherine huddled close to her papa, as if she knew it was going to be a long while before she'd see him again.

The spring weather had gone back to being cold and damp, chilling me to the bone. As we passed by all the familiar sights in Helmsburg, it seemed as if the town had lost its beauty. The whole world seemed sorrowful and dreary.

A group of nine other men were milling around the station, waiting to board the train. All of them were younger than Frank, hardly more than boys. Their families were there to see them off.

The father of one of the boys had a harmonica, and he started playing the tune, *Over There.* Several women gathered around him and started singing.

Something like that generally stirs me. But my heart felt cold and hard. It all seemed so unfair. Everything about my life seemed unfair.

Katherine reached for my hand. I knew she wanted to remind me that she and I were still together.

About that time, Clover and a couple of Frank's other sisters came rushing up, all bawling their eyes out. They crowded around Frank, hanging onto him for dear life, pushing Katherine and me aside. As the crowd around the train grew larger, Katherine and I got pushed farther and farther back. By the time Frank boarded the train, he already looked as if he was far, far away.

On the trip home, a cold rain started falling, and I could hardly make out the road in front of us. Tears poured from my eyes, mixing with the rain blowing into my face. I kept wondering how Katherine and I were going to make it through the months to come. I didn't even know how we were going to make it home.

Katherine shivered on the seat next to me, so hard that I could hear her teeth chattering. "Come here, little one," I said, stretching out my arm. She snuggled up close to me, warming herself against my body.

She was so quiet that I thought she'd fallen asleep. But all of a sudden, she said, "People die in wars, don't they?"

"Yes," I said. "That's what war is all about."

"What are we going to do, Mama?" she asked. "Whatever are we going to do without Papa?"

My heart hurt so bad for my child. "We'll just have to pray," I said.

"Of course." Katherine reached up inside the sleeve of her coat, pulled out her rosary, and started fingering the beads. I hadn't even known she'd had it around her wrist.

Truth be told, I don't know what I'm supposed to be praying for anymore. These days, I think Katherine's better than I am at figuring out such things.

1919

I hardly know what to say about this past year. While my husband was off fighting in a war on the other side of the world, I had my own battle here at home, just to keep things going from day to day. I had to learn that when a woman thinks she's running out of strength, she has no choice but to dig deep and find some more.

The very day Frank left, I had to get into the habit of doing the things he'd always done. Come evening time, somebody had to milk the cows, and the only person here to do it was me. I had to figure everything out: doing the milking twice a day, tending to the horses and the hogs, keeping the stalls in the barn cleaned out, bringing in the firewood for the stove.

Katherine helped out, of course. She knew even without me telling her that the two of us were in for a hard time, and that she needed to do her part. Knowing I could count on her was such a comfort to me.

I gave her the chore of feeding the hogs every day. And just like I did when I was a young girl, she took over the care of the henhouse. She was so particular about gathering the eggs, and I praised her for that. "If I break an egg," she told me, "that means we have one less to sell."

After her papa left, Katherine lost her childlike ways. At ten years old, she asked me all kinds of questions about the world, important things a grownup would ask. Most of the time, I didn't know how to answer her. Sometimes, she had answers to questions I asked her, from things she learned at school.

One morning when she set off for school, looking so serious-minded, I realized I hardly ever saw my child smile anymore. When I got to thinking on that, I couldn't keep the tears from coming, and I kept on bawling while I did the wash and swept the house. When it was time for Katherine to come home, I had to get myself in hand so she wouldn't know I'd been upset all day long.

Every night, Katherine would crawl into bed with me, and we'd huddle together for comfort. But first, we'd kneel together for our time of prayer. Since she was still going to the Catholic Church with Clover from time to time, she was learning to use her rosary with the proper Catholic prayers. I got to where I didn't mind it when she commenced to saying what she called a *Hail Mary*. Some days, I'd find myself repeating that prayer in my own mind. But I never could bring myself to say it out loud.

My ma and pa watched out for Katherine and me, just like I knew they would. Pa came down almost every day to see if we needed help with this or that. He'd bring a loaf of bread or a pie Ma had baked. Seeing as I hardly had the time to put a decent meal on the table, Ma had us over for supper a couple of nights a week. That did Katherine and me a lot of good, keeping company with them like that.

After Frank left, I'd wondered how in the world I was going to come up with enough money to live on. But the Lord made a way for us. I kept right on selling eggs, more than I ever did before, as Frank wasn't there to eat his share. In the spring, a couple of our sows had good healthy litters, and Pa helped me arrange for the selling of the shoats.

It wasn't more than a week after Frank left when Pa came over and said he'd been talking to a fellow by the name of George Webster who lived over in Beanblossom. He told me Mr. Webster was interested in doing some sharecropping.

"Bertha," he said, "I think this is the answer for you.

Mr. Webster can raise a corn crop on your land and keep you supplied with enough to feed the hogs and chickens."

Seeing as how I'd never be able to do the plowing and planting myself, I went along with Pa's idea.

Of course, we didn't need any corn for running the still, as Frank had shut it down before he went off to war. Even though he'd left me with everything else up in the air, he'd made sure to take care of that business. That had aggravated me, as I could tell what was most important in his eyes.

Around the middle of April, Mr. Sawyer came up the road to till my vegetable garden, for which I was mighty thankful. He wouldn't even take so much as a dozen eggs in return for his work.

A couple of weeks later, Nellie Mitchell sent one of her older boys to see if we needed our yard mowed. When I gave him fresh-baked sugar cookies for doing the job, he got a big smile on his face. I gave him extra to put in his pockets to eat on the way home.

After that, it seemed like those boys were always coming around to see if they could do something for me. More often than not, I'd put them to work cleaning out the stalls in the barn and laying down fresh straw. They'd get right at it. I started making a point of having cookies or some of Ma's fresh bread and jam on hand, knowing that would keep them coming.

I have to say the Mitchell boys behaved themselves when they were here, and I never had any trouble with them. They might get into their share of mischief, but if they put their minds to something, they get it done.

One day, I told one of them that if he'd go out and pick a bucket of wild blackberries, I'd bake some pies and send one home with him. I didn't have to tell him twice. Off he went, swinging the empty bucket. By the time I was rolling out the pie crusts, he was back with the bucket brim full.

Of course, I praised him to high heaven. He sat at the table waiting on the pies to come out of the oven, not saying anything, just grinning. Having him hanging around like that aggravated Katherine, but she was good about it and didn't let on like it bothered her. After he left, pie in hand, we both had a good laugh about the whole thing.

One morning in May, while I was doing up the breakfast dishes, I heard a gunshot. It scared the living daylights out of me. I ran out of the house and down the lane to see what was happening. And there was Mr. Sawyer standing in the road by his wagon, his rifle in one hand, the other hand holding a dead fox by the tail.

"I was just passing by," he said, "when I saw this critter running through the brush. I figured he was headed toward your henhouse."

"Much obliged," I told him. "You spared me a heap of trouble."

A month later, one of our old plow horses, Brownie, took sick and died. I was afraid Frank would get all steamed up about it when he came home, and that he'd blame me.

Right then, I had the feeling that everything else was about to go wrong on the farm. But as it turned out, that was the worst of it. Seeing as how Mr. Webster used his own horses for working in the cornfield, Brownie's dying didn't stop anything.

My pa and Mr. Sawyer dug a grave for Brownie out in the pasture. Katherine stood there watching them, tears running down her face. Out of all our horses, old Brownie had been her favorite. I had the feeling she was sorrowing over more than the horse, that a lot of things were welling up inside her.

It had been a hard winter, and her fishpond had frozen so deep that it killed off all the fish. Another year when that had happened, Frank had gone out and restocked the pond so that Katherine wouldn't be upset.

But this year, her papa wasn't here to come to her rescue. Many a summer evening, I'd see her sitting beside the empty fishpond, absentmindedly picking the weeds out of the grass.

One evening when she came in, she told me she'd seen a frog at the edge of the pond. She tried to smile, as if such a thing could make her happy. As she turned away, I heard her say to herself, "It's all I have left."

The same month Frank left, some people put together a Red Cross Society in Helmsburg. All the women around here were told they needed to do their part for the war effort. That meant knitting things for the soldiers, socks and sweaters and washcloths and such. Ma and Hazel and some of the women from church got caught up with that.

I told Ma I was already doing my part for the war by running the farm while my husband was gone. Still, she brought me over some yarn and some instructions the Red Cross had put out for doing the knitting. So, of an evening, when I was too tuckered out to do anything else, I'd sit in the front room with my yarn and needles in my lap. As it turned out, it made me feel good to help in that way.

At every one of the Wednesday evening prayer meetings, we prayed for all of the Brown County men gone off to war, naming each one of them in turn. Every time we came to the name of Frank Kelly, something in me hardened a little bit.

People would put their arms around me, getting tears in their eyes. They knew I was in need of comfort, but they didn't know the true reason for it.

I'd scold myself, thinking that I should have respect for my husband, serving his country the way he was. But I knew that he never would've gone off to war if it weren't for the fact that he had something to run from.

Last July, a traveling evangelist named Reverend Hamilton came through these parts. He stayed at the home of Reverend and Mrs. Barnes and preached at the Oak Ridge Church every night for a week. What with the strain of the war going on, those services did people around here a lot of good.

The first night of the meetings, I almost fell off my bench when I saw Sally Hawkins and her older daughter Ethel coming through the door. The Hawkins family has never been known to set foot inside a church.

Wouldn't you know it, at the end of the service when Reverend Hamilton was giving the alter call and we were all singing *Softly and Tenderly Jesus is Calling,* Sally and Ethel made their way up front, both of them bawling to beat the band. Reverend Hamilton had them kneel down, and he laid his hands on them and prayed over them. Afterwards, everyone was hugging the two women and crying over them, so happy they'd gotten saved.

I was leery about going up to Sally, thinking she might look on me as having a part in Irene's death. I was afraid she'd tell me that if I would've kept my husband at home, her daughter would still be alive. But Sally didn't seem to have that in her mind, and she was just as glad to have a hug from me as from everyone else.

Since then, Sally and Ethel have been coming to church. I'm glad about that. Still, I can't look at those poor suffering women without feeling ashamed. Sally's aged since Irene's death. She looks a hundred years old. She's always hanging onto Ethel's arm, like she'd fall over if she didn't have someone to prop her up.

Ethel looks older, too. I can tell she's settled down, and that she's given up her indecent ways. I'm pretty sure she'll never want any part of Frank Kelly again. If he ever tries to mess with her, I know she'll be giving his backside the boot.

Clover was such a help to me this past year, more than anyone else besides Ma and Pa. I'm surprised to be saying that, as she used to aggravate me so much that I dreaded the sight of her. But seeing as how she stood by Katherine and me after Frank left, she became dear to me. I got to where I was like Katherine, getting excited when I heard her motor car come rumbling down our lane.

Every time she came, Clover brought something for her niece. Katherine had gotten to the point where she didn't care much for toys anymore. She preferred books, along with paper for drawing and little tablets for writing down the stories and poems she made up in her head. Clover saw to it that she had all that.

I guess Clover didn't want me to feel left out, because she started bringing special things for me, too. Like pretty hankies and nice candies from the mercantile, or some material to make new curtains for the front room window.

One day, she said to me, "Bertha, I hate to say this, but you're starting to look like you're dressing yourself out of your ragbag. When's the last time you had something new to wear?"

I had to stop and think on that. "It's been so many years," I said, "that I can't rightly tell you."

She shook her head and clucked her tongue. "Frank, Frank, Frank," she said, as if she was blaming him for me looking so shabby.

A couple of days later, she came over with a measuring tape people use for sewing, and she commenced to wrapping it around me and taking all my measurements. She read them off, and Katherine wrote them down for her. The whole ordeal made me feel foolish.

"I'm going to have my seamstress sew you something nice," Clover said.

I hardly thought she meant that. But two weeks later, here she came, carrying a brand-new dress on a hanger. It was the prettiest color I'd ever seen, a soft rose.

"Oh, my goodness, Clover!" I cried out.

She insisted that I try the dress on right away. When Katherine saw me in it, she clapped her hands and sang out, "Oh, Mama, you look so beautiful!"

"With your brown hair and brown eyes," Clover said, "that color is becoming on you."

The skirt was so full that I couldn't imagine how many yards of material it took to make it. I was as tickled as a little girl, which made me ashamed of myself. To cover that up, I said, "This makes me look as big as a barn."

"No, it doesn't," Katherine and Clover said at the same time.

"It's a little short for me," I said. "I feel indecent."

Clover shook her head. "No, that's the fashion these days, Bertha. Skirts are getting shorter. We women are busy. We can't do what we need to get done if we're tripping over our long skirts."

I had to smile to myself, thinking that at least Clover hadn't tried to put me in breeches like some women are starting to wear.

If it hadn't been for Katherine, I would've hung that dress in my closet and never put it on again, just getting satisfaction out of looking at it from time to time. I was afraid that if I wore it to church, I'd come across as vain. And it didn't seem right to wear such a beautiful color when war widows were taking to wearing black.

But Katherine insisted that I wear the dress, saying that if I didn't, I'd hurt Clover's feelings. The first time I went to church in it, the other women said nice things about it. That made me feel good. Then, wouldn't you know it,

Clover brought me a pretty hat to go with the dress, and I started wearing that, too.

"I have to admit," I said to Clover, "that it lifts my spirits to look so nice."

She put her arms around me and said, "Sister, I'll do anything I can to help you through these hard times."

That touched me so deep that after she left, I went to my bedroom and bawled my eyes out. Then I got to thinking on how strange it was that my sister-in-law loved me so dearly when my husband didn't love me at all.

When school started in the fall, Clover took it upon herself to make sure Katherine had all the clothes she needed, down to her shoes and stockings. That took a load off my mind, seeing as I had so many other things that needed my attention.

All in all, this year would've been impossible to bear if Clover hadn't been looking out for Katherine and me. She brought a ray of sunshine into our lives during those dark months.

Clover always lets on like she's cheerful and carefree, but if you look closely, you can see the sadness in her eyes. She's past forty now, and there's no chance she's ever going to have her own child. Her curly black hair is streaked with gray, and she's starting to get lines around her mouth and her pretty blue eyes.

Even though she never talked about it with me, I knew she was worrying herself sick about her little brother off fighting in the war. I imagine she lost many a night's sleep over that.

Sometimes, I wondered whether Clover knew anything about the whole matter of Frank carrying on with Irene Hawkins, and that being the reason he'd been so quick to run off and join the army. But I thought it was best not to bring that ugly business up with her.

Three weeks after Frank left for the war, we got a letter from him. Actually, it was addressed to Katherine. That didn't surprise me, as I hadn't expected him to have anything personal to say to me.

Katherine was tickled to death, as she'd never gotten a letter of her own in the mail. It was sent from Frank's training camp in Kentucky. "They sure do work us hard here at Camp Taylor," he wrote. "They put us through drills every day, getting us ready to fight in France. The French and the British are waiting for us to come. They need our help. This American army is going to be the greatest army of all times."

He sounded excited about being caught up in something so important. It made me a little bitter, thinking about Katherine and me being stuck here on the farm.

Then Frank went on to talk about the other men there at the camp, men from all different parts of the country. Some were of different races. He mentioned Mexicans and Chinese and Indians off the reservations. "Some of these fellows hardly even know how to speak English," he wrote. "But we're getting to know each other. We have to, as we're all going to be fighting together."

Katherine folded up the letter and put it back into the envelope, handling it so carefully, as if it was something precious. "I'm going to keep this," she said. "I'm going to keep all of Papa's letters."

Then she ran up to her room to get the writing paper Clover had given her, and she sat down at the kitchen table to write a letter back to him. I helped her address the envelope to his unit in the United States Army, like Pa had told us to do.

"There," she said when she was done. "We'll have to take this to Helmsburg tomorrow so we can mail it."

"Not tomorrow," I said. "We can't take the time to go to town every day."

She stuck out her lower lip, pouting like she hardly ever does. "Maybe your grandpa will come by and mail it for you," I told her.

Every couple of days, she'd sit down at the table to write another letter. "What do you find to say to your papa?" I asked her once.

"I tell him everything," she said. "About Mr. Webster plowing the cornfield, and the litter of pigs that were just born. I figured he'd want to know all that. Of course, I had to tell him about Grandma bringing over a plate of cinnamon rolls, and how good they tasted."

"We're going to run out of money to pay for all the postage stamps," I warned her. "Maybe you'll have to put two or three of your letters in one envelope."

It seemed as if every morning, my child came down the stairs saying, "Maybe I'll get another letter from Papa today."

She pestered me constantly about going to the post office at Thompson's General Store to pick up our mail. I could only find the time to do that once every couple of weeks. But in between times, Pa would pick up our mail and bring it to us. Katherine would grab it from him and start rifling through it, hoping to find something from her papa. I had to remind her over and over that he wouldn't have the chance to answer every one of her letters.

About a month after the first letter came, another one arrived, this time from France. Katherine was so tickled that she danced around the room, not stopping until I scolded her to settle down.

"Yesterday, I stepped off the ship and into the country of France," Frank had written. "I'll tell you all about France when I come home. I can't even describe what it was like to cross the ocean. It's bigger than anything you could ever imagine."

He went on to say the French were happy to have

American troops there to help fight the Germans. "The French army looks on us like heroes," he wrote. "They're counting on us to save the day."

He sounded so proud, doing something that important with his life. I couldn't help but envy him.

But that was it. The weeks passed by, and no more letters came. After a while, Katherine stopped pestering me about going to the post office.

One day when I was fixing to go to the general store to buy a few things, I mentioned something about picking up the mail. "There's no point to it," Katherine said, tears welling up in her eyes. "Papa's forgotten all about us."

It broke my heart to know she'd given up on him. I hated him for letting her down.

In the early days after Frank left, when I was fretting day and night about how we were going to keep body and soul together, Katherine would say, "Don't worry, Mama, we'll get by until Papa gets home."

After a while, she stopped saying the last part. It was just, "Don't worry, Mama, we'll make it somehow."

Even though she didn't talk much about it, I could tell that thoughts of her papa's safety were always on Katherine's mind. One day she said, out of the blue, "What if something happens to Papa and we don't know about it? What if he gets killed and nobody thinks to tell us?"

"They always let the families know in such cases," I told her. "If a soldier gets killed in battle, or even wounded, they send his family a telegram."

To tell you the truth, from the day Frank left, I always had it in my mind that he might not come home. When the weeks passed and we didn't hear anything more from him, it started to seem as if Katherine and I were on our own for good.

Pa kept on reading the papers, trying to keep track of

where Frank's unit was in France. He'd ask if I wanted to read the news myself. I'd always say no. The list of men who'd been wounded and killed was getting so long that it took up whole pages in the paper. I couldn't bring myself to look at it.

One day when Pa was sitting at my kitchen table reading the latest news, he said, "This damn war is the bloodiest war that's ever been fought."

His words made me feel so weak that I had to sit down. Pa looked over at me, knowing he never should've said such a thing.

As week after week passed without any word from Frank, I found myself dwelling on what might lie ahead for me if my husband never came home.

I figured Pa was thinking along the same lines, so one day, I brought the matter up with him. He hardly stopped to take a breath before he answered: "If Frank doesn't come home from the war, you and Katherine will move back home with your ma and me. Then you can sell the farm and use that money for your future."

Hearing him say that eased my mind a little. It helped to know that if the worst should happen, Katherine and I would be taken care of.

One day, Pa pointed out a picture in the newspaper of women wearing something strange on their arms: black bands with gold stars. "That's what the government is telling the widows and mothers of fallen soldiers to do," he said. "Instead of wearing black dresses, they're putting on black armbands."

I wondered if he was letting me know I might have to do the same someday.

Wouldn't you know it, the next time I went to Helmsburg, I saw a woman getting off the train wearing a black armband. I told myself Ma would make me such a band when my time came. It seemed like a sure thing.

I'm ashamed to say this, but I started running ideas through my head about what I'd do when I became a war widow. The pictures in my mind became so real that I'd almost forget where I was and what I was doing.

One evening while I was washing up the supper dishes, I started picturing army officers coming to my front door, bringing me a telegram with the terrible news. *What would come next?* I asked myself.

My mind kept rolling right along. *After I get over the shock of Frank's death, I'll set about selling the farm. Pa will help with that. Katherine and I will live with Ma and Pa, but just for a spell. Then we'll go off on our own adventure, just like Frank did. We'll move somewhere else, maybe to a big city. Some place like Indianapolis. I'll find a job as a housemaid with a rich family.*

Katherine will go to good schools, and she'll learn how to live alongside highfalutin people. She'll wear fancy dresses, and she'll know how to set a table with fine china. She'll grow into such a great beauty that young men will be falling all over themselves to win her heart. She'll have an easy time of finding a rich man to marry.

She and her husband will take me into their home, and I'll live out the rest of my days in comfort, never having to milk cows or scrub clothes on a washboard or break my back planting beans and potatoes. I'll have nothing more to do than dandle my grandbabies on my lap.

All of a sudden, I realized my imagination had run away with me. To bring myself back to the here and now, I took my hand out of the dishwater and gave my cheek a good hard slap.

That shocked Katherine. "Mama, why did you do such a thing?" she asked.

"I'm tired," I told her. "I was just trying to wake myself up."

Sometimes, it seemed like the war had made the whole world go crazy. As if everything we'd ever known had been turned upside down. People around here stopped trusting their neighbors and started acting suspicious of one another.

The government had been saying that Americans should cut down on what they were eating, so as to leave more food for the soldiers. They were putting things in the paper, telling people that on certain days they should go without meat. On other days, they were supposed to give up flour and sugar and fat.

That was an awful lot to ask. People around here have a hard enough time feeding their families, and asking them to give up more didn't seem reasonable. Still, people at church questioned each other as to whether they were falling in line with what the government wanted. Being around all that talk made me uneasy.

One day when I was trying to buy a bag of sugar at Thompson's General Store, a woman I didn't even know came up to me. "You're supposed to be cutting down on sugar," she said. "For the sake of the troops." She eyed me up and down, as if she thought me being heavy meant I'd been eating more than my share of food.

I wanted to tell her that I had a husband in the war and that I was already sacrificing plenty, working my fingers to the bone on the farm while he was gone. And that the least I deserved was a little sugar in my coffee of a morning. But I didn't. I felt so ashamed that I left the store right then and there, without getting the sugar.

For the next few weeks, Katherine had no sugar for her oatmeal in the morning. She complained that it tasted bad, and that she could hardly eat it.

Practically every time he read the newspaper, Pa would comment on the fact that President Wilson didn't tolerate anybody speaking out against the war. "I don't appreciate that," he'd say. "I never agreed with this war from the start, and I have a right to say that."

But every time Pa would get going on that subject, Ma would shush him. "Be careful, Rupert," she'd say. "You never know who might be listening."

"I have a right to speak my mind in my own house," he'd shoot back at her.

But even though Pa made a point of keeping his thoughts to himself when he went to town, word must've gotten around about how he felt. One evening toward the end of summer, when Katherine and I were having supper at Ma and Pa's place, Hazel's husband Walter came by. He looked nervous.

"What is it, Walter?" Ma asked.

He glanced over at where Katherine was sitting. I could tell that whatever he had to say, he didn't want to say it in front of a child.

So, I nudged her and said, "Sweetheart, I think your grandma has some ripe tomatoes in her garden that need to be picked. How about if you go out and do that for her?"

Off she went, and Walter sat down to talk with the rest of us.

"I heard some men talking in the store today," he said. "They were carrying on about people who were going against President Wilson's war. They were saying what ought to be done to them. Terrible things."

Ma's face turned white. "Like what?" she asked.

"Like arresting them and putting them in jail," Walter said. "Or jumping on them and giving them a good beating. Or even lynching them."

He dropped his eyes, like he was afraid to look at any of us. "Then they started talking about you, Rupert," he mumbled. "They were saying you're against the war because you side with the Germans. They said maybe your name is Schneider instead of Snider, and that you need to be watched. And they said you've never once been seen in Nashville at the rallies for selling Liberty War Bonds. They were saying that instead of buying your Model T, you should've used that money to buy war bonds."

Right then and there, Ma broke down and cried in a way I'd never seen her cry before. "Oh, Rupert," she kept saying. "I warned you, Rupert."

Pa sat there quiet for a long time. Then he got up and walk out the back door. I followed him and stood at the door to see where he was going. He stopped to say a word to Katherine in the garden, then went on out to the barn. As if nothing at all had happened.

After that, I never heard Pa say a single word against the war. Nothing ever came from what Walter had overheard, and he never mentioned any more talk about Pa going on at the store. I was mighty thankful for that. I could come to terms with losing my husband in the war. But I knew that if I lost my pa, I'd lose my way in life.

In September, the newspapers started talking about the American Army fighting in something they called the Argonne Offensive. Pa told me Frank was probably in the middle of all that.

One afternoon, Katherine came home telling me that Mr. Fox had brought a map to school. "He showed us where France is," she said, "and where our troops are fighting. He said they're fighting in a thick forest, a lot like the woods we have here in Brown County. Can you imagine that?"

A couple of the children at Owl Creek School had older brothers fighting in the war. But Katherine was the only one whose pa had gone overseas.

"Mr. Fox told us how brave our soldiers are," she said. "It made me proud of Papa."

I just hoped her teacher wasn't saying too much more, things that would frighten my child and keep her awake at night.

The newspapers were saying that the Argonne Offensive was the most important thing going on in the war. They said the American troops were making good headway against the Germans. But one day when Ma wasn't around to hear it, Pa told me things over there in France were probably a lot worse than what the papers were reporting.

"The government puts things in the newspapers that it wants people to believe," he said. Then he shut his mouth, as if he'd already said too much.

"Pa," I said, "I feel like I'm living in a bad dream. Is this nightmare of a war ever going to end? Is anything good ever going to come out of it?"

"I have to think so," Pa said. "Otherwise, I'd lose all hope. President Wilson keeps on saying that peace is coming. He says this is the war to end all wars. I have to believe in that."

Ma's the type to put her arms around you if you're having a hard time of it. Pa doesn't do that kind of thing. But that day, he looked at me with softness in his eyes and said, "Bertha, better days will come. In all my years, I've learned that life brings us hard times, but that good times always follow. A person has to learn to live with both."

Then the day I'd been dreading finally came. On a chilly Monday morning in late October, just a few minutes after Katherine had headed off for school, I heard the sound of a motor car coming down our lane. I looked out the front window, thinking it would be Clover, wondering why she'd be coming at such an early hour.

But it was a car I'd never seen before. Two men in army uniforms got out and walked toward the house.

This is it, I thought. *They're coming to tell me my husband's been killed.* I felt so lightheaded that I thought I was going to pass out.

Somehow, I made it to the front door to answer their knock. "Are you Mrs. Frank Kelly?" one of them asked.

"Yes," I said. Then the other man handed me a telegram. Before I read it, he commenced to telling me that my husband had been wounded in battle, and that he'd been taken to a hospital in France. The men stood there on my porch for a minute or two, like they were waiting to see if I was going to keel over from shock. Then they left.

I went back inside and sat in the front room for a good long while, trying to take in the news.

He wasn't killed, I kept saying to myself. *Just wounded.* In all that picturing I'd done in my head, I'd always seen myself as a war widow, not the wife of a wounded soldier. When the news finally settled over me, I was mighty glad Katherine was at school. I needed time to figure out how to tell her about her papa.

I tried to think what to do next, and it came to me that I should tell Ma and Pa. I didn't have the presence of mind to hitch up the horse. So, I put on my overcoat and walked the mile to their house. When Ma looked out the window and saw me, she must've known I was coming with bad news. She stepped out on the porch to meet me and took me inside. Before I could say a word to her, she went out to fetch Pa so they could hear my news together. We all sat down at the kitchen table.

After I told them what the army officers had told me, Ma reached out to take my hand. I glanced over at her and saw tears running down her face. I realized I hadn't even cried myself.

"At least your husband is safe now," Pa said. "He's done with fighting. He won't be in harm's way anymore, and we can be glad for that."

"How do I tell my child about her papa?" I asked the two of them. We talked it over for a while. And when Katherine came home from school that afternoon, Ma and Pa were there at the house with me.

As Ma had suggested, I started out with, "Katherine, I have some good news. Your papa is safe, and he'll be coming home."

Her eyes lit up, and she was about to jump for joy. Pa held up his hand to stop her so I could come out with the rest. "But your papa's been hurt," I told her. "He'll need to stay in the hospital for a while."

I was proud of the way I put it, easing her into the bad news like that. Katherine didn't even cry. She sat there staring at the three of us while she let it all sink in. "Where is he?" she finally asked. "Can we go see him?"

"No," I said. "He's still in France. He's not able to travel yet."

"Is he hurt bad?" she asked.

I told her what the army officers had told me, that he'd been wounded in the leg by a piece of artillery shrapnel. Katherine looked thoughtful while I explained it to her.

"Tonight," she said, "when I say my prayers, I'm going to thank God over and over again for keeping Papa from getting killed."

We ate supper at Ma and Pa's house that evening, as I was in no state of mind to fix anything myself. Afterwards, Pa drove Katherine and me down to Nashville to tell Clover the news.

Clover's the type to make a big fuss over such things, and she had to cry and carry on for a while before she could settle down and talk things over. When Katherine went to comfort her, Clover pulled her onto her lap and clung to her for dear life. Of course, that got Katherine crying, too.

"I knew something had happened to Frank," Clover said. "I sensed it in my spirit."

"I did, too," Katherine said.

I wasn't sure whether she understood what Clover was saying, or whether she was just going along with her aunt to make her feel better. But seeing as how my child is so open in her spirit, maybe she does pick up on things like that.

Just two weeks later, on November 11, 1918, the entire country had cause for great celebration. Armistice Day, they called it, the end of the war. Pa said it was a day that would go down in history. He was telling us how German and American soldiers came out of their trenches and hugged each other, rejoicing together that the war was over. In the *Indianapolis Star,* they had pictures of people celebrating in cities all over the country, with bands playing and flags waving and people marching in parades.

Clover came to get Katherine and me and took us down to Nashville so we could watch the parade going through town. I'd never seen anything like it. Everyone was so happy, and Katherine's eyes were shining.

"Will Papa be coming home now?" she asked.

"It'll take some time for all the soldiers to come home," Clover told her. "And you must remember that your papa needs time to heal from his wounds."

She stroked Katherine's wispy curls back off her face, like she often does. "My dear child, you'll need to be patient."

So, as another winter set in, Katherine and I could do nothing but settle down and wait.

I thought for sure that since Frank was out of the thick of battle, he'd take to writing letters. Mr. Fox's nephew had been injured in the war. Once he was doing well enough, he wrote letters from the hospital, telling what it had been like to fight in the Argonne Forest. Mr. Fox brought the letters to school and read them to the children, as a way of teaching them something about the war.

Katherine came home and told me about that. "Mr. Fox expects Papa will write me letters, too," she said. "When he does, I'll take them to school to show everyone."

But the weeks passed, and no letters came. And once again, my child lost her smile.

Every time Clover came over to see us, I'd ask her whether he'd heard anything from Frank. She'd always ask me the same. And each of us would say to the other, "No, he hasn't written."

But one day in the middle of December, Clover answered my question by whispering, "Yes, Bertha, Frank sent me a letter."

Clover and I were sitting in the front room when she said that. Katherine was in the kitchen getting herself a drink of water. I don't think Clover meant for her to hear what she had to say, but Katherine did. She came tearing into the front room, her face looking like a storm cloud.

"Why hasn't Papa written to me?" she cried out. "Doesn't he love me anymore?"

And with that, she ran up the stairs. Clover and I could hear her wailing at the top of her lungs in her bedroom.

Never in all her ten years had I heard my child throw such a fit. Clover looked like she didn't know what to make of it. Katherine's crying was so loud that Clover and I gave up trying to talk to each other.

"I'm not of a mind to scold her about this," I said to Clover when the crying finally died down. "She's had to bear so much this year."

Clover nodded, tears in her eyes. "More than any child should ever have to bear."

We were quiet for a moment before I asked, "So, what did Frank have to say in his letter?"

Clover started talking in a rush, and I could tell she was trying to hide something from me. “As you already know, Bertha, Frank was wounded in his right thigh by artillery shrapnel. The wound didn’t heal very well. It got infected. Several times, the army doctors told Frank they were going to have to amputate, but he wouldn’t let them. He told them he’d rather die than lose his leg.”

I closed my eyes for a minute, taking that all in. Being the proud and willful man that he was, I knew my husband would never stand for losing a leg.

“On top of all that,” Clover said, “he caught the influenza. You’ve heard about how that dreadful disease spread among the troops. A soldier could be feeling fine one day, and few days later, he’d be dead. It’s nothing short of a miracle that Frank pulled through.”

Of course, I thought. *It’s no wonder my husband hasn’t written. He’s been too sick to put pen to paper.*

Right then, I was of a mind to forgive him. “Did he say when he’s coming home?” I asked.

Clover looked down and sighed, fumbling with the handbag on her lap. “Bertha, Frank told me some things in confidence. But I’ve thought it over, and I believe it’s best that I tell you.”

She looked up at me with pleading eyes. “Before I start, sister, bear in mind that war changes a man. My brother isn’t himself right now. He’s not thinking straight.”

Then I listened as Clover commenced to telling me that my husband had fallen in love with the French nurse who’d been tending to him in the hospital. “He thinks he wants to stay in France and start a life with Brigitte,” she said. “He thinks he has it all figured out. He told me he’s picked up quite a few French words, and he says he’s sure he can learn to speak that language.”

She covered her face with her hands and sobbed, as if the whole thing hurt her terribly.

Her words shocked me. But to tell you the truth, I'd already heard so many shocking things about my husband that I'd grown used to it. Clover's news didn't hit me any harder than anything else I'd heard. My first thought was that Frank could go right ahead and stay in France, and I'd get on with my life. But, seeing as how we had a child, I knew the matter couldn't be settled as easy as that.

Clover pulled a fancy hankie out of her handbag and dabbed at her eyes. "Bertha," she said, "you and I both need to understand something. After a man has been fighting in the trenches under horrible conditions, the comfort of a nurse's tender touch is going to turn him toward her. It's more than his heart can withstand. Frank isn't the only wounded soldier who's fallen in love with his nurse. Those women are used to that. They have to fend off the advances of their patients a hundred times a day."

Knowing how easily Frank turned to other women, I could picture him trying to fondle his nurse. The thought sickened me.

"Frank told me all this because he wanted my blessing," Clover continued. "He wanted me to tell him it was the right thing to do. I haven't written back to him yet, as I needed time to think on what I wanted to say to him. But I will go home and write him a letter today. I'll remind my brother that the love he thinks he has for his nurse is nothing but a flight of fancy. And that in all likelihood, she doesn't return his affections. I will remind him that he has responsibilities here at home. I will tell him that there is nothing more precious in his life than his beautiful young daughter, and that if he stays in France, he will lose her love forever."

I could see how heavy the matter weighed on Clover. It came to me that, in spite of her fickle ways, my sister-in-law was an honorable person. Even though she'd coddled her younger brother, she wasn't about to put up with his wrongdoing. She was coming down on the side of what was right.

Then Clover gave me a sly grin. “Anyway, I don’t think Frank will have a say in the matter. The army’s going to send him home, whether he likes it or not.”

She reached over and laid a hand on my knee. “Sister, promise me that when my brother comes home, you’ll never speak of this to him. His affection for the nurse will fade away in time. Just let the matter drop.”

I nodded, my insides feeling dull and heavy. I’d let matters drop so many times before. I told myself I could do it once again.

Then Katherine came downstairs, her face red, her eyes swollen, her braids a mess from burrowing her head into her pillow. Clover held out her arms. “Come here, my sweet child.”

Katherine came to sit on the sofa between us and snuggled in the crook of her aunt’s arm.

“Why don’t you go back upstairs and write your papa a letter?” Clover crooned to her. “When I go home, I’m going to write my own letter to him. I’ll send yours along with mine. And I promise you that he’ll write you back.”

Katherine nodded obediently. Clover watched her as she headed back toward the stairs. Then she looked over at me. I could see determination, strong as steel, in her eyes.

“Bertha,” she said, “I’m going to write Frank a letter, and I’m going to set him straight. I’m going to tell him that if he doesn’t pull himself together and write to his daughter, I will never forgive him. I will tell him that if he turns his back on his child, I will turn my back on him forever. He will no longer be my brother.”

She looked as if she was about to burst from the strength of her feelings. She got up, left the house, and paced up and down the snowy lane, waiting for Katherine to finish her letter.

I stood at the front window watching her, worrying that she was ruining her nice shoes. I wondered at how she'd found the strength to stick to her guns. My sister-in-law, a spoiled and flighty woman, had become a protector for my child and me.

When Katherine came downstairs with her letter in hand, she looked around and asked, "Where's Aunt Clover? Did she leave already?"

I pointed out the window. "No, she's outside waiting for you." I followed Katherine out of the house, and before Clover got into her car, I did something I'd never done before. I took it upon myself to wrap my arms around her.

"Thank you," I whispered in her ear."

In the following weeks, every time Katherine looked through the mail and didn't find a letter, she'd say, "Clover promised Papa would write to me." She'd sound sulky, as if she thought her aunt had lied to her. I'd have to remind her that it takes a long time for mail to come from overseas.

But one day in late January, Pa stopped by to drop off our mail. And there on the top of the stack was a letter addressed to Katherine Rose Kelly.

"It's a miracle!" Katherine sang out as she danced around the room. Then she sat down and read the letter out loud to Pa and me.

"Dear Katherine," Frank had written, "I'm very sorry that I took so long to write to you. As you know, I was wounded in battle and was laid up in a hospital bed for a long while. But I'm on the mend now, and I'll be coming home soon. Don't ever forget that your papa loves you with all his heart."

Katherine held the letter to her heart, her eyes shining. Pa was smiling, as if he was pleased with his son-in-law. I knew full well that letter had been written only because Clover had given Frank a good scolding. But I wasn't about to spoil the moment by telling Katherine and Pa the truth about it.

Just a week later, on February 7, 1919, the day of Katherine's eleventh birthday, I stood with Ma, Pa, Katherine and Clover at the train station, waiting for Frank's train to pull in. Katherine was bouncing up and down on her toes, saying that having her papa come home was the best birthday present she could ever hope for.

I had tried to prepare myself, picturing what I might see when Frank got off the train. Pa had warned me over and over that war takes a toll on a man. "You'll need to be ready for the fact that your husband will come home a different person," he told me. "It'll take some time for him to get back to his old self again."

I had tried to pass that advice on to Katherine. "You'll have to remember," I told her, "that your papa has been wounded. He won't be feeling well, and he'll be all tuckered out."

"But he still loves me," she said, "and that's all that matters."

I don't think any of us expected what we saw when the soldiers started stepping off that train. Three young men got off first, a sorry-looking lot, much different than the excited fellows who'd left less than a year earlier. And then, an older man got off. I didn't recognize him at first. I thought there had been a mistake, that Frank hadn't come home after all. It took me a minute to see that it was him.

My husband had always been a lean man, but now he was nothing more than skin and bones. His army uniform hung on him like a sack. He walked with a pitiful limp, favoring his right leg. His face was leathery, the skin sagging. He reminded me of his pa, Old Man Kelly.

But there was more. I could tell right away that, in terms of his spirit, Frank was coming home a wreck of a man. There was something dark about him, something that made me want to keep my distance.

I had expected Katherine to run to him, her arms outstretched, calling, "Papa, Papa." But she must've picked up on the change, too. She just stood there, her arms at her sides, as if she didn't know this stranger.

Pa was the first to speak. He stepped toward Frank, put out his hand, and said, "Welcome home, son."

Then Clover threw her arms around her brother and cried, all the while thanking God that he was home safe and sound.

I gave Katherine a nudge forward. She looked up at me like was afraid. "Go ahead," I whispered. "Give your papa a hug."

She walked up to him and wrapped her arms around his waist. I could tell her heart wasn't in it. "Welcome home, Papa," she said. Frank forced his lips into a smile and patted her head.

Then Katherine and I climbed into the Model T with Ma and Pa. Clover took Frank in her car, saying she'd follow us back home. I figured she thought none of the rest of us knew what to do with him. She was right about that.

When we all got back to the house, Clover settled Frank into his chair by the stove. Ma and I set about fixing him something to eat, but he wouldn't take anything more than a cup of coffee.

And for the rest of the day, he sat in that chair staring at nothing, saying only a word or two when someone asked him a question.

Early on, Katherine went upstairs to her room, and she stayed there most of the day. Her papa hadn't even mentioned that it was her birthday. I figured that must've hurt her terribly.

Ma and Pa and Clover stayed for supper. Clover made sure Frank ate a few bites. I was glad for that. When they were all ready to go home, I suddenly got scared. I wanted to cry out, "Don't leave me alone with this ruined man!"

To calm my nerves, I busied myself with cleaning the kitchen and bringing in more firewood. I could tell that having my husband home wasn't going to take any of the load off my shoulders. He didn't look to be in any condition to pick up with what he'd done before.

When nighttime came, I knew he wouldn't think to get out of that chair unless I told him to. So, I said, "Frank, it's time for bed." He got up and followed me into the bedroom.

It aggravated Katherine that she couldn't crawl into bed with me that night, like she'd done every night for almost a year. "I guess I have to go to bed alone," I heard her mumble as she trudged up the stairs. "It's so cold up here."

I'd grown used to falling asleep with Katherine's warm little body snuggled up to mine. Having my husband lying next to me made me feel like I was sharing my bed with a stranger.

I don't think I got a wink of sleep that first night. Frank tossed and turned and cried out in his sleep. Several times, he sat bolt upright in bed, scaring me half to death. From time to time, he got up and paced around the room. The sound of his wounded leg dragging on the floor reminded me that this husband of mine who'd come home from the war would never be the same again.

"What's the matter, Frank?" I asked the first time he got up.

"Nothing," he growled at me. So, I didn't say anything when it happened the second and third time.

In the morning, he put on his army uniform again, as if he didn't know what else he should be wearing. I told myself that when he took it off that night, I'd put it away and lay out other clothes for him.

He was able to eat two fried eggs and a slice of bread for breakfast, and I took that as a good sign. Then he went to sit in his chair again, staring around the room with his empty eyes. Not saying a word to me. Katherine acted like he wasn't even there.

After several hours of that, I figured I needed to give him a nudge. "Frank," I said, "it's time to get up and do something. Why don't you go out to the barn for a while?"

He jumped, as if my words had startled him. Then he eased himself out of his chair, groaning in pain. I knew his leg must've been hurting him. I handed him his overcoat, as I was pretty sure he wouldn't think to put it on if I didn't tell him to.

When he came back into the house an hour later, he seemed a little better. As if he was figuring out where he was and how he fit into things.

Later that day, when I went out to do the evening milking, I didn't realize that he'd followed me. Suddenly, he was standing there beside me. He took the bucket from my hand, saying, "I think I can do that." I stood back and watched him, making sure he didn't start shaking and end up spilling all the milk.

Over the next few days, Frank started asking me questions about the farm. He noticed Brownie was gone and asked where he was. I told him the old plow horse was dead and buried. He didn't seem to mind. It was like he couldn't work himself up to care about anything anymore.

Pa came down to check on us every day that first week. After a couple of days of watching how Frank was doing, he took me aside and told me we'd best allow Mr. Webster to grow another corn crop that year. "Frank's not going to get it done," he said, shaking his head. I knew he was right.

That same day, I had a talk with Katherine, telling her we both needed to keep up with our chores. "Your papa will take over when he can," I said. "He'll help sometimes, but there will be days when he won't be up to it."

Katherine wrinkled her nose, as if she was disgusted with him. "It's not fair," she said.

In the month since Frank's been home, nighttime hasn't gotten any better. He sleeps restlessly, crying out, thrashing about, getting up to pace around the room. When he starts swinging like he's fighting someone, I have to get myself out of bed before I get hurt.

Some nights, he calls out for Brigitte. He'll reach for me, wanting to hold me. That's more than I can put up with. I'll push him away, then go to sit in the front room for a while.

Sometimes, I want to let him know what he's doing, to tell him that I know all about Brigitte. But that would only make matters worse. Besides, I've given Clover my word. I've decided to go ahead and let him call out for his French nurse until she's finally out of his mind.

One day last week, he started crying in his sleep, just like a little child. "Bertha, Bertha," he said. "Help me." That touched my heart, and I couldn't stop myself from taking him in my arms and comforting him. That quieted him down. It felt good to have him need me like that.

When I woke up in the morning, he had his arm around me. I was foolish enough to think something had changed between us, that maybe he'd start taking me into his confidence. "What was the matter last night?" I asked while I was fixing his breakfast.

"Nothing," he growled. "Just leave me be." And he steered clear of me for the rest of the day, like he was ashamed of himself.

My husband's problems come up in the daytime, too. Whenever he hears a loud noise, his eyes pop wide open and he starts shaking all over. If someone next to him makes a sudden move, he's liable to swing out at them.

Two days ago, he was standing in the kitchen when Katherine came in the back door from school. The sound of the door slamming shut startled him so bad that he swung around to face her with his fists doubled up. Katherine screamed and ran out the door again. Then I heard her come through the front door and run up the stairs, crying.

We can't keep going on like this, I thought to myself. When he'd settled down some, I said, "Frank, you know you haven't been yourself since you've come home. Maybe you should go see Doc Murphy."

"And what's the doc going to do for me?" he sneered.

I could see I wasn't going to make any headway with him. And I decided right then and there that if Frank wouldn't go see Doc Murphy, I'd talk to the doctor myself.

This morning after Katherine left for school, I put on my Sunday dress and got ready to go to Helmsburg. "Where are you going?" Frank asked. He sounded uneasy, and I knew he was scared of being left alone.

Generally speaking, I know the Lord doesn't want us to lie. But I hope He allows for times when telling the truth isn't the best thing to do. "I'm going to see my sister Hazel," I said. "I won't be gone long. Just an hour or so."

I was so nervous when I sat across from Doc Murphy in his office that I was shaking almost as bad as Frank does. I was afraid I wouldn't find the nerve to tell the doctor what was going on. But once I started talking, I couldn't help but blurt out all the terrible things I'd seen and heard since Frank came home from the war. "It's like my husband's lost his mind," I told him.

Doc Murphy sat with his hands folded on his desk, a sorrowful look on his face. "Mrs. Kelly," he said, "what you're seeing is a case of shell-shock. I've talked with a number of Brown County men back from the war, and most of them are in the same condition your husband's in."

He went on to explain it all to me. "We country folk are used to living a quiet life. You must understand that the sights and the sounds of the war were terrifying, something those soldiers had never experienced before. The ear-splitting sound of the artillery—the gunfire, the mortars, the cannons. The screams of the wounded. Men gasping for air after they'd been poisoned by mustard gas. You and I can hardly imagine what it was like. Those men were living in hell.

"Mrs. Kelly, those soldiers never knew what they were facing from day to day, even from moment to moment. No doubt, there were many times when your husband thought he was facing a certain death. After going through all that, a man can never be the same again."

"What's to be done about this terrible thing?" I asked after he was done speaking.

He sighed deeply. "Nothing. Nothing can be done. All you can do is to be a comfort to him, and hope that time takes care of the worst of it."

I stood up to leave, and the doctor walked me to the door. "Mrs. Kelly," he said, laying a hand on my shoulder. "With all that's happened, I know comforting Frank is a hard thing for you to do. But you must be strong. You must be patient with your husband."

I had to wonder how much he knew about what had gone on before Frank left for the war. Probably more than I would ever suspect.

Doc Murphy's given me so much to think about. I can hardly take it all in. No matter what he's done, I guess it's my duty to take care of my husband. I can't turn my back on someone as bad off as he is. Heaven help me, I don't know how much God expects a wife to do.

1920

All the while the war was going on, President Wilson was telling us that peace was coming. He promised us the whole world was going to end up a better place. I'm thinking he shouldn't have said that, as the man clearly didn't have the gift for looking into the future.

When Pa reads the papers, he says there's still a lot of uneasiness in this country. One thing I know for sure: those of us women with husbands ruined by the war are still having a hard time of it.

Around here, Frank's looked on as a war hero. People feel sorry for him because of his injury, and they talk about the sacrifice he made for our country. No one would dare to whisper any gossip about him and Irene Hawkins. It seems that matter has been laid to rest.

But nobody knows, other than Katherine and me, what it's like to live with such a man. His leg hurts him, some days more than others. I can tell it's going to be a lifelong thing. Some mornings, he can't get himself out of bed, and I have no choice but to keep on carrying the load. But that bad leg doesn't stop him from getting around when he has something he really wants to do.

My husband feels sorry for himself. It's an ugly thing to watch, a man wallowing in self-pity like that. The way I see it, he uses his war wound as an excuse for drinking. He drinks a whole lot more of his homemade whiskey than he ever did before he went off to war.

Come to find out, he hid a couple dozen jars of whisky in the haymow before he left. He was looking ahead, making sure he had plenty on hand for when he came home. Had I known that, I would've dumped out that nasty brew and used the empty jars for canning applesauce.

It's hard not to be disgusted with my husband. When I get to where I can hardly stand the sight of him, I have to remind myself that without Frank, I wouldn't have Katherine. Life without my precious child would hardly be worth living.

Frank barely pays attention to Katherine, other than to order her do something for him. Like fetch his cane or put more firewood in the stove. She'll obey him, but otherwise, she pays him no mind. I can tell her heart has hardened toward him. Seeing as how much she loved her papa when she was little, I never imagined I'd see her give him the cold shoulder the way she does now.

But I have to say, Frank brought it on himself. He broke Katherine's heart, and he hasn't done anything to mend it.

I knew from the beginning that he never loved me. But up until he went off to war, he made his little girl feel like he loved her more than anything in the world. I despise him for what he's done to her.

I'm ashamed to admit this, but I take joy in the fact that Katherine now loves me more than she loves him. I always used to feel like I was playing second fiddle to her papa. What she and I went through together while Frank was gone brought us as close as a mother and daughter can possibly get. I'd like to think our bond will never be broken.

While Frank might've had his wicked ways before he went off to war, he was never one to let his temper fly. Since he's come home, he's taken to hollering any time something doesn't suit him. He puts me in mind of a three-year-old child living in a grown man's body.

Sometimes, he swings out at me when he's riled up. Generally, I don't get hit, as even with my extra weight, I can move faster than he can with his bad leg. But once or twice, I've gotten a good cuffing.

One evening a couple of months after he came home, I dished him up a bowl of bean soup for his supper. When he tasted it, he started bellowing that it didn't have enough salt in it, and that it tasted like swamp water. He grabbed his cane, ready to swing at me, hollering for me to bring him more salt. I jumped out of the way, telling him I didn't have any more salt in the house.

Then Katherine did something that shocked Frank and me both. Jumping out of her chair, she marched around the table to her papa and stood over him, as if she wasn't scared of him at all. "Don't you dare hit her!" she shouted at him. "If you do, I'll make you sorry for it!"

Frank stared up at her, his eyes wide with surprise. Katherine kept on shouting at him. "Mama used up every bit of salt she has in the house for that soup. If you'd get off your hind end and do something around here, then Mama would have the time to go to the store and buy more salt."

Frank's eyes welled up, and for a minute I thought he was going to cry. He pushed away his bowl of soup, then got up and went out to the barn.

Katherine went back to her place at the table and commenced to eating her own soup, as if nothing at all had happened. "This doesn't taste bad, Mama," she said. "Papa's just looking for something to make a fuss about."

I sat down to have a talk with her, trying to sound stern. "Katherine, no matter how much your papa aggravates you, you can't say such hateful words to him. I won't have that going on in my house. Do you understand?"

Katherine just tossed her head. "And I won't have him acting the way he does in MY house. If you won't get him in hand, then somebody has to."

Her words were a lot for me to take in. I had to think on them the rest of that evening and all the next day. I told myself it was high time I started putting my foot down with Frank.

As it turned out, Frank's never swung at me since then. Sometimes when he's fixing to start hollering, he'll look around and see that Katherine's right there, and then he'll shut his mouth and walk out of the house.

At such times, I have to turn away so he won't see me smiling. It's kind of funny, really, him being scared of his own child.

I have to say that Frank doesn't run off every evening after supper the way he did before the war. He's taken to sitting on the front porch on a kitchen chair, like an old man. Katherine gives him a wide berth when he's out there, going in and out of the house through the back door.

About six weeks after Frank came home, Sam Walker started coming over to see him every now and then. Sam's a burley fellow, as tall as Frank and twice as big around. The two of them started putting their heads together, conniving about something or another. Then they started going out back to the woods together.

Frank never told me what they were doing, but I knew they were making whiskey. I picked up on the fact that Sam was supplying the corn for the mash, and that he and Frank had worked out some kind of deal about that.

I've really never minded Mr. Walker coming around. Even though he drinks more than a man should, he behaves himself pretty well, and he's always respectful when he gives me the time of day. Frank has steered clear of his old buddy Zebadiah Hawkins. It doesn't take much thinking to figure out why.

But the problems came when Otto McGee started hanging around the still with Frank and Sam, trying to get in on things. Otto's an old fool ruined by whiskey. People all over the county know who he is, and no one can stand having him around. He wanders from Nashville to Helmsburg to Beanblossom. Sometimes, he even shows up as far north as Morgantown.

I've heard stories about farmers finding Otto sleeping in their shed or haymow, and them having to chase him out with a pitchfork. He'll show up at somebody's back door, begging for a plate of food. Some fellows will give him a lift in their wagons when they see him walking alongside the road. But they have to put him out pretty quick, because they say he stinks to high heaven.

My husband started coming home of an evening muttering about what a pain in the rear end the old man was, how he kept jabbering nonsense and getting in the way of what the other fellows were trying to do.

Frank wasn't so much telling me about it as he was letting off steam. "I don't know how many times I've ordered that bum off my property," he'd say to himself, "but he just keeps coming right back."

Wouldn't you know it, just about the time Frank was getting his operation up and running really well, the government came out with a new law that said people in this country couldn't make or sell liquor. Prohibition, they called it. Pa came over one morning to let me know about it. I could tell he was mighty worried.

"It's going to be a big change for people around here," I said. I couldn't even bring myself to mention how Frank was going to take it.

"Bertha," Pa said, "you're going to have to sit down and have a good talk with your husband about this."

Frank was in bed that morning, having a bad time of it with his leg. I'm pretty sure he overheard everything Pa and I were saying in the kitchen.

Pa left his newspaper lying on the table. It had a big headline saying, *PROHIBITION*.

After he was gone, Frank got up, grumbling like he always does in the morning. Seeing the paper on the table aggravated him. "What's this?" he barked.

I pushed the paper toward him. "Pa says you need to read it. It's about a new law."

He pushed it away. "I know," he said. "I know all about prohibition. They came up with that law a year ago. They're just now enforcing it. It doesn't concern me."

"But Frank," I said, "the law says...."

"I know what the law says," he growled. "And I'm telling you, it doesn't concern me."

Of course, the community was all abuzz about the new law. Some of the high-minded people at church had already been saying that drinking alcohol was a sin, and they were glad the government had finally put out a law against it. Reverend Isaac Barnes preached a sermon about the evils of strong drink, calling it the devil's brew.

To tell you the truth, I didn't think it was very Christian the way some folks were talking. They were saying they hoped the sheriff would get this fellow or that fellow for making liquor, acting joyful that somebody might get thrown in jail. Whenever I'd hear something like that, I'd be burning up with shame about what was going on in my own household.

In March, Pa came by with a copy of our weekly newspaper, the *Brown County Democrat.* When Frank saw him coming, he left the house, as if he already knew he didn't want to hear what Pa had to say.

"Where's Frank?" Pa asked when he came in. "He needs to see this."

He thumped the paper down on the table. I took a look

at it. On the front page was a story about the sheriff arresting a couple of men, Percy Slater and Dewey Armstrong, for making moonshine. Reading it made me sick to my stomach.

"See to it that Frank knows about this," Pa said.

Frank came back in after Pa left. I held my breath, not knowing what he'd do when he saw the story in the paper. He didn't bother to read it. He picked up the paper, carried it out to the burn barrel, and lit it on fire. He looked so mad that I knew I needed to steer clear of him for a while.

That evening after supper, when Katherine had gone up to her room, I decided that no matter what, I was going to have a talk with Frank. "What are you going to do about the still?" I asked him. "If the sheriff gets wind of it, he'll coming sniffing around here."

Frank got a hard look in his eyes. "Don't you worry. I'm fixing to move my still to where he can't find it."

He pushed away from the table and headed toward the back door. I knew I should leave him alone, but I had one more thing to say to him. I stood in front of the door, blocking his way.

"What about Katherine?" I asked him. "She knows about prohibition. Everybody's talking about it. They're probably talking about it at school. What will she think about having a papa who doesn't obey the law? How will she hold her head up if her papa gets thrown in jail?"

"It's none of her business," he growled. The fire in his eyes told me I'd better get out of the way before he started manhandling me.

A couple of days later, Sam Walker came over to sit on the porch with Frank. I poked my head out the front door to listen to what they were saying. I heard them talking about moving the still deeper into the woods, and closer to Beanblossom Creek so they'd have a good supply of water.

I knew the sheriff would soon hear about Frank making whiskey, but unless he could find the still, he couldn't prove anything. Knowing how many hills and hollows we have around here, and how thick the woods are, I figured Frank and Sam could do a pretty good job of hiding their operation. If the sheriff's men hunted for it all day long, it would still take them a year to find it.

I heard Sam telling Frank that the sheriff himself didn't like going into the woods because he was scared of snakes. They both threw back their heads and laughed, saying that all the rattlesnakes and copperheads in these parts would help keep the sheriff off their tails.

Two days after that talk with Sam, Frank was gone all day long. He came home late at night with mud caked on his boots and cockleburs stuck to the legs of his trousers. I figured he and Sam and old Otto McGee had been out taking care of their dirty business.

Even though I'm always caught up in my worries about Frank and his moonshining operation, there's one way we're better off than we were before the war. Frank's sisters keep on coddling him because of his war wound, and half a year ago, they got together and came up with the money to buy him a Model T Ford.

When Frank started talking about getting back to plowing his own cornfield this year, he was trying to figure out how to come up with the money for a horse to replace Brownie. He talked with his sisters, knowing they'd help him out, and they all decided Frank might as well buy a tractor instead of putting money into another plow horse.

Frank's so tickled with his tractor, a Waterloo Boy. Pa and Mr. Sawyer and all the Mitchell boys came over to have a look at it. Of course, the Mitchell boys wanted to crawl all over it and sit on the seat. Frank wasn't going to have that. He hollered at them to get down, saying he didn't want their grimy hands on the steering wheel.

Yesterday, Frank was out plowing with the Waterloo Boy. He's all set to work the field again. He says that with the tractor, he can grow an even bigger corn crop this year.

I know he's counting on putting the extra corn into making liquor. The fellows around here who have more respect for the law will be shutting down their operations. That'll leave Frank with more people wanting his whiskey.

There's nothing I can say that will make him stop what he's doing. I just take comfort in the fact that, as far as I can tell, the wives of the moonshiners aren't getting thrown into jail along with their husbands.

No, I'm not thrilled about that tractor and what it lets Frank do. But the Model T Ford is a different matter. Having our own car makes me feel like we're getting ahead in life.

At first, Frank didn't want me to drive it. But I told him I'm not going through all the bother of hitching up a horse to the carriage when we have a brand-new motor car parked by the house. And that unless he's ready to drop everything and drive me wherever I need to go, then he'd better stop being selfish and let me have a turn at it.

Little by little, I'm learning to put Frank in his place when he's being unreasonable. I've figured out that unless I start standing up for myself, life with Frank isn't going to have much joy in it.

Pa's giving me lessons on how to drive our new car. I'm telling you, I haven't had such a good time in a long while. The first time I got in that Model T and drove down Helmsburg Road, I felt free as a bird.

Katherine keeps pestering me to let her drive, too. I've told her she's not old enough. She insists that she knows a lot about motor cars from riding around with Clover. I suspect that Clover's already let her have a turn behind the wheel, and that they just haven't wanted to tell me about it.

My child's getting so smart and so capable, I hardly know what to do with her.

Mr. Fox says that Katherine's gone all the way through the eighth-grade lessons and that she's ready for high school, except for the fact that she's only twelve. So, I guess for the next couple of years, Mr. Fox will just have to look around and see what else he can come up with to keep her busy there at Owl Creek. As quick a learner as she is, he's going to have a hard time keeping up with her.

1922

These past two years, I've gotten used to Frank's new ways of coming and going. Four or five days a week, he takes off for his still buried deep in the woods. Sometimes, he leaves right after breakfast and doesn't come home until after I've gone to bed.

He keeps up with his work in the cornfield, but about half the time, the milking and the care of the animals is left to me. Having all that extra work makes me feel bitter. But I have to say that things are more peaceful in this household when Frank isn't around. I can breathe a sigh of relief when I knew he's gone for the day.

Katherine's come to the point where she doesn't even bother to ask where her papa is. She's enjoyed this summer so much. She helps me out, like she's always done. But the minute she's finished with her chores, she has her nose in one of the books Clover brings her. I like watching Katherine when she's lost in her reading. I can tell that her stories carry her off into another world.

She enjoys her drawing, too. She's gotten into a habit of packing a picnic lunch and walking down the road a little way. She finds a spot to spread out the old quilt I gave her. Then she takes out her pencil and paper and makes an afternoon of it, sketching the scenery around her.

I always fret when she's about to take off, and I tell her to be careful. But I know she's growing up, and that she likes being on her own. I'm happy to see her satisfied with her life. And I'm so glad she isn't wasting her time worrying over what her papa's doing.

Katherine's going to be starting high school in a couple of weeks. It's all she can talk about. She's a young woman now, and she's starting to get a womanly shape. Six months ago, when she turned fourteen, Clover gave her an outlandish gift for her birthday: a new wardrobe, chest of drawers, and commode for her bedroom. On top of that, she gave her a new porcelain pitcher and wash basin, along with a matching chamber pot. All this was brought over from Columbus on a truck.

I told Clover she shouldn't have done so much. But of course, she insisted that with Katherine being a teenager, she needed a proper bedroom.

Now, Katherine's fixed her room just so, and she keeps it that way, with never a thing out of place. She always has the door to the room closed, as if she's keeping out anything that doesn't belong in there. She doesn't like anyone else going into her room, not even me, because she doesn't want anything messed up.

She has her things all set for school. Three pretty new dresses are hanging in her wardrobe. Her bloomers, petticoats, and stockings are folded up neatly in her drawers. She has her writing tablets in a stack on top of the chest of drawers, along with her pencils. And she keeps her rosary right there beside them. She always takes her finger to stretch it out in a perfect circle.

It seems that when Katherine and I stopped concerning ourselves with Frank, it got to him in a way. All those years I wanted his affection, he pushed me aside, as if I meant nothing to him. But now that I can't find it in my heart to care, he seems to miss my attention. From time to time, he'll do something to force Katherine and me to take notice of him.

One evening in July, he came walking through the back door with a dead rattlesnake draped over the barrel of his rifle, knowing it would get a rise out of Katherine and me.

I jumped when I saw it, and the pan I was holding slipped out of my hand and clattered on the floor. "What on earth, Frank?" I cried out.

Katherine came running when she heard the commotion. She pointed her finger at her papa, giving him a hateful glare. "Get that horrid thing out of this house," she ordered.

He grinned, knowing he'd gotten what he wanted from us. Then he turned and took the dead snake out to the barn.

One night about three weeks ago, I was fixing to go to bed when it came to me that I hadn't seen Frank in two whole days. That seemed odd to me. When another day passed and he hadn't come home, I started to wonder whether something had happened to him.

Pa came by that evening to drop off a cherry pie Ma had baked. When he took a look at me, he said, "Bertha, I can tell you've got something on your mind. What's that husband of yours up to now?"

Pa knows to keep a careful watch on what's going on here. Plain and simple, he doesn't trust Frank to be the man of the house.

"Frank's gone missing," I told him. "I haven't seen hide nor hair of him in three days."

Pa gave a big sigh and sat down at the table to think. "Maybe we should get the sheriff involved in this," he said.

"Oh no," I said quickly, knowing that having the sheriff looking for him was the last thing Frank would want.

"Then let's give it a day or two," Pa said. "If he's not home by then, Mr. Sawyer and I will get a few men together for a search party."

Then he looked me in the eye and said, "Bertha, I want you to know that what I told you when Frank was off to war still stands. If he comes to some bad end, you won't need to worry. Your ma and I will move you and Katherine back home with us."

He got up to leave, and as he walked out the front door, I heard him say to himself, "Maybe it's high time we did that anyway." That told me he was getting fed up with Frank again.

I went to bed that night feeling comforted by Pa's words, knowing my child and I wouldn't be left alone if things went from bad to worse.

In the middle of the night, I was awakened by the sound of footsteps in the house. I opened my eyes to find Frank standing in the bedroom doorway. In the light of the kerosene lamp he was holding, his face looked hideous. It was covered with filth, and twisted with evil and fear. "Bertha," he hissed.

I thought I was looking at a ghost or a demon, and I couldn't stop myself from screaming.

He moved over to the bed to cover my mouth with his hand. He smelled terrible, a mixture of whiskey and the stench of an unwashed body. "I need you to get up," he said. "Be quiet, don't wake Katherine."

I was so scared that I couldn't move. But Frank yanked the quilt off me, shocking me enough to make me jump out of bed.

"I'm starving," he said. "I haven't had any food in three days. Fix me something to eat."

I followed him into the kitchen. He put the lamp on the table and sat down. When I took a good look at him, I saw that his clothes were grimy, as if he'd been rolling around in the mud. One sleeve of his shirt was almost torn off, and there were deep scratches on his arm and his face.

"Frank," I cried out, "have you been attacked by a wild animal?"

He didn't answer for a minute. Then he said, "In a manner of speaking, yes."

I was so shook up that I couldn't think what to fix him. Then I remembered Ma's cherry pie, and I went to the pie safe to cut him a slice. I put the plate in front of him and was about to go back to bed, but he caught my arm and said, "Stay with me, Bertha." So, I sat down at the table.

As I watched him lift a forkful of pie to his mouth, I saw that his hands were shaking, just like they'd done when he came back from the war. Chewing the food seemed to take more strength than he had, and he gagged when he tried to swallow. So, he gave up on eating and pushed his plate aside.

"Bertha," he groaned, putting his head in his hands. "I've done a terrible thing."

My heart dropped to the floor. *What now?* I thought. *What more could this man have possibly done?* I knew he was about to tell me a story I wanted no part of.

"I was out at the still," he said. "I was working alone. Sam wasn't there. But then, Otto McGee showed up. He wanted whiskey, and I gave him some, like I always do.

"After he'd drunk his fill, he started talking his nonsense, going on about me owing him money. I figured he thought since Sam wasn't there, he could get one over on the poor war cripple.

"He told me I owed him a hundred dollars for the work he'd done there at the still. I kept telling him he'd never done a lick of work for me, that all he'd ever done was get in the way. I told him that if we were talking about owing money, he owed me for all the liquor he'd drunk up."

Frank groaned again, shaking his head. "Bertha, that old fool wouldn't lay off. He just kept on arguing. I got fed up and told him I didn't want him coming around anymore, that I never wanted him there in the first place.

"That riled him up, and he came at me. I guess he thought that with my bad leg, he could give me a good licking. The old fellow's really scrappy. He might be twice my age, but he gave as good as he got. When I finally fought him off, I made a move toward my rifle and told him to get the hell off my property. He started to leave, but then he turned around and came at me again…."

Frank looked at me, his eyes begging for my understanding. As if he wanted me to tell him he couldn't have helped doing what he'd done. Then he put his face in his hands, and a sound I'd never heard before came out of his mouth. It was the pitiful howl of a man who'd sunk so low in life that he was afraid he'd never be able to pull himself up again.

I got up, picked up the plate of pie, and carried it to the kitchen sink. I felt foggy and unreal, like I'd died and turned into a ghost. I could hardly feel my feet on the floor, and when I opened my mouth to speak, my voice sounded like it was coming from a mile away.

"Don't say another word, Frank. I don't want to hear any more about this. Not now. Not ever."

I went out to the mudroom to fetch a wash bucket, hardly able to feel my hands on the handle. I filled it with water from the pump in the sink, then put it on the stove. While I waited for the water to heat up, I sat down at the table with Frank, turning my face away so I wouldn't have to look him in the eye.

"The way I see it," I told him, "it was a case of self-defense. And if this ever comes to the sheriff's attention, I suspect he'll look at it that way, too."

Frank's body sagged forward onto the table, as if he was so tuckered out that he couldn't sit up straight anymore. He buried his face in his folded arms and cried like a little boy who'd lost everything in the world.

I figured he wanted me to stay there and comfort him. But I tell you, I'd already given him all I had to give. I lifted the bucket of water off the stove and set it on the floor. "You need to wash yourself really good, Frank," I said. "You don't want those scratches to get infected." Then I left him alone in the kitchen and went back to the bedroom.

As I lay there in bed, the weight of what my husband had told me slowly began to sink in. Horror crept over me, catching every part of me in its grip. I tried to push away the ugly pictures that came to my mind, but I couldn't.

About half an hour later, Frank came into the room and climbed into bed beside me. Lying next to him made my skin crawl. I couldn't stand it, and I made a move to get up.

Frank grabbed my arm to hold me back. His touch sent chills up my spine, and I pulled away from him. As I left the bedroom, I heard his pitiful whisper: "Bertha, don't leave me."

I went to the front room to sit alone in the darkness, hearing nothing but the nighttime song of the crickets. It seemed strange to me that such an ordinary thing could keep right on going while something so terrible was happening in my life. As I listened to the chirping, it came to me that no matter what foolish or heartbreaking things we humans might do, the crickets would never stop their singing.

"Oh God," I whispered into the night. "How can a woman be married to such a man? What is it you would have me do?"

I knew I'd come to a crossroads, that I had a big decision to make. *Now's the time,* a voice in my mind told me, clear as a bell. *Like Pa said, it's high time. Time for Katherine and me to pack up and move back home with Ma and Pa. Never setting foot in this house of sorrows again. Never having anything more to do with the lawless man who's trampled on our hearts and turned our lives upside-down with his selfish and wicked ways.*

Power began to swell inside me, and I wanted to run,

run, run away from Frank. I wanted to dash up the stairs and wake Katherine from her sleep, shouting, "Get up and pack your things. We have to go."

Every part of my body wanted to run. Except for my feet. It was like they were nailed to the floor. As I kept thinking on the matter, my determination began to drain away. And I came to the point where I pitied Frank even more than I hated him.

It isn't entirely his fault, I thought. *Life has turned him into the kind of man he is. Life gave him a no-good father, not an upstanding man like my pa. Life took his mother away from him before he had a chance to know her, before she had a chance to teach him right from wrong. His silly sisters did nothing but spoil him, making him think he could do anything he wanted to do. On top of all that, being in the war ruined his mind, making it easier for him to do the terrible thing he's just done.*

Then thoughts of Clover came to my mind. *What would she do if she found out what her brother had done? She'd probably have herself a nervous breakdown. She'd suffer over it for the rest of her years.*

I knew I had to keep my mouth shut. I couldn't bring myself to destroy another person's life.

And finally, I thought of Katherine. *Oh, dear God, what would Katherine think about this? How could she ever live with herself, knowing that her papa, her own flesh and blood, was capable of doing such a thing? If I move her out of this house, she'll have to know why. And I'll have to explain it all to her.*

I pictured my sweet daughter sleeping in her pretty little room, with her things all fixed just the way she liked them. I knew it was the one place where Katherine could shut out the ugliness of the world and be at peace with herself. And I knew I didn't have the heart to yank her out of it.

I finally lay down on the sofa and dozed off a bit. When I heard Frank moving around in the morning, I got up and fixed his breakfast, just like I'd always done.

About a week ago, a couple of children came across a dead body when they were playing in the Beanblossom Creek. I can't imagine what a shock it must've been for those little ones. No innocent child should ever be faced with something so gruesome.

The corpse was hard to identify, as it had been rotting for quite some time. But the sheriff and the coroner figured that, from the size of him and the missing teeth and the shaggy hair, it had to be Otto McGee.

The body was too far gone to say for sure what caused his death. The coroner did mention that his skull was cracked in one spot, as if he'd been hit by something hard and flat. Like maybe the butt of a rifle. But more likely, the coroner said, the old man was so drunk that he stumbled and hit his head on a rock, then fell into the creek and drowned.

Everyone was satisfied to leave it at that. People have been saying that the old drunkard lived such a pitiful life that it was surprising he lasted as long as he did. I've been trying to steer clear of conversations like that.

To tell you the truth, no one cares about the loss of the old man's life, as he was nothing but a nuisance. As far as anyone knows, Otto McGee didn't have any family. So, no one had a proper funeral for him. I don't even know where they buried his body. People will soon forget about the raggedly old tramp walking up and down our county roads.

Myself, I had to take some time to think on the whole matter. Last night, I wasn't able to sleep with Frank lying there beside me. So, I got up and slipped out of the house and sat on the front porch steps for a while.

I got to thinking about how we all start out the same, as innocent babes precious in the eyes of our mothers. And then, how some lives take such a terrible turn. Tears came to my eyes, and I couldn't do anything but sit there under the stars and have myself a good cry.

1924

It's been more than four years since they passed that law against alcohol, and in all that time, my husband has managed to steer clear of any problems with the sheriff. When I got to thinking on that the other day, I had to stop and thank the Lord for watching over us. Even though I'm not sure it's right to expect God to protect someone when they're caught up in wrongdoing.

Frank doesn't go out to the still as much as he used to. Just once, maybe twice a week. He's pretty much turned the operation over to Sam Walker. I figure he's bothered by memories of that awful business with Otto McGee.

He still has nightmares about the war, and about Otto McGee, too. He thrashes around and talks in his sleep, keeping me awake for hours on end. He'll mutter something like, "Get out of here, you stupid bum." Or, "Get the hell off my property."

When he's not out in the barn or the field, he sits around the house feeling sorry for himself. I can tell he's mulling over things that've happened the past few years. He wants my pity. I do pity him, and that's the reason I don't turn my back on him. But pitying a man isn't the same as loving him.

These past two years, Frank has drunk more than he ever has. For a while, I kept telling him that drinking wouldn't help, that it was liquor that started his problems in the first place. Several times, he got angry and lashed out at me. Mostly, he just turned a deaf ear to my words.

But the last time I mentioned something about his drinking, he looked at me with sorrow in his eyes and said, "Bertha, I don't know any other way to live." I thought on that for the next couple of days, on how pitiful it is for a man to get into such a state. I decided not to bring the matter up anymore.

Katherine's sixteen now, and she's picked up on the fact that her papa drinks more than a man should. She hates it. She brings pamphlets home from school, things put out by the temperance movement, and she wants me to read them. I hardly want to look at them, as I already know firsthand about what alcohol can do to a person.

"Papa's ruining his life with the whiskey," she tells me time and again. "It's going to kill him."

Even though I think Katherine goes too far in her thoughts about alcohol, I'm glad she's caught up with that rather than the other side of things. Pa has told me stories he's read about the speakeasies in cities like Indianapolis. Speakeasies are places where people go to drink and play cards and gamble. It's against the law, and every now and then, the police raid places like that and arrest people. The young women who hang around speakeasies are shameful and indecent, with their rouge and lipstick and skimpy little dresses and bobbed hair. I'm glad Katherine has more sense than to act like that.

Pa says that out of respect for the law, he's not doing any drinking himself. "When it comes to liquor," he says, "I've always been able to take it or leave it. And I've decided to leave it completely alone." He's talked to Katherine about that, and she respects him for it.

I'm glad she has a man she can look up to, because she's ashamed of the fact that her papa is a moonshiner. Once when he was sitting half asleep in his chair, with his jug of whiskey on the floor next to him, she gave the jug a little kick and said, "You know you're breaking the law by making that nasty stuff. Why don't you just stop?"

He looked up at her with bleary eyes and mumbled, "A man's gotta do what a man's gotta do."

"Leave him alone," I told her. "It doesn't do any good to talk to him."

She looked at me, shaking her head, as if she couldn't believe his ignorance. Or mine, for that matter. "Why do you put up with this, Mama?" she asked.

I didn't know what to say to her.

One evening after Frank had been drinking in the kitchen, he fell asleep with his head lying on the table. As I did the supper dishes, I couldn't help but remember what a fine-looking man he'd been in his youth. And there he was, his mouth hanging open, the spittle drooling out, the sound of his snoring practically rattling the windows. I decided I'd best leave him there for the night.

Katherine came downstairs to sit on the front porch, something she likes to do on a summer evening. When she passed through the kitchen, she stopped and looked at her father, wrinkling her nose. "He disgusts me," she said.

I figured I should scold her for saying such a thing, although I didn't have much heart for it. "Katherine," I said, "he's your papa and you owe him respect."

"Not if he doesn't deserve it," she said.

I've never talked to Clover about her brother's drinking, although I'm sure she's noticed that he has a problem with liquor. She went through that whole trial with her pa, so she knows firsthand about that kind of life.

Sometimes, I think she feels ashamed that she hasn't been able to keep her brother from going down the wrong road. So, she tries to make it up to Katherine by bringing a better influence into her life. I love her all the more dearly for that.

Knowing how much Katherine loves to read, Clover bought her a subscription to *The Youth's Companion,* a newspaper that comes in the mail once a week. It's full of stories and poems and articles and such.

I've never seen Katherine so tickled by anything. The minute she gets her hands on the latest copy of *The Youth's Companion,* she rushes up to her room to read it from front to back, every single line. She learns so much about the world through that newspaper. Things that are beyond anything I ever could hope to understand.

She wouldn't think of throwing any of those papers out. She keeps them in a stack on her closet floor, all piled up in order. While she's waiting for the new one to come, she'll pull out an old one and read it all over again.

Once, I teased her, telling her that her room is soon going to be stacked from floor to ceiling with those newspapers. "Why don't you take some of the older ones out to the burn barrel?" I asked her.

"Are you crazy, Mama?" she said, waving one of the papers in my face. "*The Youth's Companion* has published the work of some of the greatest writers in this country: Mark Twain, Emily Dickenson, Jack London, Edith Wharton. It would be a crime to throw these out."

On Katherine's sixteenth birthday, Clover gave her a set of books written by three sisters from England: Charlotte, Emily, and Anne Bronte. Katherine busted out crying when she opened that present.

"Oh, Aunt Clover!" she sobbed. "They're my favorite authors! How did you ever know to get these for me?" She held the books to her bosom, as if they were near and dear to her heart. "I'll read them over and over again!"

Of course, Clover had to start crying herself. "Katherine, my sweet girl," she said, "what is it about the Bronte sisters that makes you love their work so much?"

"They write the way I feel inside," Katherine said. "Their work moves me."

I sat there listening to the two of them talk, feeling stupid and unlearned. To tell you the truth, I was a little jealous of Clover, with her being able to touch Katherine's heart like that. But I'm beyond the point of feeling bitter toward my sister-in-law. I know my child needs more than I alone can give her.

Many times over these past months, I've seen Katherine sitting on the sofa, reading those books with tears running down her face. Sometimes, I'm not sure I should be letting her read things that disturb her like that. But I know she'd never give up her books, no matter what I might say.

She always looks so soft and pretty when she's reading, her beautiful hair hanging down around her face, her legs curled to one side, all dainty-like. It's only when I see her lift a hand to turn the page, a hand that's dry and calloused from hard work, that I can tell she's still a farm girl.

One day toward the end of June, I got up early to go out to the garden to pick green beans, hoping to beat the heat. I was planning on spending the morning and afternoon canning them. It was one of those days I knew was going to be miserable in my hot kitchen. But I told myself I'd have to bear it. Otherwise, a whole lot of beans would go to waste.

Katherine was going to help, of course. I'd mentioned my plans to her the night before. When I came in from the garden with a bushel basket full of beans, she was sitting there at the table reading while she waited for me. I could tell she was so spellbound that the world could've been burning down around her and she wouldn't have noticed.

"What's going on in that story that keeps you so caught up in it?" I asked her.

She looked up at me and smiled. "Do you want to read it, Mama? You could find out for yourself."

"No," I said, "I'd never make it through all those big words."

"Then let me read to you," she offered. "Bring the beans, and we'll go sit out on the front porch."

So, I took a kitchen chair to the porch and sat there with a bowl on my lap and the basket of beans at my feet, while Katherine sat on the steps reading to me. The name of her book was *Wuthering Heights,* by the Bronte sister named Emily. While I snapped the ends off the beans and broke them in pieces, Katherine read for two hours straight. About a man bringing home to his family a little gypsy boy named Heathcliff. About Heathcliff and the man's daughter Catherine becoming playmates and the best of friends.

When Katherine first mentioned the little girl's name, she looked up at me and smiled. "Her name is the same as mine," she said. "Except it's spelled with a C." I could tell the two of them having the same name made it easier for her to put herself into the story.

She went on to read about Heathcliff falling in love with Catherine and having his heart broken when Catherine turned her back on him and married another man. Sometimes, I couldn't follow what was happening in the story, and my daughter would have to stop and explain things to me. She was patient with me, like a schoolteacher taking the time to make sure her student understood.

My fingers kept on working with the beans, but my mind was somewhere else, way out on the moors of England where the story was taking place. All of a sudden, I realized I'd come to the bottom of my basket. I couldn't believe how the time had flown.

Katherine said she needed to stop because her eyes were getting tired. So, we went inside to get ourselves a bite to eat. She helped me wash the beans and stuff them into the Mason jars. When we finally had the jars boiling in the pot on the stove, I said to her, "My mind's not going to be satisfied until I hear how that story ends."

Katherine laughed. "See what I mean, Mama?" And while I sat there at the table keeping an eye on the beans, she commenced to reading again. About Catherine dying and Heathcliff getting on with his life, but always sorrowing over the woman he loved.

When Katherine closed the book, she had tears in her eyes. I found myself lifting a corner of my apron to dab at my own eyes.

"It's so sad," Katherine said. "I guess that's the way life goes. One heartbreak after another. But if you're lucky, you'll find a lot of love in between."

I sat there not wanting to move, not wanting to break the spell. The story of Catherine and Heathcliff had made me forget all about the hard work and the heat. It had almost made me forget that I was Bertha Kelly.

I was still sitting there at the table thinking on the story when Frank came in from the barn. "Where's supper?" he asked.

And I realized I'd plumb forgot about making supper. "I wore myself out with doing up the beans," I told him. "I guess we'll just have to settle for bread and butter tonight. Maybe a slice of pie." Frank snorted and walked out of the kitchen.

That night, I lay in bed smiling to myself, running that story through my head. I knew something had been woken up inside me that never would be content to go back to sleep.

Even though Katherine would get wrapped up in her love stories, she didn't seem to care for boys in real life. When she was little, she'd complain to me that she couldn't abide boys. I used to laugh at that, because I knew Owl Creek School was full of ruffians who pestered and teased her and got on her last nerve. I figured that when she got older, she'd change her mind about young men.

As soon as she started up at Helmsburg High School, she made some new girlfriends, Alice Richardson, Agatha Morris, and Julia Wagner. They're girls like her, serious about their studies. Once, I asked her what she thought about the boys at the high school. She wrinkled her nose and shook her head.

Right then, I suspected she'd decided to steer clear of boys. I figured it was because she didn't want to end up with the kind of life I had with her papa.

I knew my child had a lot of love to give. I thought maybe she was going to live a life where she loved many people in spirit, but no one in the flesh.

Then along came Billy Davis, and everything changed. For a while, anyway.

Billy Davis is Hazel's husband's nephew. He's Walter's sister Margaret's boy.

I've gone to the Oak Ridge Church with Margaret Davis for a dozen years or so. When Billy was just a little tyke, she'd bring him along with her. At the Wednesday evening prayer meetings, he'd play outside in the graveyard with Katherine and the other children. He's a year older than Katherine.

The first Sunday of this past July, Margaret Davis came to church all smiles. She said she was fixing to visit her aunt up in Indianapolis that afternoon, and that her son Billy was going to drive her there.

Katherine was with me, and when she heard Margaret mention Billy's name, she gave a little start. "I haven't seen Billy in so many years," she said. Then her cheeks flushed, and I knew she had some sweet memories of her little friend.

Wouldn't you know it, when Katherine and I stepped out of the church after the service, a handsome young fellow was standing there by his car, waiting for his mother. He looked so nice in his clean white shirt and straw hat. I hardly recognized him as the little tow-haired boy I'd known years ago, as he'd grown so tall and his hair had turned dark. But I knew for sure it was Billy when I saw his big brown eyes. Those eyes had always seemed as if they could look right through a person.

Katherine stopped in her tracks, so shocked by the sight of Billy that she couldn't move. He tipped his hat and nodded at her, and she smiled at him. It seemed to me that something unseen was passing between those two young people.

Katherine had gotten used to driving our Model T, and she would always insist on getting behind the wheel anytime she and I went to church together. But after that moment with Billy, she climbed in on the passenger's side, saying, "You'll have to drive us home, Mama. I'm a bit overcome."

I had to chuckle, hearing her talk like that. I think she gets those terms from the books she reads. "What's the matter, Katherine?" I teased.

She sat there fanning herself with her hand, as if she was trying to cool down her overheated feelings. "His eyes," she murmured. "They pierced my soul." I had to bite my lip hard to keep from busting out laughing.

As I figured he would, Billy started coming over to the house to see Katherine. They'd go out for a walk, or he'd take her for a ride in his car.

He seemed like a fine young man to me. I did wonder, though, about the matter of him not going to high school. Billy's family owns the sawmill there in Helmsburg, and after he finished eighth grade, he went to work for his pa. Him not having much of an education didn't bother me, but I was a little worried about how Katherine would take it.

I kept asking Katherine when she wanted to have Billy over for Sunday dinner. "Not just yet," she'd say.

She kept putting me off, and when I finally pressed her to tell me why, she got tears in her eyes. "Papa won't make a good impression on him," she said. "I don't want Billy to think bad of me because of the way Papa is."

When I heard her say that, I had to put my arms around her and cry with her a little bit.

Yesterday evening, Billy came over to take Katherine out for a drive. He brought along a basket with a supper his ma had packed, and the two of them had a picnic. I knew that evening was going to be sad for them, their last time together for the summer.

Katherine's about to start her third year of high school. She'll be going to the brand-new school they built here last year, the brick building a little way outside of Helmsburg. It's a lot bigger than the last high school they built, and a far cry from the little country school she attended up through eighth grade.

A couple of weeks ago, we drove out there to the new high school to see it, so she could get used to where she'll be going. She was so excited about it. "Mama," she said, "I think Helmsburg is coming up in the world."

So, when she went out with Billy yesterday, I figured they'd have to talk about the matter of her getting busy with her schoolwork. I'd already told her they'd need to cut down on how often they saw each other, maybe to once a week.

About the time the sun was going down, I was out in the garden bringing in the last of the squash and cucumbers. I heard a car coming down the lane, and I knew it was Billy bringing Katherine home.

All of a sudden, I had the notion to slip around the side of the house to have a peek at them. I had an apron full of vegetables, and I knew Katherine would be ashamed to have Billy see me like that. So, I took care to be quiet.

And I came across the loveliest scene you ever could imagine. The two of them were standing on the porch. Katherine was looking up at Billy, her face so soft and tender. She was wearing a pretty blue summer dress that brought out the color of her eyes. Her blonde curls were falling down around her shoulders.

I could tell by the way Billy was looking back at her that he was totally smitten. Head over heels in love with her. The whole thing was so beautiful that it took my breath away.

He lifted a hand to twine a finger through one of her curls. Then he kissed her lips, ever so gently. He whispered something in her ear, then walked off to his car whistling a tune. As if he was the happiest young man in the world.

Katherine stood there clutching her hands to her heart, watching him for a minute before she went inside. I walked around the house and stood there in the backyard for a while, trying to pull myself together again.

"My daughter's in love," I whispered to myself. "She's found herself a young man." I thought about the sad state of affairs between my husband and me, and I told myself things would be so much different for my child. I stood there thanking the Lord for that.

When I went inside, I still had the vegetables wrapped up in my apron. Katherine was in the kitchen getting herself a drink of water, and I knew she figured I'd been out in the garden all that time. I took a quick look at her. Her eyes were soft and her cheeks were flushed, and she had a little smile on her face.

I was fixing to ask, "How was your picnic with Billy?" But before I could, she ran up the stairs to her room.

That night in bed, my mind started running away with me. I kept picturing what I'd seen on the front porch.

Around here, most girls marry when they're seventeen

or eighteen, and I figured Katherine would, too. I was happy with that idea. I knew Billy would a fine husband for her, and that he'd earn them a good living working at the sawmill. All I could think of was grandbabies playing on the floor at my feet and climbing up to sit on my lap.

But this morning, Katherine came downstairs looking out of sorts, as if she hadn't slept well. As if deep down inside, something was bothering her.

"How was your evening with Billy?" I asked her.

She shook her head. "I don't have time for this," she snapped.

"What do you mean?" I asked.

"I don't have time for Billy Davis. I'm going to break things off with him."

I thought my jaw was going to hit the floor. "Why? Why in the world would you break things off with Billy Davis?"

"I have to get on with my life," she said. "I've got to get ready for the years ahead."

"Get ready for what?" I asked.

"College," she said. "And my teaching career."

I was so dumbstruck that I just stood there staring at her.

"Mama," she said. "You need to show me how to pin my hair up properly. I'm a grown woman now."

I turned away from her so she wouldn't see the tears in my eyes. I knew my daughter would never again allow a young man to play with her beautiful curls.

1926

Last year, Helmsburg was struck by a terrible tragedy. Fires burned the town, three different times. The first fire hit the gristmill. The second one burned the feed store. Just when the town was starting to get itself back to normal, the third fire started in the restaurant, and then spread to other businesses and homes in town. When it was all over and done with, it felt as if the heart and soul of Helmsburg had been burned out.

Thompson's General Store burned to the ground. That was such a hard thing for Walter and Hazel to face. When they finally got their money from the insurance company, they moved to Nashville. They're starting up a hardware store there. I guess they think there's nothing left for them in Helmsburg.

Doc Murphy's office burned down, too. That was hard on everybody around here. We'd all come to count on going to see him there whenever we had something that was getting the better of us.

Doc Murphy's an old man now. He'd already taken on another doctor to work with him, a young fellow by the name of Benjamin Groves. After the fire, Doc Murphy said he didn't have it in him to hang up his shingle again. So, Dr. Groves went out on his own and built a new office in town. We're mighty glad to have him here.

Still, it isn't the same. The fires have ruined so much for us.

Folks around here have been wondering whether somebody started the fires on purpose. There had been bad feelings between the towns of Helmsburg and Nashville. Helmsburg had been doing so well with the railroad and all, and some people were of a mind to move the county seat from Nashville to Helmsburg.

Of course, that had riled folks in Nashville. After the fires, there was a lot of gossip going around, with people saying somebody from Nashville tried to burn Helmsburg down to make sure the county seat didn't get moved. But nobody's been arrested for that.

Ever since the fires broke out, there's been an uneasy feeling running through our community. None of us knows what's going to happen next. At the Oak Ridge prayer meetings, we've laid the matter before the Lord, asking him to watch over us during these troubled times. We've thanked God that the church didn't get burned, and that the new high school was spared.

Katherine and I cried together over all this hardship. "I remember how exciting it was to go to town with Papa when I was little," she said. "I thought Helmsburg was such a grand place. But it will never be the same again. Its glory days are over. It's the end of an era."

She had to explain to me what an era is. When I understood what she was talking about, I had to agree with her. Time never stands still, and nothing ever stays the same.

And that's not the only era that's ending. Hiram Henderson died a year ago. The old fellow keeled over from a heart attack. That made Clover the first of the Kelly sisters to become a widow. It reminded me that every last one of us is growing older by the day, marching toward our graves. Others in the family will soon be following Hiram.

All the while Clover was married to Hiram, I'd never seen much of him, as she was always coming and going without him. I think she'd already gotten used to being on her own. Truth be told, I doubt that she misses her husband very much.

Of course, everybody wondered what Clover was

going to do with Henderson's Mercantile. We all figured she'd sell the business and live on that money for the rest of her years. She did have a fellow from Columbus come to look the business over. He offered her a good price for it, and we all thought that was that. But then, she had a change of heart. She said she was going to run the store on her own.

That shocked me, and I had a hard time getting used to the idea. These days, women do things they never would've thought of doing in the past. But Katherine thought it was a great idea. She and Clover had some long talks about what it would take to run the store.

Once when I spoke up and said Clover was foolish to take on that kind of thing, Katherine put me in my place. "Aunt Clover's a strong woman," she said. "She's capable of taking on that kind of responsibility. Women in the 1920s are learning to be independent."

I've come to accept the fact that Katherine knows more than I do, and I hardly ever go against her opinion on things. Sometimes, I count on her to tell me what to do.

Here's a story about a time when my child ended up being smarter than me. Last October, Brown County held a fox hunt down south of Nashville. A lot of fellows from around here turned out for it. I heard it was such a big deal that even men from other counties showed up.

Frank and Sam Walker had been talking about the fox hunt all summer long. Frank was bound and determined to go. I was a little leery of the idea, as you never know what men might do at a get-together like that. Still, I figured it would pick up Frank's spirits to get away from the farm and enjoy himself with other fellows.

Truth be told, I was downright jealous of Frank being able to do something like that. I was getting a little down in the mouth, thinking on how there was nothing for me to do to pick up my spirits.

On the Wednesday evening just before the weekend of the fox hunt, I went to the prayer meeting feeling sorry for myself. But then, I heard people talking about something that perked up my ears. They were saying that a new preacher had come to these parts, a fellow by the name of Reverend Joshua Porter. And they said he was somebody worth listening to.

Mind you, the folks at the prayer meeting weren't talking about this out loud, out of respect for our own preacher, Reverend Isaac Barnes. But they were whispering that if you wanted to see something special, you had to go see Reverend Porter.

They were saying the man had God-given powers, that he could handle snakes and everything. He'd set up a tent out in the country south of Nashville, and he was holding meetings there. He was claiming to be preaching the one true religion. The folks at the prayer meeting said his crowd was getting bigger by the night.

When I heard all that, I felt something stirring inside me. For so many years, I'd taken comfort in going to the Oak Ridge Church and hearing Reverend Barnes preach. But truthfully, nothing Reverend Barnes ever said did much to lighten the load of sorrow in my heart. I got to wondering whether Reverend Joshua Porter might have something to say that I needed to hear.

A woman there at the prayer meeting, Imogene Jackson, kept talking to me about Reverend Porter, telling me this was something I shouldn't miss out on. Finally, I gave in and told her I'd go with her that Friday night.

So, on the very evening Frank loaded up his shotgun and his fox hounds in Sam Walker's pickup truck and headed toward Nashville, I ended up going in the same direction. Imogene Jackson and her husband picked me up in their car and drove me down to Joshua Porter's tent meeting south of town.

Reverend Porter was a tall, thin man with a big bushy beard and eyes that could bore a hole through you. When he started preaching, I could tell he had the knack for getting folks worked up. Before I knew it, the people around me were hollering and praising the Lord, raising their arms in the air. Reverend Porter said it was the Holy Ghost moving among us.

I kept quiet myself, as I would've felt foolish carrying on like that.

Toward the end of the meeting, Reverend Porter brought out a cage full of snakes. He called them serpents, which made the whole thing sound more biblical. One by one, he took those serpents out, showing everybody how he could handle them without getting bit. He said that if we trust the Lord with all our hearts, He will protect us from all evil, even the evil of a serpent's venom.

I wasn't sitting close enough to make out whether the snakes were poisonous, like rattlesnakes or copperheads. But I had to hand it to Reverend Porter. He sure could put on a show. Every time he'd pick up a snake, the people would scream and holler.

Then Reverend Porter had someone pass the offering basket around, telling us the money was going for the Lord's work. He said that whatever we gave to God, He'd return that blessing to us ten times over. I didn't have but a few coins in my purse, a dime and a couple of pennies. I gave what I had.

When I got home that night, I was so worked up that I couldn't sleep. All night long, I kept picturing Reverend Porter with his bushy beard and his wild eyes, remembering the things he said. Toward the morning, when I was starting to settle down, something about the whole matter didn't sit right with me.

When I got up, I was so tired that I could hardly get myself going. Katherine asked me what was wrong. I was thinking I shouldn't burden her, but she kept on pressing me. So, I ended up telling her all about what had happened at the tent meeting.

I hardly got two words out of my mouth before Katherine started shaking her head, as if she couldn't believe what I'd fallen for.

"Mama," she said, "this so-called Reverend Porter is talking nonsense. What he's telling people is nothing but a load of horse manure. He's playing on everybody's emotions. You need to use your reason. You need to see him for who he is, a con artist."

"But what about the snakes?" I asked her. "Doesn't him being able to handle snakes like that mean he has a gift from God?"

"I'd bet you any amount of money," she said, "that those snakes weren't poisonous. God isn't going to protect anybody who's stupid enough to play with a rattlesnake."

"You might be right," I said. "To be honest, I couldn't make out what kind of snakes they were."

She got a fierce look on her face. "Did he ask you for money?"

I hung my head. "Yes, he did. They passed the offering basket around. Reverend Porter said it was for the Lord's work."

Katherine looked so mad that I thought she was going to blow her top. "You can be sure all that money went straight into that man's pocket," she said. "Mama, your Reverend Porter is nothing but a grifter. Promise me you'll never go near that despicable fellow again."

I gave her my promise. For the next couple of days, I couldn't get over feeling ashamed of myself for being so foolish.

So yes, I'm used to my daughter being smarter than I am. I've started to trust what she says more than I trust what's in my own mind. But the day when she made that comment about Clover being a strong woman, I knew Katherine needed to hear from me for a change.

"You don't think I'm a strong woman?" I said, raising my voice a little bit. "After all I've done to keep this farm running? Taking care of everything when your papa went off to war? And now, carrying the whole load on my shoulders when he can't get himself up and around to do his chores?"

Katherine looked shocked. I was afraid I was hurting her, but I couldn't stop myself. I held up my cracked and calloused hands for her to see. "You don't think these are the hands of a strong woman? Clover's hands are as soft as a baby's bottom. She doesn't need to lift a finger to cook or clean or do her washing. She has a maid who does everything for her."

I waited for Katherine to say something, but she just turned away from me and went upstairs to her room. I felt bad, thinking I'd hurt her feelings something awful. But half an hour later, she came downstairs and put her arms around me.

"You're right, Mama," she said. "You're absolutely right. You are the strongest woman I know. If I grow up to be half as strong as you are, I'll be downright proud."

Actually, my daughter's grown up already. She turned eighteen two months ago. She's no longer a child. And I'm no longer a young woman. I just turned forty.

Last summer, between her third and fourth years of high school, Katherine worked for Clover at the mercantile. Clover praised her up and down, saying Katherine was her righthand helper. She said Katherine has a knack for running a business.

During those months, Katherine stayed at Clover's house a couple of nights a week. That was Clover's idea. She said she didn't want Katherine making so many trips back and forth. Truth be told, I think Clover just wanted Katherine there to keep her company.

The first night Katherine was gone, I lay in my bed crying, knowing my child wasn't upstairs in her room. I'm ashamed to say this, but I took to sleeping in Katherine's bed when she was at Clover's house. Just so I could feel close to her. And to get away from Frank's tossing and turning.

I know Katherine will soon be going out into the world as a grown woman. It would be wrong of me to keep her holed up in this shabby little farmhouse. She needs to get used to handling herself around all kinds of people.

With Katherine taking so well to Clover's business, I thought maybe she would stick with that for a while. As a matter of fact, I thought maybe she wouldn't even bother to finish high school.

But when I asked her about that, she said, "Oh no, Mama, I'm just working there to save money for college."

"So, will you be working for Clover next summer, too?" I asked her.

"Yes," she said. "And every summer between my years at college. Clover and I have it all worked out."

When Katherine was working at the mercantile last summer, Clover let her have anything she wanted out of the store. Of course, Katherine is too well-mannered to take advantage of her. She always waited until Clover told her to pick something out. And more often than not, she'd bring home a handful of tablets for taking notes in school.

"Why don't you pick out some material for a nice dress?" I asked her once.

"This is more important," Katherine said, holding up one of the tablets. "I'm going to need plenty of paper on hand to keep up with my teachers' lectures."

When school started last fall, she sat down at the

kitchen table with her stack of tablets. On the top of each one, she wrote her name: Katherine Rose Kelly. Then on the bottom, she wrote the name of the subject: History, English, Latin, Geometry, Art.

I can hardly believe how many notes she takes during her classes. I was always one to stare out the window and daydream a little bit during school, but I don't think Katherine lets herself do that. She keeps her mind on what the teacher is saying.

At home, she sits up in her room and copies things out of her schoolbooks. Once, I asked her why she did that. "If it's already written out in your book, why do you have to write it out again?"

"Writing things down fixes important ideas in my mind," she told me.

After just three months of school, Katherine had already run out of tablets. We had to take a trip down to the mercantile to get more. Of course, Clover gave her all she wanted and wouldn't let us pay for them.

Katherine devotes time to all her subjects, but I think she loves English the most. She loves stories, both reading and writing them. Now that she's grown up, she doesn't call them *stories* anymore. She calls what she reads *literature.* Sometimes, she talks about *the classics.* All that's way beyond me.

Sometimes, I hear her in her room reading her literature out loud. Once, I heard her talking in a foreign language. That scared me a little, hearing strange words in my own home. When she came down for supper that evening, I asked her about it.

"I was studying for my Latin class," she explained. "I was practicing conjugating verbs."

"I have no idea what you're talking about," I said.

She laughed. "That's okay, Mama."

There's so much my daughter crams into that brain of

hers. I don't see how she can hold it all. Sometimes, it seems like her brain starts to overflow, and then she has to come downstairs and tell me about what she's studying.

One day, she started telling me about the Revolutionary War. That was kind of interesting, really. The only war I've ever known anything about is the one we just came through. So, after we got done talking about the Revolution, we started talking about the war her papa fought in, the one they're now calling the Great War. I had a little bit to say on that.

Another day, she came downstairs talking about the United States Constitution. To be honest, I lost interest in what she was saying after a minute or two. I let her go on, acting like I was listening while my mind was somewhere else.

Just a couple of months ago, they held a writing contest there at the high school. Katherine wrote an essay about the Nineteenth Amendment to the Constitution. She explained to me what that amendment was all about, that it gave women the right to vote in this country.

I'd heard something about that law when they came out with it five or six years ago. But I'd never given it much thought. All the time I was growing up, Pa went out to vote whenever election time came around, but Ma never did. I just took it for granted that women weren't allowed to do such things.

After the new law was passed, some people around here were still saying it was wrong to let women vote, because a woman doesn't have the mind to understand things of the world. Ma herself didn't say the law was wrong. But she didn't feel like she wanted to up and start something new. And neither did I.

But Katherine says she's going to start voting as soon as she turns twenty-one. She wishes she could vote now.

In her essay, she came up with a list of reasons as to why the Nineteenth Amendment is a good law. She read the essay to me, even though I couldn't understand what she was talking about. She used a lot of big words, but she seemed to know how to use them the right way. I knew she did a good job, and I was proud of her.

So, I wasn't surprised when she came home telling me that she'd won first place. They gave her a little bit of prize money. Right away, she put it in her savings account for college, along with the money she'd earned working for Clover.

There was a picture of her in the *Brown County Democrat,* along with a story about her winning the contest. They mentioned something about her plans for the future, going on to study at Indiana University after she's done with high school. Not many young people around here even finish high school, let alone go to college. I cut that story out of the paper and put it between the pages of my Bible to keep it safe.

Of course, Clover was over the moon about the whole thing. She had someone come to her house with a camera, to take a picture of her standing next to Katherine with her first-place trophy. She invited Frank and me to come over to be in the picture. Frank didn't want any part of it. And being a fat old country woman, I didn't have the nerve to stand in front of a camera like that.

Clover insists that Katherine's going to be a great writer someday. She says college will give her a good background for that. That's more than I can even think about.

Whenever talk about college comes up, I get nervous. Even though Katherine's saved a lot of money, I know college costs more than what she has. And Lord knows Frank and I can't help her out. We don't have a penny to spare.

The other day, I asked her how she plans on paying for everything. She didn't miss a beat. "Scholarships," she said. "My teachers say that with my good grades, I'll qualify for any number of scholarships. They're helping me fill out the papers to apply for them."

I can tell she's dead set on going. She thinks she has it all figured out. So, I'm not going to stand in her way. Still, the idea seems outlandish to me. Something inside me wants to shake her and tell her that she's just a farm girl, and that she should give up such foolishness.

Yup, the idea of my child going to college scares the living daylights out of me. But when I see how excited she is about it, I can't help but get excited myself. I've prayed about the matter. I'll just have to wait and see what comes of it.

This past year, Katherine's begun to add weight to her tall frame. It's as if she knows can't make her way in this world being the wisp of a girl she's always been. Her hips have widened, her bosom's fuller, and her face has filled out. She has no patience for fussing with her curls. She fixes her long hair in two braids, then winds them around her head and pins them in place.

Now, she looks like a big, beautiful statue carved out of stone, so strong and sturdy that nothing can harm her. Like she's a woman to be reckoned with.

All her growing up years, Katherine had a puny little appetite. Now, she eats like she's never eaten before. Just a couple of days ago, she ate two slices of custard pie for supper. And before she went to bed, I found her at the pie safe cutting herself another slice.

"What in the name of God are you doing, Katherine?" I asked her.

"I'm hungry," she said. "I need my strength. I need all the strength I can get."

Yesterday, out of the blue, Frank said, "Bertha, I used to think Katherine favored my sisters. Now, I'm starting to think she takes after you."

His words hit me hard, and I had to go out and take a walk down the lane to think on them for a while. I cried a little bit, telling myself that I never wanted my daughter to be the plain, ordinary woman that I am, plodding along day after day like an old plow horse.

But the more I thought on it, the more I realized it didn't matter who my child looks like. She'll never be ordinary. She's going to be who God made her to be, and that's something special.

This morning when I got up, I had a little start when I looked out the front window and saw Katherine out by the fishpond, sitting on an old blanket. I figured she hadn't slept well because she had a lot on her mind, and that she was out there thinking things through. She's grown to be such a serious young woman.

The fishpond's empty now, except for the wild critters that've found their way to it. There are no more beautiful goldfish like when she was little. Frank doesn't have it in him to keep it stocked anymore. The one thing Katherine does is to make sure the pond doesn't grow up in weeds. From time to time, I've seen her out there cleaning things up. That tells me the special spot from her childhood will always be important to her.

As I stood there looking at her, I told myself I should leave her alone with her thoughts. But I just couldn't. The April air is still chilly in the mornings, so I threw my overcoat on over my nightgown and went outside to sit with her.

When she heard my footsteps, she turned around and gave me a sad smile. "Good morning, Mama," she said.

I sat down next to her, clucking my tongue.

"Katherine, what are you doing out here in your nightgown? You should have more sense than this."

I pulled her close to me and put the coat over both of our shoulders, the best I could. "You know, you used to do this when you were little. You'd come out here first thing in the morning, just to see your fish."

She laughed a little. "I know. I was just remembering that."

We sat together in the quiet. The only sounds were the birds singing their early morning songs and a squirrel scolding from the branch of a nearby tree. "Katherine," I asked, "what's weighing so heavy on your mind?"

She didn't answer for a few minutes, and I thought maybe my question had upset her. "I can't really put it into words, Mama," she finally said. "There's so much that happened in the past. So much to be done in the future. And so little time."

She laid her head on my shoulder. "It all goes by so quickly, doesn't it, Mama?"

"Yes," I said, "it surely does."

Suddenly, she sat up straight. "School!" she said. "I'm going to be late. I've got a report to give in my history class."

She jumped up and ran into the house, leaving me there alone wishing for just a few more minutes with her.

1929

Katherine is at the end her third year at Indiana University. She'll be finishing up in a couple of days. Then she'll have one more year to go before she's all done with her schooling. I can hardly believe it.

She's been living in a dormitory over there in Bloomington. She's used to it now, but it was hard for her at first. And for me, too. I tell you, I completely fell apart that September morning when she left for her first year of college.

Clover had come to pick her up and drive her over to the school. She'd gone upstairs to help Katherine carry down the things she'd packed. I was in the kitchen fixing a ham sandwich for Katherine. She had told me I was being a worry-wart, that she'd be having her lunch in the college cafeteria. But I just had to send something along with her, in case she got hungry.

Just as I was wrapping the sandwich in a scrap from an old towel, Katherine and Clover came down the stairs and into the kitchen. Katherine set down her suitcase and put her arms around me. I held her tight, and she buried her face in my shoulder. I could feel her body trembling as her tears dampened my dress. And I knew that when it came down to it, my baby girl was scared.

We clung to each other, and I started bawling like there was no tomorrow. "Mama," Katherine choked out, "it'll be so different not having you there by my side." She kissed my cheek, and then followed Clover out the front door.

After they left, the house felt dead and hollow, as if all the life had been sucked out of it. I felt so empty and lost that I didn't know what to do with myself.

I picked up a few breakfast dishes from the table and carried them to the sink. Before I put them in the dishwater, I took the cup Katherine had drunk from and held it to my cheek. Just so I could feel like I was still holding part of her.

And then I saw the ham sandwich lying on the counter. She'd forgotten to take it with her. I grabbed it and ran out onto the porch, trying to wave her down. But Clover's car was already too far down the lane, and they didn't see me.

I stood there holding that sandwich, knowing my child hadn't really needed it. Just like she didn't need me anymore. I don't think my heart has ever hurt so bad.

When they were out of sight, I kept standing there on the porch, unable to move for the longest time. "Bertha," I scolded myself, "you've got to get on with your day."

So, I went inside and rolled up my sleeves to finish the dishes. But then, I felt an urge to go upstairs to Katherine's room. Just so I could feel close to her for another minute or two.

She hadn't taken everything of hers to college. She wouldn't have had the space for all of it. Some of her high school books were stacked on her dresser, along with her tablets full of the notes she'd taken in her classes. I knew she couldn't bear to throw them out. But she wouldn't be needing them anymore, because she was moving on to higher learning.

I looked in her closet and found a couple of old dresses she'd worn around the house. They were too shabby to wear at college. And, of course, there was her stack of *Youth's Companion* newspapers. I had to smile to myself. She'd never thrown a single one of them out.

I looked around to see if I could find her set of books by the Bronte sisters. They were gone. I imagined they were so dear to Katherine that she couldn't leave them behind.

She'd made up her bed real nice before she left. She'd propped a couple of old dolls against the pillow, one Clover had given her and a ragdoll Ma had made. They were lying there so nice, with their dresses spread out just so. I'd never seen Katherine do something like that before. I knew she was wanting to keep her room as a place for remembering her childhood.

"My little bird has left the nest," I said to the empty room. "I can't keep her under my wing anymore."

All of a sudden, I felt so tired that I couldn't stand on my feet any longer. So, I stretched out on the bed and took those dolls in my arms and fell asleep, dreaming about the time when my grown-up daughter was still her mama's little girl.

That evening at the supper table, when it was just Frank and me, I got to crying again, so hard that I couldn't eat my supper. Frank usually doesn't pay me any mind, but the way I was carrying on worried him. "Bertha," he said, "you're going to have to get ahold of yourself."

I didn't even try to tell him why I was so upset. I just got up from the table and went to the bedroom, where I sat on the bed bawling into my apron.

It took me a while to get used to cooking for only two, with Katherine not here to eat with Frank and me. But for the past couple of years, I've been carrying some of what I make up to Ma and Pa.

Ma's starting to lose her strength. That's been a hard thing for me to face. I suppose every daughter likes to think her ma's going to carry on forever, doing the things a mother always does.

Pa and I have had some talks about Ma's condition. He says that by the middle of her morning chores, she's all tuckered out, and then she's done in for the day. So, every chance I get, I go up the road to help her out. It takes my mind off missing Katherine.

It hurts me something terrible to say this, but Ma's mind is slipping a little bit. One morning last week when I went up to help her, she'd just come in from the henhouse with a basket of eggs. She put the eggs in the bowl on the sideboard, like she always does. Then she sat down to rest while I swept the kitchen floor for her.

All of a sudden, she called out, "Bertha, I don't know what's the matter with me. I plumb forgot to go out and gather the eggs. Where did I put my basket?" And she got up and headed toward the door again.

I set aside my broom and took her by the arm. "Ma," I said, "you've already done that. You were coming in from the henhouse just when I got here." And I led her over to the sideboard to show her the eggs in the bowl.

She looked at me, puzzled. "How long have you been here, Bertha?"

"Just about ten minutes," I told her.

"Whew!" she said. "I don't know what's happening to my memory. It's like a leaky bucket. Things go in and come right out again."

But when it comes to things that happened a long time ago, Ma can remember just fine. I'll be washing up her dishes or sitting down with her to darn Pa's socks, and all the while, she'll be telling me the sweetest stories about when Hazel and I were little.

"When you were just two," she told me one day, "I had you out in the garden with me while I was pulling weeds. You wanted to help. So, I'd point to a weed and you'd reach down and pull it out, copying what you saw me do.

"You were just learning to talk, and it seemed like you never stopped. While I was bent over pulling the weeds, I couldn't always see you, but as long as I heard you prattling away, I knew you were right there by my side.

"I must've gotten lost in my own thoughts. All of a sudden, I realized everything had grown quiet. I stood up to look around, and I didn't see you anywhere.

"I tell you, Bertha, I've never been so scared in all my life. I dropped what I was doing and ran all over the farm looking for you, behind trees and in the bushes. I ran to the barn and told your pa you were missing. We looked in the cow stalls and up in the haymow, even though we knew you were too little to climb that far. We looked in the henhouse and the sheds. We checked the outhouse. You were nowhere to be found.

"Then we went back to the house to see if you'd gone inside on your own. We searched every room, even inside the cupboards and closets and under the beds. We couldn't find you anywhere.

"'Oh Rupert,' I cried to your pa, 'I've lost my baby girl!' I'd already lost two babies at birth. I was starting to think I was going to lose every child I ever had.

"'We'll just have to keep on looking,' your pa said. 'Let's go outside and look again until we find her.'"

As I sat there listening to Ma's story, I got so worked up and scared about that lost child that my heart was thumping in my chest. Then I had to laugh a little, knowing they'd find her. Because there I was, sitting with Ma, safe and sound.

Ma went on with her story. "Just as we stepped out the front door, we saw a wagon coming up the road. It was old Mr. Sawyer, the father of the Mr. Sawyer who lives on their farm now. And there you were, sitting on the seat next to him, not crying or anything. Just looking like you were having the time of your life.

"I ran to snatch you up and hold you in my arms, bawling my eyes out, thanking the Lord for bringing you back to me.

"'I had just passed by the Kelly farm,' Mr. Sawyer

said. 'And I saw Rose Kelly standing by the road, holding a little girl by the hand. She waved me down, and I stopped to see what she wanted.'

"'I found this precious little child,' she told me. 'Just wandering out here on her own. Do you know who she belongs to?'

"'I thought on it for a minute. Then I said, 'I think that might be Rupert and Lena Snider's baby.' Mrs. Kelly was so heavy with her unborn child that she had a hard time of it just taking a few steps. So, I said to her, 'I'm going up that way. Why don't I take her with me?'"

That part of Ma's story shook me up. I had to think on how strange it was that Rose Kelly had saved me from harm just before she birthed the baby boy who would grow up to be my husband. And just before her own death. I had to hold that thought close to my heart for a minute or two.

Ma went on to say that she'd learned her lesson about keeping a closer eye on me. She said Pa gave her a length of rope from the barn, and that when she'd go out to the garden with me, she'd tie one end of the rope around her waist and the other end around mine.

"I felt bad about it," she said. "It was like I was tying up a little calf, or something. But I didn't want to take any chance of losing you again."

I pictured that in my mind, the two of us each tied to one end of the rope, and it struck me as comical. I threw back my head and laughed, and Ma laughed along with me. That was a good time, and for a couple of minutes, I could make myself believe that nothing at all was wrong with my ma.

Sometimes, Ma's stories go back to when she was a child. Sometimes, they go even farther back, to a hundred years ago when her grandparents came up here from the mountains of Kentucky. She likes to tell about how they crossed the Ohio River, and then traveled up through

Indiana on Indian trails, making their way through the thick forests in their ox-drawn wagons.

"Times were hard back then," she's told me. "A whole lot harder than they are now. Those early Brown County settlers had to be of strong stock to survive. They had to live like pioneers for a long time, even after folks in other parts of Indiana were living an easier life."

I've heard those old stories so many times that I could tell them myself. But I never get tired of hearing Ma tell them all over again. About her grandfather almost working himself to death clearing away enough forest so he could farm his corn and tobacco. About him hunting for deer, rabbit, squirrel, and wild turkey, just so his family could have some meat to eat. About her grandmother weaving wool and flax into cloth so she could make the family's clothing. About her making quilts out of any scrap of material she could get her hands on. About her carrying water from a stream and cooking over an open fireplace.

Ma says Brown County was very wild back then. There weren't really any towns, just little clusters of log cabins here and there in the middle of the forest. Lots of wild animals lived in those woods: bears, panthers, and wolves. The wolves could be especially hard on a farmer's livestock. Ma's grandmother told her stories about how the county commissioner would pay a man one dollar for every wolf scalp he brought in. I can hardly imagine that. I don't think we've seen wolves around here in a good long while.

Ma said her grandmother told her that in the 1830's, when people decided Nashville should be the county seat, the place was nothing but a handful of log cabins. They were hoping to build it up into a good-sized town, but it was slow going. Hardly anybody had money to buy property for building a home or a business.

But during ma's childhood, things started to get better. There were gristmills, sawmills, general stores, blacksmith shops, and churches popping up all around the county. Still, most people didn't have a way to get out to the stores. They bought the goods they needed from the huckster who came to the house with his horse and wagon.

Back then, when people didn't have money, they'd use the barter system. They'd trade things like chickens and eggs for the huckster's wares. Ma said she was in charge of the henhouse when she was a young girl, and she was so proud to have eggs to trade with the huckster for something the family needed.

I can't help but feel proud when I hear those stories. Even though Ma tells the same stories over and over again, I keep on listening. Because I know there will soon come a day when she won't be able to tell them anymore.

I'm trying to keep the stories fixed in my mind. Someday, when Katherine is done cramming her head full of all her learning, she might want to hear them too.

When she was younger, Katherine had more to do with my side of the family: Ma and Pa and Hazel and her children. Of course, Clover always made sure to keep herself right in the middle of Katherine's life.

But since Katherine's been in college in Bloomington where her other aunts live, she's gotten to know them better. And she even knows some of their grown children, her cousins. I think that's made Clover jealous of her sisters. She's always wanted to have Katherine to herself. Now she knows what I've felt like all these years.

Katherine's been going to Mass with her aunts every Sunday, and at least once during the week. They come and pick her up at the college. So, she's Catholic through and through now. Even though I wish she'd been content with the Oak Ridge Church, that's not the case, and I have to accept it. Being Catholic is what she's decided deep down in her soul.

Just about the time when my heart longs to see my child so bad that I can't stand it anymore, Clover goes to Bloomington to pick her up, then brings her over to see me. Sometimes, she takes Katherine as far as Nashville, and then lets her drive out here on her own.

Whenever Katherine steps into the house, I see her intelligence shining in her eyes, and I can tell she's become a young woman who knows the ways of the world. For a minute or two, I feel afraid of her. It's like I'm not good enough to even touch her. But then she comes and puts her arms around me and says, "Hello, Mama." And then I remember that she's still my baby girl, and I feel easier around her.

Katherine's gotten used to living in Bloomington, where they've had electricity for a good long while. She's used to turning on a light switch instead of lighting a kerosene lamp. I feel bad for her, coming back to this old-fashioned farmhouse. With no electric lights. No telephone. No radio. Just an old-fashioned icebox instead of one of those new-fangled refrigerators. Just a smelly old outhouse instead of indoor toilets like they have at the college.

But after she's been home an hour or two, she'll have her hands right back in the work she used to do around the house: peeling potatoes, rolling out a pie crust, washing up the supper dishes, taking a turn at churning butter. As if she wants to let me know she's not too good for all that. Sometimes, I think she takes comfort in the old chores she knows so well. It gives her a break from the strain of her studies.

We make a point of sitting down for a long talk every time she comes home. She tells me she's working on a degree in education so she can become a school teacher. She always says she's putting a lot of time into her studies. I don't doubt that for a minute. She's worked too hard to get this chance for an education, and I know she's not going to waste it.

But she does take time to have fun every now and then. I'm glad about that. She tells me about going with her friends to watch the men's basketball games, or to hear the fellows sing in the glee club.

Her first year at college, her friends talked her into trying out for the women's soccer team. They figured that since she's a tall, strong girl, she'd be good at playing sports. But truth be told, she didn't enjoy that sort of thing very much.

"I guess I'm not the athletic type," she told me. "I'll go ahead and finish the season. But that'll be it for me."

I wasn't too happy about the idea of her running around that soccer field in those short skirts they wear. They only come to the knee. "Don't you think that's immodest?" I asked her.

She laughed. "Mama, you're so old-fashioned.

Her second year, she got involved in something called the drama club, where they put on plays. Those plays are a big thing at the college, and a lot of people buy tickets to see them. I got worried about Katherine being caught up in that sort of thing, thinking she might want to become an actress in the movies. I've never seen a movie, but from what I hear, an actress isn't the type of person I'd want my daughter to be.

"No, Mama," she said when I mentioned that to her. "I have no desire to become an actress. I just enjoy working behind the scenes, making costumes and helping people rehearse their lines."

She gave up the drama club after one year. Then this past year, she found a few things she really loves to do. She joined the yearbook staff, and she started writing for the college newspaper. To me, that sounds more like her cup of tea.

The biggest thing is that she joined the Y.W.C.A. I was so proud of her when she told me she'd been elected vice-president. I don't really understand what the Y.W.C.A. is all about, except that they want to help women live better lives. That seems like a worthwhile thing to strive for.

I asked Katherine what they do in that group. She said they put on an inspirational service there at the college every Sunday evening. And once a month or so, they have a gathering where they read stories and poetry. Literature, as she calls it. I'm sure she likes that.

When Katherine tells me about all that stuff going on at the university, it makes me think she's living in a better world than the one I live in. But after supper, she'll always say to me, "Mama, the food in the college cafeteria isn't half as good as what you cook."

It's like she wants to let me know she'll always love home life. Still, whenever she's here, I can often tell that her mind is a million miles away.

Here's a story I can't forget to mention. When Katherine came home to visit one day halfway through her first year of college, I just about fell over when I saw her. She had bobbed her hair.

"Katherine," I cried out, "what on earth have you done to yourself?"

The smile left her face, and her eyes welled up with tears. "Do I look that bad?" she asked, fingering her short hair. "Does it make me look ugly?"

Right away, I was sorry for using such a harsh tone with her. "No, sweetheart," I said, holding out my arms to hug her. "You just took me by surprise."

As I held her, I lifted my hand to ruffle her hair, just to see what it felt like. "It's almost the same as when you were a baby," I told her. "I never could stop myself from twirling my fingers through your curls." We both laughed.

When I stepped back to take another look, I had to admit the new hairdo looked nice on her. "Who bobbed it for you?" I asked.

"A couple of girls in my dormitory," she said. "They thought I looked too old-fashioned with my long hair. I was scared to do it, but then I thought, *why not try something new?* Afterwards, I had a few minutes of regret. Then I got used to it and decided I liked it. It's so much easier to take care of."

She reached up to pat her hair. "Now, I look like the other girls. But I don't think I'll keep it this way forever. After college, I'll probably let it grow long again."

I was glad to hear that. But for now, I don't mind if she wants to fit in with her friends.

I'm ashamed to say this, but I've never been over to the college where Katherine is staying. I don't have the nerve to drive over there in the Model T. I'd get lost for sure, trying to drive on the city streets in Bloomington. And I don't even bother to ask Frank to take me. That's the last place he'd ever want to go.

Nowadays, they're saying a person has to get a license to drive a car. I haven't done that, and I don't figure I ever will. I'd have to take a test, and the thought of that scares the living daylights out of me.

I drive a little way on my own around here, like up to Ma and Pa's place if I'm too tired to walk. If I ever tried to drive in Bloomington, I know I'd get in trouble with the law. I'd end up sitting in jail. And after that, I'd never be able to hold my head up again.

Frank has his license, and so does Katherine. And of course, Clover wasn't scared at all to take her driving test. She drives all over the place. Even to Indianapolis, if she has a mind to. She told me she'd help me get ready to take my driving test, but I told her no.

Time and again, Clover has said she'd take me over to Bloomington to see Katherine in her dormitory room. I keep putting her off, coming up with one excuse after another. Truth be told, I'm afraid that if I showed up there, I'd embarrass Katherine in front of her friends.

So, Clover goes over to see her, taking her things she needs, fussing over her. Acting like her mother instead of her aunt. I guess I have to let that be.

Clover said she's going to make sure I go to Katherine's graduation next year. "You'll never forgive yourself if you miss out on watching your daughter walk across the stage to get her diploma," she told me. "So, you're going, even if I have to pick you up, throw you over my shoulder, and carry you there."

"You'd never be able to pick me up," I teased her. "As heavy as I am."

She just set her jaw and said, "I'll find a way to get you there. You just wait and see."

The past two summers, Katherine lived with Clover full-time while she worked at the mercantile. I knew it was going to come to that. That leaves Frank and me living alone in the farmhouse all year round.

But sometimes, it feels like my husband isn't even there. He's quiet these days, and keeps to himself.

His war wound still hurts him, and he has trouble getting around. Some days, he can hardly get on and off the tractor. So, one of the Mitchell boys has been helping out with milking and cleaning out the stalls in the barn. Franks pays him a little for his work.

It seems like the two of them have taken to each other. It reminds me of the way Pa was with Frank way back in the day.

Once when I referred to the young man as "the Mitchell boy," Frank jumped on me about it.

"The boy has a name," he growled. "It's Elmer."

Truth be told, I can't tell one Mitchell boy from another. They're all big strapping fellows with sandy hair and hazel eyes. Even though a couple of the older ones have left home to get married, there's still a whole passel of them living with their ma and pa, Maynard and Nellie.

Most people around here do like I do, referring to the lot of them as the Mitchell boys. Frank bringing up the matter of Elmer having a name told me he's singled him out for special attention.

Maynard Mitchell can be awfully hard on his boys. Word has it that he's beaten a couple of them to within an inch of their lives. That's made for a lot of bad feelings in their family.

Elmer's on the slow side, and he doesn't catch onto things as quick as his brothers do. He'll probably never be one to get married and have a place of his own. Maynard has no use for him. He doesn't have a kind word for Elmer, and would just as soon slap him up the side of the head as to look at him.

So, Elmer doesn't think much of his pa. Instead, he looks up to Frank. That does Frank a lot of good.

It's become mighty clear to me that Frank doesn't feel worthy of being Katherine's father. He never says a word to her about college life. I can guess what's in his mind, though. He figures he's let her down something terrible, and that there's no way to make up for that. He thinks the best he can do is to stay out of her way, so as not to mess up the good things she has going on in her life.

But taking Elmer Mitchell under his wing gives Frank a chance to act like a good father. He's patient with the boy, and takes his time teaching him things. Every now and then, he'll say that Elmer has more brains than what most people give him credit for.

Since Elmer's been coming around, Frank hasn't been

drinking as much as he used to. I think maybe he wants to set a good example. He doesn't go out to the still but once every couple of weeks. He lets Sam Walker carry on with things out there.

As far as I know, Frank's never taken Elmer to the still. I don't think he wants to start an innocent young man down the wrong road like that. If I ever found out he did, I'd be likely to forget myself and give him a piece of my mind.

With Katherine being gone to college, I've taken to sleeping upstairs in her room every night. So, I don't even have the feel of my husband's body lying next to me in bed. Frank's like a shadow in my life. There are hours on end when I forget that he's around.

Last month when Katherine came home, she told me she was planning on going to something she called a prom. I'd never heard of such a thing, and she had to explain it to me. It's a highfalutin shindig where young people at the college get all gussied up and have themselves a good time, with a nice dinner and some dancing.

Of course, Clover had bought Katherine a fancy dress for the affair. Katherine brought it over to show me. When she put it on, I was shocked. It was flimsy thing with no sleeves, cut low in both the front and the back. It seemed downright indecent to me. But I've decided not to say such things to my daughter anymore. I trust she knows what's right and wrong in this day and age.

She told me about the young man named George who'd asked her to go the prom with him. I got all worked up about that, thinking maybe she'd found herself a nice fellow. Katherine just laughed at me.

"Mama," she said, "it's not like that. I'm not in love with George. And to tell you the truth, I'm not very interested in proms and parties and that sort of thing. But this is a once in a lifetime event, and I decided I didn't want to miss out on it."

Yesterday when Katherine came home again, I was all set for her to tell me about the prom. I put out a plate of cookies I'd baked just for her and poured two cups of coffee. Then the two of us sat down for a talk. I was ready to have a time of it, going over everything that had happened on her special night.

"So, how was the prom?" I asked her.

"Oh, it was fine," she said. "I had a good time."

I waited for her to say more, but she just sat there stirring her sugar into her coffee. Then she looked up at me, a little smile on her lips.

"You're never going to believe this, Mama," she said. "I can't believe it myself."

"What?" I asked. "Tell me!" My mind started racing, thinking maybe George had asked her to marry him.

She clasped her hands together, so excited. "I've been chosen for the Mortar Board!"

"Now, what in the world is that?" I asked her.

"The Mortar Board is an honor society for seniors," she explained. "They choose the members at the end of their junior year. They're selected on the basis of their service, scholarship, leadership, and character."

"And they chose you?" I asked.

"Yes, Mama," she said. "They did. Being chosen for the Mortar Board is a high honor. I hardly feel worthy of it."

I sat there dumbfounded. *How did the baby girl I gave birth to twenty-one years ago become this brilliant young woman? I don't understand the world she lives in. I don't understand where she's going in life. All I know is that she's leaving her mama sitting here with her head spinning.*

"Katherine," I said when I was finally able to talk again, "I'm proud of you. I don't know what else to say.

You just have to know that you make your mama's heart swell with pride."

"That's all I need from you," she said.

I had to notice how bright her eyes were shining, ever so much brighter than last month when she told me she was going to the prom.

This morning after church, Doc Murphy's wife Eunice came up to me and asked how Katherine was doing. From time to time, Eunice mentions that her husband has a special place in his heart for Katherine, seeing as how he was there to save her from dying when she was born. He's always looked on Katherine as a miracle baby, and he's so proud of how she's turned out.

Well, Eunice's question got me going, and I started in telling her one thing after another about what Katherine is up to at the college. I mentioned the Y.W.C.A., and what an honor it is for her to be chosen for the Mortar Board.

"Most of the young teachers here in Brown County only go to a two-year teaching college," I told Eunice. "But with Katherine going to a four-year college, she'll be ahead of the game. She'll be able to get a job anywhere she wants to go."

Eunice was smiling and nodding, like she was so happy for Katherine. But then, Margaret Davis came up and started listening in on the conversation. There's been some strain between Margaret and me ever since Katherine broke things off with Billy. As a matter of fact, there's been a bit of strain in the whole family, with Hazel's husband taking his sister's side. He looks on Katherine as being uppity, like she thought she was too good for Billy.

I've heard it said that Billy took the breakup pretty hard. Even though he went on to marry another young woman, people say he still hasn't gotten over the way Katherine broke his heart.

Anyway, when Margaret heard me carrying on about how good Katherine is doing, she had to say her piece. "College isn't everything," she snapped. "Most young people do just fine without it."

I knew she was talking about Billy and how well he's done at the sawmill, even though he never even went to high school. I figured I'd better jump in and agree with her so things wouldn't get out of hand between us. "Of course, it's not," I said. "Most people are better off not bothering with college."

I came home kicking myself, thinking Margaret Davis would never be friendly with me again. I've prayed on the matter all day, asking the Lord to help me be humble, and to forgive me for the sin of pride.

But the more I've thought on it, the more I've told myself that I have a right to be proud.

Of course, Katherine's done this herself, and she deserves the credit. But I raised her, and I'd like to think I had something to do with her being where she is in life. She's done good. And maybe I have, too.

1930

I've never expected life to be perfect. I wasn't even foolish enough to believe in that kind of fairytale when I was a little girl. But sometimes, life gets good enough to where a person doesn't have to worry day and night, and it's tempting to think things will stay that way.

It seemed like, all in all, America was doing pretty well in the late 1920s. We were building ourselves back up after the war that had wrecked so many lives, and I was starting to think we were done with hard times. Then one day in October of last year, Pa came over with the *Indianapolis Star,* telling Frank and me that the country was in big trouble. There had been a stock market crash.

I've never understood anything about investments and the stock market and that kind of thing. All I know is that many people in this country lost a whole lot of money. Some rich folks lost everything they had and ended up poor as church mice. There were stories in the newspapers about people becoming so downhearted that they took their own lives.

Pa had known Katherine had been saving up money for her schooling. The day he told us about the stock market crash, he asked us whether she still had money in the bank. His face had gone white, as if he was expecting the worst. I told him no, that she'd just taken out the last of it to pay for her senior year of college.

"Whew!" Pa said. "We dodged that bullet! She might've lost everything."

The thought of Katherine losing out on her last year of education shook me. I was mighty glad for the timing of things. I'd like to think God had a hand in it.

To be honest, this country's problem with money hasn't made much of a difference in Brown County. Because nobody around here had any money to lose in the first place. Nobody had any investments in the stock market.

Life for us has gone on pretty much the same. Except for the fact that people keep on leaving Brown County. I heard it said that in the census this year, there were barely more than five thousand people in the whole county. That's only half of the number that lived here back in the 1890s, when I was growing up. People just have a hard time making a living here. Sometimes, I get to wondering whether the county is going to die out altogether.

But people like Frank and me, who have a piece of good farmland, get by all right. We're able to raise our chickens and hogs and cows. We have our corn crop, along with our vegetable garden and fruit trees. And we always have plenty of firewood from the woods around here.

Some people aren't as lucky as we are, but they do what they can to keep body and soul together. Men who own a gun and a hound dog get all the meat their families need by hunting for deer and squirrel and rabbit. Some of them trap raccoons, skunks, and possums for their fur, and they get a little bit of money for their pelts. And their wives go out in the woods and look for something they can sell, like bittersweet, hickory nuts, black walnuts, and persimmons.

So, the people who've stayed on in this county know how to use their wits to survive. That says a lot for them.

I've worried that Clover will lose business in her store if people around here don't have money to pay for the goods she sells. I asked her about it once. She said that if she manages carefully, she'll do fine.

Here's something I'm ashamed to admit. When I first thought about hard times coming to this country, I was all of a sudden glad for the extra money that Frank makes from the still. I know how the men are around here. They're not going to give up their liquor, no matter how down and out their families might be. So, it's pretty much a sure thing that we'll have that money coming in.

It makes me feel like a hypocrite, changing my mind about Frank making his whiskey. It's strange how a person can all of a sudden start looking on something in a whole new light. Maybe I should let my husband know I'm looking kindlier on what he does, but I haven't brought myself around to doing that.

The good news around here is that Katherine graduated from college just last week. I tell you, that was really something. I haven't gotten over the whole thing yet.

She and Clover had started talking about her graduation way ahead of time. It was like they wanted to get Frank and me used to the idea of going to it.

They wouldn't have had to do that on my account, because I already knew in my heart that I needed to buck up and go. But Frank never paid any mind to all their talk. Whenever they'd bring the matter up, he'd act like he wasn't hearing a word they were saying.

One day, Clover came over and sat Frank down at the kitchen table for a long talk. I stayed out of their way in the bedroom. But I could hear everything that was said.

Mostly, it was Clover talking. She was giving Frank a piece of her mind about him not living up to what a father should be doing for his daughter. She told him that after all the hard work Katherine had put into getting her education, the least he could do was to show up for her graduation.

Whenever Clover gets going, the words fly out of her mouth like bullets from a machine gun. I was afraid Frank wouldn't be able to take it, that he'd lose his temper and storm out of the house. But he sat there and listened to her.

Finally, he said, “Okay, Clover, I’ll go!” I could tell from his tone of voice that he wasn’t happy about it.

But wouldn’t you know it, on the day of the graduation, he woke up saying his leg hurt so bad that he wouldn’t be able to get himself around. I wasn’t a bit surprised, as I figured he’d come up with something like that. I didn’t bother to argue with him.

When Clover came to pick us up, that’s when the arguing started. She wasn’t buying any of Frank’s excuses.

“This isn’t going to be hard on your leg,” she insisted. “All you have to do is get into the car, ride over to Bloomington, and sit through the ceremony. I’ve seen you do a lot more than that when you put your mind to it.”

“All that sitting will be more than I can take,” Frank shot back.

Clover just laughed in his face. Pointing to his chair in the front room, she said, “I’ve seen you sitting right here for hours on end.”

With that, Frank stormed out and went to the barn, and Clover and I both knew that was that. “Come on, Bertha,” Clover sighed. “It’ll have to be just the two of us.”

I knew she was mad as a wet hen. Personally, I didn’t mind Frank not coming with us. I knew that him being miserable all day long would’ve made me miserable, too.

I’m ashamed to say this, but I’d only been to Bloomington two or three times in my whole life. As we drove into town, my heart started pounding and I thought I was going to throw up. Cars zoomed past us so fast that it made my head spin. The buildings on all sides made me feel boxed in, like there was no way I could get out. And people were swarming all over the sidewalks, going here and there and everywhere.

Clover parked the car in a university parking lot. I’d never seen so many cars together in one place, a hundred of them or more.

She could see how shook up I was. She clucked her tongue, saying, "Bertha, Bertha, Bertha. If you'd get out more, you wouldn't end up being all worked up like this."

She took me by the arm and led me into the building where they were holding the graduation. My legs felt so weak and rubbery that I had to lean on her a little bit.

When we sat down, I looked around and saw a sea of faces on every side of me. It made me downright dizzy. I'd never been in such a crowd before. "How many people are here?" I whispered to Clover.

"Hundreds," she said. "Maybe a thousand."

Right then, I understood why Frank hadn't wanted to come along, and in my heart, I forgave him. All the people milling around would've stirred up memories of his time in the war. He'd probably been scared of losing control and acting like a man who'd gone out of his mind.

I could hardly handle the whole thing myself. Here I'd thought I'd fixed myself up nice, putting on the Sunday dress Ma had made for me a few years back. But when I saw how all the other women were dolled up, I knew I looked shabby and old-fashioned. Of course, Clover was wearing something brand new, and she looked like a million bucks.

I started thinking everyone was noticing me, looking down their noses at the stupid old woman from out in the sticks. My hands were shaking so bad that I could hardly hang onto my purse. From time to time, Clover would reach over and put her hand on the two of mine, trying to still them. "It'll be alright, Bertha," she kept saying.

All the graduates were sitting up front in their caps and gowns. I tried to spot Katherine, but I couldn't make out which one was her.

When the ceremony started, I could hardly tell what was going on. One person after another got up to give a talk. To be honest, I lost interest and was just wishing it would all get over and done with so I could go home.

All of a sudden, Clover nudged me and pointed. Katherine was walking up to the podium to give a talk. I was so shocked that I just about fell off my chair.

"She wanted it to be a surprise for you," Clover whispered.

The man who introduced Katherine said she would be speaking as a member of the Mortar Board Honor Society. Everything around me started seeming foggy and unreal, and I was in such a state that I couldn't really take in what Katherine was talking about. I know she mentioned things like courage and honor and service to others. It was so strange to hear my child's voice ringing out through a microphone, like she was someone with something important to say. When she was done talking and the people started clapping for her, I made sure to clap as hard as I could.

Soon after that, they had the graduates walk across the stage to get their diplomas. They started with the last names beginning with "A" and went on down through the alphabet. Before I knew it, the man giving out the diplomas called out, "Katherine Rose Kelly." And my tall, beautiful daughter came walking across the stage, looking so smart in her cap and gown.

Wouldn't you know it, I just busted out bawling. I couldn't help myself. Clover put her arm around me and whispered, "We're so proud of her, aren't we?" All I could do was nod.

After the ceremony was over, Clover and I had to wait around for Katherine to come and join us. When she finally showed up, we hugged her and loved on her. To tell you the truth, I was so tuckered out by then that I was all set to go home. But Clover said we had to go to her sister Ivy's house for a little while.

Frank's other sisters hadn't come to the graduation.

I'd figured it was because some of them were getting so old they would've had a hard time sitting through that kind of thing. But when we got to Ivy's house, I knew the real reason they'd stayed behind. They'd been fixing up a party, the likes of which I'd never seen before.

There were decorations everywhere: streamers and flowers and a big sign that said, *CONGRATULATIONS KATHERINE.* A table was loaded down with fancy little sandwiches and fruit and beautiful bowls of punch. And in the middle of everything was a big cake with Katherine's name written on it. People helped themselves to the food, and then they stood around eating and talking with one another.

There was another table piled high with presents for Katherine. When I saw that, I felt just awful, as it had never dawned on me that I was supposed to give Katherine a present on a day like this. I was downright ashamed, her own mother coming emptyhanded.

There were so many people there, and I hardly knew any of them. They were talking and laughing and carrying on so loud that I couldn't hear myself think. For a while, Katherine tried to take me around and introduce me to people. She'd say, "This is my mother, Bertha Kelly." But when she saw it was putting a strain on me, she stopped.

When I was able to, I took Katherine aside and told her how bad I felt about not bringing a present for her. She hugged me and said, "Mama, you've already given me everything a mother could possibly give."

After a while, someone said it was time for Katherine to open her gifts. When I saw what everyone else had given her, I was glad I hadn't brought anything. Because any present I would've come up with would've looked pitiful next to all the fine things she got.

People gave her important looking books. I remember one of them being a dictionary. She got a lot of pretty vases and candy dishes and lovely little figurines to sit on a shelf or tabletop. Somebody gave her an electric lamp with a fancy shade for her bedroom. And she got several pieces of jewelry. Clover gave her a cross on a silver chain, something that looked like it cost a pretty penny. I figured it was a Catholic thing.

Katherine was gracious about the whole affair, thanking everyone so sweetly for their presents. I was so proud of her. But all that time, I wanted to crawl into a hole and hide so she wouldn't have to be ashamed of me.

After everyone else had left the party, I helped Clover and Katherine load all the presents into the car. Then they drove me home. Katherine went back to Clover's house, where Clover has a room set up for her. She'll be staying there one more summer while she helps out in the store.

Even though I was plumb tired out, I was so stirred up that I didn't sleep a wink that night. I felt like I didn't belong in this world anymore. I told myself I was so old-fashioned and out of date that everybody had moved on and left me behind.

That feeling stayed with me for a couple of days. But this morning while I was hanging the wash on the clothesline, I took in the clear blue sky and the chirping of the birds, and I felt the strain leave my mind. Then I looked out over the pasture at the hills covered with trees. Their green leaves had just come out, making the woods look soft and fresh. And I said to myself, *this is a place where I still belong.*

I know I'll never have a big life or a fancy life. Not the important life Katherine's bound for. But I guess I'm satisfied with my own little corner of the world.

A couple of months ago, Katherine told me she'd been talking to the head of a private girls' school in Indianapolis, about a teaching job there. She was so excited about it.

She said the university had recommended her to the school as an outstanding person to fill that job.

I don't know whether she has the job yet. But I'm sure she's going to get it. It seems like everything's going Katherine's way these days. I imagine she'll be moving up to Indianapolis by the end of the summer. Farther away from me than ever.

1933

We have a new preacher at the Oak Ridge Church. Reverend Isaac Barnes passed away a couple of years ago, and a young fellow from Nashville, Harry Horton, stepped in to take his place. Some of us had a hard time with that, thinking that such a young man didn't have the wisdom to preach the word of God. I have to confess that I did my share of complaining. But in the end, he won us all over.

Last Sunday, Reverend Horton preached a sermon that touched my heart deep down. He said that when times are bleak, that's when we need to put all our trust in the Lord.

For days afterward, I kept thinking about that word he used, "bleak." And I decided that's the best way to describe my life right now. With Katherine gone so far away, Frank and I have been rattling around this old house like two ghosts. Sometimes, I wonder how much more life I've got left in me.

I guess a lot of people are feeling bleak, with the depression going on in this country. But the true reason I'm feeling so downhearted is that Ma passed away earlier this year.

Once she started going downhill, there was no turning back. She kept on getting weaker and weaker, and she fell two or three times. Pa finally decided he had to keep her in bed, as he was afraid she'd hurt herself if she tried to get up and move around.

I got to where I was spending almost every day up at my folks' place, tending to Ma and cooking for Pa. Hazel would come a couple of times a week, and her daughters Annabelle and Ruby took their turns helping out.

Dr. Benjamin Groves came out to check on Ma once

every month or so. He said she had a problem with her heart. "There's not a lot I can do for her," he told us. "Just keep her comfortable until the end comes."

And the end came quicker than we ever thought it would. Soon, Ma stopped talking and hardly did anything but sleep. It was all we could do to get a spoonful of chicken broth through her parched lips. It seemed as if she'd already left us and was standing at Heaven's door, waiting until the Lord saw fit to open it and call her in.

Here I'd known Ma all my life, her little habits and the way she thought about things. Many times, I knew what she was going to say even before she opened her mouth. I never figured I could get to know her any better than that. But I learned that when you take care of a person day in and day out, you get so close to them that it feels like your two hearts are beating as one.

So, when she passed away in March of this year, it was just about the worst thing that had ever happened to me. There were times I wished I could've died along with her, instead of having to go on living without her.

We had her funeral at the Oak Ridge Church, and we laid her to rest in the graveyard there. Reverend Horton was so good about preaching at the funeral and saying comforting words to the family. It made me feel like I could count on him to be there in times of trouble.

There must've been fifty or sixty people at the funeral, which is a lot for folks around here. Frank came, without anyone having to talk him into it. I guess he had the decency to know he owed my ma respect, after all she and Pa had done for him.

Elmer Mitchell was there with Frank, and he stuck close to his side. He watches over Frank and knows to take him by the arm if he's having trouble walking.

I was so glad Katherine was able to take time off from teaching to come down for the funeral. She was there to hold my hand for the whole thing. I don't know what I would've done without her to lean on.

But when I looked at Hazel clinging to her two daughters, both of them there to shore her up, I felt a little bitter. Hazel's girls have stuck close to their ma. Annabelle has children of her own now: Beatrice, who's five, along with two little boys. Ruby's not been married for long, but she already has a child on the way.

Hazel always seems to be holding a grandbaby on her lap. That's something I'll probably never have. I need to keep reminding myself that my daughter's cut out for a different kind of life.

I think Katherine must've sensed my bitterness. Because when we went back to the house after the funeral, she sat me down at the kitchen table for a talk.

"Mama," she said, "I know you wore yourself out taking care of Grandma in her last days. And I wasn't here to help you. I feel so bad about that."

Just having her say that lifted the resentment from my heart. It got me crying so hard I couldn't control myself.

Katherine put her arm around me. "I understand something now. You loved your mother just as much as I love you. Losing her has left a big hole in your heart."

Then she scooted her chair real close to mine and held me in her arms while I sobbed out my sorrow. "Remember this, Mama," she said. "When loved ones pass away, it's only their bodies that die. Their spirits never leave us."

I wasn't exactly sure what she meant. "I thought a dead person's spirit goes to Heaven," I told her.

"Yes," she said, "but at the same time, they're still with us. It's one of life's mysteries, I suppose."

I was wishing I could stay that way forever, heart to heart with my daughter. But then Clover came knocking on the door, ready to drive Katherine back to Indianapolis, back to the world she lives in now.

It's been three years since Katherine moved to Indianapolis to teach at the school up there. That's hard to believe.

It took some doing to get her ready to go. Truth be told, Clover did most of the helping, as I hardly knew what to do. She took Katherine to the tailor shop in Nashville and had two nice wool suits made for her, one brown and one dark blue. That's what working women wear, I guess.

With Katherine moving into the teachers' quarters, she and Clover and I sat down and went over what she would need to set up house there. Clover had plenty of extra things in her home to give Katherine. I wanted to give her something from my house, too, but everything I had on hand was too shabby.

In the end, I gave her a couple of spare towels. She acted like she was pleased. She held one of them up to her cheek, saying, "When I use this, I'll think of my mother."

Wouldn't you know it, on the day Katherine left for Indianapolis, Frank took off for the barn with his jug of whiskey. He got so drunk that when he finally came stumbling into the house, he could hardly make it through the back door. I had to grab him and sit him in a chair before he fell down on the kitchen floor. I hadn't seen him like that in a long while.

I was so aggravated with him, and downright ashamed. But I knew what was on his mind. He was remembering the little girl who'd loved him so much. And now she was going away, and he didn't know what to say to her or what to make of the whole business.

Katherine might be far away, but she keeps in touch with us. She writes a letter every couple of weeks, telling us all about her life at the school. "I pray for the two of you every day," she always says at the end. I can picture her doing that with her rosary.

She tells us about the girls she teaches, the sweet and funny things they do, along with the naughty stuff. I can tell she hates having to punish the girls. But she'll do it if they've got it coming.

She loves every last one of them, even the troublemakers. "I look on them as my own," she wrote in one of her letters.

That shook me up a little. "You're still young, Katherine," I wrote back to her. "You still have time to get married and have children of your own."

In her next letter, she came right back with an answer. "No, Mama. I won't be getting married and having babies. That's not the direction my life is meant to take."

And I thought to myself, *how does my daughter know such things? I don't know anything about my life's direction. I just get up every morning and get on with my day. Where does all her deep-down wisdom come from?*

Frank has taken to reading Katherine's letters. I'm glad to see that. But he never says a word about them.

The letters aren't the only things she sends us. From time to time, I'll open the envelope and find money. Ten dollars, fifteen dollars. Sometimes as much as twenty.

Clover has a telephone in her house now, and there are telephones at Katherine's school. So, Clover gets to talk to her niece any time she wants to. About once a month, I have Frank drive me down to Clover's house so I can talk with Katherine, too.

The first time I did that, I giggled like a little girl. Matter of fact, I was giggling so hard I couldn't get a word out of my mouth. It seemed so strange to hear my daughter's voice and know she was fifty miles away.

When I finally settled down, I talked to her about the money she'd been sending. "Your papa and I are getting by," I told her. "You need your money to live on yourself."

"Mama," she said, "I know these are hard times. I have a steady job with good pay. Not everyone is as lucky as I am. I want to make sure you and Papa are taken care of. That's my duty as a daughter."

Truth be told, with this depression going on, Frank isn't getting as much for the hogs and the milk he sells. One day, he said to me, "Bertha, our property taxes are due. And I don't know how I'm going to come up with the money for them."

Well, that sure set me to worrying. But then the mail came with a letter from Katherine, and inside was a fifty-dollar bill. Just like a miracle. Just like the Lord had dropped it from Heaven right into our hands.

Of course, I never told Katherine about all that. If she got the idea that we really needed it, she'd be sending money all the time.

Katherine's been coming home to visit three times a year, at Christmas and twice during the summer. She'll come to our house during the day, but she always stays overnight with Clover. Her aunt has a beautiful bedroom set up for her, and Katherine couldn't have any nicer place to be. It's her home when she's not at school.

A few years back, when she started staying more and more with Clover, it hurt my feelings something awful. But I'm used to it now. I know our house is too rough and rundown for her.

When she comes home, Katherine takes a Greyhound bus from Indianapolis to Martinsville. I haven't been able to talk Frank into driving all the way to Indianapolis to pick her up. He'll go as far as Martinsville. But it's usually Clover who goes to the bus station to get her.

Once, I asked Katherine if she'd thought about getting herself a car. "You could come and go whenever you want to," I told her.

"No," she said. "There's no reason to do that. My money is meant to go for other things." I thought about the money she'd been sending Frank and me, and I felt bad for taking it from her.

Soon after Ma's funeral, Hazel and I had to think about what to do with Pa. He's in failing health himself, although his mind is still sharp as a tack. He can hardly see anymore. Dr. Groves says he has real bad cataracts. It's not safe for him to be on his own at the farm.

Pa's been wanting to sell the farm these past couple of years. But he says that with the depression going on, he'd never be able to sell it for what it's worth. "I'm just going to hang onto it until this country gets back on its feet," he told Hazel and me.

So, he keeps on leasing out the land to other people who want to farm it.

Hazel and I and her girls took turns staying with Pa until we could come up with a plan for him. I told Hazel I wanted to have him come live with Frank and me.

"Where would you put him, Bertha?" she asked. "Pa never could make it up and down your stairs."

"I can put him in the downstairs bedroom," I told her. "I'll move Frank and me upstairs to the room next to Katherine's room."

Then I had to stop and think. With his bad leg, Frank wouldn't be able to go up and down the stairs any easier than Pa could. And even though I hardly pay Frank any mind these days, I knew I had to take him into account on the matter.

In the end, Hazel insisted on having Pa move in with her and Walter in their home in Nashville. I felt just terrible about that, like I'd let Pa down. During all my hard times with Frank, while he was in the war and the years after that, Pa had kept an eye on me. He'd helped me out any way he could. With all my heart, I wanted to do the same for him. And here I couldn't open my home to him in his time of need.

It troubled me so much that I finally went to talk with Reverend Horton at the church. When I poured out my heart to him, he said what preachers always say, that everything is in God's hands. That aggravated me so much that I almost got up and walked out right then and there.

Then he went on to say that Pa would be better off in Nashville anyway, as they have a good doctor over there. As if Dr. Groves in Helmsburg isn't good enough to look after Pa. I figured Reverend Horton was just being partial to Nashville, seeing as how he came from there.

The whole thing didn't sit right with me. I was feeling so bitter that I didn't go to church for a couple of Sundays. I'd look at Frank and think, *He could make it up those stairs just fine if he'd put his mind to it.* But I knew I wasn't being fair to him.

After a lot of thinking on the matter, I told myself there was nothing more I could do. Pa will live out the rest of his days in Hazel and Walter's home instead of mine. So, I'm trying to accept the way things have turned out.

But still, when I think about Ma and Pa not living up the road from Frank and me, my heart hurts so bad I can hardly stand it. Time and again, I get the notion to run up there and see how they're doing before I remember they're not there anymore.

Pa's leased out the house itself to the Jackson family. They're the ones who are farming most of his acreage now. A few years back, they had moved away from Brown County to make a better life for themselves in the city. But when the depression hit and Mr. Jackson lost his job, they decided they might as well come back to where they started out.

They're a nice family, and they appreciate Pa doing them a good turn by giving them another chance at farming. Still, I can't bring myself to be very neighborly with them.

We have some of Ma and Pa's old furniture in our house now: the sideboard, a rocking chair, an extra bed and dresser, and their sofa. Elmer Mitchell and one of his brothers carried our old sofa out of the house, and then Frank burned it. It was so old it wasn't worth anything anymore. It was already old when I moved into this house more than twenty-five years ago.

This afternoon, I talked Frank into driving me down to Hazel's house to see Pa. He'll do that for me from time to time, even though he's grouchy about it. But he won't go inside with me. He sits out in the car while I visit.

Pa can't read the papers anymore, but Hazel reads them to him. He likes that. This afternoon, he told me about an article she'd read to him from the *Brown County Democrat.* It had talked about what was going on with the Brown County State Park.

Two years ago, we were all taken by surprise when they opened a state park here. It has a lodge and cabins people can rent. And a swimming pool, of all things. I've heard it said there are miles of trails that people can hike, and nice spots where they can enjoy a picnic.

Pa was mighty pleased about all that. He said the state park will bring a lot of tourists to Brown County over the coming years. That will bring us in some money. Lord knows this county needs it.

Pa always likes to talk about politics. It takes his mind off missing Ma. He's all excited about our new president, Franklin D. Roosevelt. He says he hopes this fellow has what it takes to figure things out and get this country back on track.

1936

I'm happy to say things are starting to look up for folks around here. Our new president seems to have a heart for the people who've been down and out during this depression. Under his leadership, the government has come up with work programs for men who don't have jobs.

Something called the WPA has come to these parts. A lot of men have signed up for it, most of them fellows from local families. But they've even set up a labor camp for the homeless men who've been wandering around the county like tramps. I've heard it said each of the men get paid fifty dollars a month for the work they do, which is nothing to sneeze at.

The WPA men have been working on fixing up things in the Brown County State Park. They've cleaned up some of the cemeteries around here, and they're putting up buildings in different parts of the county. Here in Helmsburg, they're building something called a community center. That's going to be a good thing for our town.

A few years back, the government did away with the law against alcohol. Prohibition has ended. That means Frank and the other whiskey-making fellows around here don't have to worry about the sheriff coming after them.

And now, they're saying that some government program called the REA is bringing electricity to folks who live out in the country. People around here can't seem to talk about anything else. They're all wondering when the electricity will be coming to these parts. That'll really be something.

There are all kinds of stories about these government programs in the newspapers. I can hardly keep up with it all. Once when I was talking with Pa about it, I mentioned that God must be looking out for us. But Pa up and said that Franklin D. Roosevelt deserves the credit. He says Roosevelt will go down in history as one of the greatest presidents of all times.

Last year, the state did something that got everybody around here excited. They built a new section of road running from Nashville up through Beanblossom, and then on up through Morgantown. It's all hard-surfaced, so much nicer than the dirt roads we have around here. State Road 135, they're calling it. The whole thing runs all the way up north to Indianapolis and south to Kentucky.

A couple of months ago, Frank drove me down to Nashville on the new road. After I visited with Pa, we stopped by to see Clover. She was carrying on about State Road 135, saying it's going to make it a lot easier for her to drive to Indianapolis.

"This new highway's going to help Brown County open up to the world," she told us. Then she wagged her finger at me. "And that means you, too, Bertha. You've been sheltered all your life. It's high time you get out and get used to going places."

What she said scared me a little. I'd never been much of anywhere. No farther than Columbus to the east or Bloomington to the west. Never even as far north as Indianapolis. Truth be told, the older I get, the harder it is to think about going out and seeing the world.

But knowing Clover like I do, I figured she'd keep on bothering me about that idea. And sure enough, she did. She started talking about the two of us driving up State Road 135 to Indianapolis, to see Katherine at her school. "Katherine would be so thrilled," she said. "I haven't been up there to visit her in several years."

For a few weeks, I turned a deaf ear to all her

nonsense. But she kept on, and before I knew it, she was getting on the telephone with Katherine to make plans.

Two weeks ago, Clover came over to the house. "Okay, Bertha," she said. "It's all set. The last Saturday of October, you and I are driving up to see Katherine. She's expecting us. So, you'll need to get yourself around and be ready when I pick you up at nine o'clock."

I didn't bother to argue with her, even though the idea scared me half to death. I fretted about it for days, lying awake at night wondering if I could handle myself in the big city.

Today was the big day. Last night, I scrubbed myself really good in the washtub in the mudroom, wanting to make sure I was nice and fresh for the trip. And this morning after I got Frank's breakfast on the table, I did up my hair and put on my best dress. Then I sat in the front room with my purse on my lap, watching out the window for Clover's car. Of course, she doesn't drive the Model T anymore. She bought herself a new car a few years back, something called a Chevrolet.

Sure enough, at nine o'clock sharp, I saw the Chevrolet coming down the lane. I figured if Clover came into the house, she'd get caught up talking with Frank and we'd get a late start. So, I walked out the front door and stood in the yard waiting for her. When I opened her car door, I could tell she was all worked up and excited, chirping away like a songbird.

"Oh, Bertha, isn't this a lovely day!" she sang out. "The weather's perfect for our trip. Come on, get in. Let's go and have ourselves a good time."

It was one of those warm, sunny days that sometimes comes in late October. Indian Summer, they call it, the last spell of nice weather before winter starts setting in.

The reds and golds of the turning leaves were at their peak. Brown County is known for the colors of our wooded hills in the fall. It makes me proud to live here.

We had to cut over to Beanblossom to get onto State Road 135. We passed the little Georgetown School and a couple of stores, Helms' and McDonald's. Then we passed the old post office and the Georgetown Presbyterian Church. The church is standing empty now. I guess nobody uses it anymore because so many families have left Brown County. It's a sad thing to see.

A hundred years ago when Beanblossom started up, the place was called Georgetown. But when they set out to build a post office, the government wouldn't let them call it Georgetown because there was another post office in Indiana by that name. So, they had to come up with another name for the town. They settled on calling it Beanblossom, naming it after the Beanblossom Creek that runs through these parts.

People around here are used to calling the town Beanblossom now, and they don't think much about it. But folks from other parts of the state have a good laugh when they hear such a ridiculous name.

Come to think of it, we have a lot of silly names for towns around here. Down south of Nashville, there's Stonehead and Gnawbone. Who ever heard tell of something like that?

And then there's Trevlac out west of Helmsburg. Back when I was growing up, some rich people by the name of Calvert came to these parts from Ohio. They built up a little town with a railroad running through it, trying to make it something great. They wanted to name the train station after themselves, but they couldn't, because there was another depot called the Calvert Station.

So, they took their name and spelled it backward and called their depot the Trevlac Train Station. And then they called the town by the same name. You'd think they could've come up with something better than that.

About ten years after they came, the Calverts got tired of what they were doing. They dropped it all and moved back to Ohio. After they left, Trevlac pretty much ended up a ghost town.

"Isn't this highway nice?" Clover commented as we passed through Beanblossom. "It sure beats bumping around on a dirt road, doesn't it?"

I had to agree that riding on that new highway felt very smooth. I could've closed my eyes and fallen asleep, but I didn't want to miss out on seeing anything.

As we drove north into Fruitdale, I had to think it was another silly name for a town. The place got its name from all the stands alongside the road where people used to sell fruit from their orchards.

Way back when Katherine was a little girl, a couple of people got the idea of making Fruitdale into a grand town, with a train station and businesses and factories and a hotel. And a whole bunch of plots where people could build their homes. But things didn't work out like they thought it would, and the town started going downhill before it ever got off the ground. Just earlier this year, they shut the train station down.

Now, Fruitdale doesn't amount to much of anything. Just like with Trevlac, it goes to show that big ideas don't always pan out.

But I noticed that people were still selling apples in little stands alongside the road. I had the notion to tell Clover to stop, so we could buy a basketful and help some poor soul make a little bit of money. But I decided not to, as Frank and I have plenty of apples from our own trees at home. We've had such a good crop this year that I can hardly keep up with canning the applesauce.

For a while, I forgot all about my nerves, as I was so caught up with looking out the window and seeing the sights. I tell you, the time just flew by. Before I knew it, we were passing out of Brown County into Morgantown, crossing over Indian Creek on that big steel truss bridge they built two years ago. And it seemed like just a minute later, we were in Johnson County, passing through Trafalgar and Bargersville.

I had to think about how thrilled Katherine used to get as a little girl, whenever she got the chance to ride to Helmsburg with her papa. I felt just as excited as she did back then.

All of a sudden, Clover said, "We're in Marion County now, almost to Indianapolis."

And just like when I'd gone to Katherine's graduation in Bloomington, my heart started pounding so hard that I thought it would burst right out of my chest. As we headed into the city, it felt like things were closing in on me, and I had a hard time breathing.

There was commotion on every side, and it never stopped. People were milling around, going in and out of businesses and stores and restaurants. The traffic was flying past in every direction, with people honking their horns. The sound made me want to jump right out of my skin. And then, there were the stoplights, one after another, with their bright colors flashing.

I'm telling you, I just couldn't take it. I started thinking that maybe a person could get trapped in a big city and never be able to find their way out.

"Don't worry, Bertha," Clover said. "Katherine's school is on the north side, a little way out of the city. Once we're there, you'll feel better. It's a nice, peaceful place. Just close your eyes until we get there."

But I told myself I needed to buck up and get my bearings in the city. So, I kept my eyes open and kept on looking at everything. And before too long, I felt myself smiling. "I'm starting to get used to it," I told Clover.

She laughed. "I knew you'd be okay. Just think,

Bertha. Someday, you might end up living here in Indianapolis with Katherine."

Her words made me remember how I used to daydream about that kind of thing, many years ago when Frank was in the war. Then a thought jumped into my head, clear as a bell: *That will never happen, Bertha.*

The thought startled me. I don't know how it came to me. But I was sure of it, just as if it had come straight from God. Mostly, I was glad I wouldn't have to up and leave the place I'd lived all my life. But at the same time, I was sad. The sadness took hold of me so hard that I wanted to sit there in the car with my face in my hands, rocking myself back and forth.

Of course, I didn't want to make a scene like that in front of Clover. So, I just said, kind of quiet, "That's never going to happen, Clover."

I don't think she even heard me. She had her mind on watching for the road we were supposed to turn off on, the one leading to the school. "We're almost there," she said when she finally made the turn.

Before I knew it, we were pulling into a parking lot in front of a big brick building. There were a few other buildings nearby, all in a cluster, looking like they belonged together.

"This is where the headmistress and the teachers stay," Clover said. "Katherine will be waiting for us in the lobby." She opened her door and started to get out.

"Give me a minute," I said. "Let me catch my breath and take it all in."

The buildings were surrounded by big yards, still nice and green even though it was getting late in the year. Girls were walking here and there in little groups of two or three, talking and laughing. I thought maybe those big yards would be nice for running and playing, but the girls looked to be too old for that sort of thing. Katherine had told me her students were high-schoolers.

There were shade trees everywhere, so big that I figured they must've been there a hundred years or more. Their colorful leaves drifted to the ground every time the breeze blew. A few girls were sitting on blankets under the trees, enjoying the nice weather.

I pointed to a fountain in front of the teacher's building, where the water was spouting up and then falling down so beautifully. "Look at that," I said to Clover. "Isn't it something? I've never seen anything like it."

There were benches around the fountain. I thought to myself that I'd be content to go over there and sit for the rest of the day, just looking at the water. Katherine could come out and sit with me, and watching the fountain would make the two of us forget all about our worries. But I knew Clover had more in mind for us to do.

So, I got out of the car and followed her into the building. Sure enough, there was Katherine waiting for us. "Mama!" she called out. "Aunt Clover!" She put her arms around each of us in turn, kissing our cheeks.

To tell you the truth, I was a little shocked when I first laid eyes on her. I hadn't seen her for three months, not since she'd come home to visit during the summer. She'd lost weight, and her dress looked baggy on her. When I hugged her, I could feel the bones in her back.

"Katherine," I said, "you've gotten so thin. Aren't you eating?"

She winced. "I have to be honest, Mama. I've missed a few meals in the cafeteria. My workload seems extra heavy this term, and if I don't keep on top of things, I fall behind with grading papers and making my lesson plans. So, I sometimes stay in my room and work through supper."

"Don't you get hungry?" I asked her. "I start feeling peckish if I miss a meal."

She shrugged. “I really don’t have much of an appetite these days. Eating makes me feel a little queasy.”

“It must be the cafeteria food,” Clover said. “It probably gets tiresome. After you give us a tour of this place, I’ll take you and your mother out for a nice lunch. And I’m going to see to it that you eat.”

Then Katherine started leading us around the school, in and out of buildings, up and down stairs. First, she showed us the dormitory where the girls stay. She told us most of the students live there at the school. But some live out in the city, and their parents drive them to the school every day.

There were girls all over the place, going up and down their dormitory hallways, hollering to each other and giggling. They were such pretty little things. Here and there, Katherine would say something to one of the girls, calling her by name. When the girl would answer her back, she’d call her, “Miss Katherine.” I could tell they all thought a lot of their teacher, and that made me proud.

All of them gave me strange looks, as if they were thinking, *who’s this old woman walking around our school with Miss Katherine?* But my daughter didn’t act like she was ashamed of me at all. When the situation called for it, she’d introduce Clover and me, saying, “This is my mother Bertha Kelly and my aunt Clover Henderson.”

Then Katherine showed us the classrooms, taking us to hers last. “I teach English to all four grades,” she told us. “From the freshmen to the seniors.”

There were three rows of desks in the room, five desks in each row. Each desk was wide enough for two girls to sit together. I imagined how nice it would be for a girl to share a desk with her best friend, but then I thought that might lead to whispering and giggling. I figured that, from time to time, Katherine would have to separate the girls who were misbehaving.

In the front of the room was the big wooden teacher's desk, piled with books and papers. Katherine pointed to a stack of papers and sighed. "I need to get these tests graded before Monday morning. It's so hard to keep up."

That made me feel a little bad, as if Clover and I were keeping her from what she needed to do. Katherine must've known what I was thinking, because she said, "But sometimes, I just have to take a break and do something different. I'm so glad the two of you came today."

The big blackboard behind the teacher's desk was covered with writing. Katherine saw me looking at it, trying to make sense of it all.

"This is where the freshman girls were diagramming sentences yesterday," she said, pointing to one end of the board.

I had no idea what she was talking about. She looked like she was about to explain it to me, then thought better of it. She pointed to the other end of the board. "These are their reading assignments."

"It looks like you make the girls work hard," I said.

"I have to," she said. "This is a college preparatory school. The academic standards are high."

Then she looked at the blackboard and sighed again. "I need to get all this erased and washed." And I could tell she was almost too tired to do that easy little chore.

Someone had put a big red apple on her desk. I pointed it out, saying she needed to eat it before it went bad. She laughed and said, "The girls are always putting apples on my desk. Especially when they're trying to win favor from me."

Then we moved on so Katherine could show us the cafeteria. She said the teachers had to eat with the girls, to make sure they didn't get out of hand. After that, she showed us the gymnasium. "This is where the girls have their physical education classes," she told us. "But sometimes, we use it for other things, like student body meetings or the programs the girls put on."

After a while, I lost track of where we'd been and where we were going. All I knew was that I was getting hot from the warm weather and all the walking, and I had to stop and take off my sweater. Then Katherine said, "Well, I've run you around long enough. Let's go back to the teachers' quarters, and I'll show you where I stay."

We went up to the second floor of the teachers' building, and there was Katherine's room right at the top of the stairs. When I stepped inside, I saw that it was clean and tidy, just like she'd kept her room at home. But nothing in it seemed familiar to me. It made me feel confused, as if I didn't know up from down or left from right. I looked around, thinking, *this is my daughter's world now. And I hardly know anything about it.*

Katherine told us the bed, the dresser, the desk, and the bookshelves all belonged to the school. "This furniture has been used by teachers before me," she said. "And after I'm gone, it'll be used by someone else."

I did notice the pretty lamp she'd gotten for her college graduation. It looked nice sitting there on her desk. I imagined her turning it on late at night so she could have enough light to grade the last of her students' papers. I also noticed the dictionary she'd gotten. It was lying open on her desk, as if she'd just been using it to look something up.

And then I saw her rosary laid out so carefully on her dresser top, in a perfect circle. I had to smile. That was one thing that hadn't changed about my daughter's life.

"Let's go eat," Clover said after we'd had a good look around the teachers' quarters. The three of us went down the stairs and out to her car, then headed back into the city. Katherine said she was glad for the ride in Clover's Chevrolet. She said that usually when she wanted to go into the city, she had to take a taxi cab.

Before too long, Clover was parking the car in front of a restaurant. “This is an automat,” she told us. “When it comes to dining out, this is the newest thing.”

When we went inside, it took me a while to get my bearings. I’d never seen anything so strange. There were all kinds of food kept behind little glass windows. Some of it was hot food, like meat, vegetables, baked beans, and macaroni and cheese. Some of the food was kept cold, like salads, pudding, and pie.

You had to pick out something you wanted, then put nickels into a slot below that window. Then the window would open so you could take out the food. I had to watch a few other people get their food, just so I could get the hang of it.

Clover opened her purse and took out a couple of dollars, then went to the cashier to exchange the bills for nickels. Katherine and I stood looking at all the food, trying to figure out what we wanted.

“Get anything you like, ladies,” Clover said when she came back to us. She poured nickels into each of our hands. “I’ve got plenty of money. If you can’t decide between two things, then get them both. We’re not going to be watching our figures today.”

I thought to myself that no matter what Clover said, I wasn’t going to take advantage of her and get more food than I needed. I was standing there trying to decide between the roast beef and the chicken when I felt something slide around my waist. I was so startled that I jumped and let out a little yelp.

Then I heard a man’s deep voice in my ear. “I like the feel of a woman with a little meat on her bones,” he said. “The women these days are so skinny. When I see a nice plump one like you, I can’t keep my hands off her.”

At first, I couldn’t figure out what was happening. I turned to look at the man. He was a seedy-looking fellow, with a few day's growth of beard and an old fedora pulled down low over his eyes. The thing that caught my attention was his evil grin showing his crooked and missing teeth. And the smell of his rancid breath almost knocked me over.

I pushed his arm off my waist, but then he put his hand on my shoulder and kept on talking. "I'll buy you anything you want. Cake, pudding, pie. As long as you let me sit with you while you eat it."

I tell you, I'd never had anything like that happen to me in my entire life. I had no idea what to do. But right away, Clover picked up on what was going on. "Git, git," she barked at the man. She waved the back of her hand at him, like she was trying to shoo off an old stray dog. "Scram. Leave her alone."

The man shrugged and walked away. Then Clover and Katherine both busted out laughing. "My goodness, Bertha!" Clover said. "That fellow really took a liking to you."

We went ahead and picked out our food, but I was still shaking from the shock of what I'd just been through. No man had ever paid me a bit of attention, not since Frank had come over to see me when I was a girl on my parents' farm.

Then we sat down at one of the tables they had there, and all through our meal, Katherine and Clover teased me something awful.

Truthfully, I could see it was the two of them who were catching the eyes of the men in the automat. Katherine doesn't doll herself up with rouge and lipstick and jewelry. Time and again, she's told me she doesn't have patience for that nonsense. She's let her curly hair grow long again, and she pins it up like a sensible woman.

But even though she doesn't pay much attention to how she looks, her natural beauty always turns people's heads. And even though Clover's heading toward sixty, she's still something to look at, slim and beautiful in her fancy dresses.

But I went along with Clover and Katherine's teasing, batting my eyes and pursing my lips and blowing them kisses, acting like I was something beautiful. We laughed and laughed, until I thought I was going to bust. I felt so young and lighthearted. And I thought about how good it was to be in the company of other women.

After we all settled down a bit, Katherine said to me, "Seriously, Mama, you have more beauty and brains than you've ever given yourself credit for."

Her words shocked me. Nobody had ever said anything like that to me before.

I kept an eye on Katherine to see if she was eating. I could tell she didn't have her usual appetite. But she did pretty well, and she mentioned how nice it was to have something other than the food in the school cafeteria.

We finally had to call it a day, and we drove Katherine back to her school. Clover and I got out of the car to hug her goodbye. I could tell Katherine was tired and not feeling well.

"What is it, sweetheart?" I asked her.

"I have a headache," she said. "It seems like I always have a headache these days."

"You need rest," I told her. "Go back to your room and lie down. Forget about all your work. Lie down for the rest of the day."

"Listen to your mother, Katherine," Clover teased. But I could tell she was serious about what she was saying.

Katherine started to walk toward the teacher's building. But then, she turned and waved one last time, giving us a sad little smile. My heart ached to see her go.

On our way back to Brown County, Clover and I had to laugh a little while longer about the man in the automat.

Then we talked about Katherine, saying that she was working too hard and that she needed to rest more. After that, I felt tuckered out, and I leaned my head against the car window and fell asleep. I didn't wake up again until Clover turned off onto Helmsburg Road.

It was just half an hour ago when I walked into the house. I went straight upstairs to the room I've been sleeping in, the one next to Katherine's old room. I've got Ma and Pa's old furniture in there, the bed and the dresser. I changed out of my good dress and put my purse away.

Before I left the room, I stepped over to Ma's old mirror that I'd hung on the wall. As I stared at my reflection, it seemed like I was looking at someone else.

Even though the woman was fifty years old, she didn't have a whole lot of wrinkles. There wasn't much gray in her hair. Her cheeks were plump and full and had some color in them. I decided that for men who preferred women on the heavy side, she wasn't that bad to look at. And I thought, *it's a shame Frank doesn't notice such things.*

Then I got ahold of myself and said out loud, "Enough of this foolishness, Bertha. It's time to get something around for Frank to eat."

Earlier today while I was gone, Sam Walker brought over a wild rabbit he'd shot. Frank had skinned it, and just now, he asked me to cook it for his supper.

As I stand here at the stove frying up the rabbit meat and keeping an eye on the pot of potatoes I put on to boil, my thoughts keep going back to Katherine. To her sad little smile as she waved goodbye to Clover and me. In my mind, I can picture the tiredness on her face and the lines that have formed around her eyes and mouth. I know she's putting everything she has into teaching those girls. It's wearing her out.

Deep down, I know something isn't right.

1937

Lord knows I've been through plenty of trials in my life. But none of them can begin to compare to the heartache I've endured these past few weeks.

It all started on a snowy Friday afternoon in December, a week before Christmas. Frank was dozing off in his chair by the stove in the front room. I was sitting on the sofa embroidering a sampler for Katherine, thinking how nice it would look hanging in her room at the school. I was planning on it being a surprise for her.

We were expecting Katherine to come home in a few days. She'd be staying overnight at Clover's place, but I was counting on having plenty of time to visit with her.

Frank and I never make a big to do over Christmas. But Clover does. Every year, she invites us over for dinner on Christmas day. Of course, she's never the one doing the cooking. Her housekeeper does all the hard work.

I always take a little something along to help out with the meal. While I was sitting there with my needlework, I was trying to make up my mind as to whether I should bake sugar cookies or a pie from the butternut squash I had stored in the root cellar.

Every now and then, I'd turn my head to look out the front window. The snow was coming down harder and harder. I figured we had eight or ten inches on the ground, and that when the storm was all over and done with, we'd have well over a foot. The wind was blowing something fierce, piling the snow into big drifts across our lane.

"If this keeps up," I said to Frank, "we'll be snowed in. I won't be able to get out for church on Sunday morning."

He opened his eyes and grunted, then went back to

sleep. As if there was nothing going on that he needed to stay awake for.

All of a sudden, I saw headlights coming down the lane. *What in the world?* I thought to myself. *Who would come out at a time like this?*

I set aside my embroidery and got up to have a better look. The car was moving very slowly through the drifts, and I could tell the driver was having a hard time of it. But because of the flying snow, I couldn't make out who it was.

Then the car stopped, unable to go any farther. "Frank," I called out, "somebody got stuck in our lane. They're going to need help."

He opened his eyes and got up to look out the window. I went to get our overcoats from the mudroom. Then we both stepped out on the front porch to see what was going on.

The driver was trying to get out of the car, but couldn't open the door very far because of the high drifts. She finally managed to squeeze herself through the small space.

And then we saw who it was. "It's Clover!" Frank said. "What's she doing here?"

We watched Clover try to make her way to the house, but she didn't get far before she collapsed into the snow. She picked herself up, took a few steps through the drifts, then fell again.

Frank and I could see she needed help, and we went out to her as fast as we could. She was sobbing like a little child, and looked as if she was frozen through and through. We each took her by the arm and helped her through the yard, onto the porch, and into the house.

When we got inside, we saw that she'd lost one of her overshoes. Frank told her he'd look for it later. I took off her coat and her wet shoes, then helped her to the sofa and had her lie down. I covered her with a quilt, and Frank got busy putting more wood into the stove.

Then I sat down on the end of the sofa and took Clover's feet in my lap, rubbing them to warm them up.

"Clover, Clover, Clover," I said, clucking my tongue. "What gave you the crazy notion to come out in weather like this?"

"Katherine," she sobbed. "It's Katherine."

Frank dropped the piece of wood he was holding. We both stared at her, waiting for her to say more. "What about Katherine?" I asked. "Tell us, Clover."

Clover sat up, took a hankie out of her sweater sleeve, then wiped her eyes and blew her nose. "I got a call from the school just an hour or so ago," she said. "It was the headmistress. She told me that Katherine had a bad fall this morning."

"What?" I cried out. "Where?"

"In her classroom," Clover said. "Her first class of the morning. She was writing something on the blackboard. And all of a sudden, she collapsed and fell to the floor. A couple of the girls ran to get help from another teacher. The teacher got word to the headmistress, and they took Katherine back to her room and put her to bed. Then they called in a doctor."

It felt like Clover's words hit me in the chest, knocking all the wind out of me. I couldn't say a single word. *So, it's come to this,* I kept thinking. *She's worked so hard that she's completely worn herself out.*

I was surprised to hear Frank speak up. "What did the doctor say?" he asked Clover.

"I'm not sure," Clover said. "Other than that Katherine needs to stay in bed and rest. He said she's too weak to do any traveling. She won't make it home for Christmas."

Her eyes welled up again. "So now, you know why I was so foolish as to set out in this weather. I thought the two of you should hear the news right away."

"We need to go to her," I said.

Clover glanced over at Frank. I knew she was thinking the same thing I was, wondering whether her brother was ready to step up and do the right thing by his daughter. Or whether he'd settle for running off to the barn to get drunk.

Frank turned his eyes away to stare out the window, as if he couldn't bear to look at either of us. "Yes," he finally said. "We should go. But not in this weather. We wouldn't make it as far as Helmsburg Road."

"Katherine's safe," Clover said. "The headmistress is watching over her, and she's brought in the school nurse to tend to her. She'll be okay until we get there."

I wasn't about to let Clover go back out in the weather, so I insisted on her staying the night. After supper, I fixed a bed for her on the sofa. I was afraid she'd catch a chill from her time out in the cold, and I wanted her to sleep near the warmth of the stove.

When we got up the next morning, it had stopped snowing and the sun was out. We were eating breakfast when Elmer Mitchell knocked on the back door. He'd ridden up the road on his horse to see if Frank needed help.

I brought him inside for a cup of coffee. Then he took Frank's snow shovel from the back porch, and before we knew it, that big strapping fellow had most of the lane cleared out. After that, Frank said he reckoned it would be safe to start out for Indianapolis.

I was awfully glad we had the use of Clover's Chevrolet. Frank's Model T is so old that it's hardly safe to drive even as far as Nashville. Each time we make that trip, I hold my breath and pray, just hoping we can get there and back.

I had Frank sit up front with Clover so the two of them could talk. I wanted to be alone in the back seat, where I could sort out my thoughts about Katherine and do a little praying. I wasn't even interested in looking at the sights, like I'd done the first time I made the trip to Indianapolis.

When we got to the school, we all expected to walk right into the teacher's building and up the stairs to Katherine's room. But the big front door was locked. Clover pounded on it for a while, to see if she could get somebody's attention. Then Frank took a turn at it.

"Well," he said, "I guess they're not going to let us in." He looked angry, and I was afraid he'd never want to make the trip again. We headed back to the car, thinking we'd come all that way for no reason at all. I was sick at heart.

But then, we heard someone call out, "Are you Katherine Kelly's family?" We turned and saw a woman beckoning for us to come in.

"Yes, we're Katherine's family," Clover said.

"I'm the headmistress," the woman told us. "I'm so glad you're here." She led us upstairs to Katherine's room.

I could tell that climbing the stairs hurt Frank's leg something awful. I followed behind him, keeping my eye on him to see if he was going to make it. He kept right on going until he got to the top. I was proud that he was trying hard to do the right thing.

When we got to Katherine's room, there she was, lying in her bed looking so weak and pitiful.

The nurse was there with a basin of water. It looked like she'd just got done helping Katherine wash up. She stepped aside so we could go up to the bed. Frank went to one side and Clover and I went to the other.

Katherine smiled and held out her hands to us. Frank took one hand. Clover and I put our hands together to hold the other one.

"My papa," she said sweetly, sounding just like she had when she was a little girl. "And my two mamas."

Clover gave a little sob when she heard that. I wasn't even jealous. I figured that after all Clover had done for my child, she deserved to be thought of as a second mother.

"What happened, sweetheart?" I asked Katherine. "Whatever made you fall like that?"

"I've been having a hard time holding on to things," she said. "I keep dropping everything. I was up there in front of the class writing on the blackboard, and I dropped my chalk. I started to bend over to pick it up. That made me feel dizzy, and I lost my balance."

Then the nurse piped up and said, "Katherine had some difficulty with walking this morning. She's exhausted through and through."

"I guess I'll be spending Christmas here in bed," Katherine said. She tried to sound like that was nothing to be upset about. "I'll rest and sleep. By January when classes start up again, I'll have my strength back."

Frank was getting restless, as if he didn't know what to do with himself. He went to stand by the door, and I knew he couldn't wait to get out of there.

But Clover and I had to take our time fussing over Katherine. Her hair was down, spread out over the pillow in a tangled mess. The nurse brought over the chair from Katherine's desk so I could sit by the bed and brush out my daughter's hair. Just like I'd done when she was a little girl. I took care to be gentle and not hurt her.

Having her hair brushed made Katherine so relaxed and sleepy that she could hardly keep her eyes open. "I supposed we should leave you rest now," I said.

She looked at each of us, smiling. "Go on home. Don't waste your time fretting about me. Have yourselves a nice Christmas."

Clover and I kissed her goodbye and told her we loved her. Frank came over to the bed to hold her hand one more time. When we went down the stairs, the headmistress was standing in the lobby waiting for us. She looked worried.

"I'll keep you informed," she told us. "I'll call you every day to let you know how Katherine's doing."

Then Frank and Clover and I went back home. I knew the two of them were thinking the same thing I was, that Katherine's sickness might be something worse than just being tired out. But none of us had the heart to bring that up with each other.

For the next two weeks, Frank and I drove to Nashville every day for the telephone call from the school, except for a couple of times when the weather was too bad. Clover gave Frank the use of her Chevrolet so we could be sure to get to her house and back home again. She said she wouldn't be needing the car for driving to the mercantile.

"I told my manager he had to take charge of the store," she said. "At least until we get things sorted out with Katherine's health. I'm too worried to keep my mind on the business."

The Monday morning after we made our trip to Indianapolis, Elmer Mitchell came over to check on us. Frank brought him into the house, and we sat him down at the table to tell him about our troubles with Katherine.

It took a little bit for things to sink in. When he finally understood what we were talking about, he got tears in his eyes. Elmer might be dimwitted, but he has a kind heart. Frank told him it was going to take up a lot of time driving to Nashville and back every day, and he asked him if he'd mind taking over the milking every morning and evening.

"I can do that," Elmer said.

Frank reached over and clapped him on the back. "You're a good man, Elmer."

Elmer got up and went out to get right at his work, looking like he was walking on air. I could tell it made him feel important, having someone count on him like that.

I was so worried about Katherine that I put all thoughts of Christmas out of my mind. Clover's housekeeper tried to cheer everybody up by making a nice Christmas dinner. But we had a hard time enjoying it without Katherine there.

One afternoon, just after we'd come home from Nashville, Reverend Horton stopped by the house. He wanted to let us know they were praying for Katherine at the Oakridge Church. I don't know how he knew she was sick. I guess people start talking, and before you know it, word has gotten around.

I was worried about how Frank would act with Reverend Horton. He usually doesn't have a kind word for a preacher. But he surprised me. When Reverend Horton was about to leave, Frank reached out and shook the man's hand, thanking him for his kindness.

Every time we went to Nashville for one of those telephone calls, we hoped the headmistress would have good news for us. But she never had much to tell us. "Katherine's resting well," she'd say. "And we're taking good care of her."

From time to time, Katherine herself would get on the telephone, sounding weak and tired. "I don't want any of you to be worrying about me," she'd say. "I'm going to pull through. Any day now, I'm going to start feeling like my old self again."

But whenever we talked with the school nurse, she never had anything hopeful to say. One day, she told us Katherine's balance was getting so bad that she could hardly walk without falling over. She said she'd given her a little bell to ring, so that someone could come help her when she wanted to get out of bed. The nurse went on to say that Katherine wasn't able to stomach much food, and that a couple of times, she'd thrown up everything she'd just eaten.

On the first Saturday in January, Katherine's doctor got on the telephone with us. He talked with me first.

"Mrs. Kelly," he said, "I'm afraid I have bad news. Your daughter isn't well enough to return to her teaching duties this term. We need to send her home. And you'll need to see to it that she gets the proper medical care."

When I heard that, I was so shook up that I couldn't say a word to the doctor. I handed the telephone to Clover. She talked to him and then to the headmistress, to get everything sorted out.

"The headmistress was so kind," she told Frank and me when she hung up. "She said they'll have to get someone else to cover Katherine's classes this term. But they'll hold her position for her, and when she's well enough, she can go back and take over again."

I was so glad to hear that Katherine wouldn't be losing her job. "That's good of them," I said.

"The headmistress thinks highly of Katherine," Clover said. "They don't want to lose her."

After that, none of us knew what to say to each other. We just sat there in Clover's front room trying to take in the seriousness of the whole matter. "How are we going to handle this?" I finally asked.

Clover spoke up really quick. "Katherine can come back and stay in her room here."

Her words stabbed me in the heart. I could hardly stand to think of her taking care of my sick child when I wanted to do it myself. Right away, Clover knew she'd hurt me, because she reached over and took my hand.

"Bertha," she said, "I know how bad you want Katherine with you. But in her weak condition, how would she make it up and down the stairs? How would she make a trip to the outhouse in this wintry weather?"

I knew Clover was right. I was back to the same thing I'd faced with Pa. I couldn't put Katherine in the downstairs bedroom, because it would be too much of a strain for Frank to manage the stairs every day. I knew my child would be better off in her aunt's nice house, with the electricity and the bathtub and all.

Then Clover's kindheartedness came through. "Bertha," she said, "if you want to take care of Katherine, then you can stay here, too. As much as you want to. It'll probably take the two of us together to do right by her."

Frank and I hardly ever talk to each other when we're going somewhere in the car. It aggravates him if I bring something up while he's driving. But on our way home that afternoon, I just had to tell him what was on my mind.

"Katherine's done so much for us," I said to him. "Sending us money and all. She's plumb worn herself out. Partly, it was for the sake of those little girls at the school. But it was for our sake, too."

Frank nodded and swallowed hard. I could tell he was trying to keep himself from crying.

Right then and there, I knew he was no longer the hardhearted fellow he'd been for so many years. Every day, his heart was softening, growing more tender toward his child. And even toward me.

On Monday morning, two days after we talked with Katherine's doctor, Clover and Frank and I drove back to Indianapolis. Truly, I hoped it was the last time, at least for a good long while. Because that trip up State Road 135 had become something sorrowful.

When we got to the school, Katherine was sitting on her bed waiting for us. The headmistress and the nurse had packed the things she needed to take home with her. They left her pretty lamp on the desk and her books on the shelves, waiting for the day when she'd come back and use them again.

The nurse kept telling us the first thing we needed to do was to get Katherine to a doctor. As if we didn't know enough to do that on our own. I got a little aggravated with her. “We’re going to do that right away,” I snapped.

Clover and I each took Katherine by the arm and helped her down the stairs and out to the car. She’d lost so much weight that either one of us could’ve picked her up and carried her. The nurse followed behind us, in case we needed help.

On the way home, Frank sat up front with Clover, and I sat in the back seat with Katherine. She was so weak and tired that she could hardly sit up straight. I tried to have her lie down with her head on my lap, but that made her sick. “I’m too dizzy,” she said. “I’m afraid I might throw up.”

So, I helped her sit up again. “Keep looking out the window,” I told her. I’d gotten sick from car rides before, and I knew that was the best thing to do.

When we finally got to Clover’s place in Nashville, we helped Katherine into the house. She was so tuckered out that she wanted to go to bed right away. Clover’s housekeeper fixed us all a bite to eat. We tried to get Katherine to take something, but she turned it down.

“I just can’t eat right now,” she said. “I have a terrible headache. Let me sleep a while first.”

While Katherine was resting, I had Frank take me home to pack up a few things, so I’d be ready to stay at Clover’s for a while. I hated to leave Katherine even for that short time. But when I got back an hour later, she was still sleeping.

Before Frank went home again, he told me Elmer Mitchell would be staying with him while I was gone. Nellie Mitchell had taken to sending food along with Elmer every time he came over. So, I knew that between her and the other neighbors, Frank and Elmer would have plenty to eat there at the farmhouse.

Clover told me she’d been on the telephone, and that she had set it up for Katherine to see Dr. Graham in

Nashville the next morning. I was glad to hear that.

When Katherine woke up again, she was all smiles. She was able to eat some chicken soup, and said it tasted wonderful. That did my heart a lot of good. I told myself that Dr. Graham would know what to do for her. Then she would surely take a turn for the better.

The next few days, so much happened that I could hardly meet up with myself coming and going.

In Dr. Graham's office on Tuesday morning, Clover and I sat off to the side while he looked Katherine over on his exam table. Dr. Graham is a baldheaded, portly fellow. He takes his time with his patients and tries to make them feel comfortable, chatting with them about this and that. He's new in town, even though he seems like an old-time country doctor.

Clover told me Dr. Graham knew what he was doing, because he'd gone to a good medical school. While we were sitting there in his office, she pointed out the diplomas hanging on his wall.

Dr. Graham listened to Katherine's heart and lungs and looked into her throat and ears, the way doctors always do. Then he looked really close into her eyes, saying he was checking her pupils. After that, he did a test where he had her touch her nose with her finger. It seemed like she didn't do a good enough job of that, because he looked worried and shook his head a little. He had her get off the table and take a few steps across the room so he could watch her walk.

Then he turned to Clover and me. "Have you ever noticed Katherine slurring her words?" he asked.

"Sometimes when she's tired," Clover said.

Then I piped up and said, "When she's tired, she sounds like she's tipsy." Right away, I wished I would've kept my mouth shut, because I'd put my daughter in a bad light. "Of course, Katherine never drinks," I added.

Dr. Graham wrinkled his forehead and squinted his eyes, like he was thinking hard. "She's showing signs of a neurological problem," he said. "I'd like you to take her to a neurologist at the Indiana University Medical Center in Bloomington."

He took out a piece of paper, wrote down a phone number, and handed it to me. "His name is Dr. Ward. I'll be talking to him about Katherine. You can call him and set up an appointment for her."

"What's a neurologist?" Clover asked him.

"It's a specialist who deals with problems of the brain and nervous system," Dr. Graham told her.

I'd never before heard words like neurologist and neurological. They scared me. It took me a while to even learn how to say them right.

After we got home, I put Katherine to bed while Clover got on the telephone and called Dr. Ward's office. Just about then, Frank came chugging into the driveway in the Model T. I figured he wanted to know what had gone on at Dr. Graham's office.

The three of us sat down to talk. "We're all set," Clover said. "Katherine will be seeing Dr. Ward in Bloomington on Thursday morning. His office is right there near the University Hospital." She wagged her finger at Frank. "You need to come along this time."

I held my breath, waiting to see if my husband would argue with his sister or come up with some excuse. But he just shrugged and said, "Okay."

When we drove into Bloomington on Thursday morning, Katherine whispered, "This is all so familiar. It's so strange to be back here at the university."

Dr. Ward was a tall, thin, stern-looking fellow, not as

kindly as Dr. Graham. It made me nervous sitting there in the office with him. Right away, he got down to the business of asking questions.

When he had Katherine tell him about her headaches, she pointed to one side of her head and said, "They always start right here. But they take over my whole head."

He checked her over, doing pretty much the same things Dr. Graham had done. Then he said, "We need to take some x-rays."

"What for?" I asked.

He stopped for a minute, as if he was trying to think how to answer me. "To see if there are any irregularities in her brain," he said.

Right off the bat, I hated the idea of those x-rays. I was afraid it might be hard on a person to go through such a thing. I looked at Katherine, thinking that if she didn't want to do it, I wouldn't push her.

"It's okay, Mama," she said. "I'm willing to do this."

"You can go right over to the hospital and get them done now," Dr. Ward said. "I'll let the x-ray department know you're coming. Tomorrow, I'll meet with you again to go over the results."

He left the room really quick, leaving all of us sitting there not knowing what to think.

I could tell the idea of going inside a hospital made Frank nervous. He'd done real good sitting in Dr. Ward's office. But I knew that with him remembering his time in the war hospital, it might be just as well to leave him waiting in the car. We'd brought along a blanket to keep Katherine warm on the drive over. He put that over his legs to keep out the chill, and was content to sit there while Clover and I took Katherine inside.

I'd never been in a hospital before. Everything around us looked so white and clean. I was shaking a little as we helped Katherine down the hall to the x-ray department.

But Katherine put on a brave face. She said she wasn't afraid of hospitals, because she'd visited one of her students when the girl had her appendix taken out.

"Come on, Mama," she chuckled. "There's nothing to be scared of."

We all sat down in a waiting room, and then some hospital worker came to get Katherine. I was glad to see he had a wheelchair for her. I was afraid she'd have a hard time walking if she had to go too far, and that he wouldn't be able to keep her from falling.

He was whistling under his breath, as if this was nothing at all to him. I wanted to tell him that it was my child he was in charge of, and that he'd better take good care of her. When he wheeled her off to the room where they did the x-rays, I got tears in my eyes.

"I wish I could go along to hold her hand," I said to Clover. She reached out to take my hand in hers, as if that was the next best thing to do.

When the hospital worker brought Katherine back to us, I wanted to ask her all about the x-rays. But she was all done in and could hardly say a word. So, there was nothing to do but to take her home and put her into bed.

Yesterday afternoon, Frank, Clover and I all sat waiting in Dr. Ward's office. The nurse had put Katherine on the exam table. As I looked at my child lying there, too weak to sit up, my mind went back to when she was six years old, lying on Doc Murphy's table after she'd fallen and hit her head. And let me tell you, I was just as scared as I was back then.

It took a while for Dr. Ward to come in. When he finally walked through the door, I could see from the look on his face that he had nothing good to report to us. He was carrying a folder.

"I have the results of Katherine's x-rays," he told us. He took a film out of the folder and hung it in a lighted box on the wall. He picked up a pointer and outlined a big shape that showed up in white. "This is Katherine's brain," he said.

Then he outlined a dark spot on the brain. "This is the tumor that's causing Katherine's symptoms. You can see it's gotten to be a pretty good size. No doubt, it's been growing rapidly the past few months."

For a good long while, it was so quiet in the room that you could've heard a pin drop. In all my worrying about Katherine, I'd never thought for a minute about such a thing as a brain tumor. I looked at Frank and Clover. Their faces were as white as the snowflakes falling outside the office window. I knew they were as shocked as I was.

Then Katherine spoke up, hardly more than a whisper. "I'd been wondering about this," she said. "I'd been thinking this might be the problem."

Tears started pouring from my eyes. All along, my child had known she was suffering from something terrible, but she hadn't wanted to tell us. She hadn't wanted us to worry.

"What causes such a thing?" I asked Dr. Ward. "What makes a tumor grow in someone's brain?"

He didn't answer right away, so I kept on talking. "When Katherine was a little girl, she had a hard fall and hurt her head really bad. It knocked her right out, and then she wasn't herself for a week. Can something like that cause a brain tumor?"

I saw Frank wince, and I knew he was remembering the broken step Katherine had caught her foot on. I wished I hadn't brought the matter up.

"We don't know what causes these tumors," Dr. Ward said. "It could be any number of things."

I sat there feeling so helpless, thinking, *if nobody*

knows the cause, how could anyone know the cure?

Just as if he was reading my mind, Dr. Ward said, "Here's the good news. There's a doctor at our University Medical Center in Indianapolis who does brain surgery. He's had experience in removing tumors like this. So, the next thing to do is to go see him. If you all agree, I'll talk with him right away."

Then he looked at each one of us in turn. "Katherine, Mr. and Mrs. Kelly…." He sounded sad, and it made me think he had a heart after all. "We need to act on this immediately. We don't have time to waste."

Right then and there, I didn't want to wait on the Indianapolis doctor to operate on Katherine's brain. I wanted to reach in with my own hands and snatch that ugly tumor out of her head. I wanted to beat it and stomp on it and scream at it, punishing it for taking over my child's brain and making her suffer.

Dr. Ward kept on looking at us, waiting on us to make up our minds. I looked at Katherine, knowing that the decision was up to her.

"I'm ready to do this," she said in her weak little voice.

After we got back to Clover's house, I stuck close to Katherine for the rest of the day. I just couldn't bear to let her out of my sight.

Clover has plenty of bedrooms in her big house, and she had one fixed up for me. But last night, I couldn't bring myself to sleep in it. I asked her to give me blankets so I could make up a bed on the floor next to Katherine's bed. Just so I could be there in case she needed me.

When I finally got settled in, I heard my daughter's voice in the darkness. "Don't worry, Mama. I'm going to pull through this."

"If anyone can do it, Katherine," I said, "it's you."

1938

How can it be that the most precious moments of your life come when your heart is breaking into pieces? Just thinking about it, it doesn't seem like those two things could go together. A person wouldn't understand unless they've lived through such a time. Like the time I've just been through.

I have to start my story by going all the way back to a year ago. Three days after we brought Katherine home from Dr. Ward's office in Bloomington, we were off to Indianapolis again, this time to see Dr. Chang, the surgeon who was going to operate on Katherine's brain.

Katherine slept through the whole trip, wrapped up in a quilt in the back seat. She had dark circles under her eyes, and her cheeks were sunken like an old woman's. Sitting there next to her, I remembered Dr. Ward saying how we didn't have any time to waste. I had to wonder whether we were already too late, whether too much time had already gone by with that tumor growing in her brain.

When we got to the University Medical Center, Clover had a hard time finding Dr. Chang's office. With all the buildings there, she couldn't tell what was what. She was so upset from driving in circles and not getting anywhere that tears started running down her face. But she clenched her jaw and kept on trying until she figured out where we needed to go.

Dr. Chang was a Chinese fellow with little round glasses and hair as black as coal. He didn't take much time with Katherine in his office. I guess he'd already heard everything he needed to know from Dr. Ward. He had us take Katherine right on over to the hospital, saying she needed to stay overnight so they could get her ready for her operation first thing in the morning.

Clover pulled the car up to the front door of the hospital so Katherine wouldn't have far to walk. We had just gotten inside when a nurse in a white dress and cap came with a wheelchair for her. Then all of us had to go on an elevator up to her room on the third floor.

I'd never been in an elevator before. It creaked and rumbled, and I was afraid the noise would set Frank off. But he kept his cool. I suspected he'd made up his mind not to let things like that bother him.

There were a couple of other people in Katherine's room, old women lying in their beds looking like they'd come to the end. But we didn't pay them any mind, because we were so worried about Katherine.

The nurse helped her into one of those gowns they make people wear at the hospital. My poor child was so weak that she could hardly lift her arms to put them in the sleeves. As soon as she got settled into bed, she closed her eyes and fell asleep again.

Clover and I were saying to each other how much we wished we could stay with her. But the nurse set us straight, telling us there were only certain hours when people could visit, and that family wasn't allowed to spend the night there at the hospital.

Then Frank spoke up, saying we needed to go back home and tell everybody what was going on. He said his other sisters needed to know about Katherine's operation, and that we should stop by Hazel and Walter's place to tell them and Pa. He even mentioned telling Reverend Horton. He didn't say anything about having the reverend pray, but I figured he had that in mind. It surprised me, because Frank's never been one to believe in prayer.

Clover and I kissed Katherine's pale cheeks and cried over her, telling her we loved her and that we'd be back the next day. She slept through all that, and I doubt that she even heard us.

Clover was crying so hard that Frank said she wasn't fit to drive. So, she let him take a turn behind the wheel of her car. I was afraid he wouldn't know his way around the city, but he managed to get us out of Indianapolis and back to Brown County.

We all knew we had no time to rest or catch our breath. On our way down to Nashville, we cut over to Helmsburg to tell Reverend Horton about Katherine's operation. And wouldn't you know it, he was kind enough to lead us in prayer right then and there. I sneaked a peek at Frank and saw that he had his head bowed.

Then we went on to Walter and Hazel's place to tell them what was happening. Pa took the news real hard. We'd told him Katherine had been sick, but he hadn't known the seriousness of it. He closed his eyes and got really quiet while I went on talking with Hazel. But after a minute, he spoke up again.

"If you're going to be driving to Indianapolis all the time," he said, "you need to get yourselves a new car. That old Model T is liable to break down any time."

"We can't afford a new car now, Pa," I said. "We'll just have to make do with borrowing Clover's car."

But Pa said that wasn't good enough, that we should have a car of our own. He told us he had money in the bank from leasing out his farmland. "I'm old," he said. "I'm never going to need that money. It's just about enough to buy you and Frank a new car."

"We can't take your money like that," I told him. "Anyway, it wouldn't be fair to Hazel. Half of it should rightly go to her."

Then Hazel jumped in. "I want you to have it, Bertha. This is your time of need. Pa sees it as his duty to help you out."

I glanced over at Frank. He looked mighty relieved, like a big worry had been lifted off his shoulders. Pa said he'd see to it that we got the money right away.

As soon as we got back to Clover's place, she got on the telephone and talked with each of her five sisters. Her news upset them so much that I could hear them carrying on and crying on the other end of the line. Of course, that got Clover going, too.

When she hung up the telephone, she told us a couple of her sisters were coming over that evening to talk things through. The look on Frank's face told me he wasn't in any state of mind to put up with that. So, I told Clover we needed to go on home to get ourselves a good night's sleep.

Our old Model T had been sitting in Clover's driveway for the better part of a week. Frank brushed the snow off of it, and we took it on home. Clover said she'd come by in the morning with the Chevrolet to drive us up to Indianapolis.

On the way back to Helmsburg, the Model T started acting up really bad. Frank kept patting the steering wheel and saying, "Just get us home, old girl. Just get us home."

Wouldn't you know it, as we were heading up our lane, the car sputtered and died. Smoke started rolling out from under the hood, and we both knew that was the end of the Model T. Frank said we needed to get out really quick in case something was about to blow up. He said that in the morning, he'd have Elmer Mitchell push the Model T out of the way so Clover could get her car up the lane.

Truthfully, I expected to lie awake worrying that night. But I guess I was so worn out from everything that I couldn't help but fall asleep as soon as my head hit the pillow. When I woke up, I knew we were going to get a late start on our trip to the hospital. I went downstairs to wake up Frank, and we hurried around to get ready.

But as it turned out, we ended up sitting in the front room waiting for Clover. When she finally got there, she told us her sisters had stayed too late, and that she hadn't gotten herself to bed on time. She mentioned that she'd slept like a log herself. I had to think that an angel of the Lord had touched all three of us, giving us the rest we needed to face the hard day ahead.

When we got to the hospital, we were told that Katherine had just been wheeled off into the operating room. We all felt bad that we hadn't been able to see her before her surgery. A nurse took us to a waiting room, and there was nothing we could do but to sit there and pass the time.

Hours went by, and I started to feel like we were going to spend the rest of our lives in that waiting room. The longer we sat there, the more nervous we got. After a while, Clover got up and started pacing back and forth. Her doing that aggravated Frank to no end, and I could see he was trying hard not to blow his top.

When Dr. Chang finally walked into the room in his white hospital coat, I was afraid he was coming to tell us the worst. But he smiled at us and told us that Katherine had come through the operation just fine.

Clover busted out crying, and I could tell she wanted to throw her arms around the man. But she settled for shaking his hand and thanking him. Frank and I did the same.

"When can we see her?" I asked Dr. Chang.

"It'll be a while before she wakes up," he told us. "A nurse will come get you when Katherine's ready to have visitors."

Then he got a serious look on his face. "Mr. and Mrs. Kelly, I'm afraid all my news isn't good. I was able to take out most of your daughter's tumor, but I couldn't get it all. Some of it couldn't be removed without damaging healthy brain tissue. So, there's a chance that it could grow back."

Just as those words started to hit me, he went on to say, "But once she recovers from this surgery, Katherine should feel a lot better."

And I decided the doctor's last words were the ones I was going to hang on to.

So, we settled down to wait again. When I looked out the window and saw that it was getting dark outside, I figured we'd have to go home and come back to see Katherine the next day.

But then a nurse came and told us Katherine was starting to wake up. "She's responding well," she told us. "Better than we'd hoped for. There's always a chance after an operation like this that the patient will end up with some brain damage. But it looks as if Katherine's going to be her old self again."

She led us into a room where Katherine was lying in bed, her head wrapped in white bandages. She looked like she was sleeping. But when I stroked her cheek with my finger, she opened her eyes and smiled at me.

"Hello, Mama," she said. Then she looked past me and said, "Hello, Papa. Hello, Aunt Clover. It's so nice of you to come see me."

"We're so sorry we weren't here before you went to the operating room this morning," I told her.

"It's okay," she said. "I knew you were all here in spirit. I could feel you right next to me."

She reached up a weak little hand to touch the bandages on her head. "They shaved off my hair before I went into surgery. Now, my head is as bald as Grandpa's."

Clover and I laughed, and then we cried. Katherine looked aggravated. "Come on now," she said. "The two of you are going to have to get ahold of yourselves. It's all over and done with. The tumor's out of my brain, and we'll all go on from here."

Then she closed her eyes again, as if she'd tired herself

out with all the talking. And I knew none of us would ever have the heart to tell her the doctor hadn't been able to take out all of the tumor. There would be no talk of that horrible thing coming back.

A few days after Katherine's operation, Hazel and Walter came over to the house. Walter said an old fellow he'd known from their hardware store had just died, and that his children were wanting to sell his 1933 Ford Coupe.

"It's like new," he said. "The old man hardly drove it at all."

And Hazel chimed in with, "This is the car Pa wants to buy for you."

So, it wasn't but two days later when that Ford Coupe was sitting at the end of our lane next to the house. I was so proud of it that I was ashamed of myself. Of course, Frank wanted to start driving it up to Indianapolis. "We need to give Clover's car a rest," he said.

Katherine ended up staying in the hospital for three weeks. We all wished we could go see her every day, but she told us not to. "Don't be foolish," she said. "Making the trip is hard on you."

So, we ended up going to Indianapolis two or three times a week. Every time we visited her, Katherine was stronger and her spirit seemed brighter.

Soon, the nurses had her up and walking. At first, they helped her, but she wanted to do it on her own. Before too long, she was able to wash herself and change her own hospital gown. She started eating, more and more each day. The nurses bragged on her, saying how well she was coming along. "Better than most people who have this kind of surgery," they'd tell us.

We were there when the doctor decided it was time to take the bandages off her head. I could see that her hair was starting to grow back, looking like the fuzz on a peach. That seemed like a good sign to me. I told myself that before too long, her beautiful hair would completely cover the ugly scar from her operation. On the way home that day, I thanked the Lord and cried tears of joy.

When it came time for Katherine to leave the hospital, I agreed that it was best to take her back to Clover's place. I knew she'd be more comfortable there than at the farmhouse.

Her first couple of nights at Clover's house, I stayed there with her, just to make sure everything was all right. After that, I went home, but I had Frank drive me down to Nashville so I could stay with my child during the day.

The next five months were some of the best months of my life. I know Katherine felt the same. She kept getting stronger and stronger, and I could see the happiness shining in her eyes.

"I'm a lady of leisure," she joked one day. "Even though I can't wait to get back to work, it's nice to have a break. I can be lazy. I can sleep as long as I want to in the mornings. I'm starting to feel a little guilty about that."

Of course, Clover and I both told her she shouldn't feel bad about taking it easy. "You were very sick, Katherine," Clover said. "You need your rest."

"Now's the time to build yourself back up," I added. "Don't worry about going back to work until the fall."

As Katherine started putting a little meat back on her bones, Clover saw to it that she had a couple of nice dresses. She bought her a little hat to cover her short hair. The first time I saw Katherine in one of those pretty new dresses, with her curls popping out from under that hat, I thought she'd never looked so beautiful.

The weeks passed, and winter gave way to spring. The birds were singing, the tulips and daffodils were blooming.

And my daughter was blooming, growing lovelier every day. Everything in the world seemed bright and hopeful.

On a warm day in late April, Clover and I took Katherine out for a picnic in Brown County State Park. We even walked a little way on one of the hiking trails. When we stopped to catch our breath, Katherine tilted her head and looked up at the sun shining through the fresh new leaves on the trees.

"I love life!" she sang out, throwing her arms in the air. Tears came to my eyes when I thought about how close she'd come to losing her precious life.

Before I knew it, Katherine was going back to work with Clover at the mercantile, just like she'd done on her summer breaks from college.

I wasn't keen on the idea at first. "Katherine," I said, "don't you think this is too much for you?"

"Of course it isn't," she said. "I have to start using my mind again. I have to get it in shape for going back to teaching in the fall."

So, I let the matter drop. Katherine really did seem to be enjoying herself. One day, Frank and I walked into the mercantile and saw her standing there minding the till. I whispered to Frank, "You can't even tell she was so sick just a few months ago."

Looking back, those precious months with Katherine seem like a beautiful dream, something too good to be true.

But then, on an evening toward the end of July, I realized that something about Katherine was starting to change. Frank and I had driven down to Nashville to visit her and Clover. When Clover answered the door, she looked a little worried.

I asked where Katherine was. "In her bedroom," Clover said. "You can go on in and see her."

I found Katherine there with a couple of cardboard

boxes she'd brought home from the mercantile. She was sorting through her drawers and packing things in the boxes.

But she seemed unsure about what she was doing. I watched her take a pile of stockings from one of the drawers, fold them, and put them in a box. Then it was like she'd changed her mind, because she put them back in the drawer again.

"What are you doing, Katherine?" I asked.

"I'm getting ready to go back to school," she said. "I should be leaving for Indianapolis in a month."

Something didn't seem right to me. I could feel it there in the room, something bad lurking there. It gave me a queasy feeling in my stomach.

"Are you sure you're ready to teach again?" I asked her. "Don't you think maybe it's too soon?"

She turned her head to face me, and her eyes looked sick and feverish. "Mama," she said, "it's now or never. If I don't go back now, I might completely lose my nerve."

I didn't know it then, but Katherine had already started having headaches again. She just hadn't wanted to admit that to anyone.

It was a week later when Clover drove over to see Frank and me. Right away, I knew something was wrong.

"Where's Katherine?" I asked her.

"At home in bed," she said. "She's not feeling well."

Her words knocked the wind out of me, and I had to sit down on the sofa to keep from falling over. Clover sat down next to me.

"What do you mean?" I asked her.

She looked at me with sorrow in her big blue eyes. "She says her head is hurting her something terrible." Then she reached over and grabbed my hand. "Oh, Bertha, I'm so scared. Katherine hasn't been herself this past week."

Right then and there, I knew the beautiful months I'd had with my daughter were coming to an end. "We need to get her back to the doctor," I said.

Over the next week, it seemed as if we were back to where we'd started, running from one doctor to another. I was afraid Katherine might fight it, claiming that she was all right. But she went along with everything Clover and I told her to do.

We started with Dr. Graham in Nashville. Katherine confessed to him that she'd been having headaches for a month. When he pushed her to tell him more, she admitted that she'd been dizzy, and that she was having a hard time eating again. And she said something new, that she wasn't seeing things quite right.

Dr. Graham sent us back to Bloomington to see Dr. Ward. And Dr. Ward sent us back to Indianapolis to see Dr. Chang.

Dr. Chang sent Katherine to the hospital to get another x-ray. "To check on the status of the tumor," he said. His words reminded me that the ugly tumor had never been completely gone.

Sure enough, when Dr. Chang talked with us about the x-ray the next day, he said the tumor had grown back to almost the same size it had been when he'd operated on it.

"I suppose we could do another surgery," he said. "But it would be hard on Katherine to go through it a second time, and the outcome might not be as good." He looked from one of us to another. "I'm afraid the tumor is getting the upper hand. We're fighting a losing battle."

We all sat there real quiet, not knowing what to think.

Then Katherine said, "It's time to stop fighting and accept things for what they are." She sounded like she'd already made up her mind, and I knew she'd been thinking about the matter for some time.

"No, Katherine!" Clover and I said together.

"There's nothing more to do," she said, "but to let go and leave everything in God's hands."

She had her purse lying on her lap. She opened it a little, like she didn't want anyone to notice, and was fingering something inside. And then I caught a glimpse of what it was. It was her rosary. She was calling on God for strength to help her through that terrible moment. And the terrible trial that lay ahead of her.

My heart felt dark and heavy, so heavy that I could hardly breathe. *I've left so many things in God's hands,* I thought to myself. *I'm so tired of having to do this.*

"What do we do now?" I heard Clover ask Dr. Chang.

"Take her home," he said. "Help her make the best of the time she has left. You'll need to count on your local doctor to take over her care. He can give her medicine to help with the pain of her headaches."

Frank hadn't gone with us to the appointment that day, as he and Elmer had needed to mend a part of the pasture fence where the bull had broken through. On the way back to Nashville, we stopped by the farmhouse to tell him what the doctor had said.

Katherine had fallen asleep and wasn't able to wake herself up enough to go inside. "I'll stay out here with her," Clover whispered to me. "You go on in and talk to Frank."

When I stepped inside the house, my face must've told my husband everything he needed to know. Before I could say a word, he turned and limped out the back door like a broken old man, his shoulders shaking with his sobs.

For the next couple of days, I stayed with Katherine at Clover's place. I felt numb inside. Nothing I saw or heard or touched seemed real to me. It was like I was a dead person walking around that big fancy house.

I did take it upon myself to help Clover's housekeeper in the kitchen, as that gave my hands something to do. Washing a few dishes or stirring a pot of soup on the stove didn't take any thought.

I hardly said a word to Clover or Katherine. I knew that if I opened my mouth to talk about what was happening, sorrow would come crashing down on me like a wave on a stormy sea. I was afraid it would drown me.

Still, I kept watch over my child. Every night, I'd take my blankets and lie down on the floor next to her bed. One morning when I woke up from a troubled sleep, I found Katherine sitting on the edge of her bed looking at me.

"Mama," she said, "it's time to go home."

My head was still fuzzy from sleep, and I wasn't thinking straight. "What, Katherine?" I asked. "Do you want me to go home and leave you alone?"

"No," she said. "You don't understand. I want to go home. That's where I want to be until the end."

I sat up so I could talk to her better. "But Katherine, the stairs will be hard for you."

"That's okay," she said. "Soon, I won't be able to walk, and I won't have to worry about going up and down."

Then it came to me what she was saying. She wanted to spend her last days in her childhood room, the place that had been so very dear to her while she was growing up.

"When do you want to go?" I asked.

"Let's talk to Clover," she said. "Then we'll decide."

Clover didn't fight the idea. She understood what Katherine needed to do. A few days later, Frank came over with the Ford Coupe, and the three of us set off for home.

As we were leaving, Clover stood in her doorway crying. She knew her beloved niece would never again set foot in her home. Sitting there in the car, I cried along with my sister-in-law.

The first week Katherine was home, I kept thinking she was going to be there for only a few days, like she was on a break from school. It was hard to believe my child was going to be spending the rest of her life in the farmhouse with me.

She followed me from room to room as best she could, holding onto furniture or a doorframe to keep herself steady. She wanted to be a part of everything I did.

One day when I was baking a pie, she insisted on peeling the apples. With her having trouble hanging onto things, I wasn't keen on the idea of her using a paring knife. "I don't think that's a good idea, Katherine," I told her.

Still, she wanted to try, so I let her. I kept my eye on her, as I could see how clumsy she was with the knife. Wouldn't you know it, she nicked her thumb when she was trying to slice the first apple. When I took the knife and bowl away from her, I saw a tear trickle down her cheek.

"I'm sorry, sweetheart," I said. "I just can't have you hurting yourself."

"I understand, Mama," she whispered.

From the very first day she was home, I was afraid she was going to lose her balance on the stairs. So, she took to scooting herself upstairs and downstairs on her bottom, one step at a time. It struck both of us as funny.

"Remember the silly things you used to do on the stairs when you were little?" I said to her one day. "You'd crawl up on your hands and knees, lickety-split, looking like a little cat. And then you'd slide down on your belly."

We laughed together, and for a few seconds, it seemed as if no time at all had passed since then.

The day before Katherine came back home, I'd cleaned her room from top to bottom, getting it ready for her. Of course, we had to bring over all the things she'd kept at

Clover's house. Little by little, as she had the strength, she fixed up her room the way she wanted it to be. She'd put something in one spot, then change her mind and put it somewhere else. Sometimes, she'd have me help her move things around.

When she finally had everything in place, she started asking about things she'd had when she was a little girl. "Where's my old dollhouse?" she asked one day. "The one Aunt Clover gave me on my birthday when I turned four."

Truth be told, I had no idea where that dollhouse was. I asked Frank about it. He looked for it, and found it in one of his sheds. It was in pretty bad shape, with the roof coming off and one of the sides busted in. But he got to work on it and fixed it up as best he could.

Frank went on looking through the shed and found a crate full of Katherine's old picture books and some of her first schoolbooks. As we were digging through the crate, we found pieces of dollhouse furniture and a few cups and plates from her old tea set.

After I cleaned everything up, I took it upstairs to show Katherine. She clapped her hands with joy. "Put the dollhouse over against that wall," she told me, "where I can see it every morning when I wake up." I helped her sit herself down on the floor, and so very carefully, she put the furniture inside the house. Just like she'd done when she was a little girl.

She wanted to keep all those old books in her room, but she didn't have any place to put them. So, Frank and Elmer got busy and built a set of bookshelves from scrap lumber they found in the barn.

The bookshelves weren't much to look at, but Katherine was thrilled with them. She spent two or three days getting all her books set out in the proper order, starting with her storybooks on the bottom shelf and ending up with her high school and college books on the top.

Then she took the dishes from her tea set and a few old dolls, and set them here and there on the shelves in front of the books. I found some of her stuffed animals shoved into the back of the downstairs bedroom closet, and I brought them up to her. She set them around the room just so.

It took her a good long while to get everything the way she wanted it. She'd tire out in no time at all, and would have to lie down. Or one of her headaches would come. They hurt her so bad that all she could do was go to bed.

I hated those headaches. It seemed like they were taking away the precious hours I had left with my child. But at least I knew that while she was lying there in her bed, she was surrounded by all the things that had meant so much to her in life.

Katherine got to where she couldn't eat much again, and all the weight she'd been able to put on after her surgery started falling off again. That worried me something terrible. I kept trying to get her to eat more, tempting her with food I knew she liked.

One evening, I did my very best to fix a special supper for her: fried chicken, mashed potatoes, green beans, and biscuits. I'd even gone to all the trouble of baking a chocolate cake for dessert. Katherine acted like she was pleased with it all, and she tried her best to eat a little bit of everything. I knew she wanted to make me happy.

But as soon as she got up from the table, she stumbled over to the kitchen sink and threw up everything she'd just eaten. She got some on the front of her dress, and I had to help her clean up. She was crying, and I felt so bad for her.

"I'm sorry, Mama," she kept saying.

"No, Katherine," I said. "I'm the one who needs to be sorry. I made you eat more food than you could handle."

She was so done in that I had to help her scoot herself up the stairs. Then I put her to bed.

When I came back downstairs, Frank was all set to scold me. "Bertha, you know she can't eat a big meal like that anymore."

"I know, Frank," I said. "I've made up my mind not to push her. From now on, I'll just let her have whatever she wants."

I knew Katherine was going downhill a little bit every day. I was on edge all the time, watching her like a hawk. Most of the time, I couldn't see the change from one day to the next, but sometimes I could. And I'd know she'd never again be as able as she'd been the day before.

As I'd already been doing, I slept in the upstairs room next to hers. I'd lie awake for hours at night, just listening to see if she was trying to move around or get out of bed. Sometimes, she'd call out, and I'd have to bring her a drink of water or help her onto the chamber pot. Or pick up one of her blankets that had slipped off the bed and fallen on the floor.

Sometimes, I think she just needed to feel my touch, and to hear me say that I loved her.

I'd been a little worried about how Frank would take it with our sick daughter being home with us. I was glad to see how kind he was, even though he didn't say much to her. Mostly, he was really quiet in going about his business, so as not to disturb her any.

One day in early September, he and Elmer left to go someplace. I wasn't paying any mind to what they were doing. A couple of hours later, they came back into the house. Frank looked pleased with himself, and Elmer was grinning from ear to ear.

"Bertha," Frank said, "go get an old blanket. We're going to take Katherine outside."

Well, that sure surprised me. "She's upstairs resting," I told him. "She might not be up for it."

All the commotion must've woken Katherine up. I heard her weak little voice calling downstairs. "What's happening, Mama?"

"Elmer," Frank said, "go up and help Bertha bring Katherine down."

I tell you, I didn't know what to think. I headed up the stairs, and Elmer followed me. Katherine looked startled when we walked into her room.

"Sweetheart," I said, "your papa wants to take you outside for a bit."

Then Elmer just couldn't help himself. "We have a surprise for you," he said.

Katherine's face broke into a smile. Very slowly, she raised herself up to sit on the edge of the bed. But Elmer didn't wait for anything. As if she was no more than a little child, he scooped her up in his strong arms and carried her down the stairs.

When he got to the bottom with her, Frank said, "Carry her on out to the fishpond." So, Elmer didn't even bother to set Katherine down. I opened the front door for him, and he marched out onto the porch and out toward the pond. I carried the old blanket I'd brought downstairs, and Frank limped along behind me.

"Spread out the blanket," Frank said when we got to the pond. "Let Katherine sit here for a while."

I looked into the pond and saw that it was full of carp, swimming here and there and everywhere. Two or three of them were gold. The sight took my breath away.

Katherine was beside herself when she saw the fish. "Oh, Papa! Oh, Papa!" she cried out. She took to crying so hard that I had to sit beside her on the blanket to hold her up.

Then Frank did something that surprised me even more. He eased himself down to sit on the other side of Katherine. So, there we were, Mama and Papa, one on each side of our precious child. It was the first time the three of us had ever sat together like that.

Having us so close seemed to give Katherine strength. She settled down and stopped crying, and just watched the fish in the water.

"Oh, Papa!" she said again. She sounded just like she had when she was seven. "They're even more beautiful than they were the first time. I've never seen anything so lovely. Thank you, Papa, thank you!"

She reached her hand out to him. He took it and held it in his. The three of us sat there like that for a very long time. Elmer stood off to one side, as if he knew not to bother us in any way.

I've heard it said that the Lord works in mysterious ways. That day, he worked his wonders through those fish, touching hearts and healing hurt feelings. All I know is that I was thankful, more thankful than words could ever say.

After a while, Katherine started shivering, like she was getting chilled. I knew it was time to take her inside. "Those poor little fish might not make it through the winter," she said as Elmer picked her up again. And I was pretty sure she was thinking she might not make it through the winter herself.

That was the last time Katherine ever went outdoors. After that day, she barely had the strength to come downstairs. Soon, she was spending all her hours in her bedroom. And it seemed like I was running up and down the stairs a hundred times a day taking care of her.

In late September, I sent Frank over to Helmsburg to fetch Dr. Groves. Katherine was becoming so feeble that I knew we needed help from him.

When he came downstairs after seeing her the first time, he took me aside to explain what was going to happen. “With a brain tumor like this,” he said, “she’ll lose her abilities one by one, until she becomes like a helpless infant.”

His words hit me so hard that I covered my face with my hands. The kind doctor put his arm around my shoulders. “Mrs. Kelly,” he said, “this is going to be a hard road for you to travel. But by the grace of God, you’ll get through it.”

After that, he took it upon himself to come out to the house to see Katherine every week. He gave me some pills to give her when her headaches got so bad that she couldn’t stand them. I could tell her suffering touched him. He was so gentle with her.

Before I knew it, Katherine had become completely bedfast. Bit by bit, she stopped being able to do anything for herself. She lost the strength to sit up. She wasn’t able to brush her hair or wash her face. And she couldn’t hang onto a spoon well enough to lift it to her mouth.

So, I had to feed her, like I’d done when she was a baby. I’d sit on the bed and lift her onto my lap, holding her high enough so she wouldn’t choke on her food.

I’d give her something easy to swallow, like a few spoons full of broth. She’d turn her head to one side when she’d had enough. She couldn’t swallow the pills for her headaches, so I had to crush them up and put them in applesauce. From time to time, Clover brought over pudding her housekeeper had made, something Katherine had always liked, and I’d put the crushed-up pills in that.

“Now sweetheart,” I’d say, “you have to take one more bite to get your medicine inside you.” But then, I wouldn’t push her to take any more. I knew I couldn’t keep my child from wasting away.

It didn’t seem right that her body was failing when mine was still strong. Every night when I said my bedtime prayers, I’d beg God to spare her and take me instead.

I knew Frank was thinking along the same lines. One day when I came downstairs after tending to Katherine, he said, "It's not fair that someone so good has such a short life, while a worthless old fool like me keeps hanging on."

Then it seemed like he couldn't deal with what he'd just said, and he turned away from me and went out to the barn. I knew that was his way of handling his sorrow, and I let him be.

Every day, Frank would make one trip up the stairs to see his daughter. And that was it. He would say his bad leg couldn't take any more than that, and I'd go along with that idea.

But I knew it was more a matter of a weak heart than a crippled leg. Frank couldn't stand the sight of his suffering child. Every time he came downstairs after seeing her, he'd head straight to the barn. I was pretty sure he was letting himself fall to pieces out there where nobody could see him.

I've come to know that even though a man might be stronger in body, a woman is stronger in spirit. She has to be, to bear up under the sorrow life heaps upon her.

Lots of people came to visit Katherine. People from church. Girls she went to high school with. Even a few college friends. I always had to tell them not to stay long, as Katherine was so frail that she'd tire out from just a minute of talking.

Hazel and her daughters came once a week. Pa was never well enough to make it, but Hazel said he was always asking about Katherine.

Frank's sisters came over as much as they could. They wanted to take care of their baby brother, to shore him up and keep him from breaking down. They fluttered around him like little old hens. I think he was glad for their attention, but I could always tell when he'd had his fill.

Of course, Clover came almost every day. I couldn't have kept her away if I'd wanted to. She spent hours at Katherine's bedside, talking to her, reading to her. Katherine would usually sleep through all that. But I knew it comforted Clover to think she was doing something for her niece.

One day when I went upstairs to check on them, Clover was reading out of one of the books she'd given Katherine for her sixteenth birthday. It was *Wuthering Heights,* the story about the girl named Catherine who lived in England. From time to time, Katherine would open her eyes and smile a little.

Even though I had a lot to do, I just had to sit down on the foot of my daughter's bed and listen for a while, remembering the summer day she read the whole book to me while I was canning green beans.

Sometimes, Clover would take over the job of washing or feeding Katherine. She was the only person I allowed to do that. I knew I could trust her to take care of my child just as well as I did.

One day, Billy Davis came to visit. I wanted him to remember how beautiful Katherine had been when he was courting her. Before he went up the stairs to see her, I made sure her face was washed and her hair was brushed, and that she was wearing a clean nightgown.

I let him go up on his own. I figured the two of them needed to be alone to make their peace with each other.

When Billy came downstairs, I saw tears in his eyes. Right then and there, I was glad he and Katherine had never gotten married. I was thankful that he had a strong, healthy wife to raise his three children.

I went up to check on Katherine, and the first thing she said to me was, "Mama, I did right to let Billy go all those years ago."

"Yes, you did, sweetheart," I said. "You did the right thing for yourself and for him."

We let Elmer go up and see Katherine every once in a while. He's such a clumsy fellow, clomping around in his heavy boots and running into things. Over and over, I'd have to tell him to keep quiet for Katherine's sake.

One day when he came downstairs, he said, "I remember when Katherine was a little girl riding to school in the wagon. She was nice to me." Then he started bawling, wiping his eyes on his dirty shirtsleeve. I couldn't help but put my arms around the poor boy and hold him for a little while.

With all the people coming and going, it seemed like Frank and I were never alone in the house. All that commotion wore me out almost as much as running up and down the stairs to tend to Katherine. But every time somebody came, they brought over food for us. That took a load off my shoulders. And Hazel and her girls always helped out with the cleaning and the washing.

As Katherine grew weaker and weaker, she became more and more like a little child. It got to where she reminded me of when she was a newborn baby, before she filled out. Her long arms and legs were as thin and weak as noodles. Time became confusing, because it seemed as if we were back at the beginning of things instead of at the end.

Many a time, I sat at Katherine's bedside while she slept, watching her poor thin chest rise and fall with her breathing. Sometimes, I'd reach under her covers and take out her hand so I could hold it. During her growing up years on the farm, Katherine's hands had always been dry and calloused from hard work. Now, they were as soft and smooth as a baby's hands.

Sometimes during her sleep, she'd curl her hand

around mine. Just like she had curled her hand around one of my fingers when she was a newborn.

By the time Christmas rolled around, Katherine had gotten to the point where she slept most of the time. When I'd look at her, I could almost see a glow about her. She seemed heavenly. Like a weak little angel who'd fallen to earth.

Whenever she did open her eyes and look at me, it was the most precious of moments. And before she'd go back to sleep, she'd whisper something so sweet to me.

"Good morning, Mama," she said one day. "You look so beautiful. It's so nice to wake up and see your face."

I held those words in my heart, thinking on them all day long.

Another morning, she opened her eyes and said to me, "My two grandmothers came to visit me. Grandma Lena and Grandma Rose. They told me they're waiting for me on the other side."

Then she gave a little laugh. "I love them so much. Grandma Lena is the sensible one. Some people think Grandma Rose is crazy, but she isn't. She just knows things other people don't know."

Well, that sure gave me a start, her talking with people who were already dead. I'd never told Katherine that folks around here thought her Grandma Rose was crazy, as I hadn't wanted her to feel bad about where she came from. All I could think to say was, "That's nice, Katherine."

But then, I blurted out, "Tell your grandmothers that I love them."

"They already know that," she whispered. Then she closed her eyes and fell asleep again.

I sat there watching her, thinking on how I'd never gotten the chance to tell her all the stories about our people, the ones Ma had told me. But it seemed as if she already knew everything she needed to know.

When Dr. Groves came to check on Katherine the last day in December, she slept all the way through his visit.

"I can't get her to take anything anymore," I told him. "Except for a drop or two of water."

I was afraid the doctor would think I was a terrible mother, not feeding my child. But he just nodded. "That's the way it is at the end," he said. "Mrs. Kelly, your daughter won't last more than another week. So, you need to prepare yourself for her passing."

Even though I heard what Dr. Groves said, my mind just couldn't take it in. But I guess my heart understood. Because right after he left, I knew I needed to do something. I had Elmer bring our rocking chair up the stairs, the one we'd gotten from Ma and Pa's house, and I had him set it in Katherine's room.

Then I took her out of the bed, making sure she was all wrapped up in her blanket. I sat down in the rocking chair holding her in my arms, rocking ever so gently so as not to make her feel sick. Every now and then, I'd whisper in her ear, telling her I loved her.

And I kept on doing that day after day, every morning and every evening and sometimes in the afternoon.

On the morning of January 6, I went to tend to her like I usually did. Her eyes fluttered open for a few seconds, and her lips started moving. She hadn't said anything for a few days. I bent down close to hear her.

"Hold me one last time, Mama," she whispered. "Like you did in the beginning."

As I picked her up and held her in the rocking chair, I somehow knew she was remembering the day she was born, when I was cradling her in my arms. It was like those twenty-nine years hadn't passed, and I was still holding my newborn child.

Then she whispered, "Tell Papa I forgive him. Tell him not to let anything trouble his heart."

"And what about your mama?" I asked her. "Do you forgive me, too?"

"Mama," she said, "there's nothing to forgive you for."

I tell you, those were the best words I'd ever heard in my entire life. And I knew they were the best I'd ever hear in the years to come. They were the last words my child ever spoke.

I sat there holding my baby girl for hours, never wanting to let her go. But then Clover came, and together we tucked our precious child back into bed.

That night, I was so worn out that I couldn't help but fall into a deep sleep. And I had the sweetest dream about a beautiful angel floating above me, smiling down on me. When I woke up in the morning, I lay there thinking on that dream for a while, trying to hold onto it.

All of a sudden, I realized I'd forgotten everything I should've been paying attention to. I hadn't been listening for the sound of Katherine's labored breathing. I jumped out of bed, feeling ashamed of myself, thinking I hadn't been watching over my child like I was supposed to.

I ran to her room. But her poor thin chest was no longer rising and falling with her breath. I laid my hand on her cheek, the cheek that had for so long been warm and feverish. It was as cold as ice.

"Frank! Frank!" I called out. He came up the stairs faster than I'd ever known him to come. Then he went to the bed and stood there silently, looking down at Katherine, his face wet with tears.

But right then, I wasn't able to cry. I was in such a state that I wasn't understanding anything.

"I'll go get Dr. Groves," Frank said after a few minutes.

While he was gone, I pulled the rocking chair over to the bed and sat there holding Katherine's hand. I kept on rubbing it, thinking I could warm it up. Then I went to get the quilt off my bed to warm her cold, cold body.

Before long, I heard footsteps coming up the stairs, and Dr. Groves came into the room. He reached down and put his fingers on Katherine's thin wrist, checking for a pulse. Then he turned to me. "I'm so sorry, Mrs. Kelly," he said.

He went on to tell me that he would call Bond's Funeral Home in Nashville for us, and that a hearse would be coming out to get the body. Then he went downstairs, and I heard him saying the same thing to Frank.

I stayed right where I was, sitting by the bed. I just couldn't bring myself to step away from my child.

I had known Clover would come, like she'd been doing every day. Soon, I heard her voice downstairs talking with Frank. And then, I heard her soft footsteps coming up the stairs.

"Oh, Katherine!" she cried out when she came into the room. "Oh, my dear sweet Katherine!"

I got up and let her sit in the rocking chair. She leaned over the bed, stroking Katherine's cheek and smoothing her hair. "Oh, baby," she sobbed, "I'll miss you so."

Before I knew it, the men from Bond's Funeral Home were there in the room. They lifted Katherine out of the bed and carried her downstairs.

I followed behind them. I watched them lay her out on some kind of stretcher. Then they covered her up, even her face. That didn't seem right to me.

As they wheeled her out of the house, I cried out, "No! No!"

"We're awfully sorry, Mrs. Kelly," one of the men said.

Frank and Clover and I stood at the front window watching the big black hearse driving down the lane.

I felt my head starting to spin. "Why are they taking my baby girl away?" I asked.

"Because she's dead," Frank said. "Bertha, our daughter is dead."

That night, I went back up to sleep in my upstairs room, even though Frank asked me to stay downstairs with him. I lay awake listening for the sound of Katherine's breathing. Sometimes, I thought I heard it, and I'd tell myself she was still okay.

In the morning, I thought I heard her cry out for help. I jumped out of bed and ran to her. But all I saw was an empty bed. The covers were thrown aside from where the funeral home men had lifted her out. I could see a few strands of her curly hair lying on the pillow.

Then it all came to me, and I cried out and fell to the floor. "Oh God," I screamed, "I can't bear this. I can't go on without my child. Take me, too. Take me now so I can be with her."

I hardly know what happened after that. I think I must've lost my mind. I only recall little bits of things here and there. Like Frank helping me up off the floor. Like Dr. Grove's kind face looking down on me as I lay in bed, telling me he was going to give me a pill to help me feel better.

I guess everybody had to go on and make the funeral plans without me. I remember a little bit about being in Bond's Funeral Home for the wake. There were flowers everywhere. People were standing up and saying nice things about Katherine. Somebody read a letter from Katherine's school, saying what a wonderful teacher she'd been.

I remember Hazel taking me by one arm, and her daughter Annabelle taking me by the other, and them walking me up to the casket to see Katherine's body. I remember one of Frank's other sisters bringing Clover up to stand alongside me.

I remember seeing Pa sitting in a chair, looking all done in, wiping his eyes on his hankie.

The funeral was yesterday morning. They held it at the Catholic Church in Bloomington. Frank's sisters must've insisted on that. I guess it was only right, seeing as how Katherine was a member of the Catholic Church.

I remember sitting there in the front row with Hazel holding my hand. I remember a priest in a long white robe standing up front, waving his hands around and saying something I couldn't understand.

Then we took a long drive following behind that big black hearse, ending up at the Oak Ridge Church.

I was standing there in the graveyard when my mind started coming back to me. The day was bitterly cold, and maybe the icy wind blew all the fog out of my brain. I started realizing what we were doing. We were laying my child to rest there in the family plot where Ma was buried.

Not many people had come out to the graveyard. Hazel and her girls, Annabelle and Ruby, were there. Little Beatrice was there, hanging onto Annabelle's hand, her cheeks and her little pointed nose red from the cold. Elmer was there, of course, looking after Frank.

When they lowered the casket into the grave, tears poured from my eyes and froze on my face. I couldn't bear the thought of putting my poor child in the cold, cold ground.

Hazel must've known that. "Katherine is warm and safe in Heaven," she told me.

Then little Beatrice piped up and said something that touched my heart: "Don't worry, Aunt Bertha. You can count on us. We'll be here to look after you."

Such sweet things come out of the mouth of babes.

This morning, I woke up to silence in the house. The only thing I heard was the bitter January wind whistling outside my upstairs bedroom window. My mind wasn't playing tricks on me anymore. I knew my child was gone, and that she was never coming back to me.

I lay there thinking there was no reason to get out of bed. There was nothing to do. Nothing to live for.

Then I heard another sound, footsteps coming up the stairs. A few steps at a time, then stopping to rest. Then moving on up again.

And then, I heard Frank's voice from the bedroom doorway. "It's time to get up, Bertha. We have a day to face."

1942

There's another war going on in Europe, and they're sending our boys across the ocean to fight the Germans again. I guess Woodrow Wilson didn't know what he was talking about when he said we'd fought the war to end all wars.

A couple of years ago, Hazel's two boys, Walter and Ernest, had to register for the draft, just like Frank did back in his day. Ernest had his number called up a month ago. But when he went in to get his physical, they said he had a heart murmur and wasn't fit to go overseas and fight.

That seemed strange, because Ernest looks like a big strong fellow to me. But I'm glad he doesn't have to go. I wouldn't want to see Hazel being put through something like that.

I've heard it said there are some terrible things going on in Europe, what with the Jews being persecuted and killed. If Pa was alive, I know he'd be talking about it. He'd have a thing or two to say, I'm sure. But he's not with us anymore.

He passed away in the summer of 1938, half a year after we lost Katherine. I can't even tell you what it was like, losing two people I love one right after the other. I came close to the point of losing my faith, where I almost stopped believing in the goodness of God.

But after carrying bitterness around in my heart for a while, I realized that even when life loses all its joy, we have to try hard to look on the bright side of things. And we have to keep plodding on, making the best of what we have left until the Lord sees fit to call us home.

I take comfort in knowing that Pa lived a good long

life. He was an old man of eighty when he passed. There's never been a better man who walked the face of this earth, except for Jesus Christ himself.

Of course, Pa dying meant that the farm was left to Hazel and me. We decided there wasn't anything to do but to sell it. Frank and Walter got together with a real estate fellow to work out that whole business. They ended up getting a pretty good price for the farm.

So, Frank and I came into a little bit of extra money. We won't be living like rich folks, but we shouldn't have to worry too much about the years to come.

There's something else about money I should mention, something that happened even before we sold Ma and Pa's farm. A couple of months after Katherine passed away, we got a visit from a lawyer. I didn't know what to make of it when the man came to the door. I thought maybe we were in trouble or something.

Well, that lawyer sat down with Frank and me and told us that when Katherine had started teaching at the school in Indianapolis, she'd taken out a life insurance policy. And Frank and I were the ones set to benefit from it.

When he pulled out papers for us to sign, it hardly seemed real. After he left, Frank and I were so shook up that we had to sit there for a while to get our bearings.

I still can't get over how our precious Katherine took care of her parents, even in her death. You just have to marvel at something like that.

Frank had been fretting about all Katherine's doctor bills and hospital bills and the money we owed to the funeral home. He'd been saying it would take the rest of our lives to pay it all off. Well, we were able to use that life insurance money to pay off everything we owed, and we even had a little left over.

It's strange how different Frank's been since Katherine

died. He doesn't like being alone. Of an evening, he wants to make sure I'm sitting there in the front room with him. He doesn't like sleeping alone, either. Over and over, he asked me to stop sleeping upstairs. I finally gave in and started sharing the downstairs bedroom with him again.

Sometimes when we're sitting together, I can tell my husband is thinking back on his life, feeling sorry about the things he's done. It seems like when he sits still, the guilt and shame catch up with him.

It weighs down on him hard, but he doesn't know how to say anything about it. Sometimes when he looks at me, I think he's going to open his mouth and tell me something. But he never finds the words.

A couple of times, I've mentioned what Katherine said right before she passed away, that he shouldn't let anything trouble his heart. That helps him for a little while. But then it all comes back to him again.

He'll sit and watch me working in the kitchen, his eyes following me around. I think he's afraid he'll lose me, too. If I'm getting ready to walk out the back door, he'll say, "Where are you going?" Even if I'm just going out to feed the hens or to make a trip to the outhouse.

But at least he hasn't broken down like he did after the war. He's keeping up with his chores. It helps him to have Elmer around.

Frank hasn't had a drop to drink these past four years, not since Katherine passed away. As a matter of fact, he hasn't drunk anything since we first found out Katherine was sick. I'm proud of him for that.

Hazel and her daughter Annabelle come over to check on Frank and me from time to time. They always bring Beatrice with them. Beatrice is fourteen now. Even though she's just a little slip of a thing, she seems more grown up than other girls her age.

"We've come to see how you are, Aunt Bertha," she always says. Then she'll snuggle up to me and lay her head on my shoulder, and I can't help but put my arm around her and hold her tight. Even though my heart shut down after Katherine died, it's opened up enough to love little Beatrice. She belongs to Hazel, but I think of her as the granddaughter I never had.

We haven't seen much of Clover the past few years. What with Katherine dying, and then her older sister Violet passing away the following year, Clover doesn't have much strength left in her. She's turned over all the work at the mercantile to her manager, and I've heard talk that she's trying to sell the business.

But I'm telling you, Clover has always been one for surprises. One day a couple of months after Katherine died, she came driving up our lane in her Chevrolet. I went to the front window and watched her get out of the car. I saw her pull something out of the back seat. It was wrapped in a quilt, and was so big she could hardly handle it. And I thought, *what in the world is she up to?*

When I let her into the house, she set her bundle down on the sofa and said, "Bertha, I just couldn't keep this from you anymore. It needs to be in your home now."

Then she pulled away the quilt. And there was a picture somebody had painted, a portrait of Katherine when she was about seven years old. She was wearing a pretty dress Clover had given her. Her blonde curls were falling over her shoulders, and her little hands were folded on her lap just so. I tell you, seeing it gave me such a shock that I thought I was going to keel over.

Clover started talking really fast, explaining it all. "When Katherine was a little girl," she said, "I asked you if I could have my friend Mr. Elkins paint her portrait. You and Frank both said no. But the truth was, I'd already had him do the portrait before I even asked you. So, I had to keep it a secret from you. I had to keep the painting hidden away so you'd never see it when you came over. And I made Katherine promise not to tell you about it."

It took me a minute to think back on what had happened all those years ago, when Clover was all wrapped up with her friends from the artist colony in Nashville. I remembered how I'd put my foot down when she wanted to have Katherine's portrait painted, and how strange she'd acted after that. Putting two and two together, it all made sense.

"You're not upset with me, are you?" Clover asked.

"Of course not," I said. "How could I hold any of that against you now?"

"The painting should be yours," she said. "If you want it."

I took the painting in my two hands and looked at it real close. "Clover," I said, "I want this more than anything in the world. It will always be precious to me."

I put the picture down and hugged her and kissed her cheek. Then she left in a hurry, as if she'd had enough for one day. She didn't even stay around until Frank came in from the barn.

When Frank saw the picture sitting there on the sofa, he was so shocked that his face went white, and he had to sit down in his chair really quick. I told him everything Clover had said to me.

He must've sat there staring at the picture for half an hour, not saying a word. Then he asked me if I wanted him to hang it up. I said yes, so he pounded a nail in the wall, and we put it up right there in the front room.

But after a week of that, he said to me, "Bertha, I just can't abide having that picture there. Every time I look at it, my child's eyes are looking back at me. It's more than I can handle."

I had to agree with him. It was hard to look at our little girl all day long, having all that pain and sorrow stirred up over and over again. So, I tried to think where else in the house we could put the painting. I finally settled on putting it up in Katherine's old room, a place Frank never goes. I took the hammer upstairs myself and pounded in the nail, right above the head of Katherine's bed.

Now the painting's hanging there, where I can see it whenever I have it in my heart to go upstairs and visit my child. Her beautiful blue eyes are looking at me the moment I enter the room. She has a little smile on her face, as if she's welcoming me into her world.

Back in 1939, the government finally saw fit to bring electricity to the folks living out here in the country. It was done through a program called the REA.

Of course, Clover and Walter and Hazel have had electricity there in Nashville for so long I can't even remember when they got it. But getting electricity was really something for folks living in the rural parts of Brown County.

Truth be told, I wasn't keen on the idea at first. I hadn't been looking forward to anything new after losing Katherine and Pa. But Frank said we had to get on board with the idea. He said the county was making progress, and that we didn't want to be left behind.

In May or June of that year, some REA fellows started putting up poles on Helmsburg Road. Then they commenced to hanging wire between the poles.

Once when Frank and I were driving past where they were working, we stopped and watched for a little while. The men were climbing up and down the poles lickety-split, with the tree-climbing spurs on their boots. Watching them, Frank had a smile on his face. I figured he wished he was able-bodied enough to do the same thing.

Then the next thing those REA men did was to start wiring the homes of the people living on Helmsburg Road. They started on the south end of the road first.

I talked to Hannah Sawyer after their home was done. She mentioned how the men had tromped all over her house and drilled holes in the walls. I told Frank about it, saying I didn't want any part of such a thing, and that I'd just as soon leave our house the way it was.

But he said that, seeing as how we were getting older, having electricity would make our lives a little bit easier. I was pretty sure that if Pa was alive, he'd be saying the same thing. And I knew for certain Katherine would give me a talking to about keeping up with the times. That helped me make up my mind to go ahead with it.

So, a day or two later, the REA men came to our house. First, they put a meter box on the outside of the house. Frank told me it was something that would keep track of how much electricity we were using.

He was out there watching them all the while they were working. Then when they came inside the house, he followed them in and kept an eye on them. I was glad about that, because I had no idea what they might have it in their minds to do.

The men set up a fuse box in the mudroom. Then, they started going through the house like they did at the Sawyers' place, drilling holes and running wires through the different rooms. And I tell you, my nerves were so on edge that I could hardly stand it.

I'd mentioned to Frank ahead of time that I didn't want the men in Katherine's bedroom. I told him I was drawing the line at that.

There was a reason I said that. After Katherine died, I'd kept her room exactly the same as it had been when she was sick, with all her things sitting around the way she'd wanted them. I'd never allowed anyone to go in there for fear they'd ruin something. I sure wasn't going to have those REA men tromping around the room, making a mess of everything.

But Frank told me I was being silly, that if we were going to have the house wired for electricity, we needed to do the whole thing.

So, I let the men go on upstairs, but I followed them. I told them ahead of time I didn't want them to touch any of Katherine's belongings. Before I even let them into the room, I went in and took Katherine's picture off the wall and wrapped it in a blanket. I didn't want to take any chance of them ruining it. As a matter of fact, I didn't even want them laying eyes it.

Whenever the men said they needed to move something so they could do their work, I told them I'd move it myself. I had to take all the books off the bookshelves so that I could pull it away from the wall. The men stood there waiting on me, looking like they were running out of patience.

But when it came to moving the dresser, it was just too heavy for me. "We can do that, Ma'am," one of the men said. So, I had to let them.

I guess I barked at them a few times, and they looked at me like I was a mean old woman.

After the men finally left the house, I spent the rest of the day sweeping up the mess they'd left behind. The hard work helped to settle my nerves. Frank had gone outside, and I wasn't paying any mind to what he was doing.

But then he came in the back door. And wouldn't you know it, he was carrying two electric lamps, one in each hand. He had a big smile on his face. "I wanted to surprise you, Bertha," he said.

We took one of the lamps to the living room and plugged it into the electrical outlet the men had put in.

Then Frank flipped the switch on the lamp and the light came on, just like that. "We can turn this on in the evening," he said. "It'll be easier for you to see when you're doing your needlework."

We took the second lamp and set it up in our bedroom. Then Frank went out the back door again, and I thought, *What now?*

And of all things, he brought in an electric fan. "We can use this in the kitchen," he said. "It'll cool things down when you're doing your canning this summer. Or we can use it in the bedroom on a hot night."

I tell you, I was so touched that I wanted to throw my arms around my husband. But I didn't, because I didn't know how he'd take it.

The last thing I did that evening was to go up and clean Katherine's room. Then I put everything back exactly the way it had been.

Except for one thing. That pretty lamp she'd had on her desk at school had been in the closet. I took it out, set it on the dresser, and plugged it in. Then I flipped the switch, and the light filled the whole room. It shown on Katherine's face in the painting, making her look like a glowing angel.

As it turned out, we used some of our money from selling Pa's farm to buy a washing machine. It's set up out there in the mudroom. Then we got rid of the old icebox and bought a refrigerator. Both of those things run on electricity. And Frank was right. They do make an old woman's life a little bit easier.

A couple of evenings a week, I go upstairs to Katherine's room. I switch on that pretty lamp, and then I sit down in the rocking chair where I held her during her last days. I sit there in the light of the lamp, just looking around the room. Just remembering.

It often brings up tears, and I have to make sure I have a hankie with me. I don't tell Frank what I'm doing. He'd just tell me that if it makes me sad, I should stop going up there. That's a man's way of thinking.

But sitting in that room makes me feel peaceful, too. I know Katherine's dead and gone. I'm not fooling myself anymore. But sometimes, it seems like she's right there with me.

1945

After Katherine passed away, I started slacking off going to church. I'm ashamed to admit that. It just got to be too hard getting myself up and around on a Sunday morning, when all I wanted to do was to lie in bed and rest.

Besides that, all of us there at Oak Ridge were getting a little tired of Reverend Horton. He's a good man, but it seemed like he had only ten or twelve different sermons that he knew how to preach. When he'd get through one round of them, he'd go back to the beginning and start all over again. Truth be told, I lost interest in anything the man had to say.

This past spring, I heard people saying that Reverend Horton was leaving, moving out west somewhere, and that the church was bringing in some young man from Trafalgar to take his place. They were saying the new reverend had already moved to Helmsburg, and that he was just waiting to get started.

Well, hearing all that perked me up a little. I decided to get myself back to church to see what kind of preacher the new fellow would turn out to be.

One Saturday afternoon in May, Frank and I drove down to Nashville to see Clover. She's doing so poorly that we've been keeping a close eye on her. She sold her business two years ago. The person who bought her store tore it down and built another business on that spot. I think it hurt Clover to see that. Now, she talks about not having anything left to live for. That worries Frank and me.

On our way home from her house, we stopped by McDonald's grocery store in Beanblossom to pick up a few things. Frank went inside to get what we needed while I waited in the car. I was so wrapped up in my thoughts about Clover that I wasn't noticing much of anything around me. But when I glanced over at the car parked next to us, I was so startled that I almost yelped out loud.

It seemed as if there were a hundred eyes staring at me, the eyes of little children with their faces pressed to the window. I'd never seen so many children piled into one car before. They never stopped moving, squirming over the top of one another like a bunch of worms. A couple of faces would pop up in the window for a second or two, side by side or one above the other. Then they'd disappear, and others would take their places. They all stared at me with their mouths hanging open, except for the ones sucking on their thumbs.

From time to time, the tired-looking woman sitting up front would turn halfway around in her seat to swat at one of the kids. That was hard for her to do, seeing as she had a sleeping baby lying across her shoulder.

The poor thing would be about Katherine's age, I thought to myself. I couldn't imagine my daughter with such a passel of little ones.

I'm familiar with almost all the folks around here, the parents and their children. I knew for certain I'd never seen this family in these parts. Once a person had seen them, they'd never be able to forget them.

"Who are these people?" I asked Frank when he came back to the car with the groceries.

He shook his head. "I couldn't rightly tell you. But I did see a young man in the store who might be the father of this bunch."

He was getting ready to start the car, but I said, "Wait a minute. Let's see if he comes out."

Sure enough, a man who looked to be in his thirties came out of the store a minute later, carrying two paper bags heaped full of groceries. The children got excited when they saw him, and started hollering and bouncing up and down. The man put the bags in the trunk, then got into the driver's seat. The children were tapping him on the shoulder and leaning over the seat, trying to talk to him. I figured they were asking him what he'd bought, hoping for some goodies.

After we watched him drive away, Frank shook his head, as if he couldn't believe what he'd seen. "I hope all that commotion in the car doesn't get that poor fellow too rattled," he said. "I wouldn't want that family ending up in a wreck."

The next day was the Sunday the new preacher was supposed to give his first sermon.

Because I don't drive a car anymore, Frank takes me to church whenever I want to go on a Sunday morning. If the weather's nice, he'll go on into Helmsburg to pass the time, sitting with some of the other fellows on a bench outside the hardware store. Then he'll come back to get me when the service is over.

That Sunday, I made sure he got me there ahead of the crowd. I figured a lot of other people who'd been slacking off would show up at church again, just because they wanted to size up the new preacher.

I went up to sit on the second bench from the front on the righthand side. The preacher's family always sits on the front bench on that side. That's the way they do it at the Oak Ridge Church, and no one else would think to take that spot.

Just a minute after I sat down, a woman with a whole flock of children trailing behind her came to sit on the bench in front of me. I tell you, I couldn't believe my eyes. It was the same family Frank and I had seen in the car at the grocery store, just the day before.

I'd never known anyone around here to have so many

children, except for the Mitchell family. But I'd never seen all of them in one place at the same time. I tried to count the children, but I had a hard time of it because they kept bouncing around. The best I could come up with was nine, including the baby on the mother's lap.

While the other children were squirming and fussing with each other, one of the little girls, who looked to be about four, crawled under the bench and stayed there for the whole service.

I remembered how Katherine used to fall asleep under the bench at prayer meetings. But I could tell that with this little one, it was a different matter. She'd taken to crawling under the bench as a way of hiding from the rest of the family, with all their commotion and carrying on. She had her head buried in the crook of her arm, as if she was shutting out the whole world. It worried me some.

I thought about how I'd been able to devote all my attention to Katherine when she was growing up. I'd had more love to give her than she ever needed. *These children aren't getting enough of their mother's love,* I thought to myself. *Especially this little one. She's being overlooked. If somebody doesn't get this in hand, this child is going to end up as batty in the head as Irene Hawkins was after she lost her baby.*

When the service started, one of the deacons got up and introduced the new preacher, Reverend Edgar Willis, along with his wife Melba. Sure enough, it was the man Frank and I had seen at the grocery store, the one who'd driven away in the car with all the children in tow.

When he commenced to preaching, I wanted to listen. But I just couldn't take my mind off that pitiful little girl hiding under the bench.

I noticed that the three older girls in the family all had their hair done up in braids, the way I used to fix Katherine's hair. It looked like their mother had combed and braided all their hair that morning. But it seemed as if she hadn't gotten around to tending to the little one under the bench. Her braids were a mess, looking like they hadn't been touched in days.

After a while, the child turned her head a little bit to the side. I could see that her face hadn't been washed after her breakfast.

With one eye uncovered, she stared at my feet, like she was wondering who they belonged to. When she finally raised her eyes to look at my face, I smiled at her. That must've scared her. She buried her face again and kept it that way until church was over.

Even though I wasn't paying as much attention as I should've, I thought the new preacher gave a pretty good sermon. The way people were talking afterwards, it seemed like everybody was satisfied. While I was standing outside waiting for Frank to pick me up, I listened in on what a couple of men were saying to each other.

"I'd say he did a good job," one of them said. "He seems like a smart fellow."

"He must've worked on that sermon real hard," another man chimed in. "Even though from the looks of it, he spends all his time bothering his wife." Then the men all threw back their heads and laughed.

When Frank came to pick me up, I talked all the way home, telling him about the new preacher and his family. "I think the Lord is laying it on my heart to help these people," I said.

He gave me a strange look. "You never thought that way about the other preachers' families."

"I know," I said, "but this family is different."

From then on, I made a point of getting to church early, to make sure no one else took my seat on the bench behind the preacher's family. And just as regular as the sun comes up, that little girl crawled under the bench. As if she knew that was the only way she was going to get by.

After a few Sundays, it seemed like she was getting used to me being there on the bench behind her. It got to where she'd lie on her back and look up at me. Not smiling or anything. Just staring, like she was trying to figure out who I was. I'd take peppermint candies out of my purse and hold them out to her. The third Sunday of me doing that, she finally reached up a little hand and took the candy. Then she got scared, rolled onto her belly, and buried her face again.

Every Sunday morning, I looked forward to going to church, just so I could coax this bashful child into doing a little better. And all that time, the mother never even knew what was going on.

After Clover's mercantile shut down, Frank and I took to shopping at the five-and-dime store in Morgantown. One day when we were there, I came across a set of dollhouse furniture: a little kitchen table with two chairs, a sofa for the living room, a couple of beds with a dresser, and two tiny dolls to go with it all.

"Let's get this," I said to Frank.

He looked at me like I'd gone plumb out of my mind. "What on earth for?"

"For the preacher's little girl," I said. "The one I'm trying to make friends with."

Every Sunday, I'd been telling Frank about that poor child and what she'd done that day. He would always listen to what I had to say, and I could tell he felt almost as sorry for her as I did. So, he went along with me on the idea of buying the dollhouse furniture.

When we got home, I cut up one of my worn-out aprons and used the material to sew a little bag for the toy furniture. If I have to say so myself, the whole thing turned out pretty good. I was downright proud of what I'd done.

The next Sunday, I took the bag to church and held it out to the little girl. "It's for you," I whispered.

She reached out to take it. Then she buried her face.

But after a minute or so, she just couldn't help herself, and she raised up on her little elbows and looked inside the bag. Her eyes brightened up. And wouldn't you know it, she scooted out from under the bench and sat herself up on the floor by my feet.

One by one, she took the little pieces of furniture out of the bag and set them on the floor. The last things she took out were the dolls. She held them in her hands for a while, turning them over and looking at them from all sides. I could see how tickled she was with them.

Then she peeked up at me. I smiled and patted the bench, letting her know I wanted her to sit next to me. She looked away really quick.

After church was over, I made a point of letting Melba Willis know I'd given her little girl the bag of dollhouse furniture. I didn't want her to think the child had stolen it or something.

Mrs. Willis acted like she didn't know what to think. "You didn't need to do that," she said.

"I wanted to," I told her.

The next Sunday, I was so happy to see the little girl marching in with her family, holding that bag of toy furniture in her fist. She did like she'd always done, crawling under the bench first thing. But right away, she scooted on out the other side to sit on the floor by my feet. And this time when I patted the bench beside me, she came up to sit next to me.

All the while I should've been listening to her father's sermon, I sat there playing with that little girl. Piece by piece, she took all the furniture out of the bag and set it on the bench between us. Then we took turns moving the dolls from one place to another, from the beds to the sofa to the table. I made them hop up and down a little bit, like they were walking. She copied me and did the same thing.

The very best part of that whole morning was at the end of the service. “Time to put everything away,” I whispered to her.

As she stuffed the toys back into the bag, she looked up at me and smiled. It was the first time I’d ever seen that child smile. I tell you, that warmed this old woman’s heart in a way I can’t even describe.

“What’s your name?” I whispered to her.

She hung her head a little bit, like she was too bashful to talk. Then she whispered, “Lena,” so soft that I could hardly hear her.

That gave me a start, her having the same name as my mother. I had to think maybe it was a sign that I was doing right by singling this child out for special attention.

Lena and I kept on doing this from Sunday to Sunday, playing with the dollhouse furniture. Her mother didn’t seem to notice. She was too busy tending to her fussy baby and keeping her other children in line. Maybe Reverend Willis saw what we were doing from the pulpit. I don’t know.

It got to where Lena didn’t even bother to crawl under the bench. She’d follow her mother up to the front along with all her brothers and sisters, and then she’d come to sit next to me.

One Sunday, her mother happened to look around, and she saw her there with me. I could tell she was put out with the child. “Lena!” she whispered. “You get up here right now!”

Well, I wasn’t going to have her scolding the child for no good reason. I looked Mrs. Willis right in the eye and shook my head. "She's fine where she is," I whispered back. So, Mrs. Willis turned around and let us be.

One Sunday, I'd say around the end of July, Lena and I were sitting there playing with the toys. All of a sudden, she started picking them up and putting them back in the bag. Then she scooted herself close to me, laid her head against my arm, and popped her thumb in her mouth. Like she felt downright comfortable with me. I sat there dabbing at my eyes with my hankie, thinking this had to be one of the Lord's miracles.

As the weeks went past, I kept on talking to Frank about what was going on at church. It got to where if I didn't bring it up, he'd ask about it. I started getting the idea that he might want to come to church with me. But I knew he was waiting on me to invite him.

On the first Sunday morning in August, I noticed that he shaved and put on a clean shirt before he took me to church. When we pulled up to the building, I asked, "Do you want to come inside with me?"

He shrugged and said, "Sure. Why not?"

So, instead of letting me out and driving away, he went ahead and parked the car. When we were going inside, he gave a nervous laugh and said, "I hope the roof doesn't fall in when wicked old Frank Kelly walks through the door."

I could tell a lot of people were shocked to see Frank there with me. In all the years I'd been going to the Oak Ridge Church, he'd never once set foot inside it. It had almost been like I was a woman without a husband.

Frank wanted to sit in the back so as not to make a spectacle out of himself. But I told him we had to go up and sit behind the preacher's family, as that's where little Lena knew to find me.

Lena always sat on my left side. I had Frank sit to the right of me so she wouldn't think he'd taken her place.

Seeing Frank with me scared Lena a little bit. She stood there looking him over really good. Then she sat down beside me like she'd always done.

From then on, Frank came to church with me every Sunday. He never said why he all of a sudden wanted to start going, and I never asked him. I was just glad he was there.

Reverend Willis isn't one of those preachers who gives altar calls every Sunday. Just once a month or so, after an especially moving sermon. But at every one of those altar calls, two or three people go up front to get saved.

Truth be told, some people go up to the altar more than once, getting saved over and over again. I don't think that's necessary in the eyes of God. Maybe those folks think they've backslidden, but I'm pretty sure they just like the attention of getting prayed over and all.

One Sunday when Reverend Willis gave his altar call and we commenced to singing *Just as I Am*, Frank did something that shocked me. He reached over and took my hand and held it. Never in all the years we'd been married had he done such a thing.

And you know, I had the strangest feeling about it all. Something told me my husband didn't need to go up front and kneel down at the altar. The Lord was saving him right then and there.

People at the Oak Ridge Church have always had the habit of inviting the preacher's family over for Sunday dinner. It's their way of trying to get in good with the preacher. Myself, I was never one to do that because of Frank not being a church member. I was afraid the preacher would say something to Frank about him not coming to church, and that would get my husband riled up.

But it didn't seem like too many people were inviting the Willis family for dinner. That would be a tall order, seeing as how many children they have. And to tell you the truth, some of their little boys are downright ornery.

With me feeling like I needed to do something for the family, I thought maybe I should try having them over for Sunday dinner. But every which way I looked at it, I couldn't see how to work it out. Our kitchen table wasn't big enough for all eleven of them plus the two of us, and we didn't have enough chairs in the house for everyone to sit down. And I was afraid that when the grownups weren't looking, some of those children would be running up the stairs and having themselves a good time tearing up everything in Katherine's room. I knew if that happened, I'd never be able to forgive them.

After thinking it over for a while, I decided I could have the Willis family over for dessert: pie and coffee for the grownups and cookies and milk for the children. I invited them for the first Sunday afternoon in September, while it was still warm enough for the children to run and play in the yard. I don't know how happy Frank was about the idea, but he went along with it.

The first thing I did when the Willis family came over was to spread out an old blanket in the front yard, so the little ones could sit there and have their cookies.

When Lena saw me, she looked shocked, like she didn't expect to see me anywhere outside of church. I had to bend down and explain to her that this was where I lived.

The little ones gobbled up their cookies in short order, and then commenced to running around the yard. All of them were barefooted. The little girls' bare legs were full of chigger bites, some of them bloody from where they'd been scratching.

Frank decided he'd better stay outside to keep an eye on the children. He had Elmer with him. I figured that was a good idea, because if any of the kids got themselves into trouble, Frank would never be able to run after them.

I kept getting up and looking out the front window to see what was going on. Of course, the children found the fishpond right away. After Katherine died, Frank had made a point of keeping the pond stocked with carp, something he did in memory of her.

I wasn't sure how I felt about having all the little ones staring at Katherine's fish. Then it looked like one of the boys was getting ready to relieve himself in the pond, and I was fit to be tied. But Frank stopped him and had Elmer take him out back to the outhouse.

When I finally decided Frank and Elmer had everything in hand, I settled myself down and started talking with Reverend and Mrs. Willis. Then Reverend Willis got up and went outside with Frank, and his wife and I had a heart-to-heart talk.

I'd noticed at church that Melba Willis hardly ever smiled. To tell you the truth, I'd held that against her, thinking she was just a sourpuss. But when she started pouring out her heart to me, I changed my mind about her.

She told me how her own mother had died when she was only fourteen, and how she'd felt lost in life ever since then. She said that every night when she went to bed, she prayed for the strength to be a good mother to all her children, but that she knew she was falling short. Over and over, she said she wished her mother was alive so she could help out some.

All the while she was talking, she was crying off and on. She had her baby on her lap, and was trying to nurse him to keep him quiet. He kept on fussing, and it was a pitiful sight, mother and baby crying together.

Then Lena came in and stood beside her mother, like she wanted her attention. Or maybe she was just worried about the crying. Her mother was so caught up in her sorrow that she didn't notice her child. So, I took Lena on my lap.

"Lena, go outside and play," Mrs. Willis said.

"She's fine right here," I told her. "I hardly ever get the chance to hold a child on my lap."

When Mrs. Willis seemed like she was done talking, I decided it was time to tell her something about myself. I told her about how I'd had only one child, a daughter I'd loved so dearly, and how she'd died just a few years back. I told her how much I missed Katherine, every minute of every day.

Then the two of us sat there and shed a few tears together. I could feel a friendship growing between us. We would've said more to each other, but just about then, Reverend Willis brought in one of the other little girls who'd run into a tree and skinned her arm on the bark. She was bawling really hard, and Reverend Willis told his wife it was time for them to go.

Before I put Lena off my lap, she said to me, "Can we come back and see you again?"

And I said, "Of course you can." Even though I was all tuckered out from the ordeal and wasn't sure I had it in me to do it all over again.

Since then, I've had Frank take me over to Helmsburg to see Melba Willis a few times. We go when her older children are in school so she doesn't have so many underfoot. Her husband is always at work. Aside from being a preacher, Reverend Willis works as a carpenter. He surely couldn't raise that brood of children on the little bit the Oak Ridge Church pays him.

Frank never goes inside with me. He says he doesn't want to listen to two hens clucking. So, he sits in the car and waits on me.

I think he gets a kick out of seeing the little kids running and playing in the yard. They'll come to the car and climb on the running board and hang onto the open window. I think they want Frank to talk to them, but he hardly knows what to say to a child.

One day when I was visiting with Mrs. Willis, Lena came into the house with a big grin on her face. She pointed out the window to Frank sitting in his car and said, "He talked to me."

I thought I'd play along with her. "What did he say to you?"

"He said…he said…." She stammered a little bit, like she was trying to get it just right. "He said, 'Hi, Hon.'" She was so tickled about it that she could hardly stop giggling. Then she ran outside to play again.

I think my visits do Melba Willis some good. I never go without taking something for the family to eat, and I think she appreciates that.

I talk to her about taking care of the children, without making it sound like I don't think she's doing a good enough job. Mostly, I just tell her how I did things with Katherine, hoping she'll catch on to some new ideas.

Her little ones were running outside barefooted well into October, even after we'd had our first frost. Their little feet were always dirty, their soles so black I doubted if they could ever be scrubbed clean. I mentioned to Melba how I used to have Katherine wash her feet in a bucket of water every night before she went to bed.

"You could just put out one bucket of water," I told her, "and have the children line up and wash themselves one right after the other. It would go quick that way."

I got to where I couldn't stand seeing those children's bloody arms and legs from scratching at their chigger bites. So, one day I took over a bottle of calamine lotion. Starting with Lena, I rubbed the lotion on some of the worst bites. She told me it made her feel better. Then the other kids came around and wanted the same thing. Of course, I left the lotion there for Mrs. Willis to use.

One day in November when I was visiting, the little girls came in from playing outside, and their legs were blue from the cold. I thought about how I'd always kept Katherine in warm stockings during the winter.

When I got home, I went through some of Katherine's things that I'd put back, and I came up with a nice stack of stockings and bloomers. The next Sunday morning, I took them to church and gave them to Mrs. Willis for her little girls.

Truth be told, I had a hard time parting with those things. I felt a little selfish about it. I thought about taking along some of Katherine's dresses that she'd worn to Owl Creek School. But when it came down to it, I knew that seeing another little girl in one of my daughter's dresses would be more than I could bear. So, I put them away again.

This morning, I was standing at the front window watching the falling snow, thinking about that December day nine years ago when Clover came out in the storm to tell Frank and me about Katherine being sick.

And I thought about how the years keep on rolling by and everything keeps on changing. We've gone through another war. Thank the Lord, it's over and done with now. President Roosevelt died earlier this year. That was a shock for the country. And now, we have a new president, Harry Truman.

Life keeps moving on, whether we want it to or not. I'm not living the life I want. I'd give anything in the world to have Katherine back with me. But there's nothing to do but to keep on living the life I have.

1950

I am an orphan. I am childless. I am a widow.

I never imagined a day when I could say all those things about myself. Every morning when I wake up, I ask myself, "What kind of life is left for me now?"

Yes, I lost my husband. It was four months ago, in April of this year. He was only sixty-two. He never got to live to be an old man like Pa.

It all started with that tractor of his, the one his sisters bought him thirty years ago. I'd been telling him to get rid of it, because he wasn't using it for plowing anymore. He'd had sharecroppers working the cornfield for quite a few years. But every spring when it got warm, he'd get the notion to climb up on that tractor to see if he could get it started up again.

I'd always tell Frank he was too stiff and crippled to be climbing up and down on that thing. Of course, he'd always claim that he was fine. And I'd say, "You just make sure Elmer's there when you start messing around with that tractor."

Well, around the middle of this past April, Frank got up on a Monday morning feeling really good. After his breakfast, he stepped out onto the back porch for a few minutes. Then he came back in with a big smile on his face, saying it was going to be a fine day.

As he headed out to the barn with Elmer, I saw a twinkle in his eye that made me think he was up to some mischief. "Don't you be doing anything foolish," I called out after him.

He laughed at me. "Bertha, you're such a worrywart." And out the door he went.

As I cleared the breakfast things off the table and started washing up the dishes, I thought about what had happened the day before. Frank and I had gone to church together, and he'd even stayed with me for the pitch-in dinner after the service. We'd had such a nice time visiting with folks.

Thinking about all that, I couldn't help but smile. Life with my husband had never seemed so good.

But ten minutes after Frank walked out the back door, Elmer came tearing into the house with a wild look in his eyes. "Bertha, Bertha," he cried out. "You've got to come. Frank's done gone and hurt himself."

And all my good feelings came crashing down like an old barn hit by a strong wind.

I dropped my dishtowel and ran out the back door after Elmer. The first thing I saw was the tractor out there in the barnyard, with its engine running. When I got a few steps closer, I saw Frank lying on the ground beside the tractor. He had one leg bent under him in a way a leg shouldn't bend.

I ran to him and kneeled down at his side. His face was twisted in pain, and he looked like he was suffering something awful.

"What happened?" I asked Elmer.

He was so shook up that he could hardly get the words out of his mouth. "Frank got the tractor started and drove it around a little bit. Then he was going to give me a turn driving it. But he fell when he was trying to get down."

Then he started crying. "I tried to catch him, Bertha. But I couldn't. And now he's hurt himself really bad."

Frank looked like he was trying to say something. I couldn't hear him above the sound of the tractor engine. So, I bent down close to listen to him.

"I think something's broken, Bertha," he whispered. "I need to get to a doctor."

"Turn off the tractor," I said to Elmer. "Then stay here with Frank. Don't try to move him. You don't want to make matters worse."

Then, even though I was hardly familiar with driving it, I jumped into our car and raced down the road to the Sawyers' farm. I knew they were the closest neighbors with a telephone in their home.

When I told them what had happened, Hannah Sawyer went straight to the telephone and called the Columbus Hospital, asking them to send an ambulance for Frank. The hospital said they'd get right on it, and that one would be coming from Nashville. Then Mr. and Mrs. Sawyer came back to the house with me, and we all stayed with Frank until the ambulance got there.

I tell you, that was the longest fifteen minutes of my life. Frank went into shock from all the pain, and he started shivering really hard. I went to the house to get a blanket to cover him. I was so glad to hear the ambulance coming down the lane, because I just didn't know what else to do for my poor husband.

The ambulance men got Frank all loaded up on a stretcher. They knew how to move him really careful so as not to hurt him any. They told me I could ride along to the hospital with him.

Just as I was about to climb into the ambulance, Mr. Sawyer came up to talk to me. He had Elmer by the arm. Elmer's a man in his forties now, but he was crying like a little child.

"I'll be rounding up some of the neighbors," Mr. Sawyer said. "Between all of us and Elmer, we'll take care of the farm for you. So, don't worry about anything. Just tend to your husband. From the looks of things, it'll be a while before Frank's up and around again."

I was glad he said that. I'd been so beside myself with worrying about Frank that I hadn't given any thought as to how the chores would get done. It's really something how folks around here look out for each other.

When the ambulance arrived at Columbus Hospital, they rushed Frank off to get x-rays. It wasn't long before the doctor came to tell me that my husband was going to have to stay in the hospital for a while. He said Frank had broken bones in one leg, one arm, and in his pelvis. More than that, he said it looked like Frank had suffered a small stroke. He told me that was probably what made him fall off the tractor in the first place.

I guess the Sawyers must've thought to get ahold of my sister. Because after I'd been at the hospital with Frank for about an hour, Hazel and Walter showed up, along with Annabelle and Beatrice.

Not long after that, Reverend Willis came. Even though he has a lot of problems in his own family, I can tell he's truly a man of God. He held my hand and prayed with me, so earnest that I knew for sure God was hearing him.

Beatrice ended up being the one who drove me back and forth to the hospital over the next few days. She said she'd stay the night with me at the house if I wanted her to. I told her no, that I'd be fine, seeing as how the neighbor men were taking care of the chores.

To tell you the truth, I was afraid she'd be poking around the house, telling me she didn't like this or that about the way I was living. She's just twenty-two, but she's starting to act like an old busybody.

But she's got a good heart, and she made sure I had the chance to sit at my husband's bedside every day.

Hour after hour, I sat there with Frank, feeling brokenhearted over the way he was suffering. He looked so weak and frail, thin as a rail. I couldn't help but remember the fine-looking man he'd been in his youth. How whenever he'd come around to talk to Pa, I couldn't take my eyes off him. How just being near him had made me weak in the knees. I had to think how cruel time is, with what it does to a person.

I couldn't let my mind wander ahead to what might be in store for Frank and me. I knew things would never be the same again, but I couldn't let myself dwell on that. I tried to follow what Reverend Willis told me to do, to trust the Lord to carry me through one day at a time.

Frank barely had the strength to say anything, and I didn't expect him to. His body was hurting all over. The hospital had him on morphine, the same thing Dr. Groves had given Katherine in her last weeks. It made him so sleepy that the nurses could hardly wake him up to take any food.

So, on the third day he was there, I was surprised when he opened his eyes and turned his head to look at me. "Bertha," he whispered.

"I'm here, Frank," I told him.

"I need to tell you something," he said. "Before it's too late."

So, I pulled my chair close and bent down to listen.

"I know you won't believe this," he said, "but I've always loved you. I should've made a point of telling you that. I should've told you every day. But I was selfish, caught up in my wicked ways."

"It's okay, Frank," I said. "Hush now. Save your strength."

But he kept on talking. "Even though I made your life miserable, you never stopped being a good wife to me. I know you despised me sometimes, and for good reason. But you never turned your back on me. I've never deserved you, Bertha."

I tell you, I never expected to hear such words coming out of my husband's mouth. Tears poured down my face like a waterfall. I took his hand and held it in both of mine.

"Let's just love each other now, Frank," I said, crying so hard I could hardly talk. "That's what counts."

For the next two days, I kept on holding that hand. I never wanted to let it go. Every once in a while, Frank would find the strength to squeeze my hand a little, to let me know he appreciated me being there.

And it seemed as if all the love we should've shared throughout the years of our marriage passed between us those last few days of my husband's life. It was such a beautiful thing. I was completely overcome by it.

When I got to the hospital on the fifth day, the doctor was in Frank's room. He stood there blocking the way to Frank's bed. I could tell he wanted to talk with me before I saw my husband. By the look on his face, I knew things weren't good.

"Mrs. Kelly," he said, "your husband had another stroke during the night. A massive stroke. He's not going to come out of this."

I couldn't quite take in his words. "What does this mean?" I asked him.

"There's nothing more we can do for him," he said. "He won't last long. Not more than a day or two."

Then the doctor stepped aside and let me go to my husband's bedside. Frank's breathing was labored, like Katherine's had been at the end. I knew it was a sign that death was waiting just around the corner. I picked up his hand. It was limp, as if the life had already gone out of it.

It might be strange to say this, but I wasn't surprised. In the last few days, Frank and I had both known he'd come to the end, even though we hadn't said it in those terms. I took comfort in knowing that we'd made our peace with each other.

All that day, I sat there at Frank's bedside holding his

hand. When nighttime came, the nurses didn't tell me to go home. They knew I'd made up my mind to stay right there until my husband passed away.

As the hours went by, I got so tired that I could hardly hold my head up. So, I scooted my chair to where I could rest my head on the edge of the bed. But I kept holding on to Frank's hand.

I must've dozed off a little, because all of a sudden, I was awakened by a jolt of something passing through me. And I knew without even sitting up and looking that Frank was gone. His spirit had passed through me on its way to Heaven.

A minute later, a nurse came in, doing her midnight rounds. She put her fingers on Frank's wrist to check his pulse. "Mrs. Kelly," she said, "your husband has died."

"I know," I said.

They let me stay there in the room with Frank's body for a few hours. Early in the morning, someone called Reverend Willis, and he came to sit with me.

"Mrs. Kelly," he said, "you can take comfort in knowing that your husband was a saved man, and that God called him home to Heaven."

I wondered if anyone had ever told Reverend Willis about the ungodly life Frank had lived before he got himself straightened around. "Here's what I believe," I told him. "The Lord loves us all, the good and the bad. In the end, he takes all of us home to be with him."

I thought Reverend Willis might argue against that, but he nodded like he agreed with me. "God loves all his children," he said. "Even his wayward children. He does everything he can to bring his sheep back into the fold."

We sat there in silence for a while, just looking at Frank's body lying there so peacefully. All of a sudden, I had the notion to tell Reverend Willis about Frank's spirit passing through me on its way to Heaven. Then I thought better of it. I was afraid he'd think I was getting into some wrong ideas. Or that maybe I was touched in the head. I decided to keep what happened to myself.

About an hour later, Hazel and Annabelle and Beatrice came to comfort me. No one came from Frank's side of the family. All his sisters had been gone for years, except for Clover, and she'd been too sick to even get out of bed.

Finally, some hospital fellows came to get Frank's body and take it down to the morgue. Then Bond's Funeral Home came to get it. I've gotten used to how they do things when somebody dies.

As we were getting ready to leave the hospital, Hazel said, "Bertha, I want you to come stay with me for a few days. At least until you get your bearings again."

"No," I said, "I think it's best that I go back to my own home."

I wasn't sure why I felt that way. But when Beatrice drove me up to the house, I suddenly knew. Because there on the front porch steps was Elmer Mitchell. Just sitting there looking so lost and pitiful, like he didn't know what to do with himself. Like he was waiting for Frank to come home so everything would be all right again.

"Elmer," I said to him, "come inside with me."

He followed me into the house, and I sat him down on the sofa. "I have to tell you something," I said. "Frank passed away last night."

He looked at me with big scared eyes. "You mean he's dead? Frank's dead and gone?"

"Yes, Elmer," I said. "Frank's dead. He's never coming back."

And that big fellow busted out bawling like his heart was broken into a million pieces. Like a little boy who'd lost the pa he'd loved so dearly. I didn't know what to do except to put my arms around him and hold him for a while. Rocking him and patting him, like he was a baby needing his mother's comfort.

Right then and there, I knew that however hard it might be, I was going to get on with my life without Frank. But I wasn't so sure about Elmer. I knew that poor fellow would never be the same again.

For the next couple of days, Mr. Sawyer and the other neighbor men kept on coming to do the chores. I'd look out the back door and see Elmer there, stumbling around like he didn't know what to do, wiping his tears on his shirt sleeve.

One morning, Mr. Sawyer came to the back door, and I went to talk with him. "We're sending Elmer home," he said. "It's just too hard on him to be here."

We had such a nice funeral service for Frank at the Oak Ridge Church. A lot of people were there. That did my heart good. I don't think as many would've shown up if Frank hadn't started coming to church in his last years.

We laid him to rest out there in the graveyard next to Katherine. It felt right to have the two of them together.

Elmer's ma and pa were good enough to bring him to the graveside service. They knew how much he'd looked up to Frank. But he left them and wandered over to where I was standing, like he knew that's where he belonged. I reached out and took his hand, as if he was my own son.

When the men started shoveling dirt on the casket, Elmer cried out, "Oh no!" Like having Frank covered up meant for sure he was dead.

Then he said, "Frank was the best man I ever knew."

He meant that from the bottom of his heart. Frank may not have always measured up to who he should've been. But he surely did a righteous thing when he gave that poor dimwitted Mitchell boy the love and attention he needed.

Otherwise, Elmer would've gone his whole life without being cared for.

A week after the funeral, Hazel and Annabelle and Beatrice came to the house to talk things over with me. Beatrice had just gotten engaged to marry a fellow from Nashville. It's hard to believe how fast she's grown up.

And that girl is smart as a whip. So, she was the one taking charge. She wrote down everything that we said, like she wanted to make sure we got everything tended to.

Right off the bat, they all told me I should put the farm up for sale and move in with Hazel and Walter.

"No," I said, "I'm not ready for that. I'm fine right where I am."

"Who's going to do the work on the farm?" they asked.

"Frank's already had sharecroppers working the land," I told them. "I'll just keep on doing that."

"And how about the cows?" they asked. "How could you keep up with the milking at your age?"

We ended up going around and around on that idea. They wanted me to sell all the cows. I said I should at least keep one, just for the milk I drink. But Beatrice wasn't going to have that.

"Aunt Bertha," she said, "keeping one cow would mean you'd have to keep up the barn and the milk house. That's too much for you. You can buy all the milk you need from the grocery store."

That's like her, always pushing me to take on modern ways. Even though I love that girl to death, she sure does get under my skin sometimes.

I didn't even bother to argue with them about selling the hogs. But when it came to the chickens, I put my foot down.

"I want to keep the henhouse going," I said. "I've taken care of chickens ever since I was a young girl. I'm able-bodied enough to keep on doing that. I'd still like to have a few eggs to sell. People around here count on me for that."

The three of them agreed to that, even though they didn't like the idea.

Just before they left, Beatrice said, "Here's something I insist on. It's high time you get a telephone in this house. With you being on your own, it isn't safe to live without one anymore. If something comes up, you have to be able to call somebody for help."

I opened my mouth to tell her I didn't need a telephone, but she said, "Don't argue with me, Aunt Bertha. My fiancé works for the telephone company. I'll have him come over and get you all set up."

So, my life keeps on changing, whether I want it to or not. All the animals are gone now, except for the chickens. The barnyard seems awfully quiet without the cows mooing and the hogs grunting and snorting. That takes some getting used to.

I had the neighbor men haul the tractor away. I don't know who ended up with it. I don't care. I just didn't want to have it around bringing up memories of Frank's accident.

I sold the car, too. At first, Beatrice tried to make me get a driver's license so I could drive myself anywhere I wanted to go. I wasn't going to have that.

She gave in and said, "Well, I'm not sure you'd be safe driving on the highway anyway."

In the end, I had to agree with her about the telephone. It sure is nice to have it the house. Even though at first the sound of it ringing scared the living daylights out of me.

That telephone keeps me from getting too lonely. I can call my sister Hazel any time I want to, just for a chat. Or one of the ladies from church.

Mrs. Willis calls me from time to time. Even Lena gets on the telephone and says a few words to me. That always puts a smile on my face.

I'm ashamed to say this, but I've become a regular busybody. Especially in the evening when I don't know what to do with myself, I pick up the telephone and listen in on what the others on the party line are talking about. You wouldn't believe some of the things going on in people's lives. Sometimes when I'm listening, I have to bite my tongue to keep from giving those folks a piece of my mind.

All in all, I'm feeling blessed to be able to stay here at the farmhouse. Everything around me reminds me of the life I lived with my husband and child. It keeps them close to me.

Clover died just a month after Frank passed. She'd been so weak that she hadn't even been able to make it to her brother's funeral. She'd been having heart problems for years. Then she came down with pneumonia, and that was that.

My family didn't understand how much Clover had meant to me. So, I only got to see my dear sister-in-law one time after Frank died. I had to twist Beatrice's arm a little bit to get her to drive me to Clover's house.

When I walked into Clover's pretty little bedroom, she looked so sweet with her head lying on her lacey pillowcase and her beautiful bedspread pulled up around her shoulders. It looked like her housekeeper had been taking real good care of her. I was glad about that.

There was so much Clover and I could've said to each other. It would've taken hours to go over everything. But she barely had the strength to breathe, let alone talk. All she could do was smile at me. I could see in her big blue eyes that she was thinking about all the years we'd been close. All the joys and sorrows the two of us had been through together.

"I love you, sister," I kept saying.

On the way back home, I bawled my heart out. Beatrice hardly knew what to do with me.

Just a couple of days later, I heard that Clover had passed away. Her nieces and nephews were the only ones left to plan her funeral. None of them thought to ask me if I wanted to go. I guess it would've been too much to expect anybody to come all the way over to Helmsburg to pick me up and take me to Bloomington. So, I had to pay my respects to my sister-in-law in my own heart.

The evening after I knew they'd had Clover's funeral, I went upstairs to Katherine's room to have a little talk with my child.

"Sweetheart," I said, "your papa and Clover have come up there to be with you. Look after them for me. You already know Heaven's ways. You'll need to show them the ropes."

To tell you the truth, I was a little angry with God for taking Frank and Clover and leaving me behind. I was downright jealous of them for getting to be with my precious Katherine. While here I was, still having to put up with a hard life on this earth.

When I get a little down in the mouth, those thoughts always come to my mind. I mentioned something like that to Beatrice this morning when she came over to check on me.

She acted shocked. "We still need you here, Aunt Bertha," she said.

So, I suppose it's God's will to have me here a little while longer.

1951

Here it is, more than a year since my husband passed away, and I'm getting by. It's really something how other folks have shored me up during my time of need.

Reverend and Mrs. Willis have been keeping an eye on me. Every couple of weeks, Melba Willis comes over just to sit and chat.

She leaves her husband at home with the children, except for Lena. That little one always insists on coming along. She likes being helpful. If I'm washing dishes, she'll pick up a towel and dry them. Or she'll help me bring clothes in off the line.

I always send a dozen eggs home with them. I'm glad I'm able to do that.

This summer, Reverend Willis has been sending his older boys over to mow my yard. That has taken a load off my shoulders. Even though their father expects them to do it out of the goodness of their hearts, I always slip a quarter into their hands before they leave.

Last fall, the Willis boys and a couple other young men from church made sure I had enough firewood chopped and stacked to keep my stove going through the winter. I was mighty thankful for that.

Elmer Mitchell used to be the one to chop firewood for Frank and me. That big strong man could split up a log in no time flat. But I haven't seen Elmer in a long while. I guess his ma and pa got tired of having him around, and they sent him off to live on his brother's farm out east of Beanblossom. I sure do miss that fellow.

This past spring, Mr. Sawyer came up to till my vegetable garden. So, I was still able to grow lettuce, beans, peas, cucumbers, squash, and potatoes. I had enough to eat and plenty to give away. But I don't know how long I'll be able to keep that up.

I don't go much of anywhere, so I don't miss having a car. People from church take turns stopping by to pick me up for the Sunday morning service or Wednesday evening prayer meeting. Every couple of weeks, Beatrice drives me to the grocery store.

Since I turned sixty-five this year, Beatrice helped me sign up for Social Security. That's something they started up years ago when Franklin D. Roosevelt was our president. It brings me in some money every month. Because my husband was a wounded war veteran, I get a little bit of money for that, too.

Beatrice is so smart about those things. She always seems to know what I need to do next.

She still doesn't like the idea of me living alone out here in the country. Whenever she hears these old walls creaking or the wind rattling the windows, she says it's spooky. She teases me about living in a haunted house, even though she doesn't believe in that sort of thing.

Every time Hazel's family has a get-together, one of her boys picks me up and takes me down to Nashville so I can be a part of it. Like when Beatrice had her wedding last year.

It seems like every time the family gets together, Hazel's sons and grandsons get out their banjos and guitars and start playing their bluegrass music. People say Walter Jr. is one of the best banjo pickers in Brown County. All the younger banjo players look up to him and try to learn something from him. He has a good singing voice, too.

Come a Saturday night, he's playing and singing over there at the jamboree in Beanblossom. The family likes to go there to hear him. Every now and then, they ask me whether I want to go along. I always say no. I wouldn't know what to do with myself in a place like that.

But I sure do like to hear Walter and all the younger fellows in the family picking and singing when we have a get-together. They play tunes like *Mule Skinner Blues* and *Foggy Mountain Breakdown,* their fingers just flying on those strings. Then they start singing that sweet song, *You Are My Sunshine.* I just sit back and close my eyes and listen, and it takes this old woman to Heaven for a little bit.

When they start wrapping things up, I ask them to end the evening with my favorite gospel song, *Oh Come Angel Band.* Actually, it's gotten to where I don't even have to ask. They just do it for their Aunt Bertha. The song's such a comfort to me. It reminds me that it won't be too many more years before the angels come to take me home.

I have to bring up something that makes me feel a little ashamed. It's kind of funny, though, depending on how you look at it.

After we buried Frank in April of last year, we were just leaving the graveyard when Mrs. Walton from the Oakridge Church took me aside. I thought she wanted to offer me some kind words. But that wasn't it at all.

"Bertha," she said, "I need to warn you about something. In a couple of weeks, you're going to be hearing from Hezekiah Hawkins. Sure as can be, he'll start coming around to see you. And he won't leave you alone until you get real cross with him."

Then she went on to say more. "Every time a woman around here loses her husband, Hezekiah starts bothering her, trying to see if he can get anywhere with her. After my sister's husband died, Hezekiah made a pest out of himself, and she had a terrible time getting rid of him. I'm just telling you this so that when he starts up his foolishness with you, you can nip it in the bud."

I knew Mrs. Walton meant well in telling me all that. But I was a little put out with her, bringing up something like that the same day I laid my husband to rest.

Hezekiah Hawkins is the brother of Zebadiah Hawkins. Zebadiah's been gone a long time. He drank himself to death. Hezekiah's never had a problem with the liquor. I'll give him that. But he's always been a little off in the head, and the women around here have never taken a liking to him.

Any man can be aggravating, but Hezekiah Hawkins has them all beat. He's always wanted a wife. But after a woman's been around him for five minutes, she's done had her fill of him. No woman in her right mind would want to take him on for a lifetime.

But Hezekiah's never stopped trying. Since he's an old man now, too old to go after the young girls, he's trying out his luck with the widow ladies.

So, on top of being sorrowful, I walked away from my husband's grave feeling a little shook up. As Beatrice drove me home, I prayed to God that Hezekiah Hawkins wouldn't show up on my doorstep any time soon.

I knew I never wanted to go through troublesome times with another man. Not after all I'd been through with Frank. It had taken the two of us a lifetime of marriage to get to where we could be at peace with each other.

Nope, I said to myself, *I'm not having another man in my life.*

When I walked into my quiet home filled with memories of my husband and child, I said, "Another man could never belong in this house." I said it good and loud, for God and the whole world to hear.

Then, I put the matter out of my mind. Lord knows I had plenty of other business to take care of, figuring out the life of a widow lady. A whole year went by, and I never had another thought about Hezekiah Hawkins.

Then one afternoon this past spring, I heard a knock on my front door. When I went to answer it, I couldn't believe who I found standing there. As a matter of fact, I was so shocked that I almost shut the door in Hezekiah Hawkins' face.

But I didn't. I was raised with better manners than that. I just stood there for a minute taking a good look at the tall, skinny, scraggly-haired fellow.

He had a bouquet of fresh violets in one hand. He held it out to me like a little boy bringing wildflowers to his mama. I could tell he meant it to be sweet.

But I knew full well where those violets had come from. There's a big patch under the tree in the front yard that comes up every spring. He'd been out in my yard picking them before he came to the door. The thought of that made my skin crawl. I wondered how many other times he'd been wandering around my property without me knowing it.

Right then and there, I should've told Hezekiah Hawkins to go away and never come back. Make it plain and simple like that, so he'd know for sure I wasn't interested in him.

I guess I don't have it in me to be that hurtful to people. The poor man looked so earnest. Before I thought better of it, I thanked him for the flowers, and then let him come into the house to talk with me for a few minutes.

Oh boy, I shouldn't have done that. Frank was never much of a talker, and I'd gotten used to that. But the minute Hezekiah Hawkins sat his hind end down on one of my kitchen chairs, he opened his mouth and talked and talked until I thought I was going to lose my mind.

I can't even tell you what he talked about. The man could run off at the mouth from morning till night, and at the end of the day, he wouldn't have said anything worth repeating.

I kept trying to tell him I was busy, that I had things to do. But I could hardly get a word in edgewise.

After a couple of hours of that, I told him I needed to start supper, hoping he'd get the hint and go on home. But his eyes lit up, and I knew right away that he took what I said as me inviting him to stay for supper.

I told him I didn't have a lot on hand to fix. He patted his stomach and said, "That's okay. I'm not a big eater."

I tell you, I was ready to throw up my hands. I knew that man had a head full of sawdust, and that he never picked up on what anybody tried to tell him.

So, he stayed right there and watched while I boiled up and mashed some potatoes and took a little leftover ham out of the refrigerator. When we sat down to eat, I hated seeing him there in Frank's chair across the table from me.

All through supper, he smiled and smiled at me. He got a little bit of gravy on his chin that he didn't think to wipe off, and I didn't figure it was in my place to tell him about it. He just kept on smiling at me, his face shining with the grease. I could hardly look at him.

Finally, when I started clearing the dishes off the table, Hezekiah pushed back his chair and said, "I guess I ought to be heading for home now." After he was gone, I knew I was never going to put up with anything like that again.

But I guess me fixing supper for him gave Hezekiah the wrong idea. Because after that, he started driving to my house three or four times a week. It got to where I dreaded it something awful. I'd always be listening for the sound of his old rattletrap, so I could think really quick what to do to get out of visiting with him.

At first, I'd answer his knock on the door and tell him I was too busy with this or that and didn't have time to talk. He didn't seem to get the hint. He'd just come back the next day.

Then I took to not answering the door at all. I'd be really quiet, hoping he'd think I wasn't at home. That worked a couple of times. He'd stand there knocking and knocking, and all the while, and I'd be holding my breath. Finally, I'd hear him say, "I guess you're not home again." And then he'd leave.

When I'd hear his old car starting up and rattling down the lane, I'd feel like I could get on with my day.

That way of doing things didn't work for long. Because when I wouldn't come to answer the door, he took to opening it and walking right on into the house to look for me. I'd be standing there doing up the dishes, and all of a sudden, I'd hear footsteps in the kitchen. And I'd just about jump out of my skin.

"I know you're getting a little deaf, Bertha," he'd say. "You didn't hear me knock."

I tell you, the whole thing ruined my summer. It got to where I didn't want to get up in the morning, not knowing what I'd have to face if Hezekiah Hawkins showed up.

One morning last week, I was hanging the wash out on the clothesline. I was thinking about the bushel basket of apples one of the Willis boys had picked off my trees, and how I needed to cut them up and cook them down for apple-butter before they went bad.

So, I didn't hear Hezekiah coming. He must've walked through the house and out the back door, because all of a sudden, his face popped up on the other side of the sheet I was hanging up. It scared me so bad that I screamed.

That tickled him, and he laughed and laughed. The more he laughed, the madder I got. I told him I was too busy for games, and that he needed to go home.

But he wasn't about to let up. He kept ducking down and then popping up above the towels I was hanging up, like somebody playing peek-a-boo with a baby. I kept saying, "Hezekiah, get out of here." When that didn't work, I stopped saying anything at all, hoping he'd get tired of his nonsense and go away.

After I got done with the wash, he followed me back to the house. I made a point of shutting the back door in his face, but he opened it and came right on it.

I brought the basket of apples from the mudroom into the kitchen and sat down at the table to start cutting them up. He sat down to watch me. I still wasn't saying a word to him. I was acting like he wasn't even there.

I set my knife down for a minute while I went to empty my bowl of cut-up apples into the big pot on the stove. When I came back to the table, my knife was gone. I looked for it everywhere, even on the floor to see if I'd dropped it.

All the while, Hezekiah sat there with a stupid grin on his face. And I knew he'd taken it and hidden it from me.

"Hezekiah, what did you do with my knife?" I hollered at him.

He pulled his hand out from behind his back and laid the knife on the table. "I just figured a woman in an ugly mood shouldn't have a knife in her hand," he said.

I tell you, that did it. I blew my top. "Hezekiah Hawkins," I yelled, waving the knife around, "you've done gotten on my last nerve. You'd better get out of here, and don't even think about coming back. As far as I'm concerned, I never want to see your face again."

I wasn't proud of how I said all of that. But the man had pushed me to a point where I lost control of myself.

He sat there staring at me for a minute. Then he reached out across the table and put his hand on my arm. "Bertha," he said, "I know in your heart you don't really mean that."

"Hezekiah Hawkins," I bellowed, so loud the

neighbors a mile down the road must've heard me. "If you know what's good for you, you'll never touch me again!"

He pulled his hand back like he'd touched a hot stove. Then he got up and walked out of the kitchen to the front the door, muttering to himself. "My pa always said that if a man wants to be with a woman, he's going to have to put up with her bad temper from time to time."

And I tell you, it took everything in me to keep myself from snatching my cast-iron skillet off the stove, running up behind him, and whacking him in the head with it.

Last Sunday at church, just a few days after I'd chased Hezekiah Hawkins out of my house, a couple of women came up to me with big grins on their faces. They told me they'd heard Hezekiah was courting me.

I was fit to be tied. "I don't know where you heard that nonsense," I told them. "I wouldn't put up with that man for half a minute."

As soon as I got home, I got on the telephone with Hazel and told her everything that had happened. That afternoon, she and Annabelle and Beatrice came over to talk things through with me.

First of all, they had to laugh at me and tease me something awful. But in the end, Beatrice got serious and said she didn't want some old fool taking advantage of me. "He's trying to get his hands on that little bit of money you've got put back," she said. "Next time he comes around, you need to send him right back out that door."

She looked at me real stern. "If he doesn't listen to you, just give me a call. I'll come right over and give him a tongue-lashing he'll remember for the rest of his life."

She went on to say that it was high time I got locks on my doors, and that she'd send her husband over to put them on.

"I don't think that'll be necessary," I said to her.

"After the way I told Hezekiah off a couple of days ago, I doubt that he'll have the nerve to step foot on this property again."

But I was wrong. This morning, I was on my hands and knees scrubbing the kitchen floor when I heard a knock on the front door. I'm not one for cussing, but a few words flew out of my mouth that I knew I'd have to repent for later. I stayed right where I was, crouched down like a wild rabbit trying to hide from a hunter, praying that Hezekiah Hawkins would give up and go away.

Then I heard the door open, and I knew he was going to walk all over the house trying to find me. My first thought was to get out the back door.

I don't jump up to my feet so quick these days, so I had to crawl all the way over to the doorframe so I could hang onto it and pull myself up. Then I ran through the mudroom and out onto the back porch.

I could hear Hezekiah's footsteps creaking on the kitchen floor. It aggravated me to think he was tracking his dirty boots over the part I'd just scrubbed. But that was the least of my worries.

"Bertha," I heard him call out. "Where are you, Bertha? I know you're around here somewhere, because you've just been washing the floor."

I had to think really quick about what I was going to do next. I wanted to run out to the barn to hide. But I knew Hezekiah would be out the back door in half a minute, and that he'd see me and come after me.

Then my eyes fell on the root cellar just a few steps away from the house. I ran to it, slid open the door, and climbed down inside. I was just sliding the door back into place when I heard Hezekiah come out onto the back porch. I kept the door open just a crack so I could keep track of what he was doing.

"Bertha, Bertha," he kept calling. "Are you in the barn? What are you doing out there?" I heard him walk right past me out to the barnyard. It struck me so funny that I almost gave myself away by giggling.

But I tried my best to keep still. A couple of minutes later, I heard Hezekiah coming back toward the house, still calling for me. I knew he stopped to check the henhouse, because all of a sudden, I heard the hens squawking and clucking like somebody was bothering them.

Then I heard him call, "Bertha, are you in the outhouse?" And I just about doubled over laughing. Because even though I knew how shameful that would be, a man checking up on a woman in the outhouse, I couldn't help but imagine what his face would look like if he opened the outhouse door and found me sitting there doing my business.

The whole thing was so comical. Me, a woman of sixty-five, playing a child's game of hide-and-seek with a man who was making a pest out of himself. I bit my lip hard to stifle myself, but I still couldn't keep quiet. So, I had to clap a hand over my mouth. Because I surely didn't know what I'd do if Hezekiah Hawkins heard me laughing and slid open the cellar door.

My sides were about to bust from all the laughter I was holding in. It struck me that even in the middle of hardship and aggravation, life can bring you something so silly that you can't help but have a little fun over it.

Hezekiah walked right past the root cellar, saying, "Well, I guess you're not here, Bertha. Your niece must've come to take you to the store. You're getting a little forgetful. You left your bucket of mop water right there in the middle of the kitchen floor."

I heard the back door slam as he walked into the house. Then half a minute later, I heard the front door slam. And then I heard his old rattletrap start up and drive away.

I came up out of that root cellar like someone rising from the grave. I looked around taking everything in, my heart feeling lighter than it had in a year, my eyes seeing things they hadn't noticed in a long time.

And then I spotted the rosebush Rose Kelly had planted next to the cellar door. Back in her day, she'd planted flowers anywhere she could find a little bit of dirt to turn over.

I'd been wanting to get rid of that rosebush for years, because every time I'd go down into the root cellar, I'd snag my dress on the thorns. The Willis boys had run over that rosebush with their lawnmower a dozen times. And it had just kept coming back up. Several times, I'd taken a shovel to it, trying to dig the old thing up by the roots. But I never could get it all.

Here it was, late September, and all the leaves on the bush were blackened and falling off. But there on one scraggly branch was a single red rosebud, blooming out of season. It was just starting to open, so lovely and fresh. I had to stand there for a few minutes, just taking in the beauty of it.

And it came to me that even late in a person's life, when it seems like everything is over and done with, a little bit of beauty can still come. Even after someone has lost her parents and her husband and her child, something lovely and new might still show up.

1960

I've never been a sickly person. But there was a day a couple of months ago when I came down with a real bad headache, the worst I'd ever had in my whole life. I tell you, it stopped me right in my tracks. Thank God, it didn't last too long. But I didn't feel like myself for the rest of the day. I couldn't do much of anything but lie in bed.

About a week ago, the same thing happened again. That afternoon, Beatrice came to check on me, like she does from time to time. She could tell I wasn't feeling right. I told her about the headaches. Then I wished I hadn't, because she made a big deal out of them.

She asked me how long it had been since I'd seen a doctor. I told her I'd gone to a lot of doctors when Katherine was sick, but not for my own sake. She said it was high time I had a good checkup.

Two days later, she took me down to see the new doctor in Nashville, Dr. Spencer. I wanted to talk to him on my own, but Beatrice insisted on going into his office with me. She was bound and determined to say her piece.

And she sat there telling the doctor she thought I might've had a couple of strokes. I thought she had some nerve to say such a thing.

She and Dr. Spencer started talking about me like I wasn't even there. Beatrice said I was getting forgetful. Then she went on to say that I'd been cranky, and that it was hard to reason with me sometimes.

"That's not like her," she said. "Aunt Bertha has always been such a sweet person."

I was about ready to speak up and put Beatrice in her place. To tell the doctor how much it aggravates me when she comes snooping around my house and butting into my business. But then, I thought I'd just be proving her point. So, I kept my thoughts to myself.

I figured she was saying some of those things about me because her own grandmother is doing so poorly. Hazel's been going downhill real fast these past couple of years, ever since her husband Walter died. No one expects her to last much longer. Beatrice probably thinks I've got to be worse off than Hazel, because I'm the older sister. But she's wrong about that.

Then Dr. Spencer turned to me and started asking questions. "Mrs. Kelly, do you know what day of the week this is?"

"It's Wednesday," I told him. As soon as I said it, I thought I'd got it wrong, that maybe it was Thursday.

But Dr. Spencer didn't say anything about it. He went on to ask another question. "Can you tell me the month, the day, and the year?"

"It's May," I said. "But to tell you the truth, I'm not sure about the day. It's somewhere around the middle of the month."

"How about the year?"

I knew that one for sure. "It's 1960."

"And who is the president of the United States?"

"It's Dwight D. Eisenhower."

It went on like that, him asking me silly questions that everyone should know the answer to. I wondered if he took me for being simpleminded.

Then he started up with the numbers. He had me count backward from one hundred, and when he saw I could do that just fine, he told me to stop. Then he had me do the same thing, only by twos.

I used to play that game with Katherine, counting backwards. She was so good at it. She could do it with any number, lickety-split. Threes, fours, sevens, nines. I was glad Dr. Spencer didn't ask me to do anything like that. Because all I ever could do was twos, fives, and tens.

"She seems mentally sharp," he said to Beatrice. "A little bit of forgetfulness is natural for her age. I wouldn't worry too much about it."

Then he checked me over really good, like Katherine's doctors always did with her. "Her heart and lungs sound just fine," he said to Beatrice.

He had me squeeze his hand with each of my hands, one and then the other. I was so aggravated with him that I probably squeezed too hard. "Well," he said, "you sure are strong."

"She should be," Beatrice said. "She climbs up and down her stairs every day. She carries loads of firewood into the house. And she lifts buckets of water up onto her stove to heat them up for her bath."

The doctor looked at her kind of funny. "She lives in an old farmhouse that's hardly been updated at all," Beatrice explained. "She likes keeping things the way they've always been. She still uses an outhouse. But we did finally talk her into getting a new electric stove for her kitchen."

"And she manages okay?" the doctor asked.

I didn't wait for Beatrice to answer. "I manage just fine," I told him. "I feed the chickens and do the wash and sweep my floors and cook my own supper."

Dr. Spencer had such skinny arms and soft hands, and it looked like he hadn't done a hard day's work in his entire life. "I bet you couldn't do all that," I said to him.

"Aunt Bertha!" Beatrice scolded. Then she turned to the doctor. "She's not as nice with people as she used to be. I think it's because she spends too much time alone. A few months ago, my husband and I brought a television set over to her house to keep her company. She likes watching Lawrence Welk and the Ed Sullivan show."

I didn't think it was the doctor's business what I watch on television.

"I'm really worried about her living on her own," Beatrice said. "But she's stubborn. She doesn't want to leave her home."

Dr. Spencer looked at me like he was thinking really hard. "Mrs. Kelly, how long have you lived in your farmhouse?" he asked.

"Ever since the day I got married," I told him. "Back in the summer of 1907."

He nodded his head, then turned to talk to Beatrice. "Sometimes older folks don't do well if you take them out of a home they've lived in for a lifetime. I think your aunt's fine for now. Just keep an eye on her."

All the while the doctor was asking me questions, he was talking really loud. People think that just because I'm getting old, I'm hard of hearing. But I'm not. I hear a lot of things people don't think I can hear. Like what they say about me at church.

Some of those young women at Oak Ridge like to keep up with the times with the way they look. They wear those low-cut sleeveless dresses that show too much of their arms and their bosoms. They've taken to wearing tight skirts, too. Way too tight, if you ask me. I don't see how a person can even walk in those skirts.

Katherine always had the good sense to be modest. Not like these girls, showing off things a woman ought to keep covered.

From time to time, I have to say something to them about how ridiculous they look. They roll their eyes and whisper, and I can hear what they say. It isn't nice.

One Sunday, I heard a little girl say a bad word. I tapped her on the shoulder to let her know she shouldn't talk like that in the house of God. She busted out crying, then went and told her mother that I'd hit her.

People think Bertha Kelly is a just a mean old woman. Well, I know something about life, and I have a right to speak my mind. I know about loving and losing and being so brokenhearted that you can hardly carry on in this world anymore. And how you have to toughen yourself up just so you can keep putting one foot ahead of the other.

But I suppose I should learn to keep my mouth shut. Last Sunday at church, Melba Willis mentioned to me that her daughter Lena is going to school to be a nurse. It took me a minute to remember which one of her girls is Lena. Then it came to me. She was the little one who used to hide under the bench.

Well, Melba was acting like she was so proud of Lena. And I opened my mouth and told her she ought to be keeping her girls in their place, that they ought to stay home until they were ready to get married and start keeping house for their husbands.

I think what I said hurt Melba's feelings something awful. She might not want to talk to me anymore.

After I got home, I had to think on why I would say such a thing. And it came to me that if I hadn't gone along with Katherine's foolish ideas, if I hadn't let her put herself through the strain of going to college and teaching in Indianapolis, she wouldn't have gotten sick. She'd still be here with me, looking after her old mama instead of Beatrice being the one to do it.

Oh, I know the doctors have told me plenty of times that the tumor would've grown in Katherine's brain no matter where she was or what she was doing. But I've never really believed that.

The way people look at me at Oak Ridge, maybe there's no place for me at church anymore. Maybe I have everything I need in my own heart, and I should stay home and talk with God on my own. I've been thinking along those lines recently.

When Beatrice and I left Dr. Spencer's office, it was so nice outside that she drove me around a little bit, pointing out this and that. She showed me a new school there in town, Nashville Elementary. She said that's where her little ones go. She has twins, a boy and a girl.

"They're in first grade," she told me.

"When Katherine started first grade," I said, "she went to Owl Creek."

Beatrice laughed. "Owl Creek is long gone," she said. "All those old country schools are gone. Now, we have four brand new elementary schools in the county: Nashville, Helmsburg, Van Buren, and Sprunica. Our kids are finally getting a good modern education."

"Owl Creek was a good school," I told her.

She didn't say anything back to me. I knew she didn't want to bother arguing with me.

When we were heading into Beanblossom, I said, "I know for sure they were using the old Georgetown School just a couple of years ago."

"You're right about that," Beatrice said. "But it's not there anymore. Now, all the kids from Beanblossom get bused over to Helmsburg Elementary."

Then she pointed out the window. "See? They've built an Episcopal Church on the plot where the Georgetown School used to stand."

"Episcopal?" I said. "I've never heard tell of a church by that name."

"People say they're a little bit like the Catholics," she told me.

I've been in a Catholic church two times in my life: for Katherine's christening and her funeral. All of a sudden, I wondered whether I'd like to go to the Episcopal Church. I thought it might make me feel close to my daughter. But I knew I'd never work up the nerve to walk into someplace new like that.

"Do you need anything from the IGA?" Beatrice asked. "I can run in and get it for you."

The IGA is what they call the new McDonald's grocery store now. I can hardly keep up with these things.

I told Beatrice I was almost out of milk. While she was inside the store getting a gallon for me, I looked up the road to where the old Presbyterian Church used to stand. That church had been there as long as I could remember. It had been built way before my time, around the time when Ma and Pa were born.

But I knew that a while ago, somebody had moved the building back off the road a little way. And then they'd spruced the place up a bit and put a gravel parking lot in front of it.

I thought maybe I could point out something new to Beatrice. "Did you know they moved the Presbyterian Church building?" I said to her when she came out of the store.

"Of course," she said. "They did that years ago. But it's not Presbyterian anymore. The Mennonites are using the church now."

Beatrice thinks she knows everything. That girl sure gets under my skin sometimes.

Yesterday, I got my weekly copy of the *Brown County Democrat* in the mail. And right there on the front page was a story that shook me up something terrible. I had to sit down to keep from keeling over.

It was a story about Elmer Mitchell. They said he'd been killed in an accident. He was driving his brother's pickup truck and ran it into a tree. He'd died right there on the spot.

From all the years Elmer had hung around our house, I knew he never should've been driving a truck. He didn't have the mind for it. He'd hardly been able to even drive

Frank's tractor. Whenever Frank had let him get on it, he'd always kept an eye on him.

So, I know the Mitchell family wasn't watching over Elmer when they let him get behind the wheel of that truck. Maybe it's not in my place to say this, but I don't think they cared that much about what happened to him.

I know the poor fellow is in Heaven with Frank now, who was more of a father to Elmer than his own pa ever was. Maybe that's where Elmer wanted to be all along. Maybe he missed Frank so much that he crashed into the tree on purpose. But that's not for me to say.

After I read that story, I knew I needed to have a good cry, and a good talk with Katherine. So, last night I went up the stairs to sit in her room for a while. When I opened the door and saw her picture hanging there, it seemed like the corners of her mouth turned up just a little. Like she was glad to see me.

"Sweetheart," I said as I settled into the rocking chair, "Elmer Mitchell's coming up there where you are. Make sure he and your pa find each other. The two of them are going to be really happy to see each other again."

My tears started coming, but I kept on talking to my child. "It seems like I have more loved ones up in Heaven than I have left here on earth. Would you look after all of them for me? I know you've got the heart for it."

Then I bawled hard into my hankie. "And while you're at it, Katherine," I blurted out, "look out for me, too. I'm starting to have a real hard time of it down here."

1963

There's one thing about having a television in the house: you see things going on in the world that you'd never know about otherwise. It's different than looking at pictures in the newspaper. It brings everything close to home.

At first, I thought that was a good thing. Now, I'm not so sure.

Three years ago, our country elected a new president, John F. Kennedy. As far back as I could remember, the presidents had all been older fellows. But Kennedy was younger, and the women liked to carry on about how good-looking he was. He had a beautiful wife who was always dressed up in stylish outfits. And two little children, Caroline and John Jr., the sweetest things you ever did see.

A couple of months after Mr. Kennedy was elected, they showed him on television being sworn into office. He gave such a nice speech, and the people cheered and clapped for him. I hadn't heard anything like that in a long time. Listening to him stirred my heart.

After he got done speaking, his wife Jacqueline stepped up to stand next to him. The two of them looked so nice together. And the crowd cheered all the more.

There's one thing Mr. Kennedy said in his speech that people will remember for a long time. "And so my fellow Americans: ask not what your country can do for you—ask what you can do for your country."

Something like that really makes a person stop and think. They were talking about it in the newspapers the next day. I wish Pa had been alive to hear it, as he would've appreciated the president's words.

Beatrice knew how much I liked the Kennedys. Whenever there was a picture of them in the *Indianapolis Star,* she'd bring the paper along when she came to check on me. And I took to cutting out the pictures and pinning them up on my kitchen wall: Jackie Kennedy looking so pretty in a fancy evening gown; the president and his wife standing together, holding the hands of Caroline and John Jr.; the family spending time outdoors, with the parents tending to the children like they loved them so much.

They seemed like a family right out of a storybook. I think almost everyone in this country was like me, in the way we all took to the Kennedys. I'd get carried away in my mind, thinking on what it would be like to know them.

A week ago, we had a family get-together in Nashville, a birthday party for one of Hazel's great-grandchildren. I don't remember which one. There are so many that I can't keep track of them.

Roger is Hazel's youngest grandson, her daughter Ruby's boy. He's only been married a couple of years. There at the birthday party, he and his wife Vivian told everybody they had a baby on the way.

They were talking about how they needed to get a room fixed up for the baby. Roger was cracking jokes, saying how much it costs to raise a child these days, and how he was afraid he'd end up going broke.

Some of his cousins were telling Roger that he and Vivian could have the things left over from when their children were babies. A crib and a highchair, stuff like that. Roger said he'd be mighty thankful for anything anyone could give.

I sat there wishing I could help out in some way. With Hazel and Walter both being gone, I feel like it's my job to watch over the younger ones in the family. Even though I can't do much of anything for them.

All of a sudden, I remembered the chest of drawers I'd gotten from Ma and Pa's house. It's made out of oak, built really solid, good as new. A lot better than the flimsy furniture they make nowadays. And I thought maybe it was time to pass it on down to someone else in the family. It didn't seem right to have it sitting empty in my upstairs room when somebody else could get use out of it.

So, I spoke up to Roger and asked him if he wanted it. He was tickled at the idea of it. He said he'd bring a truck over to get it the next Saturday. I told him it was a heavy piece of furniture, and that he'd better bring along another fellow to help him haul it down the stairs.

Around the middle of this week, I went upstairs to clean out the chest of drawers and dust it really good, getting it ready for when Roger came to pick it up.

All in all, things were going just fine. I was looking forward to Thanksgiving coming up, and was trying to figure out what dish to take to the family dinner at Annabelle's house.

But two days ago, something happened that I never could've imagined. I'll never forget that day for as long as I live: Friday, November 22, 1963.

I was sitting in my front room watching television after lunch, that show called *As the World Turns.* Oh, I know I shouldn't have been wasting my time watching it, because I had chores that needed to be done. But the show had gotten a hold on me, and I couldn't seem to help myself.

All of a sudden, Walter Cronkite, that fellow from CBS News, broke into the program. And what he told the country shocked me like I'd never been shocked before. He said that President Kennedy and his wife Jackie were down in Dallas, Texas, and that somebody had fired shots into the car they were riding in. President Kennedy had been hit and was hurt really bad.

I tell you, I was so shook up that I could hardly take in what Mr. Cronkite was saying. He told everybody to stay tuned for more details. So, I did. I sat there like I was paralyzed, not moving a muscle. I had to know what was going to happen next. I kept praying, "Oh God, please help President Kennedy. Help him. Help him."

It wasn't too long before Mr. Cronkite told us that the president had died. And my heart just broke. It shattered like a china teacup somebody had dropped on the floor. I couldn't believe such a terrible thing could happen in this country.

I thought about President Kennedy's wife and his sweet children, and what this all would mean to them. I knew what it was like to lose someone you love so dearly, and how a person can hardly go on after that.

I started crying and praying for them. I couldn't stop. "Oh God, help them, help them, help them," I kept calling out.

After an hour or so of this, the strangest feeling came over me. Somehow, I knew I wasn't alone in my prayers. It seemed like the whole country was caught up in prayer for the Kennedy family.

And then, I found myself praying for anyone anywhere in the world going through the terrible ordeal of losing a loved one. I guess when a person's heart is broken wide open, it leaves a lot of room for God to come in.

I ended up having a bad time of it that night. I'd doze off a little bit, then wake up feeling so overcome with sorrow that I could hardly stand it. To keep myself from having a breakdown, I'd pray until I settled down enough to fall back to sleep.

The next morning, I was so tired and wrung out that I could hardly get myself out of bed. Then I remembered it was the day Roger was supposed to pick up the chest of drawers.

To tell you the truth, I wasn't up for it, and I thought about calling him and telling him not to come over. But I'd given him my word, so I decided to make the best of things.

Before I even got around to making my breakfast, Roger pulled up to the house in his pickup truck. When he and his friend came inside, the first thing he said to me was, "Aunt Bertha, did you hear about President Kennedy?"

"Yes," I said. "It's a terrible, terrible thing."

He shook his head. "I don't know what this country's coming to." He acted like he wanted to stand around and talk about it for a while. But I just couldn't. I knew if I opened my mouth about it, I'd break down all over again.

So, that was all we said about the matter. "Where's the chest of drawers?" Roger asked.

"It's in one of the upstairs bedrooms," I told him.

The two men headed up the stairs, and I followed behind. I was so tired that I couldn't keep up with them. When I got to the top, I saw that Roger was just about to open the door to Katherine's room and go inside.

And just at that very moment, I heard the sound: Katherine's voice coming from her bedroom. She was singing her favorite song from when she was in high school, *A Merry Life.*

Some think the world is made for fun and frolic,
And so do I! And so do I!

It was something she'd learned in her music class. She had loved the song so much that she'd copied down the words in one of her little notebooks so she could sing it anytime she wanted to.

Some think it well to be all melancholic,
To pine and sigh; to pine and sigh.

I tell you, I didn't know what to make of it, or what to do about it. "Don't go into that room!" I shouted at Roger.

He stood there staring at me, his hand on the doorknob. The singing was so loud, I was sure he and his friend had to hear it, too. I had no idea what they were thinking about it.

But I, I love to spend my time in singing,
Some joyous song, some joyous song.
To set the air with music bravely ringing
Is far from wrong! Is far from wrong!

It seemed like we stood there forever, with the song ringing in the air around us. But Roger and his friend didn't seem shook up by it. All of a sudden, I realized they weren't hearing what I was hearing. They were just waiting on me to tell them what to do next.

I yelled at the top of my voice so I could hear myself above the singing. "The chest of drawers is in the other room!" Roger looked at me real strange, like he couldn't figure out why I was hollering at him like that.

While the music was still going on, I led the men to the other bedroom and pointed out the chest. Roger and his buddy tried to lift it. "It's too heavy," Roger said. "We need to take the drawers out first."

So, in the middle of all the singing, Roger and his friend pulled the four drawers out of the chest and carried them down the stairs. As if nothing out of the ordinary was going on.

I stood there at the top of the stairs watching them go down, shaking my head trying to make the music go away. It started to get softer and softer, and by the time the men came back up to get the chest, the sound was so soft that I could barely hear it.

I followed the men down the stairs and watched out the front room window while they loaded everything in the bed of Roger's pickup truck. Then Roger came back into the house to thank me. "This will help out a lot, Aunt Bertha," he said.

He was so pleased about the chest that he started whistling a tune as he headed out the door. I couldn't believe my ears. It was the same song Katherine's voice had been singing, *A Merry Life.*

I collapsed on the sofa, my whole body shaking from what I'd just been through. *How could this be?* I asked myself. *Roger didn't act strange at all. He didn't seem like he'd heard anything out of the ordinary. If he'd heard Katherine's voice, he would've said something. Or he would've been so scared that he would've run out of the house. All he did was carry on with his work, joking a little with his friend.*

But how did he think to whistle that tune?

I tell you, I couldn't answer that.

I hoped Roger wouldn't make anything out of the way I'd acted. How I'd hollered at him about not going into Katherine's room. I hoped he wouldn't go home and tell the family that old Aunt Bertha was losing her mind, and that something needed to be done about her.

I sat there for a long time, trying to figure out what to do next. I thought about going to the telephone and calling Reverend Willis, telling him I needed him to come over. And then I'd ask him if he believed in spirits.

But I hadn't been to church in half a year, and it didn't seem right to expect the preacher to come calling on me when I hadn't been a faithful church member. Anyway, no preacher would think it would be right to believe in ghosts and spirits and that sort of thing. Reverend Willis would probably tell me I was trafficking in things of the devil.

I didn't want to hear him say that. Because I knew for sure that something as beautiful as my child's voice couldn't be of the devil.

I almost got up to call Beatrice, to tell her I needed to see Dr. Spencer again. But the more I thought about it, the more I decided to wait and see what would happen next. I figured the strain of hearing about President Kennedy's death had made me go out of my head for a little while. I decided maybe I needed to keep the television turned off for a couple of days. I knew they'd be showing his funeral and such, and it wouldn't do me any good to see that.

I couldn't bring myself to go upstairs for the rest of the day. At bedtime, I finally decided I needed to face things. So, I went up and stood outside Katherine's room with my ear pressed to the door. I didn't hear a thing. Then I opened the door and peeked inside. Everything was just the same as the last time I'd been in there.

I laughed out loud as I went down the stairs. "Bertha Kelly," I said, "you're a silly old woman."

I was so tired that I slept like a log last night. When I woke up this morning, my mind felt strong and clear. Still, I decided it would be best not to have anybody come to the house for a while. Because there's no telling what they might hear.

1971

These last couple of years, Beatrice has been harping on me about not getting out of the house enough. So, a few days before I turned eighty-five, she called me to say she was going to take me out for a good time on my birthday. She said we'd take a little walk around Nashville, and then have a nice lunch in a restaurant.

I told her I wasn't interested in all that, but she insisted. So, I gave in and went along with the idea. This morning, she came to pick me up.

Even though I'd been to Nashville more times than I could ever count, it had been a long while since I'd gotten out of the car and walked around town. The thought of doing that scared me a little. My legs aren't so steady these days, and I didn't see how I'd be able to keep up with what Beatrice wanted to do.

She parked the car in a lot on the north side of town. Before she helped me out of the front seat, she went around to the trunk and pulled out a folded-up wheelchair.

"I thought I'd bring this along," she said. "I didn't want you to get too tired out."

When I asked where she'd gotten such a thing, she told me her husband's mother had used it before she passed away, and that was how they'd taken her places. I guess it's my turn to be the old one they have to tote around.

Even though I was glad Beatrice didn't expect me to walk all over town, I was embarrassed to sit in that chair and have somebody else pushing me. Thank goodness there weren't too many people on the sidewalks. It's only April, a little too early for all the tourists to be here. Later in the spring and in the summer, people from out of town will be swarming all over Nashville like bees in a hive. And in the fall when the leaves are in color, so many tourists come to Nashville that it takes a person half an hour just to drive through town.

I had a sweater on, but Beatrice said that wasn't warm enough for me. So, she got a little crocheted blanket out of her car and tucked it around my shoulders. It felt nice and cozy, but I was afraid it made me look like a pitiful old woman.

With her pushing the wheelchair, we started down Van Buren Street through the middle of town. "I don't think I've told you this," Beatrice said. "Now that the twins are grown and I have time on my hands, I've been doing some volunteer work with the Brown County Historical Society. You'd be surprised at some of the things I've learned."

Here we go, I thought. *She's going to be spouting off even more than she usually does.*

"Do you know how Brown County got its name?" she asked.

Truth be told, I'd never thought of such a thing. "No," I said.

"It was named after Major General Jacob Brown. He was a hero in the war of 1812." She sounded really proud to know something like that.

I hoped she'd stop talking so I could look around and enjoy myself. But she kept on going. "Brown County was established as a county in 1836. But settlers came here before that, some as early as 1820. They came from Kentucky, Tennessee, Virginia, and the Carolinas."

"I know all about that," I said. "My ma told me stories. My great-grandparents came here from Kentucky and Tennessee."

She pointed out a building to our right. "That's where they print the *Brown County Democrat.* The newspaper was established in 1914."

"I know," I said. "I remember that. They started it up when Katherine was six years old."

She asked if I'd like to look through an antique store, and I said, "Sure." I got out of the wheelchair, and we left it by the door. Then we walked through the store with her holding onto my arm.

It was nice and all, but I didn't see what the big fuss was all about. Everything I saw reminded me of what Ma and Pa had in our home when I was growing up. I guess nowadays when people have all the modern stuff, they get a hankering for things from the past.

After we left the store, we kept on going down Van Buren Street. We passed the county jail, the sheriff's office, and the courthouse. Of course, Beatrice had something to say about all that: "Did you know that the first courthouse and log jail were built on this very site way back in 1837?"

She didn't need to tell me that. I remembered that log jail all too well, because I used to worry that my husband was going to end up inside it. But I didn't say that to Beatrice. It's none of her business.

Then she took me inside an old-fashioned general store, and after that, I was all tuckered out. I was about to tell her I wanted to call it quits and go on home.

But she had more in mind for us to do. She made a right turn onto Main Street, and we passed the Nashville State Bank and the Abe Martin Realty building. Then we turned onto Jefferson Street.

Beatrice pointed out a building to our left and said it was the public library. She said that when her twins were little, she'd bring them to the library every week to pick out storybooks to take home. She had a smile on her face, like she was thinking back on the good old times. I don't think Beatrice understands what old times are.

After that, we went in and out of a couple of shops. I

was getting so tired that everything started looking the same to me.

Then we turned onto Franklin Street and headed back to Van Buren Street. Beatrice asked me if I wanted to stop and look around in the John Dillinger museum.

"Who in the world is John Dillinger?" I asked her.

"He's a famous gangster from the 1920s and 30s," she told me. "He robbed a lot of banks. I'm surprised you haven't heard of him."

Being so tired, I got a little cross with her. "Now, why would I want to waste my time looking at things about some wicked old man?"

She shrugged her shoulders. "Okay, then. Would you want to go on down the street to the Village Candlemaker shop? You might find that interesting."

"No," I said. "I watched my ma make candles a hundred times when I was growing up."

She looked at me kind of funny. "I don't think it's the same thing, Aunt Bertha. But if you don't want to see it, we won't go there."

So, we kept going back up Van Buren Street. When we got to the Brown County Art Guild, Beatrice insisted that we stop and go inside. I was ashamed of how I'd barked at her about the John Dillinger museum and the Village Candlemaker, so I didn't make another fuss.

Of course, she started spouting off again. "Nashville built it's first art gallery in 1926. That's because of all the artists that came to the artist colony here. They built the Art Guild in 1954."

She pointed out the paintings of this artist and that artist. I couldn't keep track of what she was telling me. To be honest, I closed my eyes to rest some of the time.

But when she mentioned the name of Mr. Elkins, I opened my eyes and perked up my ears. That's the fellow who painted the portrait of Katherine. I looked really hard at his paintings, and I could tell they were done by the same person who'd done my child's picture.

Then an idea came to me out of the blue. "After I'm dead and gone," I told Beatrice, "I want you to bring my painting of Katherine here and let the Art Guild have it. That way, everybody can see it and enjoy it."

Beatrice gave me the strangest look. "Aunt Bertha, I haven't the faintest idea what you're talking about."

Then I remembered that she'd never seen the picture of Katherine. Nobody in the family has seen it. No one except for Frank and me ever knew Clover had Katherine's portrait painted when she was a little girl.

So, we stopped for a minute, and I told Beatrice the story about what Clover had done behind my back. And how she'd surprised Frank and me with the painting after Katherine passed away.

It seemed like the story touched Beatrice, as she got a little teary-eyed. "When I take you home," she said, "you'll have to show me the painting."

The thought of that made me nervous. I didn't want anybody getting their hands on that picture and taking it away from me. "Not yet," I told Beatrice. "You can see it after I'm dead and gone. It's upstairs in Katherine's old room, hanging on the wall above her bed."

"Okay," she said.

I hope she remembers what I asked her to do with it.

After we left the Art Guild, Beatrice said it was time to eat lunch, and she took me across the street to the Nashville House. Before we went into the restaurant part, we walked around the country store for a little while. Beatrice had me pick out some candy to take home with me.

"You want to see me put on weight," I teased her.

"It wouldn't hurt," she said. "You've gotten thin these past few years." She grabbed the waist of my dress to show me how loose it was. "See? Your dress hangs on you like a sack. I don't think you're getting enough to eat."

She ordered a big lunch for us, even though I would've been satisfied with a cup of coffee and a slice of bread and butter. I couldn't eat more than a few bites of my chicken and one of my fried biscuits. Beatrice had them pack up the rest so I could take it home. "It'll be enough for your supper," she said.

Just as I was finishing up my coffee, a man came up to our table and asked if he could talk with me for a minute. He said he was a reporter from the *Indianapolis Star,* and that he was writing a story about Brown County in the olden days.

"Are you a Brown County native?" he asked me.

I was downright proud to answer that. "Why, yes I am. I was born and raised here, and I've lived in Brown County all my life. Just a little way north of here on Helmsburg Road. Matter of fact, my ma and pa were born and raised in Brown County, too. So, my family goes way back."

The reporter got a big smile on his face, like he thought he'd struck gold. "Sit down and have a talk with her," Beatrice said to him. "She has lots of stories to tell."

The man sat down and pulled a tape recorder out of the bag he was carrying. "Do you mind if I record you?" he asked.

I wasn't sure about that. But before I could say anything, Beatrice said, "That'll be okay."

So, I had the waitress pour me another cup of coffee, and I started talking. The more I said, the more that came to me. The memories of family life during my childhood. The stories Ma had told me growing up, and the ones she told in her last years.

I guess I got carried away, but the man seemed to like what I was saying. I even told him the story about how I'd run off as a two-year-old, and how my husband's mother had found me. And how after that, Ma had to tie a rope around my waist to keep track of me. The reporter got a big kick out of that.

I bet we sat there for three-quarters of an hour. Whenever I stopped talking, the man would ask me another question, and that would get me going again.

Afterwards, he said he'd forgotten to get my name. I told him who I was and he wrote it down. I was feeling so good, I told him I didn't even mind if he put my name in the newspaper.

After the reporter left, I sat there thinking on what a good time I'd just had. *I can't wait to go home and tell Katherine about it,* I said to myself. I almost opened my mouth and said that out loud to Beatrice. I'm glad I didn't, because she wouldn't have understood.

Beatrice got up from the table. "Are you ready to go?" she asked me.

I made a move to stand up. But I tell you, I was so tuckered out from all that talking that my legs gave out and I had to sit back down again.

"Give me a minute to catch my breath," I said.

Beatrice looked worried. "Are you okay?"

"Just tired," I told her. "I'm not used to talking that much."

She sat down again, ready to wait on me for a while. "Aunt Bertha," she said, "it's times like this when I worry about you living alone. I just don't think it's safe anymore."

I wished I could tell her that I'm not alone. "I'm fine," I said.

"It would be so much easier for you to live someplace where you have modern conveniences," she went on. "We could sell your farm and set you up in a nice little apartment in Nashville. Or we could buy you a trailer in the trailer park in Beanblossom. With a bathroom right there in the house so you wouldn't have to make trips to the outhouse in cold weather. You could step right into a bathtub or a shower instead of lugging around your buckets of water."

"I'm just fine where I am," I told her.

But she acted like she didn't hear me and kept on talking. "Of course, nobody would be interested in your old house. They'd just bulldoze it. But they'd love to build a new home on your property. If they cleared out the brush and tore down the barn and all the old sheds, it would be a prime piece of real estate. Aunt Bertha, you're sitting on a goldmine. We could get a pretty penny for your land, and you could live in comfort for the rest of your life."

The last few years, Beatrice has never stopped mentioning how worthless my house is. She has no idea what treasures it holds.

There's always something happening around my home that seems like magic to me. Last spring and summer, I found wildflowers popping up all over the place—tiny Dutchman's breeches, pretty blue cornflowers, orange butterfly weed, big patches of daisies and black-eyed Susans. And then in the fall, the bright yellow goldenrod. I know better than to believe Rose Kelly is responsible for all those flowers on my property. But whenever I see them, I can't help but think her spirit is still living here.

If they bulldoze the house and clear off the land, all that will be lost. The Kelly family will be gone for good.

Sometimes, I think Beatrice wants me to sell my place so she can get her hands on the money. Lord knows she doesn't need it. She and her husband seem to be doing just fine. A couple of years ago, they bought a brand-new home on Artist Drive in Nashville. I was there last Christmas. Her place is almost as fancy as Clover's house was back in the day.

I know I shouldn't be having ugly thoughts about Beatrice. She tells me I spend so much time alone in my house that I've gotten suspicious of people. "You're always thinking someone's up to no good," she's told me time and again. "You know you can trust your family."

So, I kept all my bad thoughts to myself and said, "If anybody wants to buy my land, tell them I'm not interested in selling."

But Beatrice wasn't done fussing about my house. "I worry about you going up and down those steep, narrow stairs," she said. "I don't want to come over some day and find that you've fallen to your death."

"But I have to go upstairs," I said.

"What on earth for?" she asked.

I had to stop and think on what to say. "To clean. To dust and sweep."

She shook her head like she was fed up with my foolishness. "Aunt Bertha, I've told you a hundred times that I can get somebody to do your cleaning for you."

And I thought, *I've told you a hundred times that I don't want a stranger poking around in my things.* But I knew better than to say that out loud.

Truth be told, I'm not climbing those stairs to do any cleaning. Every day, I go up there and listen outside Katherine's door for a few minutes.

When Katherine was growing up, she always liked to keep the door of her room closed. She didn't want me snooping around and watching what she was doing. That hasn't changed about her. She still insists on having her door closed. If I open the door when she's in there talking or singing or laughing, everything goes quiet.

It's really something. When I stand outside the door listening, I never know what's going to come up. It's different every time.

Once, I heard her little girl voice singing her ABC song, making it fancy like she used to do, warbling like a little bird. It was so sweet that it brought tears to my eyes. Other times, I've heard her singing the nursery rhyme songs Clover used to teach her.

Several times, I've heard her reading aloud from one of her books by the Bronte sisters. I've heard her practicing her history reports for school. I've heard her conjugating her Latin verbs.

Every now and then, I hear her saying her *Hail Mary.* She sounds so holy when she does that, so close to God. It just about takes my breath away.

I hear her voice the strongest when it comes from her room. But I do catch the sound and the feel of her in other parts of the house. I've come to take it for granted that her spirit is always there with me. It's gotten to where I talk to her every day. All day long, as a matter of fact.

Usually, I don't hear back from her. But sometimes I do. Sometimes, it's just a little laugh. Every now and then, I hear, clear as a bell, "I love you, Mama."

And I say to her, "I love you, too, Katherine. I love you more than anything on earth or in Heaven."

I hope the Lord forgives me for saying that. It's not that I love my child more than God. I've just come to think of Katherine's spirit as part of God.

One day, I heard Katherine say, "Thank you, Mama." And I kept hearing that all day long. It was like she wanted to make sure it sunk in. She didn't have to tell me why she was thanking me. I just knew. She was telling me she was glad that I let her go out into the world the way she wanted to. That I let her live the kind of life she wanted to live.

Now, I understand that she was supposed to live that life, even though it was cut short. I've stopped telling myself that I should've kept a tighter hold on her. Katherine was who she was meant to be. She still is.

Mostly, Katherine and I talk to each other without words. We understand each other through our thoughts. I can always feel her when she's nearby.

As I go about my chores, she gives me strength when my old body starts to fail. When I climb the stairs, she has her hand on my arm to steady me. When I carry a bucket of wash out to the clothesline, she's holding the handle with me to share the load.

Sometimes, she plays games with me. One day when I was dusting her room, I picked up her rosary and held it for a little bit. Then, instead of laying it out in a circle, I stretched it out straight. When I went into the room a couple of days later, it was in a circle again.

Several days in a row, I tried the same thing. I'd lay it out straight, and she'd put it back into a circle. I took the rosary downstairs to the front room to see if she'd do the same thing in another part of the house. Sure enough, she did. I have to laugh every time I think about that.

Every now and then, I go out to stand by the fishpond, just remembering. I can always feel her presence there. Sometimes, I hear her whisper, "Oh Papa!" Like she's so pleased with the pretty fish he's brought her.

Sometimes, I feel Frank's presence out there with us. I give Katherine the credit for bringing him along with her. It's nice to have us all together like that.

A couple of times, she's brought Frank's spirit to me at night. Oh my, I hardly know what to say about that. Maybe it's best if I don't say anything at all. Except that I never felt anything like that in my entire life. I didn't know it was possible for a person to feel that way.

Whenever Frank comes to me, I know he's honoring the time we spent together. Even though we had so many hard times as husband and wife, he makes me feel like our years together counted for something. That they mattered to him.

The part of my husband that comes to me is pure and bright. He's lost all the ugliness from drinking and messing around with other women. He's not weighed down by the dark thoughts he brooded on after he came home from the war. The pureness of his spirit finds the pureness in mine, and we're able to love each other much more than we ever did in real life.

Hardly anyone comes to my house anymore, except for Beatrice. She thinks she has to come around every week or so to keep an eye on what I'm doing. She acts like I'm just a stubborn old woman. A stupid old woman who doesn't know what's what anymore.

Whenever I know she's coming, I have a little talk with Katherine. "Now sweetheart," I say, "don't you be getting me in trouble. You need to keep quiet when Beatrice is here. If she hears your voice, she won't know what to make of it."

And then I hear a little giggle.

When Beatrice drove me home from Nashville this afternoon, she wanted to help me into the house. "No," I said, "I'm fine."

She looked at me real suspicious, like she thought I was lying about something. "What are you trying to hide from me, Aunt Bertha?"

"Nothing," I said.

So, I gathered my strength and made it out of the car and onto the porch on my own. When I stepped inside the house, I laughed out loud. "Wouldn't she like to know?" I said to Katherine.

1976

When Beatrice came over to check on me last week, she started fussing at me the minute she stepped into the house. "Why are you doing this, Aunt Bertha? Why are you doing that?"

She walked into my kitchen and saw some old Christmas cards spread out on the table. "Why on earth do you have these cards out?" she asked. "Aunt Bertha, it's the middle of July!"

"Katherine likes to look at the pretty pictures," I told her.

I knew right away I shouldn't have said that. Because Beatrice stared at me like she thought I'd gone plumb out of my head. I wanted to tell her I have the right to bring out Christmas cards any time I feel like it. But I didn't, because I wasn't about to go and make matters worse.

I guess after she left, she had a talk with the family, and then she went to see Dr. Spencer. After that, she went to the courthouse in Nashville and got some papers. And the next day, she brought them over for me to sign.

"What's this about?" I asked her.

She looked sheepish, like she didn't want me to know what she was up to. "The family thinks you've come to a point where you need someone else to take care of business for you," she said. "And Dr. Spencer agrees with us."

I tell you, I wasn't about to sign my name on those papers. There was no way I was going to give permission to have Beatrice take charge of me, and I told her that.

She was put out with me for being stubborn. So, she went to my telephone and called her mother, hoping Annabelle could talk some sense into me.

"Aunt Bertha," Annabelle said, "we don't mean any harm by this. All of us are getting older. I'm no spring chicken myself. Pretty soon, Beatrice will need to look after me, too. There comes a time when we just can't do for ourselves anymore."

She went on to tell me that I should trust Beatrice, because she's such a smart girl and knows what she's doing. "She won't steer you wrong," she said. "She's the best one to look out for you."

I still wasn't sure, so Beatrice called her Aunt Ruby to have her talk with me. Ruby told me the same thing as Annabelle did. I figured I'd never win, with all of them against me like that. And they had Dr. Spencer on their side. So, I gave in and signed Beatrice's papers.

After I was done, she put the papers in her purse. Then she sat there at the table staring at me, like she was having a hard time bringing up something she wanted to tell me.

"Aunt Bertha," she finally said, "we need to talk about where you're going to live next. I know the last thing you want to do is leave you home. But it's too much for you to be here on your own. You're not strong enough to be mopping floors and carrying wood and hanging clothes on the line. And I just can't have you going up and down those stairs. Some of the steps are loose and rotting, and they're not safe for anyone anymore."

I almost said, "I'm not alone. Katherine's here to help me."

That would've made Beatrice think I'd gone crazy for sure. But it's true. When I feel too weak and worn out to carry on, my precious child wraps her spirit around me. Like she's holding me. Like she's giving me her strength.

"Maybe it's time to move in with a family member," Beatrice said. "My mother or Ruby would be glad to have you. And you're always welcome to stay with my husband and me. We have plenty of room."

"You can put that right out of your mind," I told her. "I'm going to say one thing: I'm not going to let myself be a burden on the family."

"Then we'll talk about other options," she said.

"I'm not up for that today," I told her. "I need some time to think about it." I said that just to get her off my back. I knew I wasn't ever going to change my mind about leaving this house.

"That's fine," she said. "I'll be over in a few days to check on you. In the meantime, you need to be extra careful. You need to promise me you won't try going up the stairs again."

"I promise," I said.

I knew I was telling her a lie. But I figured no one had a right to tell me what I couldn't do in my own home.

Beatrice always keeps her word, and she came back two days ago. Of course, she started poking around the house like she always does.

She picked up a *Youth's Companion* newspaper lying on the sofa. "What's this doing here?" she asked.

"It's for Katherine," I told her.

She looked at it real close. "It's from 1925. Why on earth are you still hanging onto it?"

"Katherine's never wanted to throw them out," I said.

She shook her head like she thought I was being ridiculous. Then she walked into the kitchen and saw the rosary lying on the table.

"What are you doing with a rosary, Aunt Bertha?" she asked. "You're not Catholic."

She reached out to pick it up so she could have a look at it, but I grabbed her wrist to stop her. "Leave that alone!" I hollered. "It's Katherine's!"

She sat down on a kitchen chair, rubbing her wrist where I'd hurt her, staring at me real funny. Like she just didn't know what to make of things anymore.

She looked down at the floor, scuffing the toe of her shoe around in the dirt. I knew she was thinking I wasn't keeping up with my housework. Then she pointed to the dishes stacked up by the sink. "That's the same pile of dishes that was here the last time I came over," she said. "When did you have your last meal, Aunt Bertha?"

I couldn't rightly tell her.

She didn't say anything else to me. She just got up and went to the telephone, and I knew she was going to call somebody to complain about me. I was so put out with her that I was afraid I'd forget myself and do something else to hurt her. So, I went to sit in the front room.

But I could hear everything she was saying on the telephone. She was asking someone if she could speak with Dr. Spencer.

He must've gotten on the line, because I heard her telling him about everything in the house that she thought was wrong. Then she went on to say that I had attacked her. She mentioned the word *dementia.*

Beatrice probably thinks I don't know what a word like that means. But I do. It's what they said about Ma at the end, when she lost her bearings and couldn't remember things right.

Then Beatrice was quiet for a while, like she was listening to what Dr. Spencer had to say. I figured he was giving her an earful.

After she hung up the phone, she came into the front room and sat down on the sofa with me. "Aunt Bertha," she said, "I hate to tell you this. But Dr. Spencer and I both believe it's time for you to leave this house. You're just not able to take care of yourself anymore."

I knew that was coming. And I knew there was no point in arguing about it. "When do I have to go?" I asked.

"As soon as possible," she said. "In the next day or two."

"Where am I going?"

"To a nice nursing home in Morgantown. We have it all worked out. They'll take good care of you there."

I figured I'd give it one last try. "And what if I say no? What if I put my foot down?"

Beatrice set her mouth in a hard line. "Aunt Bertha, you have no choice."

Beatrice came over again yesterday and today. She brought me food, and she helped me take a good bath. After she took all my dirty clothes to get them washed, she packed them up in a couple of paper bags, ready to go.

It reminded me of the day when I moved in here, when Frank's sister Violet packed up their pa's things and took him out of the house. Old Man Kelly had bawled like a baby, saying he didn't want to leave his home. Thinking back on it, I couldn't help but feel bad for him.

"What'll we do with the furniture?" I asked Beatrice. "And all the things in the kitchen?"

"We'll take care of that later," she said. "There's nothing worth anything in this house. Nothing anybody would want to steal."

"But what about Katherine's picture?"

"Oh yes," she said. "I'll take care of that in the next day or two."

She told me she knows somebody who wants to buy my land. When I asked her about the house, she kept her mouth shut. I know why. They'll be tearing this old place down, and she doesn't want me to know about it.

The story of this house is almost over. The story of my life is almost over.

This is my last night in the house.

Beatrice wanted to spend the night with me. She said I shouldn't be alone.

I told her no. And for once, she listened to me. She said she'll come to pick me up first thing in the morning.

I wanted to have one last night alone with Katherine. Even though I knew Beatrice didn't want me to, I climbed the stairs so I could sleep in Katherine's bed. One last time.

As I lie here, my child has come to spread her sweet spirit over me, like a warm blanket.

Katherine, will you come with me to the new place I'm going? Will you keep on lending me your strength? Will you help me bear the load?

You've pulled your presence away from me. It's so empty and cold in this room that I can't stand it. I've never felt so alone in my entire life.

I know it's your way of saying, "No Mama, I can't go where you're going."

I understand, Katherine. I know your spirit belongs here in this house you've known for so long. I guess I'm going to have to be on my own for a while, until the Lord calls me home and I can be with you in Heaven. I hope it won't be long.

Now, I feel your sweet warmth again. Hold me one last time, Katherine. Hold me one last time.

Author's Note

I grew up in Brown County, Indiana, the setting for this story. However, my family was not native to the area. Seven years prior to my birth, my parents and oldest siblings moved to the county, where my father, a Mennonite minister, founded a church in the tiny village of Beanblossom.

Because Brown County was so heavily forested when it first became a county, it was a difficult place to settle. It has always remained rural and sparsely populated. This is in contrast to neighboring counties: Bartholomew County, which has developed significant industry, and Monroe County, which is home to the main campus of Indiana University.

While Brown County's wooded hills, creeks, and winding roads are indelibly imprinted on my memory, I have long regretted that I never got to know the people of the county in the way I would have liked to. Our family's strict religious traditions kept me somewhat set apart from community activities.

Writing this novel has been a way of delving as deeply as I can into the heart and soul of Brown County, of embracing its history, its culture, its traditions. The story is a labor of love, a token of affection and appreciation for the place of my childhood.

Additionally, I wanted to give a voice to a woman from a generation long past. An ordinary woman who never would've attracted much of the world's attention. A woman whose outer experience was limited, but whose inner life was rich and deep.

This story consists of a little bit of fact, a whole lot of imagination, and, no doubt, a great deal of error.